Praise for P[...]

'Like a surreal cabinet of curios[...]
Bridget Collins, *Sunday Times* b[...]

'A captivating coming-of-age story with memorable characters
beautifully brought to life in a setting dripping with atmosphere.'
Daily Mail

'Polly Crosby has a remarkable gift for evoking atmosphere and place.'
Leonora Nattrass, author of *Blue Water*

'Evocative and enchanting – a future classic and a star in the making.'
Veronica Henry, *Sunday Times* bestselling author

'Polly Crosby whips up a lush, mythical world . . . realised beautifully
in vivid writing. A book worm's treat!'
Eve Chase, author of *The Glass House*

'This moving tale is set in a mesmerising world. Like a butterfly
emerging from a chrysalis, the story emerges slowly, allowing you to
immerse yourself in its wonders.'
Heat

A thoroughly compelling mystery meets a poignant love story, all
wrapped up in Polly's beautifully lyrical writing.'
Frances Quinn, author of *The Smallest Man*

'A luminous and beautiful novel that gently lures the reader into a
captivating story with a mystery at its heart.'
Jennifer Saint, *Sunday Times* bestselling author of *Ariadne*

'A bewitching read.'
Woman & Home

'A beguiling mystery from a gifted storyteller.'
Louise Fein, author of *People Like Us*

'Rich and evocative storytelling is at the heart of this beautifully atmospheric book.'
My Weekly

'Polly Crosby's shimmering writing veils a dark hint of the gothic.'
Kate Griffin, author of *Fyneshade*

'Imaginative and intriguing, this is packed with tender moments.'
Woman's Weekly

'[A] gem of a read.'
Good Housekeeping

'A magical tale, beautifully written, evocative and mysterious, and stitched through with a dark thread that I wasn't expecting. What a wonderful book.'
Anita Frank, author of *The Lost Ones*

'A hugely evocative and beautifully written dual-timeline tale of hidden stories and the search for freedom.'
Anna Mazzola, author of *The Clockwork Girl*

'In only 374 pages, Crosby succeeds in delivering a bittersweet tale of love, loss and lies that stretches across the 20th century.'
Historical Novel Society

An elegant yet earthy tale dancing between two timelines and two women trapped within the memories of the past.'
LoveReading.co.uk

'An evocatively written, haunting tale that has historic epic written all over it.'
Belfast Telegraph

Polly Crosby lives in Norfolk with her husband and son. To find out more about Polly's writing, please visit pollycrosby.com.

Also by Polly Crosby

The Illustrated Child
The Unravelling
Vita and the Birds

YA
This Tale is Forbidden

THE
HOUSE OF
FEVER

POLLY CROSBY

ONE PLACE. MANY STORIES

HQ

An imprint of HarperCollins*Publishers* Ltd
1 London Bridge Street
London SE1 9GF

www.harpercollins.co.uk

HarperCollins*Publishers*
Macken House, 39/40 Mayor Street Upper,
Dublin 1, D01 C9W8, Ireland
This edition 2024

1

First published in Great Britain by
HQ, an imprint of HarperCollinsPublishers Ltd 2024

ISBN PB: 9780008550738
TPB: 9780008550707

This book contains FSC™ certified paper and other controlled
sources to ensure responsible forest management.

For more information visit: www.harpercollins.co.uk/green

This book is set in 11.4/15.4 pt. Centaur MT Std by HarperCollins*Publishers* India

Printed and Bound in the UK using 100% Renewable
Electricity at CPI Group (UK) Ltd

To the wonderful NHS

Part One

Chapter One

The Diamond Earring

The girl climbs carefully down the chute, the flats of her palms pressed against the shiny metal. She knows from experience that she must hold her muscles taut, that she cannot give in to the ache along her shoulders. She is confident that the laundry has not yet been emptied, but still, she shimmies down a foot or two more, before drawing in her hands and knees, and she plummets.

In that moment of weightlessness, as her body plunges down, thoughts flash through her mind. How far is the drop? How hard the ground?

And then she lands with a soft thud, her body enveloped in dirty laundry. The tang of illness rises up from the sheets and blankets. She can smell the iron smack of blood, the saccharine sweetness of days-old perfume. Something sharp is pressing against her palm, and she looks down to see a golden glimmer, half hidden in the sheets. With nimble fingers, she picks it up, and pushes open the hatch. A spear of light filters into the chute.

It is a diamond earring. It glitters like treasure, and the girl pockets it.

She puts her ear to the crack, listening hard. She can hear the thrum of the boiler and far off, the chugging ventilation fan. But that is all. There is no one here now. They are all fast asleep.

Climbing out of the chute, she plants her bare feet silently on the cold, tiled floor, her skin beneath the nightdress twitching with excitement. The whole of the house lies ahead, expectant like a held breath, as if it has been waiting just for her.

Chapter Two

Agnes peered through the steam engine's smoke, narrowing her eyes against the sting of smuts as she searched the skyline. The land around them had been flat and dull for some time, with only occasional glimpses of the sea to their right. But now she could see the beginnings of a hill rising gently on their left, and an unknown feeling began to stir inside her.

There! Between the trees like a magician's illusion, the flash of a house, the gleam of a lake. And then it was gone.

The steady rhythm of the train began to ease, and as she drew her head in through the window, a tick of excitement careered through her body. They were nearly there.

She sat back down in the carriage, her stomach roiling with nerves. Would the place be as she had imagined? Would *he* be as she remembered?

As if she sensed her thoughts, her mother leant towards her, wiping a smut from Agnes's cheek, her hand lingering on her face briefly. Mother hadn't said a word since the ship had departed Calais and seasickness had ravaged through her illness-weakened body. This silence worried Agnes. Through the window, she glimpsed the flat, grey line of the sea again, like a thin, unsmiling mouth, so dissimilar to the dazzling blue ocean they had so recently left behind in the South of France. She shivered, struggling to adjust to the change in temperature. She had forgotten how much cooler England was in the summer.

As the locomotive came to a stop in a cloud of hissing steam, Agnes took a handkerchief from her carpet bag and dabbed it across her mother's forehead. Outside, they could hear doors opening and people calling.

'Come on, Mother. It looks like we've arrived.'

Her mother's eyelids fluttered like butterfly wings.

'It's all right,' Agnes said, taking her hand. 'I'm nervous too.'

On the platform, a chauffeur greeted them with a doff of his cap. She was surprised to see a white mask covering his mouth and tied behind his ears.

'Mrs Fairhaven?' he said.

It took her a moment to realise he was talking to her. She had only been Mrs Fairhaven for a matter of weeks, and as yet, no one had addressed her as such. Another thing she was going to have to get used to. She was a wife now, with a husband. Agnes tasted the word. It was so new on her tongue that it almost stung, a painful pleasure that hinted unnervingly of things to come.

As she bent to lift their cases, the man shooed her away. He hefted them up, propping her faithful old carpet bag on top, and led the women with a brisk step out of the station. She felt her mother's fragile arm link through hers, and they followed at a more hesitant pace through the gate and towards a huge motor car, a mass of chrome and curves and gleaming green paint.

'That's not for us, surely?' Agnes said.

'I can assure you it is, madam,' the chauffeur replied, his voice muffled by the cotton over his mouth, stowing the suitcases and opening the door for them.

Agnes helped her mother fold her thin frame into the car, and slid in next to her. The interior was shaded and airy. She leant back against the plush grey leather, cool against the cotton of her blouse. The car smelled expensive, like a perfumier's shop she'd once visited in France. The subtle scent of leather laced with fresh air, and something sweet-smelling that she couldn't put her finger on. She looked around for its source, and spied a small vase suspended from the car's ceiling containing a single white lily. All of a sudden, she felt far too soiled and unfashionable to be in such an extravagant, sumptuous vehicle.

Was this to be her life now? Being driven by chauffeur and referred to as 'madam'? Back in France, Christian had shown her a photograph of Hedoné House, nestled high on a lone hill set back from the Norfolk coast. It was a beautiful building, the intricate structure of balconies and verandas strung across it like a necklace. There was a lake at the front, she recalled, mirror-still, the house and the grounds encased in a circle of pine woodland like a glamorous fur stole.

But however elegant Hedoné House was, at its heart, it was still a place for those with tuberculosis to recuperate. Agnes glanced at her mother now. Her skin was very pale, and she had that high blush of colour on the sharp bones of her cheeks that indicated a fever. Christian had insisted on paying for their first-class travel, but even with this considerable luxury, the long journey of train to ship to train had worn her mother out. Not for the first time, Agnes felt relief that soon she would have some answers, and her stomach jolted at the thought that she would at last see her husband again.

She turned nervously to look at her reflection in the window, to ascertain whether the smut her mother had dabbed at on her cheek was completely gone, but the window had been wound right down.

She looked for a handle to wind it back up, but there didn't appear to be one. Instead, where she supposed it ought to have been, there was a gold roundel with a crest on it, a leaping hare, its ears poised and pointed. This was the emblem of Hedoné House, she remembered. Christian had told her that hares signified abundance, prosperity and good fortune — the perfect symbol for such a magnificent place.

How odd this all was! Like something out of a dream. She looked down at her lap, feeling rather overwhelmed at the wealth and luxury that surrounded her, and her eyes settled in embarrassment on the cheap cut of her blouse, the outdated fit of her ancient wool skirt. She put her finger to a neatly darned hole near her knee, remembering how proud she had been when she mended it. Now, it merely looked shabby and travelworn, just like her.

On the leather seat by her leg, there was a faint speckling of pink dots, like freckles. There were more of them on the padded bolster between them. Mother had noticed them, too. Little spots of palest pink, one or two a shade darker, almost red. Her mother put an experimental fingertip to one, her eyebrows drawing together, and then she whipped her hand away with a jolt. Her eyes found Agnes's, her breath coming in small puffs.

'He's the best, Mother,' Agnes said, gripping her hand. 'He'll take very good care of you.'

The car took them along a quiet lane, the line of pines Agnes had seen from the train growing closer. The road became increasingly narrow until the car was skimming the high grass verge on each side. Lord help them if another motor car should come careening round the corner. But then, this thing was built like a tank.

They began to rise steeply now, and out of the corner of her eye she saw her mother clutch at the edge of the seat, her fingernails digging into the soft leather. The chauffeur turned a tight corner, and the wind blew a sudden, vicious gust of air into the compartment. Agnes grabbed at her hat. Leaning forward, she went to pull down the screen that divided the driver's compartment from theirs, but it wouldn't budge.

'I say,' she said, tapping hard on the glass. The chauffeur's head moved slightly in acknowledgement. 'Could you close the windows? It's awfully blustery back here.'

He shook his head in response. 'Infection regulations,' he mumbled through the mask, and she sank back onto the padded seat, holding her hat in place. It didn't seem very fair: *his* windows were firmly shut after all.

The chauffeur turned up yet another small lane, this one studded with clumps of grass in a line at its centre, and then almost immediately turned again, coming to a smooth stop in front of a tall wrought iron gate, that same leaping-hare design twisted into the metal.

This must be it: the entrance to their new home. Agnes had a sudden urge to get out of the car, to pause for a moment and take stock before her new life began.

Was this really what she wanted? Back in France, with the constant warmth and dazzling sunshine, the idea had seemed so perfect, romantic almost. But now, with the cold wind surging in off the North Sea, the masks and the isolation, it all felt decidedly unsettling. In a fit of panic, she put her hand to the door to open it.

But where the handle would normally be, there was another gold roundel with a hare, leaping as if trying to escape, too. In frustration, she considered contorting herself through the window's gap, but then the gate in front of them began to swing open of its own accord, and the chauffeur pressed the car forwards like a horse exiting a stable.

Agnes glanced at her mother to see if she shared her panic. She was clutching the edge of the open window, looking with trepidation at the long, smooth road ahead. She seemed so diminutive in the vast, padded seat of the car. More unwell than ever.

Mother had not always been like this. There was a time when she was filled with so much energy, so much light and joy that it had spilled over and infected Agnes, too. But the constant gnawing of this illness on body and mind meant that there was precious little energy left for happiness for either of them. Mother was Agnes's whole life, the instigating factor in this whole plan. They needed this place, she reminded herself. Feeling her heart rate calm, she sat back against the plush seat, steeling herself for what was ahead.

The road was straight and immaculate, rising in a gentle incline, the pine trees that had drawn her eyes earlier lining each side like sentries. She searched through them, trying to see how deep they went, but they disappeared into blackness. Agnes leant forward to look out of the windscreen, searching for the house that she had glimpsed from the train. The trees broke smartly away, and a wide, gleaming vista opened up. Hedoné House stretched out in front of them in all its palatial majesty.

Her first thought was that it couldn't possibly be a sanatorium. It looked like a luxurious hotel. Indeed, it might have been plucked straight from a Swiss mountainside. It was sprawling, set high on the crest of the hill and surrounded by pine trees. The front was decorated with wooden verandas; pretty balconies dotted with what looked like deckchairs and sun loungers. And behind these were huge windows and doors, all wide open.

To their left, the lake that she had spotted from the train appeared. She could see a perfect reflection of the house in its smooth surface. Between the lake and the sanatorium, on a gentle grass slope, stood lots of small wooden chalets on wheels. Agnes turned in her seat to study them. Were they bathing machines? Beach huts? Scattered amongst them were colourful deckchairs, each with a little table next to it, a parasol above. One or two of these were in use, and Agnes caught the amber sparkle of a champagne flute, a flutter of a newspaper rippling in the breeze. Far off, she could see a glittering swimming pool, the marble tiles surrounding it so bright in the sun that it glowed.

As they drew closer to the house, a group of people playing croquet on a flat stretch of grass came into view. These couldn't be the patients, surely? None of them looked particularly ill at all. She glanced over to her mother again, taking in the handkerchief, clutched tightly in her trembling hand, and a quiver of hope traced over her skin.

Chapter Three

The car pulled up smartly in front of the house, and the chauffeur got out and began unloading their cases.

'Do we just wait?' Agnes whispered, not expecting a reply.

But her mother, until now so silent, whispered next to her, her voice as tiny as a mouse's, 'We have no choice: we're locked in.'

Agnes looked at those little gold emblems in place of handles. She tapped her foot on the floor impatiently, wondering if Christian knew they had arrived, and her stomach began again to swoop with nerves. In a flurry of panic, she pulled open her handbag and took from it a silver case. Its polish was dull from so much handling, but she could see an approximation of her face reflected in the surface, small and pinched, her hair pinned under her hat, the wave she had tried so desperately to coax into it lost forever somewhere over the English Channel. Clicking the case open, she turned instead to the pair of photographs inside.

They had been taken a few days before the wedding, on the day they had announced their engagement. She ran her eyes over her own face, the expression serious, her dark brown hair turned to monochrome in the black-and-white image. Her green eyes looked pale, too, but a tinge of shading touched her cheeks, accentuating her cheekbones and betraying her nerves.

She remembered how Christian had unpinned her hair for the photograph, his fingers lifting the tresses and laying them artfully across her shoulders, arranging it just so. It had been one of the first times he had touched her, the edge of his little finger glancing her neck. As she drank in the photograph, the memory of it sang under her skin, loaded as it was with the possibility of a new life opening up before her.

She turned to his photograph, comforted by the familiarity of the face looking out at her, steady and handsome and kind.

They had met quite by chance on the beach one day. Agnes had rented deckchairs in the hope that the proximity to the invigorating sea air would help Mother's chest. She remembered the first time she'd seen him. An enticing waft of coffee had drifted towards her from a group of people farther down the beach, and she'd glanced over. They were a flamboyant, bohemian-looking set, stretched out supinely on bathing towels under palm trees, passing cigarettes among themselves as if they didn't have a care in the world. Agnes had looked on enviously. Oh, to be so free.

Christian had been sitting among them, holding court. Even then, he had stood out, so classically, unflappably English in his well-cut pale linen suit.

'He's a doctor,' Mother had whispered in Agnes's ear, her deckchair creaking as she leant over. 'He's travelling across the Continent, looking for patients to treat at his sanatorium back in England.'

Agnes had pushed herself up in her deckchair, suddenly alert. He seemed so at home with those clever, exotic people, getting into friendly arguments with them, slipping fluidly from English to French to German. They were writers and artists mostly, she found out. A smattering of photographers and journalists among them too, and she had looked on a little jealously, watching them sip beer straight from bottles and feast on soft, ripe fruits and cheeses they'd picked from the local market. Once or twice, she thought she'd heard that telling cough amongst them, so very like her mother's, and any jealousy she'd felt was wiped away as pity rose up instead.

Once, the doctor had glanced at her, his startling blue eyes holding her gaze, and Agnes had looked away, embarrassed, aware she'd been caught staring.

On the third day, the coastal breeze intensified, the sand glittering in gritty clouds that stung at her bare arms. Unknown to Agnes then, this one serendipitous moment would go on to change the direction of her life forever. As she battled to unfold the deckchairs, the canvas flapping against the wind, a strong gust plucked the handkerchief from her mother's hand, sending it billowing across the beach.

As if he had been waiting for just such a moment, the doctor jumped to his feet and chased after it, running as a cricketer might between wickets. Snatching it up, he had returned it gallantly to Agnes's mother with a small bow.

'Beautiful day,' he'd said in perfect English, tipping his hat to Agnes with a smile, and she'd returned it, thanking him profusely.

'Please,' she'd said, surprising herself with her own daring as he began to walk away. 'Let me buy you coffee to show my gratitude.'

Over tiny cups of espresso, she had learnt that his family traced their roots back to France at the end of the Roman Empire. And indeed, however English he professed to be, there was still something rather Gaulish about him. He was tall and fair skinned with piercing blue eyes. In those fast, heady days of courtship, French words stained his lips like the blood from the rare steaks that he loved to eat.

A shout of glee pulled her back to the present, the thwack of a mallet on a ball echoing across the grounds as the croquet game came to an end. Agnes tucked the photographs away. The players had turned their attention to the car. She could hear their voices drifting over on the breeze. Her gaze flitted over each person, searching for her husband, but he was not among them. They all looked extremely glamorous. How on earth did Christian expect her to befriend people like that?

A young woman caught her eye, a little younger than herself, perhaps twenty-three or thereabouts. She was wearing a lemon-yellow sundress and huge, dark sunglasses like a film star, her gleaming honey-brown hair loose about her shoulders, the waves rippling in the wind. She was standing, like the rest, studying the car with interest. She looked vaguely familiar. Agnes averted her eyes, feeling like an exhibit in a freak show. She wondered if they knew who she was. Had they been told? Were they expecting the doctor's new wife?

There was another woman at the edge of the group, conspicuous by the darkness of her skin, and Agnes thought she saw her smile tentatively in her direction. She was wearing a cloche hat similar to Agnes's own, tipped at a jaunty angle, a single lock of gleaming black hair curled like a fern on her forehead. Agnes discreetly adjusted her own hat to match. The woman made a sudden move to walk towards the motor car, but the glamorous girl in the sundress put out her arm, stopping her.

Mother was peering up at the house, her hand still on the car's open window frame, and Agnes followed her gaze. It was a beautiful building, simple yet imposing. A decorative band of knapped Norfolk flint was wrapped around it like a ribbon on a birthday present. Slices of sunlight poured in through the open doors and windows, revealing tantalising glimpses of the interior. Agnes could see an opulent dining room, crisp white linen on the tables, the gleam of silver cutlery catching the light. Further along was a room encased in pale marble. Glittering chandeliers hung from the ceiling, and below them, plush sofas were dotted about. On the verandas, sumptuous sun loungers were lined up next to one another, ermine throws and padded cushions scattered here and there.

She pulled her eyes from all the luxury to see a woman descending the steps that led from the grand front door. She was dressed in a dark blue nurse's uniform and she too had a cotton mask covering her mouth. Her nose, poking over the top, was large and business-like, as if it were leading her towards them like a hound on the scent.

'Here we go,' Agnes whispered, half to her mother, half to herself, as the chauffeur opened the motor car's door, and she stepped out into the bright sunlight.

Chapter Four

The nurse had come to a stop at the bottom of the steps, her wiry arms folded across her flat chest. She wore a navy-blue dress cinched at the waist with a wide gold belt, a heavy set of keys dangling from one side. A white collar and short white veil finished the outfit, giving her the air of a nun, not a medic. Agnes couldn't tell if she were smiling underneath the mask, but conceded that if she was, it certainly didn't reach her eyes.

'Welcome to Hedoné House,' the woman said. 'You may call me Matron. Let me show you to your rooms.'

She clicked her fingers, and a handsome young man dressed in livery appeared from one of the open doors with a wheeled chair. He, too, was wearing a mask over his mouth. Was this how she would tell the staff from the patients, this badge of cloth half hiding their faces? He steered the chair down a slope next to the steps, and moved swiftly to collect their suitcases, and Agnes thought she saw his eyes widen in badly contained surprise at the state of her carpet bag. She felt Mother's trembling arm link with her own as she helped her into the chair, a padded winged affair upholstered in a design of blue peacock feathers, more suited to an armchair than a medical aid.

The nurse took hold of the chair's mahogany handles and began to push Mother up the slope and into a grand hallway lined with potted ferns.

'Excuse me . . . Matron?' Agnes said, trotting to keep up, the word feeling foreign on her tongue.

The thin woman came to an abrupt stop and swung round, eyebrows raised.

'Will Christian be joining us?'

'Doctor is very busy at present. He sends his apologies. He asked me to assure you that he will be along as soon as his duties allow.' She spun back around and began pushing the chair again, faster than before. 'The convalescing rooms are up on the first floor,' she called over her shoulder. 'We have a strict policy of six weeks' bed rest on arrival, during which we perform tests to assess the guest's health. I believe Doctor has already personally assessed *you*, Mrs Fairhaven, whilst on the Continent.' She said the last word as if the thought of somewhere other than England offended her greatly.

'Yes, that's right. He seemed quite sure that I was free of tuberculosis.' It had been a wonderful moment of relief for Agnes. All those years caring for her unwell parents, to find that her own body was still miraculously free of the disease.

'I'm glad to hear you *seem* very well. In any case, there will be more tests, and after that, if Doctor decides the time is right, a guest may be moved into the downstairs accommodation.'

Was the nurse talking about herself or Mother? Surely Agnes was not to live with the patients?

They came to a stop in front of a marble-framed lift with a gold metal gate. The matron took a key from a chain at her waist and slipped it into a keyhole, turning it once. She pressed the top button, and somewhere deep in the bowels of the house, the lift sighed into life.

Agnes looked around her. Two corridors led off the hall, one on each side, stretching into the distance, like a spine in the long building. When the lift arrived, Matron slid open the gate and ushered them inside. It was a large space, large enough for a bed to fit in, and covered from floor to ceiling in mirrored gold. The lift began to rise, coming almost immediately to a smooth stop. Matron pulled open the gate with her stringy arms, and they began to walk down a light and airy corridor lined with doors. It reminded Agnes again of a hotel. Sumptuous vases of lilies stood on marble planters between each door, a gentle breeze playing with their petals.

The rooms all had names. Agnes read them as they walked, noting Austen and then Keats.

'Who is the literary enthusiast?' she asked as they went past Brontë.

'Why, your husband of course,' Matron answered without turning, and Agnes sent daggers at the back of her sharp little head.

'The upstairs accommodation is named after all those great literary talents who sadly contracted TB,' the nurse continued. 'Doctor believes there is a link between the illness and a person's creativity.'

Agnes knew this already. Christian was extremely selective about who he would admit to Hedoné House. Alongside his paying guests, he offered a scholarship to gifted individuals: artists and musicians and writers who were afflicted with the disease.

She had asked him once, 'Why the creative industries, Christian? Why not people of high intellect, or those in desperate need?'

'Other sanatoria cater for the poor, Agnes. And although I value intellect, I have always loved music and art and literature above all else, as I think you do, too, which is why you are such a good fit. Call me a romantic, but I'm fascinated by the notion that tuberculosis is a creative disease. It affects so many artistic souls, and I believe there is something in the fragility of the illness that inspires a seam of creativity in people. I vowed to search the world to find the right patients, to bring them together here, to create an idyll. My hope is to cultivate a rich melting pot of discussion and debate. The patients at my sanatorium might be unwell, Agnes, but their minds still need stimulation, creativity. Hope.'

Agnes smiled at the memory. They had come to a stop outside the last door at the end of the hall, this one named Mansfield Suite.

'This is to be yours and your mother's accommodation,' Matron said, opening the door and stepping back to allow her to enter.

Agnes went at once to the huge window. It was wide open, with a marvellous view of the lake, and beyond it in the distance a glimpse of the sea. The clouds had cleared now, and the sparkling water looked just as blue as the Mediterranean. The croquet players had given up their game, mallets abandoned without thought on the lawn.

'I shall need to check your pulse and temperature.' Behind her, the matron's voice was sharp as she spoke to Mother. 'And then I will leave you to freshen up. Doctor will be around a little later. If you require tea, just press the bell.' She indicated a gold button on the wall by the bed, that same hare design that Agnes had seen in the motor car.

Mother was already sitting on the bed, her legs stretched out in front of her. She ran a hand over the soft sheet, a look of wonder on her pale face as Matron took her wrist, looking down at the watch pinned to her chest.

It might have been a beautiful room, Agnes thought, but for the large oxygen canister in one corner, and the ugliness of the hospital bed at its centre. On a table near the window was yet another vase of lilies, and she approached them in delight. Her wedding bouquet had consisted of lilies just like these. She bent to sniff one, the distinctive smell transporting her back to the day in question.

The flowers had been Christian's choice. She remembered feeling a little disappointed when she'd first seen them, for she had always thought of the lily as a funeral flower. But their creamy, textured petals had set off the expensive silk of her wedding suit perfectly, and, knowing how much they would have cost him, Agnes had forgiven him immediately.

She bent to sniff the lilies in the room, the cloying scent so strong that she wondered if they had been chosen to mask another smell. She breathed in through her nose, finding something more medical in the air, antiseptic traced with a scent she couldn't name.

'Christian gave me to understand I would need to quarantine, too,' she said.

Matron looked up from reading the thermometer. She shook it with a sharp flick of her wrist, then pointed to a door, presumably to another bedroom.

'Doctor thought you might like to be with your mother while she convalesces. He knows how close you two are.' Again, the matron's eyes lingered on Agnes, the nostrils in that large nose flaring, and she wondered if underneath the cloth mask, the woman might be sneering.

'When will I see him . . . Doctor Fairhaven . . . my husband?' she asked tentatively, stumbling over the different titles.

'Doctor is a busy man. But he knows you're here. I imagine he'll see you on his rounds if he cannot get to you before.'

All this time, the man who had brought their cases had been standing so silently by the door that Agnes had almost forgotten he was there.

'James,' the matron said, and he stiffened a little. 'Please give Mrs Fairhaven a menu. It's room service only for the first six weeks,' she said to Agnes as he handed her a thick piece of card, stretching his arm out as far as he could reach so as not to get too close, and stepping back as soon as she had taken it.

'Surely I'm not to quarantine for six weeks?' Agnes said with a start. Christian had never mentioned such a lengthy period.

'No, of course not. But your mother will need to.'

'How long will *I* be in here for?'

Matron was doling out pills into two silver cups 'That will be up to Doctor. Now, your meal choices.' She nodded at the card in Agnes's hand. 'When you've chosen, simply ring for a member of staff, and they will come and take your order.' She indicated the gold button by the bed again. 'Dinner is served at six o'clock. Open up, dear,' she added to Agnes's mother, tipping the jewelled array of tablets into her waiting mouth. Mother swallowed obediently, taking a sip of the water that Matron pressed to her lips.

'Now your turn, Mrs Fairhaven,' she said.

Agnes looked up, alarmed. 'But I'm not unwell.'

'No. But you *are* in quarantine. And for that to end we need you in tiptop condition.' She passed the silver cup to Agnes.

'What are they?'

'Cod liver oil, magnesium, calcium, omega three. Those little gilded ones are thiamine. We cover them in gold to take the bitter taste away.'

'Not real gold, surely?'

Matron met her gaze. 'Yes, real gold. Taken together, these tablets will make your hair shine and your nails grow strong. Doctor likes us all to be at our best.'

'Does he take these, too?'

'I couldn't say, madam.'

Agnes looked down at the tablets. 'Thank you,' she said, and then, girding herself for a fight, 'I'll take them later.'

Matron's eyes locked briefly onto hers, but she only opened a leather book and began to make notes.

'Let's take you to the bathroom, Mother,' Agnes said, going to help her up.

'No need, Mrs Fairhaven,' Matron said. 'Mother really shouldn't be getting out of bed.'

'But *Mother* might need the toilet.'

Matron produced a bedpan. 'We shall help her from now on,' she said sweetly.

Agnes was about to protest, but Matron was already pulling back the bedcovers, and she turned to the window to give her mother a modicum of privacy. It was a bright summer's evening, the birds singing joyfully outside. With a stir of air, Matron bustled past her and began closing the windows one by one.

'I thought the windows were meant to stay permanently open,' Agnes said. 'To air the lungs?'

'Indeed, but only during the day,' she said, locking them with a little gold key. 'My charges on the quarantine floor require a good night's sleep. We have lots of owls round here. They can be quite vocal. And the deer in rutting season are awfully loud.'

'I'm sure Christian said—' Agnes started, but her words were drowned out by a screech as Matron dragged the curtains across the windows, her stringy arms tight with cords of muscle. The room became all at once very dark.

'Agnes?' Mother's voice drifted out of the dark. 'What's happening?'

'It's all right, Mrs Templeton,' Matron said loudly, as if Agnes's mother were deaf.

There was a click, and the light of a bedside lamp filled the room. Matron's severe face was softened by the glow. The gold belt at her waist glinted in the light, and Agnes saw for the first time that the design upon it was the golden hare, the emblem of the sanatorium, its beady eye staring straight at her.

'At night, the chill can have a debilitating effect on the guests,' Matron explained. 'Especially on those who are extremely ill.' She looked pointedly at Mother, before turning back to the curtains, fussing over the folds to ensure they were straight.

Was Mother extremely ill? Fear trickled over Agnes, and the fight that had reared in her drained away. She was exhausted. She realised that arguing with the nurse in her current state was only going to end one way. Better to rest and recuperate, and speak to Christian in the morning. He had obviously employed this woman for a reason. Better not rock the boat yet.

'I will see you both bright and early,' Matron said, going to the door and unlocking it. 'Goodnight, Mrs Fairhaven, Mrs Templeton.'

Agnes turned. Now was the time to make a good impression, to demonstrate what an asset she could be. 'Matron?' she called. The matron raised her eyebrows. 'Thank you, for all you've done. Mother and I are so happy to be here.'

The woman stood stiffly for a moment, a touch of crimson colouring her cheeks. Clearly, she wasn't used to being thanked. She gave a perfunctory nod, before disappearing through the door, and Agnes let out a breath of relief.

Looking over at her mother, Agnes saw she had fallen asleep, her head lolling awkwardly on the plump pillow.

Chapter Five

In her own bedroom, Agnes unpinned her hat and placed it on her bed, relieved to see that it wasn't a hospital bed, but a luxuriously large divan. She found the bathroom behind a door back in her mother's room, and splashed her face, washing away the hours of train travel.

'You're here,' she whispered, grinning at her reflection in the mirror.

She knew that there would be plenty more testing situations to come, that this was only the start, but she was ready for the challenge. Slotting into a perfectly oiled machine such as Hedoné was bound to ruffle some feathers, Matron's included. But Agnes was not stupid. She knew how to tread lightly, how to ingratiate herself to people. She had no plan other than to fit in, to survive this strange new life until it wasn't strange anymore. Mother was her priority, as she had always been, and this place was their salvation, however out of her depth she felt right now.

Too pent up to sit still, she went to the door that led to the balcony, but found it locked. She leant out of the open window, looking to her left and right. It appeared that each room had a private balcony, but nobody was out there. Perhaps all the doors were locked.

It was very quiet out in the grounds, too. Where *was* everyone? Quickly, Agnes checked on her mother, and seeing that she was sleeping peacefully, she went to the door they had come in through, itching to explore. Perhaps she might even bump into Christian, she thought with a jolt of nerves. A fleeting memory came to her, of her husband's fingers, slipping beneath the beaded cuff of her wedding jacket, sliding back the fragile silk until her bare wrist was exposed. The flash in his eyes as he raised it to his mouth, dabbing at the vulnerable skin with the coral tip of his tongue.

The feeling it had elicited came back to Agnes now, like a chord, pulled taut in her body, the string of a harp, plucked and released, plucked and released, and she felt her face grow warm at the memory. It had been their first moment alone as husband and wife, a dark corner of the hotel, the warm, balmy night smelling of roses and sunset.

She looked down at her wrist now, feeling the echo of her dormant pulse just beneath her fingers, as if her body was waiting for him. She pressed the pad of her thumb insistently into the flesh. Soon, soon.

With renewed excitement, she went to open the door, but when she tried to turn the handle, she found that this door, too, was locked. A tingling sense of alarm rose in her, and she hurried to her own room, searching for another way out, to no avail. Agnes sat on the edge of her bed and picked up the menu she'd dropped there. Perhaps she should eat something, fortify herself for what was to come. Christian might come by at any moment, and it would be good to be as refreshed as possible.

There was no gold button by her own bed, so she went back to Mother's room, noting with relief that the earlier tinge in her cheeks was a little less pronounced now. The gold circle made a satisfying click when she pressed it, and somewhere far away she thought she heard a bell ring. Agnes bunched her hands together, waiting. She wondered how many staff Christian had here.

Less than a minute later there was a knock on the door, followed by a click as it was unlocked. It opened straight away.

A maid stood in the hallway.

'Good afternoon, ma'am,' she said. Her voice was soft, muffled by the mask over her mouth. She had a much kinder nose than Matron's, and Agnes stepped forward, thrusting out her hand.

'Good afternoon, I don't believe we've met. I'm Agnes. Agnes Fairhaven . . . Doctor Fairhaven's new wife.'

The maid took a step back, leaving Agnes's hand hanging in the air. In embarrassment she let it drop back into place.

'I'm afraid we don't make physical contact with the guests,' the maid said politely. 'Infection control. Matron likes us to maintain a distance where possible. What may I get for you?' she said, lifting a notebook and pen.

Flustered, Agnes looked down at the menu. 'Let's see, I'd like to order lamb cutlets with braised red cabbage for dinner tonight, and smoked haddock chowder for my mother. And could I have a pot of tea sent directly, please?'

The girl wrote this down. 'And wine with your dinner, madam? May I recommend a bottle of the Sancerre?'

'Oh.' Agnes was not used to wine, but she supposed it would go nicely with the lamb. And perhaps her husband might be here by then, and they could share a glass on the balcony. 'That would be lovely, thank you.'

The girl nodded, then turned to go.

'Actually,' Agnes rushed forward, 'I need to come out, too, I need to find my husband—'

The girl put a hand across the doorway, barring the way. She looked troubled. 'I'm sorry, madam, but no one is allowed out during the convalescing period. It is a time for relaxation and recuperation. Guests mustn't overexert themselves.'

'But I'm not convalescing, and I'm not a guest. Least, not in that sense of the word. I'm here with my mother, as I'm sure you know.'

The girl looked uncomfortable. 'This is a quarantine area, madam,' she whispered. 'I cannot let you out, it would be more than my life's worth. You might be carrying illnesses that could endanger the guests.'

'Oh.' Of course. 'Not even on the landing? Out there?' She pointed to the crack in the door.

The girl shook her pretty head so that it drooped like a snowdrop. 'I'm afraid not. They're the doctor's orders. I'm very sorry.' Without waiting for an answer, she quickly pulled the door closed before Agnes could reach it.

'Damn it!' Agnes hissed in frustration. Behind her, her mother stirred at the sound, but she only mumbled something in her sleep and rolled over with a sigh.

Agnes went to the window, her pulse flickering beneath her skin. Surely Christian didn't mean for her to be locked away like this? It must be a simple misunderstanding. Carefully, she put one leg over the window frame, then the other, dropping down onto the balcony on the other side. The breeze was strong here, ruffling the beautiful furs that were strewn across a wooden sun lounger. She went to the edge of the balcony, searching for a fire escape, but there was none. The drop to the ground felt perilously far.

'Damn it,' she said again, louder this time. Somewhere far below, she thought she heard someone chuckle, only for it to be cut off by a rumbling cough.

The swimming pool she had glimpsed earlier glowed a perfect

azure blue. From up here, she could see it was in the shape of a leaping hare, the water lit from beneath by hundreds of underwater bulbs so that it shone, bright and inviting. A white diving board stretched out from the hare's tail, over its flank and belly.

With a start, Agnes saw that the grounds were no longer deserted. While she'd been inside, a group of people had congregated down by the lake. One man had a saxophone. He lifted it to his lips, playing a volley of discordantly beautiful notes. The woman she remembered with the cloche hat was there, too, her willowy body seated on the edge of the jetty, her feet in the water. Her hands were tapping the planks of the wood either side of her as if they were the keys of a piano. A red-headed man sat a little way from the others, hunched over a sketchpad on his lap, his hand moving fluidly across the page.

She could not see the glamorous young woman in the lemon dress. Agnes scoured her mind to think where she had seen her before, to no avail. The little group seemed so at ease with themselves, lost in their own little bubble, the women sharing the men's cigarettes and batting them playfully on the arms. They reminded her of that group on the beach in France when she'd met Christian. A sudden sting of jealousy pierced Agnes as she watched them from her elevated viewpoint, a familiar sensation creeping over her, of always being the one on the outside looking in.

How many of these patients were Christian's specially selected scholars? What were the talents that had earned them a free place here, allowing them to embrace their creativity and benefit from the world-class scientific treatments on offer? Or perhaps they were all paying guests, able to afford the substantial price tag of Hedoné themselves. One or two might be lords or ladies; they'd even had a princess stay here briefly last year, Christian had told her.

Agnes shook her head in amazement. She had known that the

lifestyle would be incredibly luxurious. In France, her husband had talked of the excessive manner in which the guests were accustomed to live: the champagne, the rich, exotic food, the legendary parties that sometimes went on through the night. Privately, she had wondered just how healthy all of it could be on already strained bodies, but when she'd broached it with Christian, he had only patted her hand.

'I don't expect you to understand,' he'd said, and perhaps he was right. What did *she* know of excess, after all?

Christian's ethos was that these people deserved the best. He explained that many of them soon got bored with the constant supply of luxuries, and their thoughts turned to finding healthier pursuits, of which there were many on offer at Hedoné. And for those who were too unwell to ever leave, why should they abstain from the one thing that gave them pleasure?

But whether rich or talented, *all* of these people were from a world Agnes had never known. It struck her again how healthy they looked. She had expected to see wheelchairs, oxygen canisters, sickness and illness at every turn, but these people looked normal. Better than normal; they looked wonderful.

Her husband had boasted, of course, about how healthy his patients were. She thought back to one particular day in France, remembering the tiny restaurant he had taken her to for a late lunch in a secluded cove close to Juan-les-Pins.

The walk there had felt treacherous atop a cliff, winding down to a secluded beach. Palm trees and tall, windswept pines shaded their table as Christian ordered *rascasse farci* for them both. The wine he had chosen had made her head swim pleasantly, so that she could barely focus on the conversation, until one word drew her back.

'. . . I am delighted to say he's now cured.'

'Cured?' she said, louder than she'd intended. She thought of

Mother, the racking cough, the thin, fragile bones. 'But, I thought that was impossible.'

'Nothing is impossible,' he said. 'Except, it seems, finding the right sort of person to share my successes with.' He held her gaze as he said this, and Agnes felt lost for a moment in those startling blue eyes, not quite daring to believe the insinuation.

'You see, I was married once before, but she passed away, leaving me and my young daughter, Isobel, alone. Meredith, my late wife, died from tuberculosis. It was she who spurred me on to open Hedoné.'

'Christian, I'm so sorry.'

He shook his head. 'For years I couldn't think of marrying again, but when at last I felt able, I realised that finding a suitable wife would be . . . difficult. Not everybody is suited to a life in a sanatorium, however luxurious the lifestyle. You know yourself how horrific this disease can be, Agnes. Most people prefer the sick to stay out of sight and out of mind. I've wondered sometimes if I'm destined to be a bachelor forever because of the vocation I felt I had to pursue. That is, until I met you.'

Agnes stilled.

'You are kind-hearted, and you have this incredible inner strength, demonstrated by the excellent care of your mother. You would not be shocked by the illness you see at Hedoné, I'm sure.' He cleared his throat. 'My daughter is eight years old now, and she needs a mother to nurture her. And I need a wife,' he added, meeting Agnes's eyes. 'A partner to share in all my success. Your mother will be taken care of. She will have access to *all* the latest modern treatments.'

'And the cure?' Agnes asked hopefully.

'The cure is still in its infancy, but I cannot see why she could not benefit, if the tests show she's suitable. She would need to rest first of course, to promote recovery. My treatments comprise—Ah, scorpionfish!' he exclaimed, snatching up his napkin as the food arrived.

Agnes waited for him to continue, but the sight of the fish had made him quite forget his train of thought.

He helped her remove the bright orange head of her own fish, its eyes staring milkily up at her, and she thought on the proposition he had just made, if proposition it was. She was under no illusion that he was in love with her. The kindly platitudes were merely a way of demonstrating his belief in her suitability for the role. Offering up that first tender mouthful of fish, he fed it to her from his fork, and it was that moment, on that balmy, sun-kissed afternoon on the French Riviera, that she had first glimpsed a future charged with hope.

The glamorous crowd at the lake got to their feet and made their way to the house, and Agnes melted back into the shadows of the balcony, suddenly shy. Would some of these people eventually be cured? Could her mother be too? This had been her hope, in those hot, yearning days in France. But still it had felt just out of reach, a dream not yet realised. But now she and Mother were here, and their future was spread before them.

On the lawn close to the house, Agnes saw that a lone deckchair was still occupied. A large, tasselled parasol hid the face of whoever was sitting in it, and as she watched, a slim arm stretched out, lifting a cocktail glass from a side table. The bright yellow liquid winked in the sun, and she caught a glimpse of the person in the chair, a pair of long legs unfolding to one side.

It was the glamorous girl with the sunglasses. She stood up, stretching as if she had recently awoken. The cocktail in her hand perfectly matched her lemon-yellow dress, and Agnes wondered if she had chosen the drink for that reason. She reminded Agnes of a model, everything about her perfectly proportioned, her movements calculated, as if she was used to being looked at. There was a chill in the air now, and the girl slipped a cashmere shawl over her shoulders and began to make her way to the house. Halfway across the lawn, she spied Agnes up on the balcony and changed direction.

'Mrs Fairhaven,' she called up from the path below, removing her sunglasses. Her eyes were big and brown, her lips a perfect smiling bow.

'Yes!' Agnes said, surprised. This woman knew who she was. She stepped forward, resting her hands on the railing.

'What a treat to be able to chat with you, the other guests will be wild with envy,' the woman said. 'It's awfully awkward talking in this fashion, isn't it?' she called up. 'But of course, we'll have plenty of time to get cosy soon enough. Doctor says it won't be long before you're afforded more privileges. You'll be one of us before you know it. We can't wait to meet you properly, I'm very much looking forward to taking you under my wing.' She smiled that Hollywood smile again.

'Thank you,' Agnes said, taken aback. Had Christian really told this glamorous young thing that much about her?

'I'm terribly sorry,' the woman said, her liquid brown eyes unblinking. 'We haven't been properly introduced. I'm Juno Harrington.'

Juno Harrington. The name rang a bell, and Agnes scoured her mind to place it.

'Agnes Fairhaven,' she said. 'But of course, you already knew that,' she added.

'Yes, indeed I did.' Juno laughed. She put her head to one side as if she was studying her. 'I can see exactly why he likes you,' she added, the words coming out in a sigh.

What an odd thing to say, Agnes thought. 'I'm sorry, what—'

'Must dash,' Juno interrupted. 'I take an age to dress for dinner, and I must be punctual today: I've got my eye on the lobster, and last time the Americans got in first. If I'm not quick, I'll be left with oysters again.' She made a face. On anyone else, it would have looked ugly, but on her it was merely charming.

'Of course. Enjoy,' Agnes said.

The young woman disappeared into a room directly below hers, and from her mother's room, Agnes heard a knock on the door. Hastily, she clambered back over the windowsill, snagging her skirt on its sharp edge.

'Come in,' she said, smoothing down the wisps of hair that had blown free from her pins on the balcony.

The door swung open, and there, bearing a tea-tray laden with cups and saucers, stood her husband.

Chapter Six

Doctor Christian Fairhaven stood on the threshold, his startling blue eyes boring into her.

'Darling,' he said, his face grave with worry. 'There has been a misunderstanding.'

Agnes, who had been all set to pour her frustrations about the living arrangements out to him, was suddenly tongue-tied. She had quite forgotten how he made her feel.

Christian laid the tray on a table in the corner of the room. She followed him over and sat down as he began to pour the tea. Agnes had only ever seen him in the pale linen suits he had favoured in France, but now he was wearing a well-cut suit of dark grey cloth. When she'd imagined him at work, she had always pictured him in a white doctor's coat. He didn't look like a doctor at all, more a wealthy banker or a fashionable aristocrat.

'They locked the doors, Christian,' she said as he passed her a cup. 'I know we need to be in quarantine for the sake of the patients, but even the balcony door is locked.'

'I know, and that was entirely my fault. I had instructed Matron to unlock the balcony for you, but it appears she disobeyed my orders.'

Matron. Of course. Agnes thought of the sharp-nosed nurse, the way she had sneered at her earlier. She took a sip of the tea. It was refreshingly zesty, a perfumed Darjeeling if she wasn't mistaken, and she felt herself somewhat revived.

'We keep the balcony doors locked when guests first arrive, you see. Often, they're so unwell that they can't get out of bed anyway, but the first rule of Hedoné House is recuperation, and that begins in bed.'

'But as I said to the maid, *I'm* not ill.'

'No, you're right, and I promise I shall have a stern word with Matron. She sometimes forgets who is in control here.'

Ah! Agnes thought. *That's how it is.*

Christian was looking at her, a long, searching look, drinking her in.

'What is it?' she asked, patting her hair self-consciously.

'You are just as beautiful as I remember,' he said quietly.

Agnes wanted to drop her head in embarrassment, but she found she couldn't look away. She stared back at him, like a deer caught in the moonlight. Deep inside her, a squirming ribbon of excitement pulsed.

Across the room, Mother mumbled in her sleep, and the moment was lost.

Christian pulled out of his pocket a little gold key with a golden hare dangling from it.

'Here,' he said. 'This key will open the door to the balcony and enable you to take air outside.'

'Thank you,' she said, her fingers closing over it.

'Soon, I promise, you'll be out of this room and allowed into the rest of the house. You'll be an integral part of Hedoné! I can't wait to show you what I've done here. You're going to love it, I just know you are. The music! The intellectual conversation!' He placed his cup and saucer on the table with a delicate clink and took her hand in his own. 'I'm so sorry for the confusion over the locked doors, my darling.'

'No, it was my fault. In my excitement at being here I had forgotten that this resort was primarily for the wellbeing of the sick. It's not as if you didn't warn me that I would need to quarantine.'

'I thought it might bring comfort to you and your mother to be in adjoining rooms while your period of isolation lasts. Heaven knows this place can come as quite a shock to the uninitiated. I was hopeful that your mother's presence might be a welcome familiarity, and vice versa.'

'That's very kind,' Agnes said. She looked down at their linked hands, the gold of their wedding bands glinting in the sunlight. 'I still can't believe we're husband and wife.'

'Nor can I,' Christian said, smiling, and excitement tumbled again in Agnes's stomach. 'And soon,' he added, 'you'll be able to move into our cottage. We shall be a proper family.'

A proper family. Christian had talked only sparingly of his daughter, Isobel. Agnes knew that she was eight years old, and that her mother had died when she was younger. She had never thought much about motherhood before, her whole life being dedicated to taking care of her own mother, but now that it was being thrust upon her, she was quite looking forward to the challenge.

'I can't wait to meet her. Though I'm a little nervous. I want to make a good impression.'

Christian looked momentarily baffled, and then understanding dawned on his face. 'Oh, you mean Iso!' he said. 'Of course, you shall meet her soon. But she lives in the main house with her governess, not in the cottage with me.'

'Oh.' How strange, Agnes thought, not to live with one's own child.

Seeing her expression, Christian elaborated. 'I'm terribly busy, running Hedoné. It made sense, stationing her in the house. But now perhaps that you're here, we might rethink things. I'm sure she cannot wait to meet you either. I shall arrange it as soon as you're settled.' He lifted her hand to his lips, his eyes on hers.

'You're not wearing a mask,' she said, noticing for the first time.

'No. Only the live-out staff wear masks. It protects them and the guests.'

'Does Matron live out?' she asked hopefully.

'No. But she likes to set an example to her household. Now,' he said, getting up, 'let me see to my patient.'

He crossed to the bed, and Agnes was momentarily disappointed she was no longer the focus of his attention. Then she chided herself: her mother was the reason that they were here, after all. And she was in the best hands now.

Christian took the leatherbound book from the bedside table and began reading Matron's notes. 'Your mother's settled in well,' he said quietly so as not to wake her.

Agnes smiled with relief as he began taking her mother's pulse, those same fingers that had recently touched Agnes wrapping themselves around the frail wrist. In sleep, it was easy to see just how much the illness had ravaged through her. This place was her last hope, this caring, gentle man the one person who could help, and gratitude bloomed in Agnes's heart as she looked on.

Christian went to wash his hands, rolling down his sleeves as he emerged from the bathroom. 'Now,' he said, crossing to her and placing a hand on her cheek. 'As for you, good food and good sleep are what you need, doctor's orders.'

He was so close she could smell the warm, spicy scent of him, a lemony sharpness deep within it. He pressed his lips to her forehead, before walking to the door.

'Must you go?' she said, hurrying after him, hating the feebleness in her voice.

'Alas, my love, while you're in quarantine I cannot stay for too long in the same room, just in case. It could endanger the guests.'

He opened the door and stepped out into the hallway. Agnes hung back, frustrated that she was prohibited from crossing the threshold.

'Am I to stay in here for long?' she whispered.

'Tomorrow we shall assess you, and then if all is well, you will be able to join me in our cottage.' He smiled a dark, secretive smile. 'In the meantime, if you need anything, anything at all, don't hesitate to ask.'

He extended an arm towards her in what Agnes assumed was an embrace, and she responded in kind, but he was only pointing to the call button on the wall. When she turned back, he was reaching for the door handle.

The soft thud as the door clicked into place sounded expensive to her ears. On the bed, Mother stirred, stretching against the silky sheets.

'Agnes?' she said, her voice laced with confusion, and Agnes turned from the door with a sigh, and went to check on her mother.

Chapter Seven

At precisely six o'clock, a maid arrived with a hostess trolley bearing two silver platters, each topped with an ornate silver cloche. Two large glasses of milk and two crystal glasses were set next to a wine bottle, shivering with condensation in a silver ice bucket.

The maid set a tray on Mother's lap and stepped back. 'Bon appetit,' she said to them before leaving, the words sounding forced in her local accent.

The food smelled wonderful. Mother took a suspicious sip of her chowder, her eyes closing in pleasure as she tasted it.

They ate their meals in contented silence. After the long journey from France, with only an increasingly stale baguette and a hunk of brie to sate her, the lamb cutlets tasted like heaven to Agnes. She took a sip of the wine. It was cold and sharp, with an earthy freshness that made her turn her head to look out over the lake.

As she put her knife and fork together, the gold wedding band on her hand caught her eye, and she smiled, thinking fondly of her late father's ring. She had worn it for a while after his death, until circumstances had forced her to sell it.

Her family had never had much money, but they had always managed. That was until Father died, and Mother grew sick. Then, things had taken a turn for the worse. Agnes, their only child, had tried her best to keep the household together: she was good with a needle, mending clothes seamlessly, breathing new life into tired outfits. But their increasing poverty soon became hard to hide. Bills piled up. When their water was cut off, they could no longer keep themselves or their clothes clean. Agnes tried to no avail to disguise the musky scent that rose from her mother's festering skin. When she realised she couldn't stop the spread of illness that was thriving in such unhealthy, desperate conditions, she knew they had no choice. They left in the night, rent unpaid, leaving no trail.

Agnes sold her father's wedding ring to pay for their passage to France, and then later, her mother's too, to free up some money for their living expenses. After that, they had nothing. She took in sewing, but each visit to the *docteur* drained her of what little she'd saved, and she took to obtaining cheap, illegal morphine instead to curtail her mother's pain.

One night, when Mother was especially sick, Agnes had loitered down an alleyway, contemplating buying the heroin that she knew would blot out all of Mother's pain. How much of the drug would it take, she had wondered briefly, to end her suffering altogether? Horrified at the path her thoughts were taking, she'd turned back to the hotel, only to see the door of a rundown house opening, a pretty young Frenchwoman blowing a kiss to a man as he hurried away, still buttoning up his fly.

For a moment, Agnes had contemplated her choices, before shock and disgust with herself sent her running back to her mother, a cruel homesickness spreading through her for the lush, green landscape of England that she had left behind.

And now of course, here she was. This was her home now. Christian did not need to know the details of her past life. She'd made sure that all he'd seen was a respectable young woman, fallen on hard times. He had never seemed interested in her background anyway, and for that she was eternally grateful.

From what her husband had told her about Hedoné, Agnes had anticipated that it would be very different to what she was used to, but she'd had no idea it would be *this* luxurious. Luxury to Agnes meant sheets free of bedbugs and two meals a day. It had meant regular medication for her mother instead of waiting for when it was absolutely needed, clothes of good enough quality that they lasted years. But this . . . this was a different world altogether.

She thought with trepidation of the cottage Christian had talked about. *Our* cottage, he had called it. There had been affection in his voice, a gentle touch, loving words that she had not expected. This was a marriage of convenience for both of them, and yet . . .

Could their union be more? Might Christian really have burgeoning feelings for her? Agnes had given up on the idea of love years ago, yet there was something about him that made her feel *seen*, made her feel alive for the first time in years. Soon, she would be properly embedded in this new life, settled and safe. She needed to show him she could be the caring, nurturing wife and mother he so obviously needed. Her gaze settled on the silver cup, and she quickly tipped the contents down her throat before she had time to think about it, swallowing the tablets with a gulp of wine.

Tired after her meal, Mother soon started snoring softly, and when Agnes was sure that she was settled, she took the little golden key that Christian had given her and slipped behind the thick curtain, unlocking the door to the balcony.

As she stepped outside, the haunting sound of a flute floated up from below. She hadn't heard it when she was in the room, the closed windows blocking out all sound. She peered over the edge but the veranda below was hidden from view. The music was beautiful, sad and low, the long notes piercing the black night. Agnes supposed she would hear music like this often, what with all the musicians that Christian had acquired on his travels.

She looked up, suddenly alert to another sound. A soft crackling, like kindling catching fire. On the balcony to the left, a dot of red glowed in the black. It flared then grew dim, dancing in the air like a firefly.

'Hallo?' she called, and the red dot stopped moving. Then, the sound of footsteps, and a voice calling back, 'Hello.'

A woman emerged out of the darkness. She looked a little younger than Agnes and was spectacularly thin. A black lock of hair was curled perfectly on her smooth brown forehead, and Agnes realised it was the woman she had seen at the game of croquet, and then afterwards, down by the jetty, her slim fingers tapping the wooden boards as if they were the keys of a piano.

'How nice to have a neighbour at last,' the woman said.

Her voice was soft and musical, with a peculiar mixture of accents, and Agnes thought she detected American along with something European.

'I can't believe they've already allowed you out on the balcony,' the woman added, taking another pull of her cigarette, the black of her silk robe flashing in the moonlight. 'It took weeks before I was given that privilege.'

She turned back to the window, the cigarette in her hand sending out a spray of gold sparks. With great effort, she managed to push back a section of the heavy curtain. A ray of light filtered out from the bedroom inside, settling on her face so that Agnes saw her properly for the first time.

She must once have been very beautiful, but now she was gaunt and emaciated, her eyes far too big for her face. It gave her the look of a fawn, all limbs and jutting bones. The result was a peculiar sense of innocence that made Agnes want to gently scoop the woman up like a child and whisper words of comfort.

'Come closer,' the woman said. 'I can't see who I'm talking to.'

Agnes took a step forward. The balconies were separated by a large gap, and the light from the window only just touched the edge of hers. The woman's eyes widened in surprise when she saw her.

'You look well,' she said.

'Oh, I am, I think,' Agnes said, her cheeks flushing, embarrassed by her good health.

Understanding flashed across the woman's features. 'You're the doctor's new wife,' she said. 'I saw you in the Rolls earlier.'

'I suppose I am,' Agnes said. 'My name's Agnes.'

'Sippie,' the woman said, picking a speck of tobacco from her lower lip. Leaning across the two balconies, she stretched out her hand and Agnes took it. In the spear of light, she noticed that Sippie's nails were round and bulbous.

'They're not piano-playing hands by a long shot,' Sippie said, grimacing. 'But they do the job.'

'You're a pianist? I'm sorry, I didn't mean to stare. I'm afraid I'm having a little trouble adjusting to it all.'

'That's all right. I was the same. It's enough to drive you mad, in the beginning. But I've been here long enough now that it feels like home. They've told me I'm to move downstairs full time tomorrow,' she added, brightening. 'So it'll be much more peaceful for you up here.'

'It's actually rather nice to have someone to talk to,' Agnes admitted. 'I imagine quarantine can be a lonely place on one's own. How long have you been here, Sippie?'

'Oh, a while. I arrived the day of the silver jubilee.'

Three whole months, Agnes thought, shocked. She remembered, their street had held a jubilee party, their old house festooned with bunting. It had been a few days afterwards that she and Mother had upped and left for France in the middle of the night. She thought fleetingly of that house now. It had only been rented. Christian had asked if she wanted their belongings collected and sent on to the sanatorium, but she had declined. There would be nothing of worth left there now, not after the way they had departed. And even if there had been, she did not want him to see the sad state she and Mother had been living in before he met her.

'Did they celebrate the jubilee here?' she asked Sippie.

'Oh yes. It was all very surreal, I can tell you, arriving to see everything painted silver to mark the king's anniversary. Even some of the guests.' She gave a smoky laugh. 'Though other than a brief glimpse of it all from the car, I didn't see much else. I was whisked up here and put on bed rest for eight weeks. They needed to feed me up, you see.'

She looked like she still needed feeding up now, Agnes thought. But Christian knew best.

'I've been slowly integrated with the guests over the past few weeks. And they finally told me today that they think I'm well enough to come out of quarantine fully. I can't wait to get immersed in the lifestyle here properly, start my journey to getting better so that I can get out of here.'

'You don't like it at Hedoné?'

'It's not so much that I don't like it, it's just, it's not real life, is it?'

'No,' Agnes agreed. Sippie was right. Every moment since she stepped off that train had felt the opposite of real. *Surreal*, she thought.

'Besides, I want to be one of your husband's success stories, cured of this illness.'

Agnes's heart gave a pulse of excitement. She glanced back through the window to where her mother lay. 'Has he cured many of his patients?' she asked lightly.

'Some. His reputation precedes him, of course. It's why I came here.' The young woman took a breath, her thin ribs rising and falling visibly beneath her robe, as if even this short sentence had depleted her lungs of oxygen. 'I'm hoping I can be one of them. I want to get back out there.'

'Where is "there"?'

'Oh, Paris at first, then Madrid maybe. I'd love to see Italy, too. I used to travel all over Europe, singing – though I came here on a piano scholarship. Playing piano is nice and all, and I appreciate what your husband is doing, but standing in front of a crowd, just you and the microphone, everyone looking up at you, that's my real passion.'

Agnes could well imagine this delicate young woman, all soulful eyes and gleaming skin, her hands clasped on the microphone as she crooned into it, her voice low and heady.

'Did you always want to be a singer?' she asked, intrigued.

'Oh yes. Since I was a little girl. My aunt, who took care of me, she was not a nice woman. She could be tender when she wanted to be, but oh, she could be cruel too. And we were so poor. All I wanted was to get away, you know? Use my voice. I hate to think what would have happened if I hadn't.'

'Where do you think you'd be now?'

Sippie folded her arms across her chest. 'Oh, I don't know. Still in America, probably. Cleaning and cooking and married with six babes of my own. But still singing.' She touched the balcony balustrade with the palm of her hand, as if for luck. 'Always singing. It's a part of me.'

46

'I'd love to hear you sometime.'

A cloud drew over Sippie's face. 'I don't sing. Not anymore.'

'Not at all?'

Sippie shook her head. 'To sing is to have hope. I resolved never to sing again unless I knew I was leaving this place.' Her gaze settled on the swimming pool, the azure water perfectly still, shining out of the darkness. 'Happy the hare at morning, for she cannot read the hunter's waking thoughts,' she said, a watchful, wounded look in her eyes.

A chill breeze reared up as if from nowhere, rippling the pool's surface, and Agnes shivered. 'What a melancholy line,' she said.

'It is rather, isn't it?' Sippie nodded towards the pool. 'A guest drowned in there. Did you know?'

'God, how terrible.' Agnes followed her gaze. The water looked so perfect, so inviting.

'It's by Auden, that quote,' Sippie said, making an effort to pull her eyes from the pool's azure surface. 'Do you know him?'

'The poet? Yes, of course.'

'There's a writer here who is friends with him. They correspond with one another and share their ideas. It feels kinda fitting for Hedoné, I think.'

'Oh? In what way?'

'I suppose I felt a little hunted, like a hare, when I first came here. Doctor found me in Paris, you see. I was in a bad way at the time. The TB pandemic had really hit the city the winter before, and I lost a lot of friends to it. I suppose I was at a sort of crossroads in life, I think,' she paused, raising her eyebrows. 'Whether or not to continue on with it at all, I mean?'

'I'm so sorry,' Agnes said.

Sippie dismissed her sympathy with a wave of her hand. 'Doctor heard me sing and play piano in a jazz bar, and he invited me here. I actually thought for a moment before I realised who you were, that you might be a scholar too.'

'Oh? Why is that?'

'I don't know, it's just, you seem a bit more like me than most of them.'

Agnes felt Sippie's eyes flash to her modest blouse and her travelworn hair in need of a cut. She managed a small, 'Oh.'

'I have offended you. I'm sorry. My aunt always told me I was too direct.' She looked at Agnes, her soulful eyes glinting in the moonlight. 'It was meant to be a compliment, I promise.'

'Then I shall take it as one,' Agnes said, grinning, and the woman reciprocated it.

'What are they like?' Agnes asked. 'The other guests, I mean?' She was thinking of that glamorous woman in the yellow sundress, Juno Harrington. The name stirred at her memory again like a word on the tip of her tongue.

'They're very nice. Extremely rich, some of them. But you have to be, generally, to come here, don't you?' She put another cigarette to her lips. 'Sorry, would you like one? I can throw one over.'

'No, thank you.'

'Not very sensible with my condition, I know, but I'm going to die anyway, so . . .'

She shrugged, and Agnes felt again a keen sense of pity for this thin, fragile young thing. 'I was thinking more about the proximity of the oxygen canisters in the bedroom, actually,' she said.

'Ah yes.' Sippie looked down at the cigarette in her hand as if she couldn't remember why she had lit it. She stubbed it out on the edge of the balcony and dropped it over the side.

The sound of a saxophone drifted across the grounds towards

them, discordant and jarring as if the performer was still practising the piece. It was oddly moving, and Agnes peered through the dark, thinking of the man she had seen earlier down by the lake.

'They never stop rehearsing,' Sippie said with a smile.

'Isn't it a bit dark out there to play an instrument?'

'Oh, the guests are all encouraged to be outside as much as possible. All that fresh air is good for the constitution. And they're all night owls here anyway, you'll barely see a glimpse of them before lunchtime.' She yawned, clapping her hand over her mouth. 'Apologies. I on the other hand am no longer a night owl. They wake you up so early here in quarantine, my bedtime seems to beckon earlier and earlier. And it's surprising how exhausting doing nothing all day can be. Goodnight, Mrs Fairhaven, it's been nice to talk to you.'

'Goodnight, Sippie. Sleep well.'

'Oh, I will.' She smiled before disappearing through the curtains of her bedroom and pulling them closed, plunging Agnes back into darkness.

Chapter Eight

Agnes stayed out on the balcony for a while longer. Somewhere below her in the house, the flute she had heard earlier started up again, this time accompanied by a piano and the deep bass of a trombone. She thought she heard the soft, low murmur of voices, deep in the house, punctuated by laughter, and she had that feeling once more, of being on the wrong side of a pane of glass, her hands cupped to help her see in.

She wondered what her husband was doing now. Had he finished his work for the day? It was strange, she felt as if she'd got to know Christian so well during their time on the Continent, yet she barely knew anything about his day-to-day life here.

Agnes looked down at her wedding ring, glinting in the moonlight. Soon, her marriage proper would begin. The thought made her stomach flip with both pleasure and apprehension, and she swallowed the feeling down. She supposed she ought to try to get a good night's sleep, prepare herself for whatever the morning might bring.

As she went inside and locked the door, the sounds she had heard from out there vanished into a muffled silence. In bed, she thought she could feel the edges of a percussive beat of music start up somewhere directly below her. It sounded marvellous, and she pulled the covers up to her chin, listening, imagining all the glamorous guests down there, draped elegantly across the sofas she had spied on arrival in that marble-covered room.

She tried to sleep, but everything that had happened since she'd arrived played out in her mind, and she lay, staring up at the ceiling. This might be one of the last times she would lie alone in her bed. The thought, both exciting and frightening, did nothing to help aid her sleep.

In France, their marriage had been consummated perfunctorily, both of them shy, the weather that night so warm that the touch of skin to skin had felt unwelcome. But here, they would have time to make sense of what their union could become. She thought of the feel of Christian's blue eyes on her earlier, and a thrill of something unknown flickered, but she pushed it away. This was only ever going to be a marriage of convenience, for both of them. She must not hope for anything more.

With this thought, exhaustion finally pulled her eyelids closed, and swiftly and readily she slept, the scent of the lilies – so like the ones she had held at her wedding – rippling through her dreams.

Agnes was woken by a thin shadow across her face. Opening her eyes, she saw Matron standing in her bedroom doorway, silhouetted by the lamp from Mother's room.

'What time is it?' she asked blearily.

'Six o'clock,' Matron replied in a bright voice.

Agnes groaned. Still half asleep, she got up and went to the bathroom, coming to a stop in the doorway, taken aback by the opulent splendour that she had failed to notice the night before. The floor and walls were encased in marble, the bath set low to the ground. The room smelt divine too, a mixture of lavender and roses. Bottles and tins of heavenly scented lotions and soaps lined the shelves. From the bedroom she could hear Matron giving a protesting Mother a bed bath, and as she entered, she saw that last night's supper had been cleared, and breakfast was laid out on the table, orange juice, a bowl of muesli, slices of Swiss cheese and Bavarian ham, and a large glass of the obligatory milk, cool and creamy. Agnes's stomach rumbled at the sight of it.

'Come, eat,' Matron said, laying a bed tray over Mother's lap. 'You must both build yourselves up. You are a little too thin for my liking, Mrs Fairhaven.'

Stung, Agnes pulled back her chair. Matron would find herself underweight, too, if she had spent every penny on keeping her mother alive.

'Do remember to drink your milk, ladies. Milk is full of nutrition. It is produced by our own herd of Jersey cows. Doctor recommends two pints daily for all guests.'

A knock on the door, and a maid entered.

'I'm to take your measurements, madam, for your wardrobe,' she said.

'My wardrobe?'

'Yes, madam.' She unrolled a tape measure, holding it up to show her.

'Right. Shall we?' Agnes said, directing the young woman to her bedroom.

When she emerged a little later, confounded by the extraordinary number of measurements required, she found Christian at her mother's bed. He had removed her bed jacket and was easing her forward, tapping at her back. She searched his face, looking for a reaction, anything that might betray his thoughts, but he was so difficult to read. She remembered, a day or so before they were married, he had been stung by a jellyfish in the warm shallows of the Mediterranean. He hadn't made a sound, despite the great red welts rising on his skin.

Christian took the stethoscope from around his neck, placing it in his ears. He pressed the other end to her mother's chest, warming the cold metal in his hands first, she noted with fondness.

'Breathe in,' he said, lapsing into silence as he listened.

Agnes caught sight of her own reflection in the mirror above the mantelpiece. She had thought the cotton two-piece smart and fashionable when she put it on this morning, but now it felt a little dowdy, the pale green leeching her of colour, giving her skin a sallow and sickly appearance, and she turned away.

Christian was wearing a different suit today, this one a shade darker so that it deepened the blue of his eyes, making them look almost navy. Agnes's gaze traced the muscles beneath the thin cotton of his shirt, taut and well-formed.

'Right,' he said suddenly, straightening up, catching her staring at him, and she dropped her head in embarrassment. He strode towards her, taking her hands and looking her up and down. 'You are positively radiant this morning, darling. A fragile beauty. The perfect English rose. Isn't she, Matron?'

Agnes was sure she heard Matron snort from behind her mask.

'Now, Mrs Templeton,' Christian said, turning his attention back to Mother. 'Let's get you down to have an x-ray, so we can see those lungs properly.'

Her mother nodded, and Agnes marvelled at how calm and kindly he was, so different to Matron's stiff, outdated authority yet more forceful by far. It was a strange kind of power.

'We'll need to x-ray you, too,' Christian added, turning to her.

'Me?' Agnes said in surprise. 'But I don't have tuberculosis.'

'I'm sure you're right. From my assessment in France, you did indeed appear perfectly healthy. But you've been living in close proximity to your mother for a long time, and to your father, too, before he died. We need to make sure. And we have the most modern technology here.'

'But I really don't think—'

'Don't argue with Doctor, Mrs Fairhaven, he's only thinking of what's best for you.'

'I'm not arguing with him,' Agnes said through gritted teeth. 'I'm only questioning him. I'm trying to understand.'

Christian smiled. 'I myself have precautionary x-rays every six months, as does Matron. That way, should any infection be present, we will know at the earliest opportunity, and should have every chance of eradicating it.'

'Of course,' she said, adding, a little acerbically, 'it will be nice to escape this room for a while.'

Matron gave her an appraising look, and Agnes regretted her words at once: comments like this might not endear her to her new husband. She glanced at Christian, but he appeared not to have heard. He had opened the door, and she looked out at the landing, suddenly nervous at what the x-ray might betray.

'Once we have the results,' he said, his hand warm on her back, 'it should significantly speed up your quarantine period.' He smiled, a small, hopeful smile.

'Come along, ladies,' Matron said. 'Let's get those lungs looked at.'

Chapter Nine

It was an odd feeling, leaving the bedrooms of Mansfield Suite, even though it had been less than twenty-four hours since Agnes had first entered. Matron had brought the wheeled chair for her mother, and she sat in it, elegant as a queen, her hands folded meekly in her lap as Matron pushed the chair on ahead, leaving Agnes and Christian to follow.

'How did you find your first night?' he asked her, his voice low.

'I've had better,' she said, and he laughed.

'Was the bed not to your liking?'

'Oh no, it was gloriously comfortable. I suppose it's just being somewhere so new and different.' Christian nodded. 'What's *our* bed like?' she asked, daring herself to brush the back of her hand against his. Ahead of them, Matron strode on, oblivious.

'Oh.' He looked down at the plush carpet, the skin around his collar flushing becomingly. 'It's a good solid Victorian thing.'

'Where is the cottage?'

'It's in the grounds, behind the main house. I used to have rooms here, near the staff quarters, but I realised they probably weren't conducive to a healthy marriage. I think you'll like it,' he said, glancing at her and looking away, embarrassed. 'It's far more private than my old bachelor rooms.'

He took her hand as they neared the lift. It felt elicit, this touch, here in the sanatorium, as if she were holding the hand of her doctor, not her husband. Matron had already taken Mother down in the lift, and Christian produced a little gold key, just like Matron's, and slipped it into the keyhole, pressing the lower gold button.

'Why do the lifts need keys to access them?'

'Oh, just a quarantine precaution.'

'To stop new patients from potentially infecting the others, you mean?'

'That's right,' he said, smiling at her.

'But couldn't they just use the stairs?' she said.

'Hedoné House has no stairs.'

'What? None?' Christian must have misunderstood her question. He must think she meant a staircase for the patients. What kind of building relied only on a lift? 'But there must be a service staircase somewhere?'

'Hedoné was built with the most up-to-date, modern technology,' he said, his smooth voice reassuring. 'Many of our patients would struggle with stairs. A lift provides a simple, safe and effective way to travel between floors.'

'But what happens if there's a power cut, or a fire?'

'We have an emergency generator. And of course, there are plans in place should they be needed: the staff are well trained. Hedoné is perfectly safe, my love.'

But surely it couldn't be, Agnes thought. If the most unwell patients were kept upstairs, how on earth could they move them safely?

'May I have my own key for the lift?' she asked him. 'I feel a little anxious, knowing I can't get off this floor.'

Christian laughed, touching her cheek lightly, as if she were a child that had said something precociously funny. 'Agnes, how would it make you safer? You're locked in your room. You would have no way of accessing the lift, even if you had a key.'

'Oh. Of course,' she said, looking down at the carpet. She hadn't thought of that. How foolish of her.

Christian touched her chin, tilting her head up, his warm hand steady on her jaw. 'Of course you shall have a key,' he said, his smile tender and secretive, as if he could see things in their future that she could not. 'Just as soon as this x-ray confirms your good health.'

'Thank you, Christian.'

The lift arrived at that moment, and he dropped his hand, the cool air rushing over her skin where his touch had been. They stepped inside, and he leant round her to press the button, his body so close that she could feel the warmth of him, smell that heady concoction of spices that reminded her of their first few days together in France. When she looked up, it was to find his eyes locked onto hers, his lips parted. She had a sudden, depraved urge to lean in and take his lower lip in her mouth. The softness of it, the way it trembled, and she realised she was trembling too. She felt her own lips part, saw his eyes settle on her mouth, her breath pooling out in one long exhalation, and somewhere deep within her, desire trembled, aching to get out.

The lift came to a jolting stop, and Christian pulled away, sweeping his hand over his face, the spell broken. Behind him, through the metal gate, Agnes could see the grand entrance hall that she remembered from yesterday.

'I'm so sorry,' Christian said in a hoarse whisper. 'It's just so hard to control myself around you.'

'Why do you have to?' Agnes asked in a small voice, not understanding.

'We can't . . . do anything . . . until you're out of quarantine. It would put my patients in too much danger.'

'Of course,' she said, turning away from him to hide the flush of blood in her cheeks. Clearing her throat and swallowing down her shame, she peered through the grid. 'Where is everyone?'

It was very quiet, no staff or guests anywhere. At the centre of the hall, a Lalique vase stood on a marble plant stand, a huge bunch of the obligatory lilies arranged inside it.

'The guests will all still be slumbering, I expect,' he said. 'Most of them keep very late hours.'

'And the staff?'

'Oh, they're here, but they're very discreet. Hedoné House is like a hotel in that respect.' He pressed the gold button again, and the lift shuddered back into life. 'You can measure the quality of the staff by the infrequency with which you see them,' he added with a grin.

Agnes saw with surprise that they were travelling down to another floor, the bright hallway disappearing above them. She hadn't realised the house had a basement. The lift grew dark, and in the gloom, she noticed that the gold buttons had the same hare design on them as the call button in the bedroom.

'Why did you choose this for the sanatorium's emblem?' she asked, touching the shining gold roundel.

'Now Agnes, remember what I told you in France: we prefer not to call it a sanatorium,' Christian admonished. 'It's a retreat, a private health spa for the creative elite.'

'That's a long title.'

'Well, we tend to just call it "Hedoné",' he said, smiling at her. 'Or just "The House" is fine. We don't like to remind our guests why they're here, however fortunate they are to be in our care.'

'No, of course not,' she said, shaking her head. There was so much to learn.

The lift came to a stop, and Christian pulled back the gate, ushering her out.

'All our medical rooms are down here,' he said, striding ahead.

This floor was markedly different to upstairs. There was no natural light, for one, the corridors lit by pretty sconces along the wall. Agnes balked at the thought of being trapped down here if the lift broke. There must be another way out, surely? A strong breeze caroused down the corridor, playfully lifting her skirt. Dotted along the wall at regular intervals were little metal grids. She put a hand to one and felt the force of the air press against her palm.

'Is there some kind of ventilation system down here?' she asked, hurrying after him. She passed door after door, each one with a name stamped regimentally onto it.

'Yes, there is,' Christian said, surprised by her interest.

He had come to a stop at a door halfway down the corridor marked 'X-ray'. Everything down here was so much more functional, Agnes thought, hearing the hum of a boiler coming from somewhere farther along. Christian knocked and entered, and she followed him in, blinking at the sudden brightness.

It was the most unusual room she had ever been in. It was a small, square space, lit by powerful overhead strip-lighting that emitted a low buzz. At one end was a wooden structure about the size of a door. Her mother was standing in front of it, Matron fixing a white rectangular screen against her chest.

'All ready for you, Doctor,' she said.

Agnes looked on with fascination as Christian checked that her mother was correctly positioned, then he went to the other side of the room, where a large lever was mounted on the wall. Thick, curled wires spiralled directly from it and across the ceiling to the x-ray machine that encased her mother.

'Step back, Agnes, over here,' he said, pointing to a line marked on the floorboards, and she obeyed, her feet behind the line, watching with trepidation. Her mother's eyes were a little wider than normal as she took in what was going on. With a click, all but one of the lights went off, plunging them into gloom.

'A deep breath please, Mrs Templeton,' Christian called, and Agnes's mother did as she was asked.

He pulled the lever down, and a loud fizzing sound filled the room. The white plate in front of Mother's chest began to change, a fuzzy image appearing. It looked like a pair of wings, Agnes thought, and she realised suddenly that this was Mother's lungs. She stared, transfixed by their beauty.

Did every person have these incredible, intricate things inside them? The lungs had such beautiful patterns in them, little cloudy swirls. She had been led to believe that lungs were simply balloons, but these, these were incredible.

Christian lifted up the lever, and the fizzing sound abated. Mother let out a breath, her chest heaving at the effort of holding in the air for so long. Matron turned the lights back on, and Agnes blinked in the brightness as Matron unlatched the white plate, and guided her mother out from the machine.

'Are you all right, Mother?' Agnes said.

'I'm fine,' she said, a little breathlessly.

'Your turn now,' Christian said, beckoning Agnes over.

She stepped up against the wooden panel, her heart in her mouth. Christian moved the plate into position, directing her arms and feet to the correct place. He was as close as he had been in the lift, so close that she could see the colour of his eyelashes, pale brown, almost blonde in the stark overhead lighting. The plate was tight against her, and she felt the pressure of being sandwiched between the two surfaces. It wasn't uncomfortable as such, but it made her heart rate speed up, feeling as if she were trapped.

Agnes wondered why she felt so nervous. It wasn't the procedure she was worried about, she realised, but the result. Christian had already performed checks on her, all of which seemed to confirm she did not have TB. But what if, after all this, the x-ray machine picked up things he had not been able to detect? What then of her marriage, of her and her mother's care? She pushed the thought away, concentrating on the here and now. There was no point in getting ahead of herself. There was a click as the door closed, and she looked up to see that she and Christian were alone in the room.

'Are you ready?' he asked her, still so close, the only thing separating them the white plate. She nodded, her eyes on his. 'Deep breath then,' he said, crossing the room and switching the lights off before pulling the lever down. That same high fizzing sound began again.

Agnes imagined a warmth in her. She thought of the delicate lines of her lungs forming on the plate at her chest. What did tuberculosis look like? Was it a pretty disease or an ugly one? She held her breath, feeling the mounting pressure in her lungs as the air struggled to find anywhere to go. Black spots began popping in front of her eyes, but still she held her breath, feeling the pressure of the plate against her. The image of her mother's lungs danced in her vision, and the room swam out of view, and then the buzzing sound faded away, and she found herself back in the room, limp and sweaty.

Christian was at her side, uncoupling her, pulling her drooping body from the machine. He settled her in a chair, his hand supporting her wilting head.

'Oh, my darling,' he said. 'Are you all right?'

Agnes lifted her head. It felt extraordinarily heavy. 'I'm okay,' she said weakly. 'Just a little faint. A glass of water, perhaps?'

Quickly, Christian got to his feet and left the room, coming back with a glass. He knelt down in front of her, helping her to sips. He still hadn't turned the lights up. Beginning to feel better, Agnes looked over at the white plate. Etched onto it now was an echo of her own lungs. They were filled with delicate lines like the veins of a leaf, hazy white bars traversing them that must be her ribs.

'A perfect pair of lungs,' Christian said, following her gaze. His voice contained a hint of relief. 'No sign of tubercles whatsoever.'

She let out a gasp. 'Oh, thank God.'

'You know what this means?' he said, a throatiness to his voice that she hadn't heard before. 'You're healthy. You can come out of quarantine. You can be my wife.'

There was something in his expression as he said this, that same flash of desire she had felt in the lift, and Agnes's joints flooded with an alacritous tingling.

Christian helped her to her feet, his hand lingering on hers. 'Come,' he said.

The corridor was empty. Matron must already have taken Mother back up to her room. At the lift, they waited in silence for it to arrive, an awkwardness between them, as if his words had marked a change in their relationship but neither of them was quite able to work out how to cross that boundary.

In the lift, Agnes was aware of how still Christian's body was, how close he was standing. It felt as if every tiny movement was magnified. His fingers went to the band of his wedding ring, twisting it nervously, and without thinking, she took hold of his hand and brought the ring to her lips, kissing the gold.

She could feel the warmth of his skin at the edge of her mouth, and before she knew what was happening, he was pushing himself forward, and his mouth was on hers, hungrily, desperately kissing her, his hands caught in her hair, and her breath that had before been light and careful became low and heady with desire as it tangled with his.

The lift came to a stop, and Christian broke away, his hand to his mouth as if he couldn't quite believe what he had done. They had stopped in the entrance hall. There was still no one about, the lilies sitting starkly on their stand at the centre.

Christian cleared his throat. 'I have some time,' he said, his voice husky. 'If you'd like to see your new home?'

'That would be wonderful,' Agnes said, suddenly shy again, smoothing her loosened hair and running her tongue over her lips nervously.

Chapter Ten

It was a perfect, still morning, dew drenching the lawn. The road that they had come up yesterday stretched ahead, disappearing in the pines, as if the world beyond had ceased to exist. Near the swimming pool Agnes could see a rose garden, dots of pink and red and white, a confetti of rose petals floating on the water's surface.

'Such beautiful grounds,' she stuttered, looking at the lake. 'It looks so different when one is actually in it. From upstairs it just feels like a pretty picture.'

'The layout was designed by one of my first guests. He was an architect.' Agnes noted the past tense with sadness. 'Come. This way,' Christian said, offering her his hand.

They turned left and skirted the front of the house. The ground floor here was composed of large French doors, each one open wide. They passed the dining room that she remembered from her arrival. Inside, staff were busy laying the tables, polishing silver and standing crystal decanters of juice on the perfectly pressed tablecloths. An enticing smell drifted out, something buttery that reminded Agnes of the boulangeries in France.

Christian led her through the grounds, pointing out places of interest. Ahead of them on the lawn stood what she at first assumed were guests, but she soon realised her mistake. They were statues, about twenty of them in all, twice as tall as real people, all standing in different poses. As they approached, Agnes saw that they weren't the traditional statues that you found in museums, but modern, almost abstract figures made in pale, smooth stone, some with no facial features at all. And yet, they seemed to convey so much more emotion than the unsmiling statues one saw in galleries and wealthy houses. She wanted to stop, to place a curious hand on their smooth bodies, but Christian pulled her onward.

They were drawing closer to the pine trees at the back of the house now, and Agnes noticed for the first time a small pathway that led right into them.

'Are we to live in the woods, like Hansel and Gretel?' she asked.

'I told you it was private,' Christian answered with a wink, picking up his pace, and her stomach rolled over in nervous excitement.

He led her beneath the pines, and she gazed up to the sky in awe, taking in the trees' soaring majesty. They were so tall that she felt all of a sudden shrunk into a miniature version of herself, dwarfed by the imposing trunks with their shivering needled tips. As they drew further into the woods, she was surprised that it didn't appear to grow any darker, the pine trees planted in regimental lines, aisles of sunlight pouring down onto them, as if in a church.

At last, the trees came to an end, and Agnes saw ahead of them a little cottage.

'Welcome to your new home,' Christian said, and, scooping her up, he carried her, laughing, to the door. Fumbling with the key, he pushed it open and swept her over the threshold, stopping her laughing mouth with a kiss as he set her on her feet.

He stood back, a nervous silence replacing his laughter, and Agnes looked around her. The sickly smell of lilies pervaded the room, radiating from the many vases placed on tables and shelves, so many that she wondered for one dreadful moment if someone had died. Lilies gave the wrong impression in a sanatorium. Far better that they have sprigs of lavender or bouquets of roses. Sunflowers and daisies, warm, happy flowers with no connotations of illness or death.

The front door had opened straight onto a small sitting room. It was quite a modern cottage, presumably built at the same time as the main house. A huge chimney breast dominated the room, made of the same knapped Norfolk flint that she had seen adorning the outside of Hedoné House. It was all tastefully decorated, simple, yet cosy.

'Well?' Christian said behind her, the nerves evident in the tremor in his voice. 'Shall we be happy here?'

Agnes stroked the nap of a soft white fur draped across the sofa, noting that there was no hint of anything medical about the place. No clinical beds, no oxygen canisters, no little gold buttons with hares on them glinting at her from across the room.

She turned to face him. He was watching her cautiously, searching her face for a reaction.

'Yes,' she said. 'Yes, I think we shall.'

'Papa?'

'Ah,' Christian said. 'Isobel.'

In the doorway across the room stood a little girl, and Agnes's heart gave a tick of surprise. She had not expected to meet her stepdaughter so soon. She looked to Christian, unprepared as to how she should behave.

'Iso, why aren't you with your governess?' he said, exasperation on his face.

'She said I could start my lessons late today.'

'Well, I suppose now is as good a time as any to introduce you both. Agnes, I'd like you to meet my daughter, Isobel Fairhaven. Iso, this is your new stepmother.'

The little girl came forward. Agnes's first impression was that she looked younger than her eight years. She was small and fragile-looking, her hair a bright, white blonde. Up close, her skin was almost translucent, her eyes a strange silvery grey.

'Pleased to meet you,' the girl said, dipping into a little curtsy.

'And I you,' Agnes said.

It was such an alien feeling, conversing with a child, and she felt tongue-tied. How did one talk to them? There was something curiously watchful about her, as if she were an adult in a child's body. It must be odd, being the only little girl in a whole mansion full of adults. Agnes parted her lips, trying to summon up meaningful words. After all, wasn't this part of the reason she was here? To mother this delicate little thing?

But Christian got there first. 'Did Miss Rose really say you could delay your school day?' he asked, a touch of weary frustration in his voice. 'Or did you give her the slip again?'

'She wanted me to do Latin.'

'That is no reason to run away, and you know it,' he said sternly. 'Back you go, Iso. And if I hear you've run off again, there will be consequences.'

The girl turned her solemn eyes on Agnes. Dipping into another curtsey, she flitted across the room and was out of the door before Agnes could say goodbye.

Agnes looked at the space she had been with a tinge of disappointment. She was not foolish; she had not expected the little girl to fling herself gaily into her arms, but the meeting had been so unceremoniously quick, and she so unprepared. Why had Christian terminated it? Did he not want to observe how they were together?

Perhaps he was only thinking of Agnes after such a long journey, she decided. There had been a lot to take in in a very short time, after all. She should feel relieved.

Christian was looking at his watch. 'I'm afraid I've run out of time, my darling. Come, I'll walk you back to the house.' He took her hand, locking the cottage up behind them.

'She's a spirited young thing,' he said as they walked back through the trees, their fingers laced together. 'I sometimes think I allow her a little too much freedom. It's been hard, since her mother . . .'

Agnes nodded, wondering how on earth she would begin to mother such a flighty little girl. Had Isobel not been given any boundaries in her life? Back in France, Agnes had asked often about Isobel, trying to build a picture of the child, but Christian never dwelt long on her. Perhaps, she thought, he did not know her well enough himself to answer her increasingly thorough questions.

'Iso copes well with her loss,' Christian said. 'The innocence of youth, it helps one heal so quickly. She struggled initially, after Meredith died. We both did. I had her buried nearby. I wanted Isobel to be able to visit her grave, I thought it might help with the grieving process. But she is such a wayward child. I do hope that your being here will bring her out of her shell a little.' He lifted her hand to his mouth, kissing the wedding ring on her finger.

'I shall try to be a good mother to her,' Agnes said.

'And perhaps a mother to our own child, one day, too,' he said, catching both her hands in his. Pulling her to him, he pressed his lips against hers. 'Tell me, are there any signs that you might be . . .'

'No, not yet,' she said abruptly, a little embarrassed by the direction the conversation was taking.

'Then we must work hard to change that,' he said with a grin. 'I must admit,' he added, pulling away, 'I was terribly pleased, and a little relieved, to find you completely free of tuberculosis.'

'But you seemed so sure that I was healthy.'

'Oh, I was sure you were,' Christian said, coming to a stop on the shingle in front of the house. 'But until I x-rayed you, I had no *scientific* proof. I have a theory about how your immunity to the disease came about.'

'Oh?'

He started walking again, and Agnes followed him up the steps to the house.

'I believe that some people are simply unable to contract it. I'm not sure if it's in their genetics, or if it's some kind of protection that emerged from an earlier illness. A long time ago, we discovered that smallpox could be stopped by introducing a small amount of the illness into the body. Many doctors and scientists have been postulating for a long time now that the same might be true of tuberculosis. Indeed, there have been experiments in this field for a few years.'

Agnes, distracted afresh by the towering beauty of the entrance hall, looked back at him, her hand trailing through the featherlike fronds of a fern. 'But surely it's a dangerous thing to experiment with, introducing illness to a healthy body?'

'Indeed, most unethical. Which is why, two years ago, I chose to experiment on myself.'

Agnes stared at him. 'Christian, you didn't?'

He nodded, grinning at her. They had reached the centre of the hallway now, the ghastly stench of lilies pervading the great space.

'But you see, my dear Agnes, it worked! I haven't worn a mask around these people in all that time, and yet I am well. I believe that I'm protected, unable to contract it.'

'Is this experiment part of your cure?'

'No, no. It would only work on those who don't currently show signs of TB.'

'What is the cure, if you don't mind my asking? You mentioned an operation . . .'

'Yes, that's right. It's a simple little procedure, but in combination with everything else, it seems to be key.'

'Can I ask exactly what it entails?'

'Alas, only I am party to the details. Even Matron doesn't know the full facts. I have experienced times in my medical career, Agnes, where saying too much too soon can be detrimental.' He took her hand. 'You'll know soon enough. But what I really wanted to say to you, darling Agnes, is that just as I believe I am immune, I think you might be, too.'

She looked up at him in surprise. 'What makes you think that?'

'Well,' he ran a hand over his face, thinking, 'you nursed your father for many years until his death, and you have cared for your mother too, and yet you are perfectly healthy.'

Agnes clung to his words. Here was yet more hope that she had been so desperate for in her darkest days looking after Mother. The desire for a whole life free from the illness that had eaten away at both her parents. Now all she needed was for her mother to be cured, and then all of her prayers would be answered.

'Hedoné House is at the forefront of research in this field,' Christian said excitedly. 'In fact, I have arranged for some eminent scientists and investors to visit, in order to present them with my ideas. You have joined me here at such an exciting time, my love.'

He caught her hand, kissing her on the cheek. She could feel the hum of excitement radiating through his jawbone. She felt his palm press gently to her stomach.

'And soon, there will be a little Fairhaven in there to continue the line,' he whispered. 'Strength and beauty and immunity all parcelled up in one perfect package.'

Agnes looked down at his hand, resting against her cardigan.

For a long time now, she had believed her sole job on this earth was to care for her mother, and to try to remain free from TB for as long as possible so that she could carry this out. And then she had found Christian in France, and everything had suddenly, irrevocably changed.

She was still getting used to being a wife. The notion of becoming a mother felt alien, particularly so soon after meeting her own, fully formed stepdaughter. Agnes was not even sure she *wanted* to have children of her own, especially here, in a house full of sickness and fever.

And yet, it was obvious that Christian did. And keeping Christian happy was her job now. The most important job of all, if she wanted to remain here.

Christian hadn't noticed her silence. From a pocket, he pulled a small set of keys, dangling from a golden hare keychain. 'As promised,' he said, handing them to her. He went through them, showing her which one was for the lift, which for their own cottage and which for her mother's room.

The sound of hurrying footsteps, and Matron came striding towards them from a corridor. 'Doctor, I've been looking for you. You're needed in Chopin Suite.'

'Alas, work calls,' Christian said to Agnes. He kissed her goodbye, smiling that dark, secretive smile of his, and her stomach somersaulted again as he strode off down the corridor with Matron.

Alone in the entrance hall, she paused for a moment, taking stock. She put a hand to her mouth, remembering the way Christian had kissed her in the lift earlier, as if he couldn't help himself. Her lips felt different, bruised, and swollen. It was a strangely pleasant feeling.

She had not expected any of this: this emotion that flooded through her, that had seemed to flow from him, too. Was this what a marriage should be like? A union not just on paper, but something more tangible, more sensual? Could her new life have more meaning in it than she had dared to hope?

She looked around the hall. The ceiling was extraordinarily high and made of gold glass, with sweeping, almost abstract lines depicting Grecian figures. While they had been at the cottage, a new vase of lilies had replaced the old one, artfully arranged at the centre of the room. These ones were orange and pink and smattered with dots of crimson that made Agnes think queasily of blood. Their thick, syrupy scent curdled the air, and with a sudden burst of irritation, she marched forward and pulled them, dripping from the vase. She looked around for a bin to put them in, but other than the copious ferns in pots, the hall was sleek and empty. She set off with them down the corridor in the opposite direction to that of her husband, leaving a spatter of scented water in her wake.

This corridor was in complete contrast to the one below in the basement. It was much wider, and bathed in sunlight. She came to a double door on her right that led into the dining room. Inside, she saw staff placing fresh vases of flowers at the centre of each table. Agnes noted with relief that they weren't lilies this time, but little Michaelmas daisies.

To her left, opposite the dining room, was a door with a plaque that bore the words 'Doctor Christian Fairhaven' in gold lettering. Christian's office would surely have a bin, she thought. The lilies shook a powder of bright yellow pollen into the air as she tried the handle, but it was locked, and Agnes stood for a moment, gathering her thoughts. She saw that the door at the end of the corridor was open a crack, and she set off towards it.

It was a library. As she entered, Agnes looked around her in awe, taking in the walls and walls of books stretching so high that they were lost to the shadows. The shelves were punctuated by floor-length windows on three sides, all thrown wide open, the library running from the front of the house to the back. To her right, she could see the lake at the front, and to her left, the pine trees that led to hers and Christian's cottage. The windows ahead looked out onto acres of green parkland; the sculptural statues dotted across it.

She spotted a wastepaper basket in one corner, and dropped the lilies into it, dusting her hands of pollen. Selecting a book at random from a nearby shelf, she slid it out, enjoying the dense weight of it, the warm leather, soft in her hands. Sinking into an armchair, Agnes opened the book and put it to her nose, inhaling deeply. It was the smell of luxury, of time spent in leisurely pursuits with no interruptions – an indulgence she had never known before.

Turning to the first page, she began to read.

'There you are,' Christian said some time later, and Agnes looked up from the book, surprised to find herself in the library. He was standing in the doorway behind her. 'I thought I'd lost you,' he added with a nervous laugh.

'Everything all right in Chopin Suite?' she asked him.

'Yes, disaster averted.' He sank down in an armchair opposite her. 'It's lovely to see you taking an interest in the books here. I knew of course that we shared similar passions, but I can see already how well you're going to fit in here.' He drummed his fingers on the leather arms of the chair. 'Agnes, I have a proposition for you. I've held off asking before, because I wasn't sure how rested you'd be after your journey. And of course, there was the small matter of the x-ray's result. But since you are in remarkably robust health, I wanted to put something to you.'

Agnes remained silent, waiting for him to continue, but inside, her heart began to beat faster.

'This afternoon, the delegation of scientists and investors I told you about are arriving for the weekend. I'm hoping that they will be so impressed with what I'm doing here that they'll want to invest in the place – both financially and scientifically. I'm hosting a welcome dinner this evening, and I'd love for you to be there at my side.'

'Tonight?' Agnes felt the beginnings of panic rise in her throat. 'I'm . . . I'm not sure, Christian,' she said, her mind racing. 'What do I know about Hedoné? Or about science. Or investments?' She gave a small laugh. 'Wouldn't it be wiser to do these things on your own, at least until I'm better acquainted with your work?'

Christian leant forward, touching the tip of a finger to her knee.

'Oh darling, you don't need to understand it!' he said. 'It's your moral support I'm after, not your intellect. I've been planning this weekend for a long time, and to have someone at my side tonight would make the world of difference.'

He stood, pulling Agnes to her feet.

'You do something to me, Agnes,' he murmured. 'You bring a calmness to me. I cannot fathom how.' He kissed her gently on the lips. 'I must be off, I have so much to do before they arrive. Why don't you go and take lunch with your mother in her room? I'm sure she's eager to hear all about your morning. And then you can go back to the cottage for the afternoon, rest up a little and settle in properly. It's your home now. With me,' he added, flashing that tender, secretive smile again, his eyes tracing her body, and despite her panic, Agnes felt that now-familiar tick of desire deep in her belly.

'Dinner is at seven,' Christian said. 'I may not have a chance to see you again before that, but I shall be waiting for you in the dining room, I promise.'

He put his hand on her waist, guiding her out of the library. In the entrance hall, he called the lift for her, dusting a soft kiss on her cheek as the lift's motor hummed into action.

'Until this evening,' he said.

Chapter Eleven

Ascending in the lift, Agnes wondered how she would feel, going back into the claustrophobia of the quarantine bedroom. She rubbed her thumb over the key that Christian had given her. It was a far more palatable prospect, knowing she could leave at any time.

In Mansfield Suite, she was relieved to see that Matron was not about. Mother seemed well rested. She was back in her bed after her x-ray, sitting propped up with pillows. Already, she looked much better than when they had arrived, and as Agnes pulled up a chair, she sighed inwardly in relief.

Up here, there was far less pressure to keep up the pretence of being the perfect wife. It wasn't that she didn't want to be Christian's wife, but the title came with all sorts of caveats, some of which she was only just beginning to understand now. She had never dreamed that her second night would involve hobnobbing with scientists and investors, but she knew that if she wanted to make herself indispensable to her husband, then she must go through with it. Agnes wondered whether to confide in her mother about her worries over tonight's dinner, but she did not want to upset her fragile health. Instead, she filled her in on everything she had seen and learnt that morning.

'Have you met your new stepdaughter yet?' her mother asked. 'It will be lovely to have a child in the family again.'

'Christian introduced me earlier. She seems a little . . . wilful,' Agnes said, trying to be kind.

'All children can be wilful if they're not given the right conditions to thrive in. She will be like a plant that has not been watered, Aggie. You must nourish her, that's all. Spend time with her. Get to know her likes and dislikes.'

'I already know that she doesn't like Latin.'

'I seem to remember you didn't either,' her mother said, laughing, and Agnes smiled. Perhaps Iso and she had more in common than she thought.

At the cottage after lunch, Agnes opened the door nervously, wondering if Isobel might be lurking again, but the house was silent. She saw with a jolt of pleasure that her cases had been brought over, her ragged old carpet bag looking particularly forlorn, and she felt a wave of affection for it, like seeing an old friend.

She quickly explored the rooms that she hadn't had time to see earlier. In the bedroom, she found an evening gown in dusky pink satin laid out and a pair of heels to match. The dress was a beautiful, flowing thing, the fabric gathered at one shoulder and held there by a sparkling brooch in the shape of a circlet. Christian had left a little aigrette for her, too, the tiny paste jewels on it sparkling in the soft bedroom light. A note pinned to the dress read, 'The first of many. Cannot wait to see you in this. C.'

She spent the afternoon resting, as Christian had instructed. In the evening, she pulled on the shimmering gown, carefully zipping it up, before securing the aigrette in her hair, the fine strands of the egret feather betraying the nervous tremor in her hands.

Just before seven o'clock, Agnes closed the door of the cottage, picking her way towards the main house in her heels, the pine-needle-covered floor soft underfoot. Her stomach roiled with nerves at the thought of the evening ahead.

'You will be fine,' she repeated under her breath to herself as she walked. 'You are Mrs Agnes Fairhaven, wife to the eminent Doctor Fairhaven. You are *meant* to be here.'

She reached the entrance hall just as a gong sounded, the sonorous reverberations setting the Lalique vase ringing, and she saw that it had been refilled with new flowers. Pale pink roses this time, she noted thankfully, the exact colour of her dress. The ghastly stench of lilies had gone, replaced by their much more delicate perfume. She wondered, as she detached one from the bouquet, if they had been grown in Hedoné's rose garden.

There was no one about, and Agnes tucked the flower into her hair and stood, unsure whether to wait for Christian, her stomach flipping over once more. She wrapped her arms about herself, the tips of her fingers touching the naked skin of her back, sending a stipple of goose bumps across her body. Catching sight of her reflection in the mirrored interior of the lift, Agnes stepped closer, captivated by what she saw. It did not look like her at all, not even an echo of the poor spinster in darned clothes who had befriended the dashing doctor in France, and she felt a rush of jubilation.

She turned this way and that, admiring herself. The dress fitted perfectly, and she wondered if Christian had a seamstress tucked away somewhere in the house, working diligently to alter it for her on time. As she moved, the iridescent sparkle of the comb in her hair caught the light, and the thought came to her half-jokingly that they might actually be real diamonds.

'You can do this,' she whispered, smiling at her reflection. Patting her hair one last time, she strode towards the dining room before her courage could fail her.

It was the first time that she had been inside this room, and she was surprised by how large it was. The walls were covered from floor to ceiling in opalescent glass panels that reminded her of the vase in the entrance hall. The room was empty of dining tables but for one long trestle table laid for thirty at its centre. Already a clutch of what must be the invited party were mingling in the space, glasses of champagne in their hands while waiters circled with trays of hors d'oeuvres.

There was a grand piano in one corner, and Agnes saw with a start that the patient she had met in quarantine – Sippie, she remembered – was seated at it, playing a gentle piece of classical music. Her hair had been sculpted into a gleaming, immaculate bouffant, a lotus flower pinned to one side. As Agnes went past, Sippie looked up, and Agnes saw that she was wearing a mask. The young woman raised her eyebrows, the smooth skin beneath that pretty, fernlike curl on her forehead wrinkling, and gave a small shrug as if to say, *Surely the delegates should be wearing these, not me.*

The room was filling up now, the hum of voices drowning out the soft chords.

'Ah, and here she is,' came Christian's jubilant voice. 'Everybody, may I introduce my new wife, Mrs Agnes Fairhaven.'

Here we go, she thought, hitching a smile onto her face.

As each of the scientists and investors came forward to take her hand, Agnes saw with a tinge of disappointment that every single one of them was male. A second gong rang out, and everyone grew silent. A waiter cleared his throat.

'Gentlemen, please take your seats.'

Agnes took her place to the left of her husband. She found herself sitting opposite a large man who introduced himself as a doctor at a sanatorium in Austria. He had managed to procure a whole plate of hors d'oeuvres, and was busily working his way through them, his lips glistening with traces of oil from the smoked salmon.

'Room for one more?' a familiar golden voice purred from the doorway.

Juno Harrington strolled into the room, completely aware of the spell she was casting over the table. Her dress was a dark shade of silver, almost transparent as to be nearly indecent. It clung to her contours as if she had been dipped in melted pewter. The men's eyes lingered on her as she crossed the room, and the man sitting next to her empty chair stumbled to his feet to help her into the seat.

'May I introduce Miss Juno Harrington,' Christian said. 'Her father is the pharmaceutical genius Maximillian Harrington. Juno is one of our most esteemed guests here at Hedoné.'

There was a murmur of appreciation among the party, and as the buzz of conversation around the table grew, Juno turned to the man on her left who had helped her to her seat, fixing him with her smouldering gaze. 'Tell me *everything* about yourself,' she said in a voice as smooth as molten gold. 'You must be *awfully* clever.'

Agnes stifled a cough of laughter, surprised by the woman's brazen confidence. If only she could channel an ounce of that.

Christian turned to her, his eyes raking her body in the pale pink silk, and Agnes felt suddenly naked under his gaze.

'You look incredible,' he whispered. He had a rose in his lapel, pale pink and paper thin, and he reached up and touched the matching one in her hair and smiled.

'It's a beautiful dress, thank you,' Agnes said, embarrassed by his gaze. 'The same colour as your rose.' She touched it with the tip of her finger, and he caught her hand in his own and brought it to his lips.

'I prefer what's underneath it,' he murmured, making Agnes blush. 'A rose coloured-dress for my English rose.'

When every seat was filled, the waiters leapt in and began filling up everyone's glasses. Christian pushed his chair back, champagne flute in hand.

'Now that we are all here, I would like to start by making a toast. It is so wonderful to welcome so many of you here to Hedoné House. As you know, I have long held a dream of creating a private and luxurious health spa for those with tuberculosis – not only for the ones who can afford it, but also for the creative elite, to nurture and encourage their talent. I hope that your short time with us will allow you all a little glimpse of what we are trying to do here.'

Agnes brimmed with pride as her husband talked. He was smiling round at the gathered men with such confidence. She thought of her mother, upstairs, already so improved in only twenty-four hours. What incredible treatments might Christian have here that Mother might benefit from?

'Tuberculosis is not a pretty word,' Christian said, continuing his speech. 'The current wave of the TB pandemic feels in some ways like a very modern illness – a part of so many of our lives – yet it is important to remember that tuberculosis has of course been around for centuries. It was described by Hippocrates as far back as four hundred BC. Our rich history of literature, art and music is peppered with those suffering from the disease, Keats, Modigliani and Chopin to name but a few.

'We cannot deny that TB is an ugly and dangerous disease, and yet, it is in its strange, clawing depths that so many creative people have produced their best work. The poet Percy Kelly said that at his most unwell, he possessed an unnatural and keen excitement. Emily Brontë grew stronger mentally as she declined physically.

'It struck me a few years ago that I might be in a position to bring these things together, to create an environment to support and encourage raw talent, whilst making the often painful lives of those affected as comfortable as possible. Hedoné House is at its heart a sanatorium, yes, but it is a sanatorium with a difference. It boasts luxury that many of us can only dream of, and it inspires and nurtures our guests to reach for the stars. We operate a scholarship policy here that enables those of extreme creative talent to stay for free, to work on whatever project that fascinates and captivates them, and to support them in any way we can.

'But more than this, Hedoné is a place of miracles. I should like to announce my first tentative steps in finding a cure for tuberculosis. I am not at liberty yet to disclose the full details, but rest assured, your input – both scientific and financial – will be going towards the most cutting-edge developments.

'So, let us raise a glass, first to your good selves, for coming all the way to this small corner of Norfolk to indulge my little venture, and also to the guests – for here they are considered *guests*, never *patients* – and the incredible, breath-taking future before them.'

Christian raised his glass, his toast echoing back to him from around the room. As he sat down, he placed his hand briefly on Agnes's, his eyes glittering, and she smiled back at him.

The scientist opposite Agnes had nearly finished the platter of delicacies, his moustache twitching as he finished chewing on the last morsel of beef.

'Geddes tells me you're a fan of Forlanini's artificial pneumothorax, Doctor Fairhaven,' he said.

'Yes. Many of my guests have benefitted from it, Miss Harrington here among them.' Christian indicated Juno with a tilt of his head, a smile on his lips, and she looked up and smiled in return.

'And can you breathe all right, miss, with only one lung inflated?' The scientist was still chewing furiously, looking a little too hard at Juno's chest.

'Oh, absolutely, sir. I imagine I'd find the corsetry of modern underwear a little uncomfortable, but the marvellous thing about Hedoné is that one can wear what one pleases beneath one's clothes, and nobody bats an eyelid.'

Agnes's eyes went from Juno to the scientist in incredulous disbelief. She took a gulp of wine.

'Now, tell us more about this cure, Fairhaven. That's why you brought us here, isn't it? To enlighten us all?' There was a murmur of agreement among the men.

'Ah yes.' Christian looked down at the table. Was Agnes mistaken, or was he blushing? 'It's very early stages at the moment, and I have to admit that it is not suitable for every TB case, but I'm very proud of the results I've been getting thus far.'

'Don't leave us in suspense,' said a corpulent man with a port-wine birthmark on his cheek. 'Let us in on it, then.'

'Alas, until I've fully concluded my tests, I can't reveal too much.'

'Or don't want to,' the man said with a smirk. 'It could be a good money-spinner. Especially with someone like Maximillian Harrington on board. At least tell us what form of cure it comes in. Is it a medication? A therapy? An operation?'

'It's a combination of all three, actually,' Christian said, and Agnes sat up with a pulse of excitement. She was suddenly glad she had come tonight. This cure, after all, was the very catalyst that had set her and her mother on the path to Hedoné.

'But rather than tell you, I think I'll let the guests' health speak for itself,' Christian said. 'You'll get to meet many of them over the course of your stay here with us.'

'Well, I think that's rather cruel,' the man with the birthmark hmphed. 'Luring us all the way out to the very edge of England with the promise of a cure, like dangling a carrot on a stick.'

'Of course,' interrupted a man with a head of curly hair, sitting at the end of the table, 'cure or not, we aren't that far off from a vaccine.'

'Now, now, don't forget the Lubeck disaster, old chap,' chided another.

'What's the Lubeck disaster?' Agnes asked. Across the table, the men all stopped eating, looking up at her as if she had grown two heads, and she felt her cheeks flush unbecomingly. She dropped her head.

'Forgive my wife,' Christian said with a small laugh. 'She is almost as new to Hedoné's delights as all of you are. I'm encouraging her to take an interest in the place, to really get beneath Hedoné's gilded surface.'

The men smiled indulgently and went back to their food. At the piano, Sippie swept her hands across the keys, plunging the room into a haunting version of 'Salut d'Amour', and Agnes sent her an appreciative smile.

Christian began a long and complex discussion with the man to his right, and Agnes sat in silence, cheeks still warm from her faux pas.

'How do you feel about your husband's endeavours here, Mrs Fairhaven?' said the man seated to her left, and she turned to him in relief. He was a nice-looking gentleman, with a kind, open face.

'I imagine it must be quite difficult, what with your own mother a patient here, trying to tread the line between your two roles. Though,' he lowered his voice, 'Doctor Fairhaven is obviously getting results. I suppose he won't let us in on it before he has a chance to patent it.' He placed a slightly too warm hand on Agnes's bare arm. 'I'm sure *you* could let me in on some of the doctor's secrets though.'

'I—' Agnes began.

'My wife and I have only been married a few weeks, Mr Parkinson,' Christian interrupted, no trace of a smile on his face. 'I haven't had the time to fill her in on all my plans just yet.'

At that moment, the waiters began bringing out the first course, and Agnes turned away from the man in relief. A contented silence spread throughout the room as the delegates sampled the exquisite fare, but Agnes stirred her food around her plate, her appetite gone.

'Darling?' Christian said, putting his hand on her shoulder, making her jump. 'May I introduce Doctor Camberwell, the head of the European Tuberculosis Foundation.' He indicated the large man with the port-wine birthmark on his cheek. A feathery-looking toupee on his head lifted in the breeze from the open doors. 'Leonard, my wife, Agnes.'

The doctor took her hand, bringing it to his meaty lips.

'Enchanté,' he said, his bulbous eyes glistening like a dead fish's as he studied her. 'You're quite right, Fairhaven,' he said, nodding at Christian. 'She is the epitome of the English rose, just as you alluded. Slim and demure, yet sophisticated too, and under that delicate beauty, extremely healthy, I'll wager. Well done, old chap, well done.' He smiled benevolently down at her. 'I imagine she will produce beautiful children, too. Tell me, Mrs Fairhaven, will we be hearing the patter of little Fairhavens running about the place before too long?' His gaze travelled down Agnes's body to her stomach.

'We do hope so, don't we, darling?' Christian said, following the man's gaze, and Agnes folded her arms across herself.

After dinner, the party got to their feet, mingling once more. As yet more wine was brought out on trays. Agnes remained at the table while the waiters cleared it around her, not wanting to join in with the conversation in case she made any more careless errors. Juno had no such scruples. She was standing at the centre of a circle of men, her laughter tinkling across the room, and Agnes looked on, trying to learn from Juno's assertive example, admiring her confidence and the way she seemed so at ease in every situation.

Sippie was playing a jazz number now, the notes discordant and jarring, and suddenly the room felt too bright, too overwhelming. Everywhere she looked, Agnes saw more men in suits, felt the press of their bodies around her, the warmth of the room suffocating. Christian was in the middle of a crowd of braying men. He would not miss her, not now she had done her bit.

Quietly, she got to her feet and made her way to the door, ready to make her excuses, but nobody questioned her. Out in the corridor, she wondered whether to go straight back to the cottage, but her body felt coiled like a spring, and she turned towards the library instead.

Inside, it was cool and dark in comparison to the heat and energy of the dining room, and Agnes sank down with relief into an armchair, taking a deep breath, feeling her heartbeat slow. She saw that a table had been laid out, with a large cut-glass decanter filled with brandy, and a set of glasses. It had not been there before, she was sure.

And then, from the corridor, there came a buzz of male voices, her husband's among them, oiled by champagne and pride. 'I should like to take you chosen few somewhere a little quieter, so that we can talk in more privacy, and more depth.'

Agnes could hear footsteps now, growing louder, and she jumped up, feeling her new heels digging into her feet. The handle of the library door began to turn, and she hurried to the end of the room, the thought of spending more time with these men exhausting.

Slipping through the open French doors, she hurried out onto the lawn, the darkness swallowing her whole.

The day had cooled, the night air brushing her skin, soft as moths' wings. Agnes pulled off her heels and walked, barefoot, down to the lake. At the jetty, she came to a stop, looking back at the house. Most of the delegation were still in the dining room, but in the library at the end of the house she could make out Christian and a clutch of the more vocal of his guests, glasses of brandy already in hand.

The evening had been a success, she could tell. The view through the open library doors was beautifully lit, reminding her of a play she had been taken to as a child, a treat from a kind customer of her father's. She watched the men as they each took the cigar that Christian offered, lighting up and puffing contentedly. She was too far away to hear their conversation, but she caught snatches of it drifting out across the grounds, words she had heard from her mother's doctors over the years, *droplet infection, phrenic nerve crush*.

Christian strode to the French doors. His face was turned away as he said something to the men, but Agnes caught the tail end of it as he turned back to pull the doors closed.

'. . . it's like experimenting on guinea pigs,' she thought she heard him say. There was a burst of appreciative laughter from the room, and then the doors were closed, and all sound was blocked out.

Agnes sat, gazing at the lake. *Like experimenting on guinea pigs*. What a horrible term that was. It was quiet out here, but for the occasional odd sound coming from the woods, and she remembered Matron on her first night, locking the windows to prevent the calls of the owls disturbing their sleep. Yet, as she listened, it didn't really sound like owls. Least, not any owls she had heard before. Curious screeches echoed through the trees, and far off, she thought she heard the rustle of branches, as if something large was being pursued. A deer? The noises came again. It sounded more like laughter than anything else.

There followed a piercing sound, like a scream, raising her heartbeat for a moment, and it took her a second to realise it was just a violin, the long notes off key, rising and falling and cutting sharply through the air. Perhaps the unruly noises that Matron so disapproved of were not made by the birds at all, but by the guests. Sippie had said that they were all night owls here. The trees by the lake shook again, and Agnes wondered if Matron had lied.

Yawning, she gathered up the edge of her dress, the hem already sopping from the evening dew. She made her way barefoot back to the cottage, her mind on nothing but the soft, welcoming comfort of her new bed.

Chapter Twelve

The Turquoise Hairpin

The girl tiptoes lightly through the basement, relishing the peace and solitude that this floor has brought to her night-time wanderings.

Tonight, the floor above is off limits. Her father is hosting a dinner for a delegation of important men, and it has run late into the night. She spied on them out in the grounds earlier in the day from the safety of an empty quarantine bedroom. They seemed very boring. Not enigmatic like her father. Not artistic like many of the guests.

Passing the x-ray room and the boiler room, the cleaners' cupboard and the laundry, the girl comes to a stop at the door at the end. Above it is the word 'Infirmary'. Cautiously, she peeps through the small pane of glass.

She knows, from years of visiting this room, that it is meant only for the sickest patients. Of all the rooms deep in the bowels of the house, it is the most clinical, the most like a hospital, and yet still she is drawn here. When she first came to Hedoné, the bed at its centre was occupied by her mother, but now, it is usually empty.

As quietly as she can, the girl opens the door, and slips inside.

She likes to come here sometimes, to remember who she used to be — not just a young girl, pitied because she has lost her mother. Not simply the only child in a houseful of sick adults. At night, she is no longer Isobel Fairhaven, the doctor's daughter. At night, she has no name. Or rather, she can pretend to be whoever she wants. Sometimes, in the darkness of the corridors, she feels like she has no body at all, as if she is a part of the walls of this place, stitched into its very bones.

She crosses to the bed, and ducks down, looking underneath. This room, like all the rooms in Hedoné, holds vestiges of the people who have been here before her. Today she spies something half hidden under the wainscot, and she crouches to pick it up. It is a turquoise hairpin. A single hair still hangs from it like a golden thread. Tucking it away, the girl climbs onto the high hospital bed, her feet kicking the empty space beneath, and looks about the room.

This is the last place she saw her mother, three years ago, yet it feels so much longer. Sometimes, she struggles to recall her face, yet down here it always comes to her, as fresh as if she had seen her just yesterday. She remembers, Papa told her that Mama was too ill to move into the nicer rooms at the top of the house, the ones that she so often prowls through now. Instead, she was shut away down here, her daughter forbidden to visit her. It was then that the girl discovered the laundry chute. The lift shaft. The hidden gaps and hollows that enable her to move invisibly through the house. In the time she has been here, she has discovered many of the house's secrets.

But there are still secrets left to uncover.

Isobel lays a hand on the sheets. The bed is freshly made, neatly turned down and folded tightly underneath. The metal rails can be lifted on either side to keep the patient from falling out. Now and then she has seen other people in here. Guests who are very ill. She likes to watch over them at night, to maintain a vigil when no one else is here. Most do not get better.

Those people are remembered in a special glade in the woods. It is a peaceful place. Her mother was the first, but now she has been joined by many more. Isobel likes to study the names on the headstones, trying to put a face to each one.

Many people have been in this bed, more than she can count, but tonight, there is no one but her. The girl's legs swing to a stop. She listens. Around her, the house's heart seems to beat, regular and slow, in time with her own.

Chapter Thirteen

Agnes woke the next morning to find herself alone in her new bedroom. The delegates' party had gone on late into the night, and she'd heard Christian come to bed at around two, rousing her from the deepest of sleeps with the touch of his hand on her bare skin.

She reached out now to her husband's pillow, the indent he had left there still warm. She was aware of the sheets, rumpled and twisted beneath her, her body filled with a pleasant ache, and she lay back against the pillow and closed her eyes, letting the intoxicating memories of last night's union wash over her again.

She felt a shadow looming over her, and she opened her eyes to see Christian, standing by the bed.

'You're awake,' he said, smiling.

He was already dressed, and, suddenly shy, Agnes pulled herself up, folding her arms across her body self-consciously, aware of how translucent her nightdress was in the stark light of morning.

'I was hoping you might wake me,' she said, not daring to meet his eyes. She could see a dusting of stubble on his cheeks and chin. He must be busy if he hadn't had time to shave.

'You looked so peaceful I didn't want to disturb you. Now, I've asked Matron to give you directions for your morning walk. I would show you myself, but I have meetings all morning with the delegates.'

'I'm to go on a walk?'

'Indeed you are.' Christian ran a hand through his hair. 'It would be all too easy to spend your time lounging by the pool and eating too much delicious food. I find the best way to counteract the indulgent lifestyle here at Hedoné is to get one's heart rate up, and it makes sense to get into good habits early on, don't you think? The air here is so invigorating, so health-giving.'

Agnes was a little bemused by this abrupt change in tone from lover to doctor, but she supposed it was something she was going to have to get used to, that it came as second nature to someone so caring to always be searching for ways to ensure she was well looked after.

Christian sat down on the bed next to her, stroking a finger down her stomach, the touch making her quiver with desire.

'We must take extra special care of you, my darling: keep you in the peak of health. Matron will meet you on the steps at the front of The House at nine. I must be off, I've a busy day ahead.'

'Christian,' she said as he went to get up. 'The dinner last night. Did I . . . did I do all right?'

'You were a complete success,' he said, and he leant towards her, kissing her full on the mouth, his warm hand on her stomach again, and this time her body rose to meet his touch, as if it had a mind of its own.

She felt Christian's mouth break into a smile against hers.

'More of that tonight,' he whispered. 'I promise.'

'May I . . .' she asked, as he went to leave, 'may I go and visit Mother again today?'

'Of course, my darling. I think that's a splendid idea.'

Another smile, and he was gone, and Agnes lay back in bed. She placed a hand on the flat of her belly, remembering the conversation last night with that odious toupee'd man about children.

Could they have made a baby last night? Her mind flashed forward to a few weeks' time, to telling Christian the news, his excitement, his palpable bliss, and despite her indifference to motherhood, Agnes felt a twinge of excitement.

At just before nine, she let herself out of the cottage dressed in a new blue wool suit. A selection of outfits had appeared miraculously in her wardrobe last night, and as she walked through the woodland, she ran a hand admiringly over the striking red-and-green buttons. Ahead, she could make out the low bulk of the main house in the distance, a looming shadow beyond the trees. The lace of her new silk blouse frothed at her neck, tickling at her throat, and she reached up absently and tugged at it with a finger.

Matron was waiting for her on the front steps, as Christian had promised, eyeing the watch strapped to her uniform and tapping her foot impatiently. Agnes imagined her mouth, hidden away beneath that mask, the lips pursed as she watched her approach, as thin as the rest of her.

'Time for your morning perambulation, Mrs Fairhaven,' Matron said, turning on the spot and pointing to the right, past the guests' bedrooms. 'If you take yourself that way, and bear right around the end of the house, you'll find it's a brisk forty-minute walk. Please do not stray from the path. Our gardeners work tirelessly to ensure Hedoné remains picture perfect. Now, if you don't mind, I have important duties to attend to.'

Without waiting for a reply, she turned and walked smartly back up the steps.

Insufferable woman, Agnes thought. She looked out over the estate, breathing in the fresh morning air. The dense, mellow smell of the pine trees was tantalisingly strong here, and she set off in the direction Matron had indicated, skirting the front of the house.

As she walked, Agnes noticed that the windows and doors that led to the guests' bedrooms were all flung wide open and it was impossible not to spy a flash of the interiors as she went past. One bedroom had blue wallpaper decorated with great silver birds, another boasted a huge ornate mirror in the shape of a lotus flower. In yet another, she thought she saw a naked leg, half-flung from the bedclothes, and she turned away in embarrassment. As she came to the last room, below her mother's quarantine suite, she remembered that this was Juno Harrington's bedroom, and she imagined the beautiful girl in there, that molten pewter dress from last night abandoned over the back of a chair as she slumbered on.

Did Christian visit these bedrooms on his rounds? She thought of him scooping Juno's shiny brown hair aside and tapping at her back with his warm fingers as he had done with Mother, bending close to her chest to listen to the whisper of her lungs. How difficult it must be to separate patient from friend when you lived in such close proximity to the people you treated. And yet Christian was nothing if not professional.

It was very quiet out here, the only sound the crunch of her shoes on the gravel path. As she rounded the end of the house, she was confronted by yet more pine trees, the sun still so low that their shadows stretched long and dark across the grass. The walk that Matron had directed her to led, not to the trees, but away, round the back of the house, the gravel path neat and pristinely kept. She stood for a moment, listening to the call of rooks in the canopy, and then she stepped off the path, ignoring Matron's orders, and started towards the trees.

At the edge of the woodland, Agnes came to a stop, glancing

back at the house. Matron might be in any of the rooms at this very moment, looking out. A surge of irritation swelled up inside her. She was the doctor's wife for goodness' sake; she could go where she pleased. Quickly, she slipped in between the trees, standing in the cool, dark shadows.

These woods felt different to the ones near her cottage. Was this an actual footpath, or simply made by the deer and rabbits who lived here? She began to make her way along it, the smell of pine sap all-consuming. Ahead, a fence emerged from the gloom, not pretty and perfect like everything she had seen so far in Hedoné's grounds, but ugly and scarred. It was made of chicken wire, presumably to stop the rabbits from getting through and nibbling at the perfect, manicured lawns, yet it was high — too high to step over. It looked as if it had been repaired here and there, wire twisted together like badly sutured wounds. Farther along, she spotted a fresh cut in the wire, large enough for a person to climb through. A rabbit had not done this. She made a mental note to tell Christian. Perhaps the local children liked to dare one another to sneak into the grounds.

She was about to turn back, when up ahead she heard the unmistakable sound of a twig snapping. It took Agnes a split second to make up her mind. With difficulty, she pushed her way through the slit in the fence, her new skirt catching on a sharp wire, and she swore quietly under her breath. The path on the other side rose steeply, and she set off, searching the trees for whatever it was that had made that sound.

She walked for a good quarter of a mile. After a while, she noticed the light getting brighter ahead, and she found herself emerging into a large formal garden surrounded by an oval of pines. Sunshine poured down, and here and there, yew trees grew, sculpted into the shapes of birds and animals. Between these were a number of gravestones: smooth, flat slabs inset neatly into the grass, constructed from marble and granite, with beautiful, flourishing script. Some had ornate scrolls and delicate pictures on them, flowers and butterflies, and one had what looked like real gold inset into the carved lettering. As Agnes began to walk among them, she realised that they couldn't be graves, they were far too close together. Was this a memorial garden, then?

She was distracted by a glimmering spangle of light on the ground near one particular stone, the earth around it still devoid of grass. The marble was pristine, glowing white in the sunlight. Above the inscription carved into it was a small golden hare, just like the one on Hedoné's emblem.

She crouched down to read it. The words were framed in a rectangle of sparkling gems, and it was these that were catching the light, fracturing into bright drops that covered the ground like fragments of broken glass. She ran a hand over them, feeling their hard sharpness under her palm.

Elizabeth Thackeray

1911–1935

'One should die with memories, not dreams'

Agnes's heart clenched for this poor, poor girl. Elizabeth Thackeray had only been twenty-four years old. What memories could such a short life have given her? She can only have only died a few months ago. As Agnes looked around at the other memorials, she saw that all of them were dated within the last three years. How many of these patients were still fresh in the minds of the current guests back at the house?

She got to her feet and carried on, winding around the memorials, noting with another pang of sadness that many belonged to people in their twenties and thirties. She came to a stop at a familiar name, set into one corner of the glade.

Meredith Fairhaven
1901–1932
Loving wife and mother

This was Christian's first wife. The memorial was not as extravagant as some of the others, though it had a quiet air of dignity about it. It was well tended, the grass around it cut neatly, the stone polished, and Agnes thought fondly of Christian coming here, whispering words to her, bringing news of their daughter and of his great project on the other side of the trees.

'I shall do my best to take care of your daughter, Meredith,' Agnes whispered. 'To love her as a child needs to be loved.'

Behind her, she heard a noise from within the trees and she spun round, but there was no one there, only bright sunlight slanting down into the glade. A deer, perhaps, or a squirrel. On the other side of the glade, a rose bush tangled with a large holly tree, the delicate scent of the late summer blooms rising into the air. Two more stones stood here, set slightly apart from the rest of the garden, not nearly as ornate as the rest. Curious, Agnes went over to them, and immediately saw why they were separate: in front of each was a long, low mound. These were graves.

The closest one was covered over with grass, but the farthest was sparser, glimpses of bare earth still visible among the emerging shoots. A dandelion clock blew seeds into the air. She crouched down and read their names: Elsie Clements and Betty Simpson.

They were both so young, younger even than Elizabeth Thackeray, only eighteen and nineteen respectively, and it came to her that even at Hedoné House, despite its modern advances in treatment, the death rate must still be high. Agnes gave a shiver, thinking of the possibility of her own mother's grave being dug here one day. Christian's cure had obviously come too late for these patients. Was Mother too ill, too old to benefit, too?

Kneeling down next to Betty's gravestone, she put a hand on the warm granite, struck again by how stark and plain it was. There was no epitaph, no poem or saying, no mention of God or of peace. Not even an RIP. Just a name and a date. Why had these two women been laid to rest here? Had they no family, no church of their own to welcome their bodies back to? Perhaps they had been penniless scholars, with no money for their own burial back home, wherever home had been.

Again, Agnes thought she heard a soft rustle somewhere nearby, and she straightened up, searching the trees around her.

There was something odd about this place. It was beautiful, in the same slightly eerie way that all graveyards were. But this layer of luxury felt at odds with its purpose. It was not something one usually found in village churchyards. Down at the house, the opulence felt fitting, but here, it was paper thin, as if the whole place had been smothered with gold leaf so fragile that it might peel away at any moment, revealing the death and decay beneath.

She supposed that the garden was hidden away from the house on purpose, that the guests might not even know of its existence. But if this place was not for their benefit, then why was it here at all?

Except, of course, it seemed that at least one person knew about it. Agnes thought of that slash in the fencing. Whoever had cut it, *they* had had the urge to come back again and again, slicing through the wire each time it was repaired.

What was it about this place that had drawn them back? But she already knew the answer to that; she could feel it herself right now: all these names, all this death, threaded through with glitter and glamour, so intoxicating, so terribly, addictively compelling that you could do nothing but come back again and again.

She glanced over at Meredith Fairhaven's memorial. Had this garden been Christian's idea? Perhaps he had begun it when he placed his wife's stone here. A cold shiver touched Agnes's shoulders, and fighting the urge to break into a run, she turned and retreated slowly into the woods.

On the walk back through the pines, she had that same feeling of someone watching her, pursuing her softly through the trees. When at last she glimpsed the brightness of Hedoné's grounds, relief clouded over her, and she hurried out into the sunshine.

Chapter Fourteen

Agnes emerged into the grounds, seeing that they were deserted, the guests all still asleep. Ahead, the sight of the house was a comfort after the shadowy walk back. Out of the corner of her eye, she caught a bright flash of colour, darting among the trees, and she came to a stop, shading her brow.

'Isobel?' she called.

The girl stepped out from beneath the trees further along, and relief tumbled in her stomach. Nothing sinister chasing her after all, then, only a child.

'Hello there,' she said with a smile as her stepdaughter approached. 'Were you following me?'

Iso's silvery eyebrows drew together, a look of hesitation in her unusual eyes.

'It's all right, I'm not angry. I think I heard you earlier, didn't I? In that garden in the woods?' She wondered briefly if it had been Isobel who had sliced the wire fence so many times.

The girl looked down at her hands, a daisy between finger and thumb, the translucent petals squeezed of life.

'I won't tell,' Agnes said, glad of the chance to bond with her. 'Were you visiting your mother's grave?'

The girl looked at her, her eyes narrowing. 'My mother's not there.'

'Well no, I suppose not in that sense, but—'

'I just go there sometimes,' she said with a shrug. 'To get away from my governess.'

'Ah, I see.' Agnes smiled. 'Miss Rose doesn't know the place exists, is that it?' She was rewarded with a small smile.

'You won't tell her, will you?'

'Of course not, Iso. May I call you Iso?'

The girl nodded.

'You must miss your mother.'

Iso shrugged. 'Sometimes when I go there, I tell her things,' she said. She stooped to collect up a twig from the grass and began picking away at its bark, and Agnes felt a streak of pity for this odd child.

'It's good to talk, isn't it?' she said. 'You know, Iso, I'm here, if you ever want to talk about anything. It doesn't have to be about important things. I'm a good listener.'

Her heart clenched as the little girl continued to scratch away flakes of bark. One lodged deep under her nail, and Agnes winced.

'Careful,' she said. Taking the girl's hand, she pulled the sliver of wood gently out. 'There.' She closed her fingers over Iso's, stroking the cold skin. 'It's nice to visit the graves of those who are no longer with us, isn't it?' she said, choosing her words carefully. 'I used to do that with my father sometimes. Chat away to him about my life.'

'Where's your father?' Iso asked, looking up at her, and in the bright sunlight, Agnes saw that her eyes were not silver-grey, as she had previously thought, but blue, a shade or two paler than Christian's.

The question caught in Agnes's chest, and she pondered how best to answer. 'Well, he passed away a few years ago. He's buried in a churchyard in Bedfordshire. But I suppose that's just a marker for him on earth, a place I can go and mourn him, like the memorial garden is for you. He's not really there. He's in heaven, just like your mother.'

A whisper of confusion passed over the child's face. 'I'm meant to have declensions next,' Isobel said, scowling at the thought, and Agnes breathed a sigh of relief at the fleeting attention span of children.

'Don't you like declensions?'

The girl shook her head. 'I thought I might go and swim in the lake instead. Don't tell my governess.'

'Are you sure that's—'

But before Agnes could finish, the girl had run off, heading towards the smooth body of water.

She wondered if she ought to stop her, or at least check that she was all right. Would Christian approve? He had warned her that she was a little spirited. Perhaps he meant that Agnes's job here was to tame her. But to do that, she must first gain the girl's trust. She imagined Iso did not have many people she could trust here, she certainly didn't seem close to her father, from what little Agnes had seen of them together. It was a start at least that the child had confided in her.

She set off back to the house. The sun had risen high in the sky now, the day a beautiful one, and she felt a pang of regret as she left the bright sunshine for the cool of the entrance hall. As she walked across the polished tiles, brushing stray pine needles from her shoulders and trying to tuck away the loose thread on her skirt that had snagged on the wire, she nearly collided with Matron, hurrying out from the corridor that led to Christian's office and the dining room.

'Ah, Mrs Fairhaven. Your mother has been asking after you.'

'I was just on my way. How is she?' Agnes said.

'She has a slightly raised temperature.'

A ribbon of alarm trilled through Agnes, and her mind began to run over all of Mother's regular symptoms, the tiny changes that indicated her health might be in decline.

'Has she an increased cough with it? Difficulty breathing?' she said, pulling out the golden hare keyring, cursing herself for going for a walk when she should have gone straight up to see her. She went to summon the lift, but found Matron blocking her path.

'Did you have a nice promenade?' the nurse said.

'Yes, fine. Matron, I need to see—'

'Take a tumble, did we?' the woman interrupted, arms folded over her measly bosom, still planted between Agnes and the lift. She was eyeing a grass stain on Agnes's new skirt, the loose thread hanging there. 'Were my instructions not clear?'

'Sorry?' Agnes stopped trying to get past, looking at the woman in exasperation. How much authority did Matron have around here? Must she follow every bit of her advice to a T?

'I wasn't aware that the walk I told you about took you into the woods,' Matron said, picking a pine needle from Agnes's hair and scrutinising it. 'Did you not hear my directions correctly? Perhaps we should get Doctor to check your hearing after you've seen your mother.'

Agnes felt a spark of fire ignite. 'What a good idea,' she said, anger rising. 'In fact, I think I'll go and see him now. I can find my own way up to my mother's room in a moment, thank you.'

As she started towards Christian's office, she felt Matron snatch at her wrist, and she looked down to see the woman's skinny fingers gripping her bare skin. Matron was surprisingly strong, the wiry cables of muscles in her arm flexing.

'Doctor is not to be disturbed,' Matron said in a controlled whisper.

They held each other's gaze for long seconds, silent fury bubbling between them, and then Agnes became aware of a soft click of heels on tiles behind her, and Juno Harrington appeared from the corridor that led to Christian's office, wrapped in a Chinese silk robe, her immaculate hair tousled.

'Agnes, darling!' she said, a soft blush of pink creeping swiftly across her cheeks. 'What a treat to see you again so soon.'

There was a sheen of sweat on the young woman's brow. Was she feverish, Agnes wondered, or just embarrassed to be caught *déshabillé*? Whichever it was, she had to concede that Miss Harrington still looked glorious.

Juno came to a stop at the lift, and her face broke into a frown as she saw Matron's hand clutching at Agnes's.

'Matron dear, what on earth are you doing to poor Mrs Fairhaven? Stop being so beastly and let her go, or you'll frighten her off, and then where will poor Doctor Fairhaven be?'

Matron gave the woman a withering stare that suggested this was exactly what she wanted to happen, but she reluctantly took her hand from Agnes's wrist and turned towards the lift with an audible huff. Juno shot a look of venom at her departing back, raising her eyebrows to Agnes in a show of mutual dislike, and Agnes thought, well, at least we have that in common.

'What a wonderful outfit,' Juno said, and Agnes looked down at her suit, brushing away another pine needle, suddenly aware of the grass stain at her knee, the thread that was fast becoming a hole. 'He really wants you to look the part, doesn't he?' She gave her soft, melodious laugh.

Agnes could smell her expensive perfume, its powerful scent bringing to mind the lilies that were everywhere, but with something sharp in it, too, like sweat, breaking through the saccharine sweetness. She reminded herself that Juno, despite her beauty and casual elegance, was as unwell as all the other guests.

'Are you coming up to see your mother, Mrs Fairhaven?' Matron said stiffly from the lift, her stringy arm holding the gate open. 'Any longer and I believe she might think you've quite forgotten her.'

Wordlessly, Agnes stepped into the mirrored compartment, fixing her gaze on Matron's detestable reflection as she pulled the gate closed.

'Until next time, then,' Juno said, as the lift began to rise, and Agnes thought she saw her wink, before the hallway and the glamorous young woman slid slowly out of view.

Upstairs, Agnes hurried along the hallway after Matron, reaching Mother's door just as the nurse unlocked it. She hastened inside, panic rising, only to find her mother sitting up in bed, flicking through a magazine.

'Mother,' Agnes said, hurrying to the bed.

'Aggie! How nice to see you.'

'Are you all right? Matron said you had a fever.'

Matron's voice called out from the bathroom where she was washing her hands, 'I said "a slightly raised temperature".' She emerged, going to the open window, through which the sound of splashing and laughter could be heard coming from the pool, and she peered out, scowling, as if she did not approve of guests that were too well for bedrest.

'But as I made demonstrably clear downstairs, your mother is perfectly fine. I have given her some analgesics to bring her temperature down. Everything is under control, though I would appreciate it if you don't get her too worked up.' She flashed a glance to the window again, and Agnes frowned. Did Matron dislike the guests so much that she wouldn't begrudge them a little fun once they were well enough for it?

When she had gone, Agnes's mother gave a rumbling laugh. 'She's a fine one, isn't she?'

Agnes pulled up a chair to the bed, shaking her head. It was laughable, really. 'As long as she's looking after you properly,' she said.

'Oh, she is. And how are you, Aggie?' She rested her hands on the open magazine in her lap, eager to hear. 'Are you being looked after? Tell me about your adventures.'

It was so lovely to see her mother so animated, the effervescence that Agnes remembered from before she was ill evident in the lightness of her voice, the enthusiasm with which she observed her daughter, and Agnes was reassured.

'I . . .' she began, and then she stopped. Gazing out at her from the magazine was a familiar face. She stared at the photograph, at the perfect waves of hair, the sardonic smile. Above it, read the headline, 'Famed socialite breaks off engagement after illness'.

'May I see that?' she said, pulling the magazine towards her.

It was unmistakably Juno Harrington. The young woman was smiling at the camera, her sultry lips pouting just a little. Her face was thinner than the woman Agnes had seen downstairs at the lift just now, her hair not quite so lustrous, but there was no doubt that it was her. Quickly, she scanned the article.

Glamorous it-girl turned actress Juno Harrington has broken off her much-publicised engagement to Lord Todmorden after taking up residence at a luxurious health spa for the past three years. Miss Harrington was admitted soon after the release of *The Lady of Paris*, her first prominent cinematic role. Friends say Juno, the daughter of the multimillionaire pharmaceutical magnate Maximillian Harrington, is in very good health. However, rumours abound that something more sinister is afoot.

Of course! Agnes had seen the very same image of Juno at the time the film came out, though since her life did not allow her much time for leisure, she hadn't been to see it. How terrible for Juno to be packed off here just when she'd begun to make it. She studied her perfect face, and that peculiar perfume she had smelled down by the lift filled her nostrils again, like lilies laced with an underlying sickliness.

Poor Juno. Was she very ill? Doubt about Christian's methods rose unbidden once again. Could all the excess here really be good for these people? Surely it was more likely to hinder their progress, rather than help it? Was that why Juno had been up at such an early hour, dressed only in that pretty silk robe? Had she been burning the candle at both ends, and waking, feeling unwell, gone to see Christian to get something to make her feel better?

The gravestones flashed into Agnes's mind again, and she thought of the guests she had met and was yet to meet: the Americans and the Europeans, those with titles and those with scholarships. The rich and the poor, the clever and the creative. She reminded herself that many of them were so ill that they would never leave this place. However incredible Christian's cure was, at this infant stage it wouldn't yet be suitable for everyone. Which of the guests' names would appear next on a memorial stone in the garden at the top of the hill?

Lost in thought, she barely heard her mother's cough, but she felt her head jerk up automatically, reacting subconsciously. Two bright spots had appeared on her mother's cheeks, a tell-tale sign that the fever was setting in. Quickly, Agnes found a thermometer and placed it under her tongue. Her mother did not argue. She looked a little pale.

Agnes sat, the magazine forgotten, waiting. At last, she took the thermometer from her mouth, looking at it with a frown, then leant over and pressed the gold button. Almost immediately there was a knock on the door, and to her relief, Matron appeared.

'What is it?'

'She's extremely feverish,' she said, lifting the thermometer for her to see.

Matron went swiftly to her mother's side. She took her face in her hands, kneading her neck with her fingers, then she felt for her pulse. Agnes could see the silent panic in her mother's eyes as she let herself be examined.

Without speaking, Matron pulled a medicine bottle from a pocket in her uniform and drew up a pipette of liquid, releasing it onto Mother's tongue, then she went to the oxygen cylinder across the room and wheeled it over. She uncurled the tubing and placed the rubber mask over her mother's mouth and nose, securing it in place with an elastic strap around her head, and Agnes saw that immediately her breathing seemed to improve.

'I don't understand,' she whispered. 'It was so quick. And she was so well yesterday.'

Under the cloth mask, it sounded like Matron tutted. 'I was informed by Doctor Fairhaven that you understood this illness.'

'I . . . I do.' But she also understood her mother. Whenever a fever had taken hold before, it had been slow to start and quick to abate. But this felt too sudden. Agnes knew how dangerous a raised temperature like this could be, taking hold of its victim without mercy. A high fever was the single biggest indicator of advancement of this cruel disease. If not controlled, it could be fatal.

'This place . . . it's meant to make her better. It's why she's here.' She was aware she sounded like a petulant child. She swallowed back her tears.

Something in Matron's face softened. 'You know that fevers

come and go, Mrs Fairhaven. We are not miracle workers here, but I promise you, we *do* know this disease. Your mother is in safe hands. Look at her, she is already improving.'

Agnes had to concede that she did indeed already look much better, the colour returning to her skin. She was already half asleep, the medication Matron had administered taking effect.

'Now, why don't you go and freshen up, and then I suggest you leave your mother to sleep. I fear your visit has been a little too much excitement for her for one day.' She pinned her with her stern gaze, eyebrows raised, and reluctantly, Agnes got to her feet.

In the bathroom, she gazed at herself in the mirror. Her body felt weak and insubstantial, as if *she* had been struck with a fever, not her mother. She filled the basin with water, steam rising like perfume, and splashed her face. Blinking water from her eyelashes, she pulled a towel towards her, then came to a stop.

The mirror had fogged up from the steam, and in it, she thought she could make out some words, traced into the silvered glass. She leant closer, peering through the steam.

Don't trust them.

The towel fell from her grip, landing in the basin of water. Swearing under her breath, Agnes pulled it out, dripping. When she looked up again, the condensation was vanishing away, the mirror clear once more.

Was it a joke? Surely this message hadn't been intended for her? She took another towel and dried her face, trying to slow the beating of her heart. It was probably just a feverish delusion of the patient in here before her mother. She could imagine how quickly a sense of claustrophobia and unease could set in while in quarantine, being ill and alone in a place where doors were locked and visitors banned. TB was a complex illness, she knew, bringing with it a whole host of other disorders: malaise, anxiety, depression. On rare occasions, it could even spread to the brain.

She twisted the tap once more, hot water streaming into the basin. The mirror misted up, those words appearing again, as if by magic, and she stared at them, trying to understand.

'Don't trust them,' she whispered to herself.

But don't trust *who*?

Chapter Fifteen

Agnes left her mother to sleep, as Matron had decreed. She didn't want to give the woman any reason to go to Christian. Her marriage was still in its infancy, it would not do to put a foot wrong. Not while she was getting to grips with the place. This was her home, now, after all.

She wondered what to do with herself. Coming to a stop outside her husband's office, she knocked softly, hoping he wouldn't mind her disturbing him during working hours.

There was silence for a moment, and she wondered if he was in, but then she heard footsteps, and the door opened.

'Agnes,' Christian said. 'What a pleasure. Come in, come in.' He was wearing a white doctor's coat, a stethoscope hanging round his neck. There were dark shadows under his eyes, but his smile seemed genuine, and she felt at once soothed by the familiarity of his kind face.

It was a beautiful room, every surface filled with complex, intricate scientific models that ticked and whirred. A large partners' desk stood at the centre, papers spread across it. Agnes admired Christian's medical degree certificate, hanging in an ornate gold frame on the wall.

'How was your walk?' Christian asked her.

'Illuminating,' she said, truthfully.

'And what can I do for you?'

He looked distracted. She glanced at the pile of papers on his desk, awaiting his attention.

'I'm sorry, I wasn't sure where I ought to go now. I've visited Mother, you see, and I didn't want to go somewhere I wasn't wanted.' She thought she saw a flash of irritation cross his face. 'You're busy,' she stammered. Backing towards the door, stuttering out apologies, she collided with the edge of the desk.

There was a clatter, followed by a great, splintering crash. The sound rang out through the room, and she turned in horror to find a metal tray, its contents upended onto the floor.

'Oh my goodness,' she said, her hands to her mouth. 'I'm so sorry.'

Christian had crouched down, carefully scooping the contents back into the tray. Slivers of broken glass glittered on the floor. Amid the wreckage, Agnes could see a number of glass syringes, the liquid inside leaking out.

'What are those?' she asked.

'It *was* the guests' evening medication,' Christian said. 'Not to worry, I shall have Matron draw up some more. We have plenty.'

She crouched down to help scoop up the shards of glass. 'What medicine is it?' she asked, though she thought she already knew – Mother had had many painkilling injections in her time. But it wouldn't hurt to play ignorant. And showing an interest might endear her to him.

'Medical morphine of the highest quality,' Christian said.

Agnes looked at the shattered remains, thinking how much these medicines would have cost her and her mother had they needed to pay for them. There were many, many syringes. More than there were patients, she estimated.

Christian put the tray back on his desk, going to a basin and washing the spilled medication from his hands, gesturing for Agnes to do the same.

'Why don't we go and introduce you to some of the guests,' he said. 'That should keep you out of trouble for a time.'

She glanced at him to see if he was angry, but he was smiling at her.

'Are you sure I'm ready?' she said, thinking apprehensively of that sparky group of men and women she had seen from the quarantine balcony on her first night.

'Of course you are. Come on,' he looked at his watch, urging her on, 'I need to be back soon; I'm scheduled to meet the delegates a little later.'

He led the way, out of the office and down the corridor.

'Is it safe for the guests to be around me?' Agnes said. 'Ought I perhaps to wear a mask?' She thought of Sippie last night at the piano, that horrible mask covering her delicate face.

'No, no,' Christian said distractedly. 'There's no need. Come.'

They emerged into the entrance hall, the vase at its centre now filled with fresh sunflowers, twenty or thirty of them, bright and brash, their thick, prickly stalks somehow not quite genteel enough for their surroundings.

Christian led her to the open front door and down the steps. To their left, Agnes could see some of the guests in the dining room, enjoying a late breakfast. A few others were stretched out in deckchairs and in those strange open cabins.

Crossing the lawn, Christian pointed out little dots of gold far off in a distant meadow. 'Our Jersey cows,' he said proudly. 'They supply all of our milk. And there's the generator,' he added, pointing to a building in the trees beyond the lake. 'And next to it you can just see the artificial-light therapy room. Beyond that, at Hedoné's border, is the carriage house, where our vehicles are kept.'

Agnes took it all in, wide-eyed. 'It's incredible,' she said.

They made their way towards the swimming pool, an occasional shriek of laughter drifting over to them as a guest splashed someone sunbathing, and Agnes felt her nerves rise. It was one thing to meet the guests fully clothed, yet another to have to converse with them half dressed.

Sensing her falter, Christian took her hand, squeezing it reassuringly. 'They won't bite,' he whispered.

As they drew closer, she saw that there were eight or nine people round the pool, a couple more swimming. Juno Harrington unfolded herself from a lounger as they approached.

'Darling Agnes,' she said. She was wearing a glittering emerald swimsuit, and she placed her hand lightly on Agnes's shoulder, leaning in to kiss her on the cheek, before wiping away the residue of her shimmering lipstick. Startled by the overfamiliar touch, Agnes gave a cough of uncomfortable laughter.

'Behave, Juno,' Christian said.

'Sorry, Doctor. I just know how excited everyone has been to finally meet your new wife.'

Her sultry eyes didn't leave Agnes's face as she said this, and in embarrassment, Agnes looked away, her gaze running awkwardly over the bodies that lounged by the pool. The guests were for the most part thin and gaunt, the swimsuits and summer clothing revealing rake-thin bodies that in other seasons might have been better disguised. Agnes wished she was wearing sunglasses to hide the shock that she knew must be visible on her face.

'I would like to introduce my wife, Agnes Fairhaven,' Christian said to the guests. 'She is still very green to the ways of Hedoné, so I hope I can trust you to be gentle with her.'

At this, all the guests got to their feet, following Juno's example and taking her hand, or leaning in to kiss her on both cheeks so that she was sure that she must have three or four different shades of lipstick on her face. Sippie was the last to greet her, and Agnes was thankful that she didn't try to kiss her, merely took her hands in her own and smiled that calm, reassuring smile.

'It's lovely to see you down here,' she said.

'Now,' Christian said. 'I really must go and attend to business. The delegates will be leaving soon.' To Agnes he said, 'We're to dine with the guests tonight at seven. I'm afraid I'll be too busy to come back to the cottage in between, but I shall see you in the dining room then.' He kissed her lightly on the cheek, his warm hand low on her back, whispering in her ear, 'I can't wait.'

To the guests he said, 'I leave Mrs Fairhaven in your trusted company. Remember: be nice.'

Agnes watched Christian leave with a feeling of mounting panic.

'Come on,' Juno said, linking arms. 'Now the fun begins!'

After the initial buzz of excited intrigue on her arrival, the guests all settled back round the pool, picking up conversations and books.

'Come, sit,' Juno said, patting the empty lounger next to her, and Agnes did as she was bid. The sun was hot, beating down, and she began to regret her choice of clothes. Rolling up the sleeves of her blouse, she tugged the wool skirt a little higher up her legs. The water glittered as people swam and dived, and she remembered suddenly what Sippie had told her, about the woman who had drowned here. How sad, to think that such a place of joy could also be a site of such tragedy.

Next to her, Juno stretched out supinely, purring like a cat. Turning her head, she regarded Agnes through her sunglasses.

'We're having a bit of a party tomorrow night,' she said. 'Why don't you join us?' Her glasses were so dark, Agnes could see nothing of her eyes.

'Christian hasn't mentioned it,' she said.

'Oh no, he wouldn't. He rarely comes to these things. A sort of doctor-patient breach, I suppose. But you're very welcome. It might give you a bit more of an idea about how Hedoné *really* works.'

'In that case, I'd be delighted,' Agnes said.

Juno smiled. 'Wonderful. It'll start late, probably about midnight. Over in the woods on the north side of the grounds.' She slipped her glasses down her nose, looking at Agnes as if for the first time. 'We must get you a swimsuit ordered,' she said, running her eyes over Agnes's body. 'You'll melt in all that wool if this summer gets any hotter.'

'I must admit, I do feel a bit guilty, relaxing out here, while Christian and Matron and all the staff are working so hard.'

'Enjoy it while you can,' said a young red-haired man sitting on the diving board. He had a soft, lilting Irish accent. 'You'll be pregnant before you know it, and then there'll be no time for relaxation.'

There was a chorus of 'Georgie!' among the guests, and the man gave an affable laugh, shrugging his shoulders, the movement drawing attention to his protruding ribs and the swollen, distended stomach beneath.

'I'm terribly sorry, Mrs Fairhaven,' he said. 'I forget what sophisticated company I keep these days.'

Agnes smiled, but inside she felt only pity for the man. His poor body was even more gaunt than the rest of the guests', his milk-white skin beginning to turn a paler shade of his hair in the strong afternoon sun. In the crooks of his arms, she thought she could see little pockmarks that looked like scars.

'Don't listen to Georgie,' Sippie called from the other side of the pool. She was sitting on the edge, cooling her legs in the water, her hands on the tiles, moving her fingers along them just as Agnes had seen her do at the lake on her first day, and Agnes got up from her lounger to join her.

'You played beautifully last night,' she said, easing her feet, still sore from last night's heels, into the water. 'What did you make of the delegates?'

'In truth? Rather stuffy,' Sippie said, and Agnes laughed.

The afternoon passed in pleasurable luxury, and she lost track of the time, chatting amiably with Sippie until the sound of a gong reverberated across the grass from the house.

'Time to dress for dinner,' Juno said.

The guests all got to their feet as one, as if in some strange Pavlovian reaction, and Agnes wondered if they all might start salivating any moment. She got up as well, supposing she ought to go and change, too. Last night's beautiful gown would have to manage another night, though she had a terrible feeling that it might still be where she'd left it, in a crumple on her bedroom floor.

As they all walked back towards the house, a muffled knocking echoed down from one of the upstairs windows.

'Isn't that Leopold Rackham?' Sippie, said. 'Up there in Keats.'

Agnes followed her gaze. In an upstairs room two doors down from her mother, a pale face flashed briefly at the closed glass door. She wondered if he was rattling the door handle, just as she had done only days before. The windows to his room, although open, appeared to be locked in position, allowing air in through only a small gap.

'I thought he'd left,' Sippie said. 'I hadn't seen him for a while.'

The other guests murmured their agreement. They had stopped on the lawn now, looking up at the window. A sudden loud banging rent the air. The man was clearly visible now. He had a chair in his hands, and he was hurling it repeatedly against the glass.

'Oh law,' Sippie said.

With a great cracking sound, the glass ruptured, the pane splintering down onto the balcony. Rackham clambered out through the window frame and ran to the edge of the balcony.

'It's all a ruse!' he shouted to them.

'What on earth?' one of the guests whispered.

'You hear me?' Rackham continued. He sounded half-drugged, his voice slow and slurred. 'It's all nothing bu—'

But what it was, they never found out. From behind him, the door opened, and Matron appeared. Quickly, she directed two strong-looking men dressed in livery to contain the patient, and he was pulled back inside, still mindlessly ranting.

'What was all that about?' Agnes said.

'Tuberculosis can affect the brain,' Juno said with a shrug. 'Looks like he's gone mad.'

The guests fell silent, staring at the gaping void that had been Rackham's window.

'Honestly,' Juno tutted, her honeyed voice breaking the quiet. 'What a ridiculous show.' She started towards the house again, calling over her shoulder, 'Agnes darling, I wonder if I might borrow you for a moment before you go and dress?'

'Of course.'

Agnes hurried forward, and Juno linked arms with her, clasping her close with sisterly affection. Her hands felt marble cold.

'Will he be all right?' Agnes asked, looking up at the shattered window.

'Oh, he'll be fine. Matron knows how to handle him.'

'What do you think he meant just now?'

'Who knows? Rackham's always been full of hot air,' Juno said dismissively. 'The wine probably wasn't up to standard or some such rubbish.'

But all the same, a shimmer of unease trickled through Agnes as she thought of that message on the mirror in Mother's bathroom. *Don't trust them.*

'What room was he in, last time he was in quarantine?' she asked.

'Oh, the one above mine. He used to wake me up early every morning doing some kind of frantic exercises, thumping down from my ceiling. That, or he and Matron were engaged in a rather passionate affair.' She laughed, but Agnes did not join in.

Could it have been Mr Rackham who wrote the message on Mother's mirror? But if what Juno said was true, and the TB had reached his brain, then it really was no more than the ramblings of a madman. Poor chap, Agnes thought.

They had reached the house now, and Juno opened a little gate that led onto the veranda beneath Mother's room.

'Welcome to Paganini Suite,' she said. 'All the guests' rooms on this floor are named after famous musicians and composers who had tuberculosis. Doctor likes to remind us how many exceptionally talented people had this godawful disease, in the hope that their brilliance will rub off on us.' She laughed softly through her nose. 'It seems tuberculosis loves to wipe out anyone with a penchant for creativity,' she added. 'Which is why I am glad to be completely without talent.' She gave another careless laugh as she ushered Agnes in through a shimmering curtain of organza.

It was not, as Agnes had expected, a bedroom, but a sitting room.

The walls were composed of a dark and leafy mural, like an exotic jungle. Tigers and monkeys and snakes eyed her from all around, and huge flowers in shades of orange and crimson burst from the walls as if they were growing into the room.

'Don't you just adore trompe l'oeil?' Juno said. 'It takes one away from reality. Sometimes I just sit here and imagine I'm far away in the jungles of deepest Borneo.' She gazed at it for a moment, lost in the beautiful artwork. 'I had Georgie paint it.'

'The man at the pool just now?' Agnes said. 'He's an artist?' She remembered him now on that first day, sketching down by the lake.

'Yes – part of the scholarly lot that Doctor likes to collect on his travels.' Juno gave that soft, mocking laugh again. 'Before that, I had every wall coated in real feathers. Ostrich and flamingo. And before that . . .' she paused, thinking. 'Do you know, I can't remember.'

'How long have you been here?'

'Since spring '32. I was here in the early months, even before Doctor Fairhaven came. I like to think I've been instrumental in making Hedoné what it is today. You know,' she added with a sly smile, 'famously infamous.'

'What do you mean?'

'Well, rumours abound about it, didn't you know? Whispered in the highest echelons of society. Of course, Doctor Fairhaven's renown in the field is undisputed, but no one seems to know *everything* about the place. That would spoil the surprise when you got here.'

'The surprise?'

'What *really* goes on here,' Juno said, her eyes sparkling.

'And what does really go on here?'

'Nothing sinister, darling, I promise. Just, oh, I don't know, the sheer volume of champagne shipped in each week, for example, or the fact that the staff are so very discreet. That sort of thing.'

'They are?'

'Oh yes. The rich and famous feel inordinately safe here. They can let their hair down in the knowledge that nothing will ever be leaked to the outside world.'

'But, what about when the guests leave? Don't they let on about everything they've learnt?'

'Do you know, it's very rare that *anyone* leaves. Most come here and realise they're on to a good thing. If they leave, they generally hold onto their secrets in case they ever want to come back.'

Agnes was suddenly overcome with the realisation that this incredible place that they were discussing was her *home*. Everything that Juno had outlined, it was hers for the taking. Never again would she have to worry about finding enough money to pay the rent or feed herself or her mother.

She was not prone to fancy, but from that first moment she'd seen Christian in France, she had known, hadn't she, that she was on the verge of something incredible? A feeling so unlike her that she'd followed the compulsion without question.

And now, that moment had germinated, flourishing as lushly as the mural that surrounded her in this room, yet far more real. She was here indefinitely. Even if Christian managed to cure her mother, then they wouldn't leave this place like other cured guests. Her marriage had tied them to Hedoné forever.

'But what about those who've been cured?' she said. 'They won't ever come back here, will they? They could spill Hedoné's secrets without fear of retribution.'

Juno had gone to a mirrored glass cabinet in a corner. She pulled it open, revealing a vast array of bottles and glasses.

'I suppose those that have been cured are so very grateful, they would never compromise Doctor's trust in them by gossiping about his sanatorium. Drink?' she added, tapping her long nails on the cabinet's mirrored interior.

'Yes, thank you,' Agnes said, and as the young woman expertly mixed and shook and stirred, she gazed around the room, taking it all in. Large potted ferns, their fronds curled like ammonites, were arranged around a suite of silk sofas and armchairs, a messy pile of magazines spread across them. At the centre of the room, a leopard-skin rug took pride of place. Agnes couldn't pull her gaze from its glassy, staring eyes.

Juno poured their drinks into two delicate glasses. Dropping an olive into each, she handed her a glass, taking a deep sip from her own.

'I wonder if you might help me with something,' she said, beckoning to her as she went through to the next room.

Agnes took a sip of the drink and screwed her face up at its briny taste. She put the glass back in the cocktail cabinet and followed Juno, avoiding the leopard-skin rug lest it snap at her heels as she went past.

Juno's bedroom was far grander than Mother's, the walls steeped in gold leaf.

'Yes, yes, I know,' Juno said. She was sitting on the edge of the bed, kicking off her shoes as she looked about the room. 'It is a bit over the top, but I do love a touch of excess.' Seeing Agnes hovering by the door, she patted the bed. 'Come in, don't be shy. Oh good, it's arrived,' she added, seeing a silver tray on the bedside table, a small syringe resting on a napkin at its centre.

This must be the pain medication, Agnes thought, like the syringes she had inadvertently broken in Christian's office earlier. Except that the liquid inside this one looked different, shimmering with a strange luminosity. Too late, she averted her eyes, realising she had been staring.

'It's all right,' Juno said. 'You can look.' She had picked the syringe up, and Agnes watched with fascination as she pushed the needle into her arm and pressed the plunger.

'What is it?' Agnes asked.

'Gold.'

'Gold?'

'Yes. It's a relatively common treatment, but here, Doctor makes the gold concentration much higher. We might all look pale and pasty on the outside, but inside we shimmer with excess.' She laughed, then before Agnes had a moment to avert her eyes, got to her feet and let the Chinese robe she was wearing fall to the floor, stepping smoothly out of her swimming costume at the same time.

Agnes looked away quickly, but not before she noticed that one of Juno's shoulders drooped markedly lower than the other.

'I know, I'm a frightful sight,' Juno said, still standing there, brazenly naked. She turned to a mirror, gazing at herself. 'It's the artificial pneumothorax. The lung on this side is deflated,' she said, clapping a hand to her left breast.

Agnes remembered the term from the delegates' dinner the night before. She was still averting her eyes, not sure where to look.

Juno continued gazing at herself in the mirror. 'Years of dieting in an effort to be thin, and it turns out all one really needs do is catch the white plague,' she said with a sad little laugh, the fragile sound of it cracking in the air between them. 'Now I eat everything put in front of me, and I wouldn't know a curve if it jumped up and bit me on the derriere.'

Agnes didn't know how to reply to this. She could feel Juno watching her now, waiting for her reaction. Stooping to pick up the shed swimsuit, still warm from its contact with Juno's body, Agnes draped it over a nearby chair.

'It's a beautiful room,' she said, truthfully.

'Daddy called it my "boudoir" when he last came to visit,' Juno said. She sounded sad. Lifting down an evening dress from the back of the door, she gazed at the gilt splendour all around her as if for the first time. Stepping into the dress, she crossed the room and presented her back to Agnes. She had not bothered to put on any underwear.

'Would you mind awfully zipping me up?' she said.

The dress rippled with white feathers at her neck. Even here, at her back, Agnes could see the delineation of her ribs. She pulled the fabric's edges together, her fingers brushing Juno's spine where it protruded in great, knobbled lumps. Juno's skin felt stone cold.

'I didn't think family was allowed,' Agnes said.

'As a rule, they're not. But my father has invested a lot of money in Hedoné, so he has stakeholders' privileges. I don't think Doctor would dare say no to him, to be honest. And besides, he likes to check I'm being properly looked after.'

She turned to Agnes and smiled, though it didn't quite meet her eyes, then she crossed the room, disappearing through another door. Agnes heard the turn of a faucet. 'Can I be of any more help?' she called out.

'Oh no, I'm fine,' came the muffled reply, as if Juno had already forgotten she was there. 'You go on and dress. See you at dinner!'

Agnes let herself out through the little gated veranda. The sun was low in the sky now, and the air had taken on a perfumed, drowsy thickness, the scent so rich it clouded her mind. As she made her way back to her cottage, she wondered why she had been invited back to Juno's rooms. Surely a maid could have helped her with her clothing? It occurred to her that Juno had wanted to shock her. But something about the woman had felt a little melancholy, too, as if her glamour and bravado was just an act, and beneath it a very different Juno Harrington existed, if only she would let people see.

Chapter Sixteen

Back at the cottage, Agnes found a new dress waiting for her, laid out on the bed. Her pale pink gown from the night before had been taken away, and she wondered who these ghostlike people were who waited on them. Christian had been right – it was so rare to see the staff, unless one was needed, in which case they appeared instantly.

Agnes realised she was exhausted from her afternoon fraternising with the guests. She barely had enough energy to trudge back up to the house, let alone spend the whole evening chatting politely with yet more people. But she knew it would appear rude if she did not show her face. And besides, she was looking forward to seeing Christian's expression as she entered, wrapped up in this new gown. And she had to admit, the anticipation of sitting through dinner, with the knowledge that once back at the cottage she would present her back to him, just as Juno had to her, and feel his hands slowly unzip her, felt deliciously erotic.

At the house, the dining room looked different, lots of small tables instead of one long one down the centre. Already, a few guests were inside, sitting in pairs or on their own, the room thrumming softly with their voices. Agnes thought she could hear some

German speakers and perhaps some French too among the English.

Across the room, near the open doors, a large table was set for eight. Most of these seats were already filled, and Agnes spied Sippie sitting among the guests. When she saw Agnes, she beckoned her over, lifting the place card next to her own.

Agnes wove between the tables, the guests nodding and smiling as she passed, and she commended herself on recognising some of them from her day out in the grounds.

Sippie rose to her feet and pulled out Agnes's chair for her. She was wearing a simple dress, far less extravagant than many of the costumes all around them, but still, she shone. Her sleek black hair was pinned up, that single dark curl gleaming against her forehead. She was so graceful, Agnes thought as she sat down, her body at once sinuous and almost liquid, and she thought of her playing the piano, those tender, delicate hands flitting over the keys.

She looked down in bewilderment at the array of glinting knives and forks in front of her. A small card menu had been placed artfully on her folded napkin, and she ran her eyes over the selection, written in gold, the now ubiquitous hare gleaming at the top. Unlike the menus in quarantine, this one was in French. Agnes studied the choices, thankful that her rusty French had improved during her time on the Continent.

SAUMON, SAUCE HOLLANDAISE

✣

POULET DE PRINTEMPS ROTI
ASPERGES, SAUCE MOUSSELINE
SELLE D'AGNEAU A L'ANGLAIS

✣

PUDDING D'ETE A L'ANANAS

'It's all a bit much, I know,' Sippie murmured, nudging her elbow. 'Don't worry, you'll soon get used to it. Oh look, here comes the mistress of the house,' she added, and Agnes looked up to see Juno entering the room.

She had not paid much attention to Juno's dress earlier, but now she saw it was even more elaborate than the molten silver gown she had worn the night before. The skirt was simple, black and sinuous, but the bodice was composed entirely of white feathers. As she approached, Agnes saw that the feathers were in fact an actual stuffed bird, a seagull perhaps, or an avocet. It clung to her chest, its wings outstretched, stroking her bare shoulders, its beak indecently close to her throat.

Juno placed her hand on Agnes's shoulder, and Agnes half rose to meet her as she leant in to kiss her on the cheek. The feathers tickled at her clavicle.

'Don't you brush up well?' Juno said approvingly, folding herself daintily into the seat opposite.

There was no sign of the vulnerability that Agnes had glimpsed briefly in her rooms earlier in the evening, but her eyes looked a little red, and she wondered if after she had left, the young woman had given in to that melancholy that had touched her so briefly during their conversation.

Juno picked up her menu, studying it with her pretty frown. 'Why do they insist on writing these damn things in French?' She dropped it on her napkin with a sigh, giving a nearby waiter a withering look, as if it was his fault. 'Oh good,' she added, plucking up the name card from the seat next to hers at the head of the table. 'I see Doctor will be joining us.'

The dining room was filling up now. A group of four tanned

American youths came in, their voices loud and rambunctious over the polite chatter.

'Good god, look at those suits,' Juno said witheringly. 'Do they think they're still in the Deep South?'

Beside her, Agnes felt Sippie stiffen. 'Are lots of the guests from foreign climes?' Agnes asked Juno.

'Oh, a few. There's a Swede here somewhere, I think, and many are European, but they mostly keep to themselves. We even managed to secure an Indian princess last year.'

'Cultural bingo,' Sippie murmured to Agnes with a raised eyebrow. 'Tell me, Juno,' she said more loudly, 'does one score more points the darker a guest's skin is?'

Juno smiled coldly at Sippie, but she didn't reply.

'Champagne, madame?' a waiter said quietly at Agnes's shoulder, making her jump.

'Oh. I'm not sure.' She had only had champagne once before, a few small sips on her wedding day. She had been too fraught with worry last night to notice what she was eating or drinking.

'Go on,' Sippie said, lifting her own glass, her slim collarbone jutting awkwardly, revealing its sharpness beneath her gleaming skin. 'It's awful nice.'

'Well, all right then.' Agnes watched as the pale amber liquid frothed to the top of her glass.

'Salut,' Sippie said, clinking her glass to Agnes's.

She took a sip. It was cold and sharp, the bubbles pleasingly volatile on her tongue. The feel of it as it slid down her throat was like velvet. A gentle glow of wellbeing spread slowly through her, and she sat back in her chair, listening to the guests chatter around her. She became aware that the sound had changed, ramping up an octave, and she looked around to see that Christian had entered the dining room.

He was dressed, like many of the guests, in a dinner suit. But unlike the other men, whose bodies had been ravaged by illness, he looked wonderful, his broad, muscular back filling the fabric pleasingly. A tingle of desire traced itself up Agnes's body. She took another sip of champagne, watching him as he stopped at each table, working the room, his presence commanding total attention as he chatted briefly, shaking hands here and there.

He arrived at their table and briefly put a hand on her shoulder before going round to each guest, exchanging pleasantries. When he came back to Agnes, he sat down at the head and kissed her full on the lips.

'Darling,' he murmured.

Immediately, a waiter rushed forward and filled his glass with champagne.

'I trust they've been looking after you,' Christian said loudly, raising an eyebrow at the guests around the table. A rumble of laughter followed.

'Very much so,' Agnes said.

'You look beautiful by the way,' he said, lowering his voice. Across the table, Agnes felt Juno go still.

The waiters brought out the first course then, tiny plates edged with gold, at the centre of which were shavings of pink salmon drizzled with a rich yellow sauce.

As she took her first bite, Agnes's eyes closed in wonder.

'Marvellous, isn't it?' Sippie said. 'I'll always remember my first meal here.' Her eyelids fluttered at the memory, the dark lashes sweeping her cheekbones. 'Utter ambrosia.' Opening her eyes, she gave Agnes a smile, her small, elfin face so friendly that Agnes beamed back.

'You said Doctor Fairhaven found you in Paris,' she said.

'That's right. I was on a tour of Europe. I used to sing at jazz clubs all over, but this damn disease had begun to make that quite tricky.' She put her hand to her throat, a fleeting look of regret washing over her face. 'So now I play piano instead,' she said brightly. 'You don't need good lungs to play piano,' she added, for a moment sounding every bit of her Black American roots, and Agnes imagined how beautiful her voice must have been, flowing smooth and enticing out into the smoky jazz clubs in Paris. How cruel a disease, to rob this young woman in such a visceral way.

'Sippie is being modest,' Christian interrupted. 'She is an incredibly talented pianist.'

The young woman dipped her head in acknowledgement.

'Are there lots of musicians here?' Agnes asked.

'A few,' Juno said. 'There are writers too, and artists of course. There's Georgie down there.' She pointed to the red-headed man Agnes had met earlier. He was busy attacking his salmon with gusto. 'He's the one who painted that wonderful mural in my sitting room. Many of the people here have found projects to keep them occupied. Not just the scholars, but the paying guests too.'

'And what's your project?' Agnes asked her.

'Oh, to admire everyone else's,' she said to a titter of laughter around the table.

'Miss Harrington is a most supportive patron,' Christian agreed, wiping his mouth with his napkin. 'And of course, it is due to the incredibly generous investment from her father that I have been able to make Hedoné the place it is today.'

He lifted his champagne glass. 'To Juno, who like Midas, turns everything she touches to gold,' he said, inclining his head.

After a moment, Juno lifted her own glass too, her eyes lingering on Christian, and Agnes thought she could see vestiges of that same sadness she had noticed in the young woman's face earlier.

She raised her own glass along with the others, murmuring, 'To Juno,' but her puzzled gaze stayed trained on Miss Harrington long after everyone else had begun to talk once more.

Chapter Seventeen

The next morning, when Agnes woke, Christian was sitting on the edge of the bed. She smiled sleepily up at him, wondering how long he had been there, watching her.

'I'm late,' he said, straightening his tie. 'But I shall see you back here tonight at about eight o'clock.'

'We're not dining up at the house tonight?'

'No. I thought we'd have dinner here alone instead. Let the guests have some time away from us, and us from them.'

He ran a finger down her collarbone, trailing to a stop at the dip of her breasts, and she felt a pulse beat somewhere deep within her belly. He pressed his lips to hers, the kiss long and lingering, and Agnes lay back in bed, listening to the silence of the cottage, wondering what to do with herself all day.

Pulling back the quilt, she placed her feet on the carpet, her toes luxuriating in the thick pile. She would start the day with her prescribed morning walk.

Out in the grounds, Agnes set off in the direction of the statues on the lawn, curious to see them up close. But when she reached them, she found that she was not alone.

Her stepdaughter was standing in their midst, gazing up at the tall, sculptural figure of a ballet dancer. Her hair was damp, tangled and knotted, drying in silver waves down her back, and her dress was wrinkled, the hem sopping and dusted with mud.

'Hello, Iso,' Agnes said. 'Have you been swimming again?'

The child smacked at a mosquito on her skin. 'Shh,' she said, putting a mud-stained finger to her lips. She glanced over her shoulder, looking out between two statues. 'I'm hiding from Miss Rose,' she whispered. 'She won't find me here; she's scared of the stone people.'

'Scared of them?' Agnes looked at the statues encircling them. She hadn't thought of them as frightening before, their perpetual stillness radiating calm, not fear. But looking at them now, tall and forbidding, she thought she could see why the governess might find them so. They reminded her a little of a postcard she had seen once of the carved figures on Easter Island, their faces almost abstract.

Iso was looking up at the ballerina statue, its leg stretched out above her in an arabesque. Kicking off her shoes, she placed her hands on the raised leg, and swung up onto it, her toes clenched against the cold stone. Agnes watched her as she straightened, her heart in her mouth in case the girl fell, but she was very agile. Stretching out her arms, she began to walk along it, lithe as an acrobat.

Agnes sat down in the shade of a nearby statue, leaning back appreciatively against the smooth, cool stone. She closed her eyes. A soft thud, and she felt the press of the girl's bare leg against her own as she sank onto the grass by her side. Agnes opened her eyes.

Isobel was sitting, cross legged, her dress rucked up, picking at the blades of grass with well-chewed fingernails. It was an odd feeling, Agnes thought, this unsolicited touch, though not entirely unpleasant, like having a butterfly settle on one's hand for a moment, and she found she wasn't sure what to do with herself. Iso was humming a nursery rhyme under her breath, and Agnes looked down at the small, silvery head, at the vulnerable parting at her crown. She had a sudden urge to run her hand over the child's hair, just to see how warm, how alive, she felt. A browning water lily petal had pasted itself to the girl's bare leg, and a feeling came over Agnes, a tight, clenching warmth, caught somewhere between pity and love.

Would Isobel have had a governess if her mother were still alive, she wondered. Perhaps she would have been sent away to boarding school instead. Surely it would be better for her, to be away from this place, to grow up with other girls her age, instead of among sickly adults? Her world was so small here. Christian must have wanted to keep her close after Meredith died, his last remaining link to her, but was it fair on the child?

'Do you have any hobbies, Iso?' Agnes asked. 'Painting or drawing, perhaps, or reading?' She wondered if she might procure some materials for the girl, help widen her outlook a little.

Iso didn't answer straight away. Plucking a long grass stem from the ground, she wrapped it round her finger like a ring. 'I like to write,' she said at last.

'Oh lovely! Stories, or poems?'

'Letters, mostly.'

'It's good to keep up your correspondence. Who do you write to?' Perhaps she had grandparents, distant cousins.

'My mama.'

'You . . . write to her?' Agnes said, her voice rising in surprise.

Iso nodded again. She pulled the ring tight, the skin beneath losing all colour, and Agnes waited for her to explain, but she only began humming the nursery rhyme again.

'What a pretty ring,' Agnes said. 'Shall I adjust it a little for you?' Carefully, she loosened it, smoothing away the indented line it had left. To her surprise, the girl's fingers closed over hers, holding onto her hand tightly. Her palm was sticky and damp, and as she squinted up at Agnes in the sunshine, her sour little face broke into a smile, and she was suddenly extraordinarily pretty.

Was this the face of Meredith Fairhaven, Agnes wondered? The woman Christian had loved so much and lost? She didn't know what his first wife had looked like; Christian did not keep any photographs of her in their cottage, and she couldn't remember seeing one in his office either. Perhaps he thought it might be seen as a slight to their own marriage, a sentiment Agnes could appreciate, even if she did not wholly understand the reasoning.

Beside her, she felt the girl stiffen. Iso was scanning the distant grounds, her small hand in Agnes's going still.

'Miss Rose,' she whispered, whipping her hand away and springing to her feet, and then she was off, darting across the grass in the opposite direction to her governess, her sylphlike body light and quick.

Agnes watched her go, thinking. She and Isobel shared more than she realised. They had both lost parents to this cruel disease, but both remained healthy, living among the sick. Christian had tried to give the child structure and routine, controlling her as best he could, but still Iso pushed against it, escaping every chance she got. It struck Agnes that here, too, she and her stepdaughter were the same. Christian and Matron had tried to provide Agnes with routine, to help her fit into this strange new place, yet here she was, just like Iso, hiding among the statues, escaping from this peculiar, unorthodox life, if only for a few peaceful minutes.

Chapter Eighteen

That afternoon, Agnes lay in a sumptuous bath back at the cottage, scented oils perfuming her body, the warmth of the steam enveloping her as she reclined.

She had never had time to herself like this before. The luxury of having someone else be responsible for her mother still took her breath away. At first, the thought of all this time to herself had frightened her, but now she wondered just how she had managed all those years on her own.

She thought of Christian and she, alone here all evening, wondering if tonight would be the night that they conceived a child. She had never paid particular attention to her monthlies, often surprised when they arrived, like some mysterious magical happening. But living with Christian meant that she couldn't help becoming more attuned to her body. He had told her not to worry about dates and timings, but it was difficult to forget these things when one's husband's language was peppered with words such as 'luteal' and 'follicular'. Still, every union between them carried a small chance, she knew, and even if nothing came of it, Agnes found she was enjoying the act simply for what it was.

She had never had much interest in the idea of sex before. It felt like something she had missed out on earlier in her life, too busy caring for her parents to socialise much, and then it was too late. The first and only time anyone had shown any interest in her had not ended well. It had been just after her father died. Walter was a nice young man who worked at the local tax office. Back then, of course, Mother's TB was still undiagnosed, though Agnes supposed that it was probably already twisting and burrowing inside her.

She and Walter went out a few times, and though the evenings spent together were pleasant enough, they were hardly scintillating, with Walter talking monotonously of tax breaks and deductions. When he asked her to marry him, she supposed she ought to say yes. They began to plan their wedding, and he had even agreed to move into Agnes's house once they were married, so that Mother could continue to live with them. But then, her mother had begun to cough.

Walter's interest in Agnes had grown lukewarm, until he called off the marriage altogether. It was never discussed, but Agnes understood. She supposed it was only a matter of time before she herself grew ill, just like her father and mother before her. And yet, here she was, three years later, still as strong and healthy as ever.

She and Walter had never consummated their relationship, but thinking back now, the idea of undressing in front of him would have felt rather like doing so in front of one's brother. With Christian, it was different. Agnes looked at the clock, eager for their evening to begin.

At eight o'clock, there was a knock on the cottage door, and she opened it wearing only a chemise and transparent silk robe over the top.

But instead of her husband, it was a young man in livery bearing a single silver cloche on a platter. Agnes pulled her robe tight about herself in embarrassment.

'Doctor Fairhaven sends his apologies,' the man said, averting his eyes. 'He says he'll eat in his office up at the house tonight as he's very busy, and not to wait up for him.'

'Oh,' Agnes said, trying to hide her disappointment.

The waiter stepped over the threshold and set the meal on the table. The food looked exquisite, but she did not feel hungry, so she went to the sofa, turning on the wireless, and tried to lose herself in a play instead. At ten o'clock, Agnes went to bed.

She awoke sometime in the early hours to find her husband still missing. She pictured him in his office, paperwork strewn across the desk, blearily sipping a cup of coffee as he rubbed his tired eyes in exhaustion.

From somewhere outside, she thought she heard a low, monotonous beat. Slipping out of bed, she padded to the window, pulling up the sash and leaning out.

There it was again, and with a jolt, she remembered that tonight was the party that Juno had invited her to. In the excitement of thinking about a night in with her husband, Agnes had clean forgotten about it. The music was coming from the north, deep in the woods she had not yet explored, and, curiosity overtaking her, she pulled on the first dress she could find in the wardrobe. Letting herself out of the cottage, she shivered as the warm night air licked beneath the fabric.

As she emerged into the grounds, she came to a stop, spellbound by the beauty of the landscape ahead. The front of Hedoné House was lit with golden floodlights. It looked like a beacon soaring into the dark sky. On the grass, the statues in the shivering moonlight could almost be mistaken for real people, frozen in time. The beat was louder here. She could just make out a glimmer of light from the woods at the north end of the estate, the pulsing music percussive and enticing, and Agnes started towards it.

As she reached the woodland, she saw that the light came from a string of bulbs tied high in the trees. They shone onto the ground, illuminating a path, and she began to make her way through, the lights flickering above her like fireflies.

The beat of the music was slow and heavy and repetitive, inciting in her a soporific wooziness as if she had drunk a glass of champagne. Ahead, she could just make out a clearing. Flashes of colour and movement flitted across it.

The glade was set about with sofas and cushions and Oriental rugs. Here and there, huge, fringed parasols provided cover, and yet more strings of lightbulbs hung high above, crisscrossing the circle, making the vast space feel more like a cosy room.

The guests — almost all of them at a count — were in here. Some were dancing, their bodies fluid and trancelike. Others were stretched out on the sofas and rugs. Here and there, Agnes noticed clothes strewn across the floor. Her eyes settled briefly on a woman reclining on a great pile of cushions. Her dress was unbuttoned, pooling about her waist, and Agnes saw with shock that her chest was bare. The woman was sucking on the mouthpiece of a strange, ornate pipe.

Agnes looked from face to face, searching for her husband until she was sure that he was not among them. Her attention was caught by a movement out of the corner of her eye. Two men were sitting on a sofa, one wearing a peacock feather headdress, its shimmering mask covering his eyes. Sitting next to him was the young artist, Georgie. Unable to tear her eyes away, Agnes saw the masked man gently roll up the young man's shirt sleeve. She saw the taut muscle of Georgie's bicep, the glint of a needle sliding expertly into flesh, and then the masked man leant in, kissing him slowly as he pushed the glass plunger of the syringe.

From somewhere nearby, a piano started up, the notes lacing themselves into the beat. The tempo began to rise, and people's dancing intensified. Agnes felt suddenly dizzy, the whole scene seeming to press itself against her, pulsating with the beat of the music like something out of a dream. The man in the mask had withdrawn the needle. He tossed the syringe carelessly onto the ground.

'You came, then.'

The voice was so close that Agnes jumped. She turned to find Juno, ravishing in a glittering sequinned dress.

'I wasn't sure if you would.' She smiled, that slow, licentious smile. Taking Agnes's hand, she led her into the clearing and pulled her down onto one of the sofas.

'What is this place?' Agnes said, looking around.

'It's where we come at night, once the grown-ups have gone to bed,' Juno said with a small shrug, tucking her long legs beneath her. 'To play,' she added, that smile flickering about her lips.

Agnes glanced again at the two men on the sofa, a fresh syringe in the older man's hand. She felt Juno's gaze on her face, studying her like a hawk.

'What is it they're injecting?'

'Morphine. One can have all kinds of enlightening conversations under its influence.' Juno turned to watch them, a hungry expression on her face. 'There's something quite wonderful about losing one's inhibitions like that. Our truths become so much easier to bear.'

She was smiling, but beneath it, her face had taken on that same sadness that Agnes noticed before, as if she was looking wistfully back into her past. Or perhaps, Agnes thought with pity, simply seeing a glimpse of her future.

'You take it for fun, not medicine?' Agnes said.

Juno nodded. 'Morphine has some very pleasurable effects. It's named after Morpheus, the Greek god of dreams.' She paused, assessing Agnes's face. 'Are you shocked, Mrs Fairhaven? It's a lot to take in, for someone like you.'

What did Juno mean by this? Agnes had seen enough of her now to know that what she said and what she meant were often two different things.

I must be careful, she thought. In truth, she was not shocked by what she had learnt. She had seen enough drug misuse in France to know it went on, and that night when she had considered buying heroin for her own mother would haunt her for the rest of her life. At least here the medication was properly regulated.

'I suppose I just don't understand why everything about this place has to be so cloaked in secrecy,' she said.

'Oh, it's really not all that secret,' Juno said, her eyes glittering.

There was a bloom of pink on her cheekbones that looked more natural than her usual perfectly applied blusher, and Agnes wondered if she had taken some of the morphine too.

'I mean, take the name of the house. Hedoné. It's from the ancient Greek, meaning pleasure, but we couldn't exactly call it "Pleasure House" now, could we? People would have raised eyebrows. Even you must know what a house of pleasure is, don't you, dear Agnes?'

She gave that mocking laugh of hers, her eyes glittering dangerously. Lifting a glass of champagne from a nearby table, Juno took a deep gulp, and Agnes wondered if it wasn't morphine that was making her conversation so barbed, but alcohol.

The young woman uncurled her long legs and got to her feet, pulling Agnes up with her. Lifting a manicured hand, she brushed a pine needle from Agnes's hair, her palm lingering there. She was so close that Agnes could smell her perfume, the clotted reek of lilies on the verge of turning. Or perhaps it was just the smell of sickness.

'The truth is, Mrs Fairhaven,' Juno said, her voice like cream, 'the whole world operates on these things, on sex and pleasure. I dare say even you are driven by your base needs and urges sometimes.'

Agnes stood, paralysed to the spot, the party's sounds and sights whirling around her as Juno trailed an ice-cold finger down her cheek. She took a step back, breaking the thread that hung, taut between them.

'I assure you, Juno,' she said with a nervous laugh. 'My base needs are not that vulgar.'

'So, you and Christian haven't made love then?'

The mocking edge in Juno's voice was gone, replaced by that same vulnerability that Agnes had noticed before. What was this, *jealousy*? The light from the bulbs above picked out the sharp bones beneath Juno's skin, making her sickly face look almost skeletal.

'It's none of your business what my husband and I do,' Agnes said, suddenly angry, not caring that she showed it, wanting only to wound this woman who lorded it over everyone else. 'Just because you're too unwell to have a husband of your own, doesn't mean I have to go and divulge . . .'

She stumbled to a stop, realising what she had said.

Juno had taken a step back, as if Agnes had slapped her. She slumped down onto the sofa in slow motion, her body drooping in on itself to reveal that awkward lopsided gait.

'Juno, I'm so sorry,' Agnes whispered, sinking down next to her and putting an arm awkwardly around her shoulders. For a moment, she felt Juno crumple against her, allowing herself to be held, but then she stiffened and pulled away.

'It's all right,' she said quietly. 'You're right, of course. We're all dying here. It's easy to forget, amid all this luxury, that we guests are here because we're a little more mortal than the rest.'

She looked genuinely upset, but try as Agnes might, she could not shake the feeling that this was just another part of the woman's act. It had been clear from the start that Juno was an integral part of Hedoné, not just from the money her family had invested, but in the day-to-day running of the place. How much influence did she have over Christian? Agnes knew she must try and repair the damage. If this got back to him . . .

'I shouldn't have said that,' she whispered. 'I don't know what came over me. The truth is, Juno, all this, it's been so much to take in. I . . . I wanted to thank you, for taking me under your wing, inviting me to this party. It's made me realise how little I know of the ways of the world, how ignorant I am to it all.'

Juno looked up at her, her head tilted to one side, as if she was trying to get a measure of her.

I've taken it too far, Agnes thought.

'Oh, don't you worry, Mrs Fairhaven,' Juno said at last. Her voice sounded confident, but her eyes still looked wounded. 'Innocence is a good thing here, I promise you. It's better not to know about everything that goes on.'

What does *that* mean? Agnes wondered. Was it a threat?

'What do you—' she began, but the young woman had got to her feet. She crossed the glade, coming to a stumbling stop at the trees. She looked so fragile, so vulnerable, standing there in the shadows, and Agnes felt once more the woman's inexorable pull. She wondered whether to get up, to plead with her to stay, but before she could decide, Juno had turned and disappeared into the darkness of the woods.

Chapter Nineteen

The Kingfisher Blue Sequin

Isobel is sitting in the driver's seat of the Rolls when she first hears the hypnotic music. She takes her small hands from the tan leather steering wheel, and opens the driver's door to listen.

So many of the guests here are musicians. Isobel is learning to play the piano, but her fingers are awkward and cumbersome on the keys in comparison to theirs. The distant music is calling to her, and she hops out of the car, drawn towards it as if bewitched.

The sound is coming from the trees far to the north, and as she crosses the grounds, she senses movement ahead. She ducks behind a statue.

Juno Harrington flits across the grass in a beautiful blue dress, the sequins catching the moonlight. She reminds Isobel of a kingfisher she glimpsed once over the lake, a flash of breath-taking colour.

Isobel has always felt a certain protectiveness over Juno. Juno was already living at Hedoné when Papa took this place on. Unlike some of the other guests, who look at Iso with disdain as if she is intruding on their perfect world, Juno takes the time to talk to her, slipping her stolen barley sugars from the bowl of sweets in the salon. Once, she asked Iso to call her 'Auntie', but Isobel cannot bring herself to do it.

Sometimes, Iso lets herself into Juno's suite at night and stands at the foot of her bed, watching her. Juno's breaths when she sleeps are slow and ragged, and once or twice, she has witnessed her in the throes of a terrible nightmare, kicking the covers from her thin frame, sweat coating her luminous skin.

Juno is the most beautiful and elegant of all the guests, but there is something about her that frightens the girl, too. In her dreams, Iso mixes Juno up with her mother. She always wakes from these dreams guilty and confused.

As Juno passes, Iso sees that her make-up is smudged beneath her eyes, blending with the dark hollows. Her face looks frightening, like a skull almost devoid of skin. She has never seen Juno like this. A sequin detaches from Juno's dress, spinning down to the grass. Iso waits until Miss Harrington is out of sight, then she darts out, her keen eyes spying it glinting in the darkness. She slips it into a pocket, then continues on towards the woods and the music, staying clear of the bulbs that light the path into the trees. Keeping to the shadows, she comes at last to the edge of the clearing.

It is a party. Not the kind that her governess organises for her birthday, with cake and party hats, the only guests her father's patients. This is a grown-up party. Isobel has witnessed parties like this before. Her father used to go to them sometimes, but now he stays away as if he is sickened by the behaviour of the guests. Isobel knows she must be careful, for if her father knew of half the things she'd seen, he would lock her up and never let her out. Just like he did with her mother.

She watches the musicians, looking longingly at a saxophone, its golden brass gleaming under the string lights, the pearl keys opalescent. She tries not to stare at the other goings on in the glade, the things she doesn't understand, yet is compelled to look at anyway.

She is just about to leave when she spies someone lingering in the shadows a little way away.

Her stepmother.

Iso has not yet decided how she feels about this woman. There are times when she sees her from far off across the grounds, and thinks for a heart-skipping moment that her mother has come back for her. But when she draws closer, the resemblance melts away.

Agnes is leaning against a tree. She is barefoot, like Isobel, and it is this, more than anything else, that endears the woman to the girl in this moment. Her stepmother is whispering to herself. Unable to make out her words, Isobel tiptoes closer.

'Stupid, stupid.' Agnes's voice is so low that Isobel can barely hear her. 'Don't let her get under your skin. She was goading you, that's all.'

She begins to pace between the trees. 'But why did she say all that tonight? Was it just to shock me? Or was it more than that?' Her voice is strangled now, her eyes sparkling with tears. 'She was drunk and jealous, that's all. That has to be all. But still, if she complains to Christian . . .'

Isobel does not know what her words mean, but she knows when someone is in distress. She wonders whether to go to her, to offer her comfort, but then her stepmother gives her head an angry shake, her face contorting, and, frightened, Iso retreats into the trees.

No one in the glade sees the young girl as she flits anxiously through the woods, unsure what to do with herself. But if they *were* to spy her, they would think her only a mirage. A dancing, wisping fever dream, brought on by their own excessive emprise.

Chapter Twenty

When Agnes left the woods in the early hours, she reached the cottage to find that Christian was still not home. She knew that he kept his old bachelor rooms at the house, and she presumed he was staying there, that he hadn't wanted to disturb her.

As she set out on her walk the next morning, she felt grateful: she needed time to process what had happened. She had let her guard down last night, and in front of the one person with the most influence here. Agnes was not usually easy to anger, but there was something about the way Juno spoke to her that made her feel so small.

Innocence is a good thing here, she had said to her. *It's better not to know about everything that goes on.*

What had she meant by such a barbed comment? Agnes was smart enough to understand that Christian would not tell her everything about his practices here. There was the doctor's code of ethics to consider, but even apart from that, he was not the kind of man to view her equally. Perhaps all marriages were spun with soft little lies like this, threaded through so delicately that it wasn't until you'd spent decades together that you realised it was the lies uniting you, not the truths.

She came to a stop on the lawn, letting the sparkle of the sun on the lake's surface calm her. Up in her mother's quarantine suite, she saw Matron at the window, gazing out over her domain. Below on the ground floor, Sippie emerged, yawning, onto the veranda of her new bedroom, and Agnes changed direction towards the house, deliberately ignoring the nurse's pointed glare above.

'Sippie,' she called, raising a hand.

The young woman turned at her name, her emerald-green robe billowing in the morning breeze.

'Mrs Fairhaven,' she said, a cigarette held aloft.

Agnes was surprised to feel the beginnings of a grin stretching across her face. There was something about this woman that drew her. A shared outlook, perhaps, as if they were both often on the edge, observing the rest.

'Welcome to my new rooms,' Sippie said, spreading her arm out to the open French door behind her. 'Lord, I thought I'd be stuck up in quarantine forever. Care to take coffee with me, Mrs Fairhaven?'

'That would be lovely,' Agnes said.

Unlatching the gate that led onto the veranda, Sippie picked up a little handbell. She gave it a shake, the tinkling peal drifting across the grounds and sank gratefully down into a chair, indicating that Agnes should do the same. 'How is your mother?' she asked.

'She's as well as can be expected.' Mother had picked up quickly after her fever, just as Matron had assured Agnes she would.

'That's good news.' Sippie's headscarf shone blue green in the sun. 'You know, I do sympathise, my mother had this damn disease, too.'

'She did?' Agnes noted the past tense with a pang of empathy.

'Mmm hmm. A long time ago now. I was only four years old when I lost her. Of course, there was nowhere like this place back then, and even if there had been, she wouldn't have been rich or talented enough for a place in it.'

Agnes put a hand gently on Sippie's knee. 'I'm so sorry,' she said.

Sippie shook her head. 'Oh, it's okay. I barely have any memories of her, I was so young. At least you've had time with your own mother. Treasure that, Mrs Fairhaven.'

'Oh, I do.'

'It's strange, what memories you cling onto, isn't it, and what little things can bring them back? I remember sitting on my ma's knee, sorting through the necklaces in her jewellery box, rolling those beads between my fingers. I can still feel my mother's arms around me as she hummed a song. The rumbling vibration of her poor lungs.' She shook her head, and her hand went to her throat where a single bead was strung on a silver chain. A disc, thin and pale as ivory. 'All those different beads, shell and bone and amber and glass . . .' She drifted off, gazing at a distant point on the horizon.

'Is that one of them?' Agnes said, nodding at Sippie's necklace.

Her fingers closed over the single bead. 'Ostrich shell. I had a whole necklace strung with them, it was my favourite of all her jewellery. After she died, my sisters and I left to live with an auntie, and I took the necklace with me. I wore it every day for years, but then it broke.' She pressed her hand to her throat, as if the thought of this final bead loosening and falling was too painful.

The waiter arrived then to take their order.

'Coffee please,' Sippie said, smiling up at him. 'How are you settling in?' she asked Agnes when he had gone. 'You've been here, what, a week?'

'Almost,' Agnes said. Was it really barely one week? A part of her felt she had lived here for months. 'It's been a lot to take in,' she said truthfully. 'Christian told me what it would be like, of course. But it's just so different to anything I've experienced before. The level of luxury, it's all a little mind-boggling, if I'm honest.'

'Don't worry, that stage will pass, I promise you. Soon you'll be thinking it's normal.'

'Juno invited me to a party in the woods last night,' Agnes said. 'I'm not sure what her intention was, whether to shock me, or to impress me. I didn't stay long.'

'Oh yes, those parties are legendary.'

'Were you there last night?' She tried to remember if she had spotted the pianist, but the night had been a swirl of sound and smells and colour, and all she could picture was Juno's glittering eyes, that cold, bony finger trailing down her cheek.

Sippie shook her head. 'I'm still on quarantine hours, lights out at nine, doors locked. But I've heard all about them. Which were you, then – shocked, or impressed?'

'I'm not sure I was either. Bewildered, more than anything.'

Sippie laughed. 'Good answer. You know, that sort of party isn't that different to the world I knew before I arrived. Though with plenty more money thrown at it, I'm sure.'

She rolled up the sleeve of her velvet robe, presenting her arm to Agnes. In the crook of her elbow was a scattering of little scarred dots, pale against her skin.

'Heroin,' she said, by way of explanation. 'I used to inject it directly into the vein instead of the muscle, like they tend to do with the narcotics here. You get a stronger hit that way.'

'Are you still . . .' Agnes trailed off.

'Using it? No. I stopped when I came here,' she said, pride lacing her voice. 'I quit cold turkey, clammy and goose pimpled as a plucked bird for roasting. Turned down all the painkillers and everything. That's why I was so long up in quarantine. I refused to leave until I knew I could trust myself. It was hard, even with Matron's support.

But imagine how much more difficult it would be trying to do that out in the real world on your own.'

'It's admirable, Sippie,' Agnes said. 'What made you decide to stop?'

'I want to be cured,' she said with a shrug.

'Has Doctor Fairhaven indicated that it's possible?'

'If I really look after myself, yes. I'm doing everything he's asked of me.' Her face took on a steely look of determination, her usually smooth brow creasing below the headscarf. 'It'll be difficult enough to go back out there — to the real world — without adding addiction into the mix.'

Agnes had noticed that the guests often used terms like 'the real world' to describe the world outside of the sanatorium. Hedoné was a bubble, a self-governing state with its own laws and rules. How far did this concept extend?

'But if you were cured, surely it wouldn't be all that hard to live away from here?'

Sippie lit another cigarette, considering her through the smoke. 'A woman on her own, faced with every hardship we don't need to worry about in here: earning an income, finding food and a place to stay. Not forgetting our safety.'

She was describing the life that Agnes had feared she would herself face once her mother died. Agnes might not have this disease, but it had taken away her future, nonetheless. And now, conversely, this same illness had given her a home and security for the first time in years. A number of times since she got here, Agnes had found herself feeling thankful for this place's existence. The thought of returning to her old world beyond Hedoné's borders felt more frightening than ever.

She looked down at her wedding ring, twisting it on her finger. Last night's fit of anger had been stupid and dangerous. She mustn't let her emotions get away from her like that in the future.

'Mrs Fairhaven?'

Agnes looked up. 'Sorry, I was miles away. It must have been terribly hard out there for you.'

'Add to that the colour of my skin,' Sippie said. 'And you've got a melting pot of disaster.' She took a draw on her cigarette, lapsing into silence.

People had begun to emerge from their rooms now, Agnes could hear the clink of juice being poured into cut-glass tumblers in the dining room. She breathed in the delicious smell of bacon and croissants and coffee.

'Sometimes I crave the world out there,' Sippie said, her voice a little wistful. She was staring at the sea, her hand at her clavicle, worrying at the bead there. 'And yet, I imagine that when you're back out there, all alone, you desire nothing more than to return here.' She shivered, grinding out her cigarette in a marble ashtray. 'There's a waiting list as long as my arm for this place. If I left, I'd never be able to come back. So I must ensure I'm cured before I make that choice.'

Agnes looked out over the beautiful grounds. Perhaps she was naïve, but who in their right mind would ever want to leave such a place? *She* certainly didn't. Going back to her old life felt like a terrible backwards step, sliding to the bottom of a snake in a board game, when before she had nearly reached the top of the ladder. It had taken so much luck to get here. So many chance rolls of the dice.

She admired Sippie's bravery, her hopes to return to the real world. But perhaps when you were sick, the only thing that kept you going was the hope of getting better. For someone like Agnes, why would she want to go anywhere else?

The waiter arrived then, bringing a steaming pot of coffee and two cups, a tiny petit four balanced on the edge of each saucer.

'I still don't understand why the staff all wear masks,' Sippie said in a stage whisper to his departing back. 'I presumed at first it was because they might pass dangerous illnesses on to us, but the longer I'm here, the more I see that's just the innocent's view. It's the opposite: they wear the masks to protect themselves.'

'But you're not *that* contagious, surely?' Agnes said. 'Especially outside.'

'I know. It's ridiculous. I blame the matron. She seems to make up most of the rules here.'

'Does she?' Agnes asked innocently, pouring the coffee into the two cups, and adding cream from a little jug.

Sippie nodded. 'And most of them just to inflate her own ego, no doubt. She was desperate to hang onto me in quarantine. Her face when I left was a picture! She loves rules. Your husband too, if you don't mind me saying. They might call us guests, but they never let us forget what we really are.' She sighed, taking another sip. 'Do you know, I stayed in a sanatorium in Germany once where they called the patients *haftlinge*: inmates. Can you believe it? I ought to say thank you to Mr Hitler for making my decision to leave that country so much easier.'

Agnes nodded. 'Whatever trials we face here, it's nothing compared to what's going on over there.'

She lifted her cup to her lips, then changed her mind, wrinkling her nose at the smell, its bitterness too much on an empty stomach. Popping a petit four into her mouth instead, she closed her eyes, relishing the sweetness as the crystals of sugar dissolved on her tongue. In the silence, she thought she heard a sound coming from the next room along. Juno's room. She turned to Sippie.

'Would you take a walk with me?'

Chapter Twenty-One

They hurried past Juno's open door before the woman had time to emerge.

'I have nothing against Miss Harrington,' Sippie confided as she took Agnes's arm, 'but between you and me, she does like to take centre stage.'

Agnes grinned conspiratorially.

'It's going to be a hot one today,' Sippie added, tugging at the collar of her robe. 'Shall we walk under the trees for a bit of shade?'

They crossed the grass, approaching the trees that led to the memorial garden, and Agnes peered into the darkness, searching for the path she knew was there. She wondered if Sippie knew of the garden's existence. Might the pianist be able to tell her a little more about it?

'What are you looking at?' Sippie said, following her gaze. 'Is that a footpath? It looks nice and cool. Shall we go explore?'

Agnes paused. She did not like the idea of lying to this woman, but she didn't want to upset her either. And yet it felt wrong, leading her up there without mentioning what lay in wait at the top.

'What is it, Mrs Fairhaven?' Sippie said, a dash of frustration in her voice.

'There's a memorial garden up there,' Agnes admitted at last.

Sippie turned to look into the trees. She was silent.

'Have you been up there before?' Agnes asked.

'No, but I've heard of it.'

'We could walk somewhere else,' she suggested.

But Sippie did not move. 'You know, I think I should like to take a look,' she said.

'Are you sure?'

She nodded, her jaw set rigidly.

They set off, Agnes slowing her pace to match Sippie's as the hill grew steeper, aware that the young woman's breathing became more laboured the further they climbed. When they reached the wire fence, Sippie came to a stop, a small frown puckering her forehead.

'We don't have to go on,' Agnes said.

'I want to,' she answered, pushing determinedly through the cut in the wire.

As they reached the garden, a flash of movement caught Agnes's eye. Iso was crouched at her mother's grave. She sprang up when she saw them, eyes narrowed, and quickly flitted away through the trees, but not before Agnes had time to glimpse a tight curl of paper grasped in her hand, a ribbon tied round it, trailing behind. Iso took a different route to the one they'd climbed, disappearing down a well-trodden path into the trees, as if she did this often. Did that mean it was not she who kept cutting the fence?

Agnes watched her leave a little regretfully, her mother's advice ringing in her ears. She should have called out and tried to stop her. She needed to find a way to reach her stepdaughter, and this would only come by spending time with her. But perhaps now was not the moment, she thought, looking at Sippie.

She was standing at a memorial, her face solemn as she looked down at it. When Agnes approached, she saw that it was the one she remembered from her last visit, the sparkling gems inset all around the inscription.

'Elizabeth Thackeray,' Sippie said.

'Did you know her?'

'Not really, no, but this is the girl I told you about; the one who drowned herself in the swimming pool.'

'I hadn't realised.' Agnes looked at the stone with renewed sadness.

'The diamonds are dazzling, aren't they?'

'Do you think they're real?'

'I suspect so,' Sippie said. 'Rumour is Juno helped pay for them.'

'They were friends?'

'Oh yes, good friends, apparently. It was Juno who got her a place here. The other guests told me that she was never quite the same after Elizabeth went.'

'Did your paths ever cross?'

'Only the once,' Sippie said. 'And that was from my quarantine balcony. But she was a beauty. She had real grace, real poise, you know? I know everyone swoons over Juno, but Lizzie had real old-fashioned glamour. I could tell, just from that one meeting. She was a burgeoning starlet before she came here, apparently, following in Juno's glamorous footsteps. She'd just had a call-back for her first film when she was diagnosed, and she was packed off to Hedoné instead. So sad.'

'You told me before she had drowned, but I didn't realise it was suicide.'

'Yes.' There was a hardness to Sippie's voice.

'But surely this place might have offered her a cure. Why do you think she did it?' As soon as she'd said it, she realised how crass it sounded.

'We all have our demons, I suppose,' Sippie said. 'Hers just . . . took her over.' She lit a cigarette, cupping the flame to shield it from the breeze. 'This place is disturbed,' she said, smoke flowing over her teeth. 'Like some kind of trophy garden. I see why they've hidden it away like this: there's something a little perverse about encountering the names of the previous occupants of your own bed, I can tell you.'

'I'm sure,' Agnes said softly, thinking of that message on the mirror of her mother's bathroom. *Don't trust them.* Had it been written by one of these people?

Sippie moved on, stopping at a memorial nearby. 'The first Mrs Fairhaven,' she said softly.

'The enigma,' Agnes said, joining her, and Sippie looked up questioningly. 'Oh, Christian doesn't talk about her much,' she explained. 'And I don't like to pry. I wish I knew more about her. I want to help little Iso, and to do that, I need to understand what happened.'

'Well, I came here long after the first Mrs Fairhaven went,' Sippie said. 'So all I know is second hand, but I heard she died soon after the doctor came to Hedoné, that she was so ill with TB that she never made it out of the infirmary down in the basement. Apparently, when he found her body, little Isobel was curled up on the hospital bed with her.'

Agnes's heart clenched. Poor little child. What would that do to someone? No wonder she searched for answers by coming here.

'I'd speak to Juno if you want to know what she was like,' Sippie said. 'She was already a patient here when Doctor Fairhaven took it over. She convinced her father to invest a huge amount in the place, knowing he wouldn't dare say no if it might cure his only child. Apparently, she's always had a hand in how the place is run. Many of the luxurious touches you see at Hedoné came from her.'

Agnes sighed inwardly. Juno. Of course. A breeze rose up, harrying the pine trees, stirring the long grass at their feet, and she gave a shiver. Sippie flicked her cigarette to the ground, grinding it with the toe of her slipper. She pulled her robe tighter about herself. They strolled through the garden, past the holly tree to the graves.

'These are the only two graves up here, aren't they? Isn't that a bit odd?'

'Perhaps they didn't have any family to go back to,' Agnes suggested.

Sippie crouched down to Betty Simpson's grave. It was greening up now, barely any earth showing at all. 'This one is very recent,' she said, touching a hand to the new shoots. 'I don't remember a Betty in my months at the house. Perhaps she was in a quarantine room further along from me and never made it downstairs. What a sad thought.' She stood up. 'They feel a little out of place here, don't you think?'

'What do you mean?'

'Well, look at all the memorials: they're beautiful, aren't they? And they reek of money. They must all be paid for by Hedoné, of course. So why are these two graves so different? So . . . cheap looking?'

Why indeed? Another question to put to Christian, Agnes thought. But not yet. It would not do to disrupt her fledgling marriage with talk of secret graves and sick young women. She had a sudden urge to leave this odd place, to emerge out into the warm sunshine of the grounds.

'Come on,' she said to Sippie. 'Let's go.'

Chapter Twenty-Two

After the memorial garden, Agnes felt suddenly desperate to see her mother, guilt bubbling up at the thought of all the leisure time she had been enjoying without her. It was a novel feeling, being able to forget about the disease that gripped the person you loved, but those memorial stones and the discussion with Sippie had brought it all rushing back. What was she doing, basking in all this freedom, when her mother's time was ticking away in that room, all alone?

She managed to avoid the matron's punctual visits, and she and her mother spent the morning reading snippets out to each other from magazines, and choosing the most elaborately titled meals from the lunch menu, laughing between themselves when they couldn't work out exactly what it was that they'd ordered. In the afternoon, they sat in companionable silence, each lost in a book. When Agnes next looked up, her mother's head was nodding, her eyes closed, and she reached over and slipped the book from her hands. Quietly, she got to her feet, intending to leave.

'You're not off already, are you?' Mother said, her head snapping up, suddenly awake.

'I thought you were sleeping.'

'Merely resting my eyes.' She smiled. 'Tell me about Christian,

Aggie. How does he fare, now you've seen him in his working environment?'

Agnes settled on the edge of the bed. 'Well, he's extremely conscientious, as I knew he would be. Very busy, too. Sometimes I don't see him from morning to evening, other than a glimpse in a corridor.'

'Conscientious is good, but you need to remind him you're here. A marriage will not bloom if it isn't tended to.'

She patted Agnes's hand, her kind eyes crinkling into a smile, and Agnes took the frail fingers in her own, rubbing some warmth into them.

That evening, Christian surprised her by coming home early, and they dressed for dinner together for the first time. Her husband produced another new dress, this one a delicate shot silk the colour of moss, and Agnes stood obediently at the mirror while he looped each button into place at her spine.

'Christian, about Mother . . .'

'She seems well, doesn't she?'

'She does. I know you said she must meet certain criteria before she could be put forward for the cure. She certainly seems stronger now than she has for a long time. Does that mean we can start thinking about it?'

'I don't see why not.'

In a rush of gratitude, Agnes spun round, her relief raising the colour on her cheeks. She flung her arms about his neck, kissing him enthusiastically.

'Steady on, old girl!' Christian said, laughing.

'It's just such wonderful news!' she said. 'I don't suppose you can tell me more about what it involves now, since my own mother might be having it, I mean, it seems only fair.'

Christian smiled indulgently. 'Well, since it's you. It's a multifaceted treatment. Good nutrition, gentle exercise and fresh air. But the crux of it is a small operation. Each of my cured patients have had it.'

'Is it dangerous?'

'Well, all surgery comes with risk, but no, as long as she's fit enough beforehand. We must ensure she continues to grow stronger, and then we can start to think seriously about it.'

Agnes nodded eagerly. 'Who of your current guests has had this operation? Has Juno?'

'No. Sadly she is not eligible to be put forward for the cure.'

'Oh, that is sad.'

She thought of the woman last night in the woods. She had worried that Juno might have complained to Christian about their conversation, but he had not mentioned anything. She turned back to the mirror to allow him to continue to secure her dress, and as their eyes met in the glass, his warm fingers caressing her skin, Agnes felt reassured.

How sad that Juno could not benefit from his wonderful new treatment. Perhaps she did not have as much power over Christian as she had led Agnes to believe. Comforted by this thought, and thinking of her mother's sage words earlier, Agnes reached up a hand, and twined into her husband's.

They walked in silence to the main house, taking a route that wound round the lake, enjoying the peaceful calm of the evening while the guests all readied themselves in their bedrooms. The house looked resplendent, but Agnes's eyes were drawn to the gaping window in Keats room. It had been boarded up now, an ugly scar marring Hedoné's beautiful exterior. A cool breeze blew across the lake, and she pulled her ermine stole tighter about her shoulders.

'Who was up in Keats when the window got broken?' she asked

Christian. 'We saw him do it.'

'Leopold Rackham. He'd been down in the infirmary, but we moved him up to quarantine to assess his health before we reintegrated him.'

'I didn't know there was an infirmary here.' She began mentally running through the rooms of the house.

'No, I don't suppose you would have. It's at the far end of the basement, past the x-ray room.'

'Did you find out what he was shouting about when he broke the window?'

Christian's eyelids fluttered. 'I have no idea,' he said. 'The man was raving. Tuberculosis can have an unfortunate effect on the brain. He must have been hallucinating.'

'Is he a scholar?'

'No, no. Son of a lord. Extremely entitled, but he's rather unwell. He was delirious when Matron got to him. He'd cut himself quite badly on the glass. But not to worry, he's sedated now and we're taking good care of him.'

'Is he in there?' she said, nodding at the boarded-up window.

'Gracious no!' He kissed her bare shoulder where the stole had slipped. 'He's locked down in the infirmary again. You're quite safe.'

Agnes thought with a shiver of those windowless rooms down there. 'Darling,' she said, thinking of her own mother, 'don't you think the most ill patients should have natural light and fresh air? Isn't it a bit wrong to shut them up in dungeon-like rooms as if they were prisoners?'

Christian came to a sudden stop. In the fading blue light, his face was a shadow, but she had been sure for a moment that she'd seen a snarl of resentment cross his features, before it was gone.

'Look,' he said, sweeping a hand through his hair. 'I know some of our practices are a little . . . unusual, but they are all in the patients' best interests, I promise you.'

Agnes bent to pluck a daisy from the edge of the path, allowing her silence to speak for her. Better that she didn't pose a threat, that Christian thought of her as meek and quiet as a mouse.

'I'm the first to admit that what I'm doing here is experimental,' he went on. 'But it is reaping huge rewards. The number of people being cured here is incredibly high in comparison to other sanatoria.' He took her hands, the daisy spiralling to the ground. 'I promise you, dear Agnes, the patients are in the best hands here. There is no danger to them or to you: I control everything here. Everything.'

He sounded so confident, and despite her doubts Agnes knew she must not try to persuade him otherwise, for doing so would disturb the delicate fronds of their marriage before they'd had time to unfurl, to grow fecund.

'When I first met you,' Christian said, drawing her close to him, taking her silence as acquiescence, 'I saw how you cared for your mother, how you always put others before yourself. It was how I knew you would fit in so well here, how I knew you were exactly what this place needs – what *I* need. You are so willing to learn what I teach you, to help me in any way you can. These people are not just my patients, Agnes, they are *our* patients. Mine and yours. You are a mother to them, as I am a father. Just as one day soon we will be a mother and father to our own offspring.'

She looked down at their joined hands, at the matching gold wedding bands glittering in the last of the setting sun. Christian dropped a kiss on her collarbone, and despite herself, she felt a shimmer of desire.

From far off in the house, the gong for dinner resounded. She could see the guests emerging from their bedrooms. Sippie was walking with the saxophonist Agnes had seen on her first night. A little farther along, the group of American youths strode on exuberantly, patting each other on the back and stopping to adjust each other's bow ties. One of them put his hand to his mouth, a racking cough doubling him over.

'Come,' Christian said, pulling her on. 'We shouldn't be late. I'm glad we've had this talk. It's important to be able to speak candidly with each other.'

But as they drew closer to the house, Agnes found herself dwelling, not on the conversation she and her husband had just had, but on that brief moment when she'd pushed him a little too far and his face had changed, as if a mask had slipped, and for a moment, he hadn't resembled her husband at all.

Chapter Twenty-Three

The Gold Signet Ring

Isobel has been visiting the man in the infirmary bed for a few days now. The night she discovered him hidden away down here, she had been frightened. He'd been ranting at the wall, the oxygen mask on his face slick with condensation, and when he saw her, he asked if she was a ghost. This made the girl laugh. She feels like a ghost sometimes, drifting about the sanatorium, revealing herself only when she wants to.

He told her his name was Leopold. Leo for short. She knew he was dying. They all died down here. She had gone to the kitchens and brought back a jar of blackcurrant preserve, remembering those times when she was small and sickly, and her parents had fed her spoonfuls of sweet, sticky jam. It had always tasted like nectar, taking away the bitter taste of the medicine they'd given her.

It feels strange, feeding a grown man, but he is so weak that he's barely able to hold his head up, and so she must do it for him, making smacking noises with her own lips to encourage him to swallow, wiping away the excess jam from his chin with the edge of the spoon. He has lost weight, even in the short time he's been down here. His fingers are so thin that the gold signet ring on his left hand is too big.

It sits on the table next to the bed, and Iso eyes it as she tends to him.

'Ruse,' he whispers between mouthfuls, his stained teeth shining purple.

'Ruse?' she whispers back.

'No cure,' he says, his voice clotted with blackberries. 'We all die.' He sighs, a painful, high-pitched noise, then begins to weep.

The girl has seen her father cry before, soon after her mother left them, not long after her grave appeared in the memorial garden. She has learnt from those times not to interrupt, that this man might get angry with her, just like Papa did. Instead, she screws the lid back on the jam jar. The man's eyes close in contentment, and when he is not looking, she slips the ring from the bedside cabinet and places it on her own finger. A small payment for her diligent work.

The man does not open his eyes again, his poor, broken body craving sleep, and Isobel steps quietly away, leaving him to his grief.

In the corridor, she goes to the laundry chute, listening. She is out early tonight, but they are all at dinner, so she is safe. Placing her bare feet on the chute's slanted surface, she ascends, past the ground floor, up to the quarantine area. Here, she jumps down onto the plush carpet, enjoying the way it feels between her toes. The sickly smell of lilies drifts down the corridor as she makes her way to the door at the farthest end. Here, she knocks gently.

'Are you awake?' she whispers.

'Yes,' comes the frail reply. Isobel pulls a key from her pocket and slips inside.

Iso likes this old lady. She is the oldest person in here by far, the oldest person Isobel has ever seen. She is sitting up in bed, as if she has been waiting for her. Pulling the quilt about her, she smooths it down and smiles a crinkly smile.

'Hello, dear child,' she says warmly. 'Tell me what adventures you've been up to since last I saw you.'

Iso tells her of the party and the musicians, of her visits to see her mother's grave. She tells her about the lessons she dislikes with her governess, about her difficulties learning piano. The old woman's face creases up with a smile as she listens.

'And have you seen much of your stepmother?' she asks her. 'Has she been spending time with you?'

Isobel pauses. She knows that this woman is Agnes's mother. Her stepmother spends a lot of time up here. A small needle of jealousy glitters through Isobel's body. How wonderful to be able to visit your mother every day. But she does not want to offend this sweet, kind old lady.

'She is very busy, learning the ways of Hedoné, I think,' she says, diplomatically.

The old woman frowns. She gives a sigh, but it breaks into a rumbling cough, and she lifts a monogrammed handkerchief to her mouth. Iso sees the pain pass over her face.

'Would you like some jam?' she asks her. She still has some left from her trip to the basement.

'Jam?'

'It always makes me feel better when I'm unwell,' Iso explains.

'Well, in that case, why not? It would be nice to have the taste of something so simple, instead of all these rich, luxurious foods they give me here.'

Going to the bathroom, Isobel rinses the spoon that Leo used, priding herself on her knowledge of cross-infection rules. Back in the bedroom, she gently spoons the jam into the old woman's mouth. Mrs Templeton sips at it appreciatively, the soft skin of her jaw as fuzzy as a peach.

'Thank you, Isobel,' she says. 'You are quite right, it is delicious.'

Isobel grins.

Chapter Twenty-Four

As she and Christian entered the dining room that evening, Agnes saw with some trepidation that Juno was already seated. She hadn't set eyes on her since their conversation in the woods, and with a quick, reluctant breath to ready herself, she crossed the room.

Christian had taken his place at the head of the table, and Agnes sat down next to him, a waiter tucking her chair in. Juno was sat to her right, and she wondered a little cruelly if the young woman had come early on purpose, to ensure that their place cards were next to each other. Reluctantly, she turned to her, not quite sure of her reception.

'Good evening, Mrs Fairhaven,' Juno said, placing a hand lightly on Agnes's arm.

The touch reminded her of the trail of Juno's finger across her cheek at the party, though Agnes could sense no trace of that night's vulnerability in the Juno before her.

'Good evening, Juno.'

'I'm sorry for my behaviour last night,' Juno said, lowering her voice, the mocking tone that so often laced her words not there. To her left, Agnes sensed Christian half-watching them.

'I had a little too much champagne,' Juno went on, 'and I have a tendency to get carried away when that happens. I do hope we can 'forget it all and be friends.'

'Of course,' Agnes said, picking up her menu as the table began to fill up. Sippie sat down opposite, giving her a smile as she lifted her own menu.

'Actually, I wanted to say how sorry I was to hear about your friend, Elizabeth Thackeray,' Agnes said to Juno. 'I gather you two were close.'

She wasn't sure why she had said it; only that Juno's apology did not feel genuine, just another part of the young woman's act, and she felt a streak of satisfaction as Juno's hand tightened painfully on her arm.

'How did you hear about her?' Juno said, her voice low.

'I saw her memorial earlier, up in the woods.'

The woman's eyes widened, glittering with emotion.

'It must have been terribly hard,' Agnes added.

'It was a difficult time,' Juno admitted. 'It's always sad, when we lose a friend here. We were very close, Lizzie and I. They tried their best with her, of course, and she was showing signs of improvement, but some people just don't want to be saved.'

'I'm so sorry,' Agnes said again, meaning it this time.

Sippie was unfolding her napkin and smoothing it out in her lap. 'I sometimes think I'd rather not know when someone here dies,' she said, overhearing them. 'I'd rather just believe they've left Hedoné. You know, gone on to wonderful, glittering things.'

The gathered guests around the table nodded in agreement.

'Like those two girls in the woods,' she went on. 'What were their names, Agnes? Can you remember?'

'What girls?' The softness in Juno's voice had disappeared.

'Betty someone, wasn't it?'

'Betty Simpson and Elsie Clements,' Agnes said. She felt Juno's gaze on her, eyes narrowed, her pretty head on one side.

'Doctor?' Juno said suddenly. 'Do you know these names your wife's been asking about?' There was something hard in her voice, as if the molten gold inside her had solidified.

'I . . .' Christian's eyelashes whirred as he scoured his thoughts.

'Some of your first guests, weren't they? They came here long before you arrived from what I remember; before you turned this place into the success it is today.'

'Yes, that's right. Not scholars, and not rich by any means. Very poor, in fact. But I allowed them to stay. It would have been cruel to turn them out just because they didn't fit my guest profile. They were both very young. Terribly sad, and no family to send their bodies back to . . .' He trailed off, taking a sip of champagne.

Juno raised her glass. 'To all those we have loved and lost,' she said, looking at Christian.

As one, the table raised their glasses in a toast, the sentiment taking hold across the room until everyone was murmuring the heartfelt words. Christian took a moment to lift his own glass, but when he did, his voice was among the loudest.

After dinner, they moved into the salon. It was a strikingly handsome room with large geometric mirrors set into the marble walls, rising like skyscrapers to the ceiling. Waiters went around silently filling up glasses, and people sipped as they talked, the warmth of the wine flushing their already bright cheeks.

As it grew dark outside, fringed lampshades cast golden pools of light, giving the impression that the space was made up of pockets of dark opalescence. Agnes sat back, content just to listen as they spoke of hopes for the future, projects and dreams, and a fondness for the little group spread through her. They were all such fascinating people, both the scholars and the wealthy, their brilliance only magnified by each other's company. There was an unbuttoned-ness about them all that Agnes had never seen before, an ease that meant she had never once felt unwelcome, despite sometimes feeling out of her depth. And to think that on her first day here she had worried what they might think of her.

She sipped her champagne, enjoying the feeling of wellbeing that it cast over her. Aware of her husband's eyes on her from across the room, she lifted her gaze and searched for him, finding him at last sitting on his own, staring at her intently. Agnes could feel the alcohol thrumming through her veins, and as she raised her eyes to meet his, she thought suddenly of Mr Rackham, down in the infirmary, those words he had used, both shouted and written on the mirror. *It's all a ruse. Don't trust them.*

What had he meant by them? It would be quiet in the basement now, she thought, with Matron off for the night and all the guests here. Mr Rackham would be all alone down there, poor thing. Perhaps she should go and talk to him, ask him what he had meant.

Agnes looked down to find her hand already in her purse, fingering the set of golden keys. Christian was deep in conversation with Georgie now, he would not miss her, not if she was quick. And if anyone asked what she was doing, she was still new enough to feign ignorance, say she had simply got lost.

Out in the corridor, she could feel the wine she had drunk surging in her blood, and she swayed slightly. It was a stupid idea to go and talk to that man now. Christian had told her he was raving; he might even be dangerous. But something about the way he had shouted so passionately from the balcony nibbled at her brain, sending out fracturing fingers of thought, like the panes of glass that he had shattered. She was perfectly within her rights to go down to the basement, and yet, something told her Christian would not approve. Pulling the little set of golden keys from her purse, Agnes set off unsteadily towards the hall.

It was quiet out here, her heels clicking pleasantly on the tiled floor. In the entrance hall, she stopped at the lift and inserted the key. Once inside, she slid the gate closed and pressed the down button. Nothing happened. She pressed it again, but the lift remained stationary.

Feeling a little foolish, Agnes stepped out again, her brow furrowed. What was she doing wrong?

Just at that moment there was a burst of chatter from the corridor, followed by footsteps as a group of guests emerged into the hall.

'We've been sent to get you,' Sippie said. 'We're all going outside for a nightcap.'

Agnes allowed herself to be led through the hall, tucking the key away in her purse as discreetly as she could. Glancing back at the lift with a puzzled frown, she followed the guests down the steps and out into the cool night air. Behind her, she heard Christian call her name, and she turned to see him standing at the top of the steps. He looked so handsome, so very *right*, and she glowed with pleasure as he came down to join her.

'I'm afraid it's time for my wife and I to depart,' he said, taking Agnes's arm and kissing her.

They bade the guests goodnight, watching them trot merrily across the grass to the lake.

'Best not get *too* friendly with them, darling,' Christian murmured.

'I'm not,' Agnes said in surprise.

'Good. We must have some boundaries, after all. You're my wife. Not a patient. Don't forget that.'

Agnes looked at him, unsure if he was joking. She felt his hand tighten momentarily on her arm, before he relaxed his grip and smiled his customary easy smile.

'Come, my dear,' he said. 'Bedtime.'

Part Two

Chapter Twenty-Five

Autumn drew breath, bringing with it cooler evenings and shorter days, and Agnes settled into the rhythms of Hedoné. Each morning she picked her way across the dew-drenched cobwebs that laced the grounds for her morning walk. The statues were strung with them too, silvery threads of silk stitched from one to another, so that negotiating them was like walking through a fragile labyrinth. Once or twice, she saw Matron at her mother's window. The woman always gave her a stiff nod of acknowledgement, which Agnes had no choice but to return.

The guests went about their usual routines. The musicians honed their craft in the music room and out in the grounds. Easels were set up across the lawn, great parasols shading the artists beneath. Waiters criss-crossed the grass at all hours of the day and night, bringing drinks and tempting foods on silver platters. There were daily light therapy sessions, cold water swimming in the lake, guided walks and outdoor meditation classes, the latter of which Juno often attended. Agnes saw her regularly, far in the distance, eyes closed and back straight, trying to perfect the breathing techniques that her meditation teacher had taught her.

In the evenings there were music recitals under a cooling, star-gilded sky, beautiful compositions drifting across the lake, tangling with the lilies and the sparse branches of the pine trees. The resident writers held literary salons where they shared their latest work, Sippie sometimes accompanying them on the grand piano. The readings grew rowdier and more salacious as more magnums of champagne were consumed.

Once or twice on these late nights, Agnes thought she spied Isobel, up and about far later than a child ought to be allowed. On one of these occasions, she'd tried to follow her, intending to find out just what she was up to, but she lost her somewhere in the rose garden, as if the girl had simply turned into mist. Agnes wondered whether to mention these sightings to Christian, but she didn't want him to think she disapproved of his parenting style. And what harm was the child doing, really? In any case, Agnes was spending more time with Isobel during the day – sitting in on her lessons and going on walks together – and the late sojourns didn't seem to affect the girl's energy. On the contrary, she was always bright and engaging whenever Agnes saw her. It was a relief. Perhaps Iso was at last beginning to warm to her new stepmother.

In the evenings, Agnes and Christian usually dined at the main house, but sometimes they ate alone in their cottage. These were Agnes's favourite moments. Christian let his guard down at home in a way he couldn't at the main house. Once or twice, she suggested to him that Isobel should join them for dinner so that they could begin to be a proper family, but for various reasons not at all clear to her, he refused. He always had an excuse at the ready: Isobel's mealtimes were much earlier in the day, or, as a newly married couple, it was important that they spend some time alone.

'She's far happier dining in her own room with her governess,' he said to her once, but Agnes suspected that it wasn't Iso who preferred this arrangement, but Christian. She imagined that he could see echoes of his first wife in his daughter's face, though this was only conjecture, for Agnes had still not found any photographs of Meredith. She wondered if time spent with Isobel was painful for Cristian. But it was only going to get more so as the young girl grew up?

In recent days, Agnes had seen her stepdaughter out in the grounds, her little hand in Juno's as they walked together, talking animatedly. It had taken her a moment to realise the feeling inside her was jealousy. Surely the girl should be spending time with her *own* family, not with the patients of her father's sanatorium?

But as much as her husband's lack of interest in his daughter worried her, Agnes knew that her place was to support him, not try to change things. And besides, she thought guiltily, having Isobel spend more time with them in the evenings would surely postpone the inevitable, wonderful ending to each day, where the first touch of her husband's welcoming fingers made her unfurl like a rosebud opening up to the sun, and she and Christian would tumble, sated, into bed.

There was of course one thing that overshadowed these pleasurable pursuits. Agnes had still not managed to conceive. Every morning, when Christian woke her with a kiss, his warm palm cupped to her stomach, he whispered excitedly, 'Do you think that was the night?'

She wondered sometimes if her husband knew her body better even than she. She awoke often to his hands on her skin for the second time, and in her drowsy, half-slumbering state, desire overtook her again, rising like the slow twist of smoke from an extinguished candle.

Surely she must fall soon? Christian had done his best to hide his disappointment when she told him they'd failed to conceive on their wedding night, but nonetheless she could see it in his eyes, the bright blue dimming just a little. A tiny voice in her mind kept niggling at her as she lay, sated in bed each night. *It's because you're ill*, it whispered cruelly. *Deep inside you, it's twisting and burrowing, just like your mother before you.*

But Agnes did not feel unwell. As she lay, listening to her breaths, searching in them for the changes that she suspected might be hiding there, she thought back to her mother before she was diagnosed. For her, the illness had begun with a change in her breathing and a feeling of restlessness. An effervescent, hopeful energy, as if something extraordinary might happen. Ever since that moment, whenever Agnes had felt the first stirrings of hope within her own body, she'd banished it, frightened of what it might become. Hope was a dangerous emotion.

She was not due another chest x-ray for months, but what would happen if, still clearly unfruitful, she stepped into that godawful machine and her lungs appeared clouded and mottled on the plate, just like her mother's? Would Christian still want her as his wife?

In spite of these worries, Agnes felt settled in her new life. And though the weather began to grow colder, noticeable in the cool plumes of breath that clouded the air on her morning walks, the sun continued to pour down onto the glorious grounds for a few hours in the middle of each day, cradling the resort from the threat of the coming winter.

On one such afternoon, Agnes walked contentedly across Hedoné's grounds, admiring the glitter of the swimming pool, its ripples catching the bright sunlight as a few of the guests enjoyed the last of the summer's warmth. Slipping beneath the trees, she climbed the path to the memorial garden. As she strolled between the manicured yews and roses, she came to a stop at the glittering marble memorial belonging to Elizabeth Thackeray. Now that she knew what had happened to her, it felt important to acknowledge the young woman's life, and she lowered her head for a moment, paying her respects.

Meredith Fairhaven's memorial looked neat and well tended, and a spark of hope kindled in Agnes that now the cure for her mother was imminent, she might never have to fear seeing her name here, too. From her recent visits up to Mansfield Suite, she had seen that the enforced bedrest and nutritious, health-giving food was doing her mother wonders, but she could tell that Mother was growing bored of her isolation. Agnes worried for her sanity, shut up there all alone, day in, day out.

She had asked Christian if Mother might be moved downstairs, but he'd pointed out that despite maintaining a plateau of relatively good health, the illness was still exhausting her poor tuberculous body, evidenced by the fact that she slept so much of the day, and had failed to put on any weight.

Agnes glanced across to the two pitiful paupers' graves, feeling a renewed sadness that no one had mourned them enough to pay for a proper burial. Despite Christian's explanation about these two women, she couldn't shake the feeling that there was still something about their presence here that didn't make sense. She must try to find out what.

As she went to leave the glade, she noticed a new memorial stone had been added on the far side of the garden, and she felt her heart sink at the sight of it. It must belong to someone who had passed away just before she arrived, for Christian would have told her if someone had died more recently, wouldn't he? Curiosity overtook her, and she picked her way over to it, shading her brow to read the name etched upon it.

Leopold Rackham

1903–1935

May he rest in peace

Agnes stared at the stone in shock. Poor Mr Rackham. She had been meaning to visit him for days, but had been so caught up in her own new life she had not yet managed it. And now she never would. Had he died all alone down there?

Why on earth hadn't Christian told her of the man's demise? Did he think it might worry her, bringing to mind the possibility of her own mother's death? He can't have let on to the guests, either, or she would have heard about it by now.

She remembered what Sippie had said, that night at dinner, *I sometimes think I'd rather not know when someone here dies. I'd rather just believe they've left Hedoné.*

Perhaps her husband had taken Sippie's words at face value. Or perhaps the truth was much sadder than that. Agnes glanced back at Meredith Fairhaven's memorial. She knew that men often preferred to keep a stiff upper lip rather than speak of difficult subjects. She thought of what Christian had been through with his first wife and this illness; how he must be reminded each day as he tended to the health of his guests.

Was that why he had said nothing? And if so, could Agnes find a way to reach him, to draw out the emotion that she knew must be inside, or was it buried too deep for even his own wife to unearth?

Chapter Twenty-Six

The next day, the rain came. Most of the guests stayed in their rooms, the doors and windows open to the sound of the incessant downpour. A handful of the French guests played rummy in the salon, and Agnes heard snippets of their conversation as she passed, going in search of Sippie.

She found her in the music room, tackling a difficult sonata. She listened for a while, but seeing the concentration on Sippie's face, ducked back out of the room, not wanting to disturb her. In the library, she stood in the open doorway, watching the rain over the lake. When it seemed to ease a little, Agnes slipped out into the deserted grounds.

She walked around the lake, keeping to the trees for protection as the rain drew slowly to a stop. Above, the low, grey cloud refused to move, blanketing the grounds in its gloom. She struck out onto the lawn, taking a breath in through her nose. She had always loved the smell of grass after a rain shower. Mother's chest had always been better after a storm, too, as if the humidity in the air had opened up her lungs, helping her to breathe. Idly wondering if this theory was worth pursuing, Agnes made a mental note to talk to Christian, just as a crash of thunder cracked overhead. Rain came pelting down again so suddenly that for a brief moment, she found she couldn't breathe.

She ran for the cover of the pines down past the lake, but the storm was so insistent that even there, she found she had no shelter. Further along the treeline, she could make out the ghostly shape of the artificial-light room, the rain bouncing off its glass panes in an aura of mist. There was a light on inside. It was much closer than the house, and she broke cover and ran towards it, her hands over her head.

Pulling the door open, she barrelled inside, laughing to herself, water dripping from her hair and clothes. She had been right; she wasn't alone. Isobel was stretched out on her stomach on the floor, propped on her elbows, absorbed in a drawing. She looked up briefly, then returned to her work.

It was extraordinarily warm in the little room, the heat coming from what looked like a very modern chandelier, quite low to the ground, with long telescopic arms coming off it like a spider. One of these was directed at a large sharp-leafed potted plant in the corner, an unripe pineapple at its crown.

Agnes looked around the room, taking it all in. The floor was tiled in a mosaic pattern depicting the sun, its beams of light spreading out in thick yellow rays across the floor. Along one wall stood a strange, lidded bed that reminded her of a coffin, the lid lined with lightbulbs.

She crossed the room, leaving soggy footprints in her wake, and looked over the young girl's shoulder to see what she was working on. It was a scientific study of the pineapple plant, each part labelled in careful, solid handwriting.

'What terrible weather,' she said conversationally. 'I think I shall wait in here for it to stop, if you don't mind, Iso. I shan't disturb you,

I promise.'

The girl gave her a fleeting smile before returning to her work, and Agnes sank gratefully down onto a comfy chaise longue. Around her, the panes of glass were fogged with condensation. Stretching out, she turned on her side, half-watching her stepdaughter through fuzzed eyelids. Iso was wearing a daisy chain on her head like a crown, her silver hair hanging down in straggly ringlets around her face. Her tongue appeared, caught between her teeth as she concentrated on the drawing.

Agnes closed her eyes, basking in the heat, listening to the sound of the rain on the glass roof. She felt sleep pulling at her, luring her in, and with a sigh, she let her arm drop down, dangling from the edge of the chaise. A soft shuffle, and she felt the touch of a warm body against her. She half-opened her eyes.

Isobel was still immersed in her drawing, but now she was sitting with her back against Agnes's arm. She could feel the insistent press of the little warm body, the thrum of life that flowed effervescently through her, and a surprising rush of love enveloped her. Slowly, she began to tease her fingers gently through the white-blonde hair, working apart the tangles. Iso gave a small sigh of pleasure.

The glasshouse door opened again, the roar of the rain intensifying briefly, and a large, ungainly umbrella burst through the door with a clatter, spraying droplets of rainwater over them both. There was a click, and the umbrella collapsed.

'Juno,' Agnes said in surprise, sitting up.

The young woman seemed equally surprised to see Agnes. 'Hello, Mrs Fairhaven,' she said.

Agnes felt suddenly awkward. They had barely talked since their conversation at dinner about Elizabeth Thackeray and the two graves. Miss Harrington's moods seemed to swing like a pendulum from effusive to waspish and back again in a matter of moments. Which woman would she encounter today?

'I didn't know you came in here,' Juno said, shaking the excess water from her umbrella and propping it against the wall.

'I don't, as a rule. But I got caught in the downpour.'

'Iso and I always come here on days like today. Don't we, darling?' she added, dropping a kiss on the top of Isobel's head, but the girl didn't look up, too immersed in her drawing.

Juno sat down next to Agnes, leaning back against the cushions and closing her eyes with a sigh. 'The lights in here are so good for one's mood, I find.'

The umbrella dripped rain onto the floor, trickles running in rivulets between the tiles. Up close, Agnes saw that Juno's lips under the bright red lipstick were chafed and sore, the pale pallor of her skin beneath the powder bluish and papery, and she closed her own eyes, not wanting to be caught staring. Tiredness overwhelmed her again.

Outside, the rain slowed, then stopped, and then there was only the scratch, scratch of Isobel's pencils on paper, the tick of the UV lamp as it worked its magic on both humans and plants.

Time passed. Agnes did not know if she slept, half-aware of the woman next to her, so close that her hip bone jutted uncomfortably against her own. She became aware of the soft rustle of paper, the patter of feet on tiles, the whump of the door opening and closing, and she opened her eyes.

Iso was scampering away across the grounds, her abandoned pencils scattered across the floor.

'She does that,' Juno said quietly. 'Disappearing like a little wood sprite.'

Her face was reflected in the misted panes of glass in front of them, watching Isobel's progress across the wet grass with a wide-eyed, mournful expression. She sighed, resting her head on Agnes's shoulder, and Agnes felt a sudden dart of pity for this strange, difficult woman.

Juno would never have a child of her own. She had broken off her engagement to come here, searching fruitlessly for a cure that had so far eluded her. These moments with Isobel might be the closest she would ever get to motherhood. Gingerly, Agnes took Juno's cold hand in her own, then rested her head gently against Juno's, her eyes on the child, far away now, disappearing off against the storm-dark sky.

Chapter Twenty-Seven

The rain continued relentlessly for two more days, preventing the guests from spending time outdoors. Matron went around with an expression of gloom on her face, as if angry with herself for not being able to control the weather.

As soon as the first ray of sunlight shone down, the guests poured out into the grounds, hungry for fresh air and space to breathe. They were rowdier than usual, like caged animals finally released. The Americans threw themselves joyfully into the lake, yells of glee ricocheting off the house's walls. The artists began painting landscapes farther and farther from the house, and beautiful music drifted once more across the lawn.

Sippie and Agnes sat at a table near the lake, playing chess. Sippie had been quieter recently, spending more time in the music room, practising ever more complicated pieces. Agnes did not push her to talk. She sensed that Sippie, like herself, sometimes found solace in isolation.

It was Sippie's turn to move. As she lifted a knight, her hand paused in mid-air, distracted by something over Agnes's shoulder.

'Someone's in trouble,' she said quietly.

Agnes turned. Matron was hurrying towards them over the

grass. It was so rare to see her outside that for a moment she looked incongruous, like seeing the x-ray machine plonked on the lawn.

'Mrs Fairhaven,' she said when she reached them, a little out of breath.

'Is everything all right?' Agnes said, her heart beginning to patter.

'If you'll come with me, I'll explain on the way.'

Agnes glanced at Sippie, then followed the nurse back across the lawn, feeling a burgeoning sense of alarm.

'Is it Mother?' she said as she caught her up, but Matron did not answer.

There had been talk of her mother moving out of quarantine, but it had been set back a few days by a cold that had gone to her chest. Though Agnes was disappointed that yet again she would be confined to the quarantine floor, privately, she'd been a little relieved. She had noticed that the guests downstairs – though not as needy as the quarantined patients – did not get such complete attention, and she worried that Mother would not fit in well with the excesses that came with being on the ground floor. Christian assured her that Mother would not be expected to partake in anything she did not feel comfortable with. But still, the change would be a big one, and Agnes had felt reassured that she would remain under Matron's care for a little longer.

As they neared the house, she realised that the nurse was not heading to the main steps, but towards the library.

'Matron, why are we going this way?'

The woman did not answer, hurrying on. As they drew level with the library doors, Agnes lunged forward, grabbing her shoulder, pulling her to a stop.

'What's going on, Matron?'

The woman turned. 'I wanted to tell you privately,' she said in a low voice. She took a quick breath. 'I'm afraid your mother is not well.'

Panic filled Agnes's head like a white cloud, but it was soon eclipsed by a single, primal need: she must see her mother. Pushing past Matron, she ran up the library steps, hurrying towards the passage that led to the entrance hall.

Matron caught up with her at the lift, Agnes scrabbling with her key, trying to jam it into the keyhole, but her hand was shaking too much.

'Here,' Matron said, taking it from her and turning it smoothly.

They rose up to the quarantine floor in silence, worry and guilt tumbling in Agnes's stomach. She had not been to see her mother for two days, the hours filling up so fast that when she reached the evening, she realised with a flash of guilt that she hadn't once thought about her during the day. As soon as the lift came to a stop, she hurried along the quarantine floor with Matron following behind. At her mother's door, Agnes heard a muffled wet cough from within. Matron glanced sharply towards it too, a glint of alarm in her eyes.

'When did she start coughing like that?' Agnes whispered. She knew that cough. It had always preceded a bad episode of health.

'Yesterday morning. Doctor thought it best not to worry you.' Seeing her face, Matron added swiftly, 'We all know how quickly a patient's health can change: she may just as quickly improve.'

Agnes felt anger spark like electricity. Why had Christian not told her? She yanked open her bag, searching for her keys, remembering too late that Matron had taken them at the lift.

'Let me inside,' she said, rounding on the nurse, a desperate mix of fury and panic in her voice.

'You know that's not quarantine protocol. Not when patients are this ill.'

'Please, Matron.'

Something in her voice made the nurse relent. 'All right,' she said. 'But you'll need to wear a mask. You know as well as I do that any virus from outside could make her much, much worse.' She indicated a basin at the end of the corridor. 'Wash your hands. The masks are in the cupboard there.'

Agnes did as she was told, rummaging furiously through the neatly ordered thermometers and strange medical contraptions before she found the masks, tying one securely at the back of her head. It felt strange, this thin covering over her mouth, and she wondered how Matron could stand it, day in, day out.

The nurse opened the door to her mother's bedroom, and all thoughts of the mask dissolved as Agnes stepped inside.

A fire was crackling in the grate. Across the room, her mother looked as if she was asleep, her breathing slow and shallow. She rushed to the bed, looking on in shock. It had only been a short time since she'd last seen her, and yet she looked different: smaller somehow. Shrunken.

'Mother?' Agnes whispered, searching her pale face, the eyes flickering under the lilac eyelids. She glanced back at Matron. 'Can she hear me?' she asked.

'She may be able to. She's not unconscious, just very, very tired. Her body is working extremely hard.'

'But Christian can fix this,' Agnes said. 'Can't he? Why isn't he here, tending to her?'

'Doctor is a very busy man,' Matron said, but the words felt like lines she had rehearsed, like a poor imitation of Juno.

'He said he would look after her,' Agnes whispered.

Something in Matron's eyes softened above the mask. 'We *are* looking after her,' she said, and her voice was more tender than Agnes had ever heard it. 'We are doing everything we can.'

'But he promised,' Agnes said, tears filming her eyes. 'He was going to cure her.'

The look in Matron's face changed, a hardness coming over it, but she did not contradict Agnes. 'You mustn't stay here for long, but I shall give you both a little time.'

Agnes felt her briefly clasp her shoulder, then heard the door close. She gazed at the husked body lying in the bed, so small she looked like a child. She did not need the matron to tell her how incredibly hard her mother was fighting; Mother had fought so hard for so long. Agnes took her hand, the skin cool and paper thin in her own warm one. A clock ticked, and the fire crackled, the sound somehow too cheerful. She gazed at her mother's sleeping face, thinking of the day she had been diagnosed, the acrid tang of disinfectant that had filled the doctor's office, the hard wooden seats.

She remembered her mother sitting next to her, nodding meekly as the doctor explained the implications of the disease on her body. She remembered looking down at the handkerchief she was clutching as they received the news, and seeing with a jolt that it was one of her father's, his initials, LT, stitched into a corner. His death, only two months before, still so raw.

'Since you cared for your father, too, madam,' the doctor had said to Agnes, fixing her with his stern gaze, 'there is a risk that you have contracted tuberculosis as well. I trust that you will impart this information to your husband. And remember, you should be careful near any children you may have. I would advise against hugging or kissing them.'

'I don't have a husband, or any children,' she had said, her fingers gripping the handkerchief tightly, and he'd looked at her over the top of his spectacles, his gaze like an x-ray.

'Probably for the best,' he had said.

This illness was the root of every evil that Agnes had been dealt. It had robbed her of her father, making them poor, stripping her of any worth other than to care and nurture as best she could. It was the reason her fiancé had ended their engagement. And now, it was taking away the only person that she truly loved. She rested her cheek on the quilt, closing her eyes, and focusing on the rise and fall of her mother's chest as her poor, broken body worked so hard to breathe.

'Aggie.'

Agnes's eyes sprang open. Her mother's sunken face was lined with worry.

'What's wrong?' Her voice was barely a whisper.

Agnes swallowed back her fear, her eyes glistening. 'Nothing,' she said, fixing a smile on her face. 'Nothing important. I wanted to come and see you, that's all.' She swallowed again, failing to conceal a small sob, and she felt her mother's hand close over her own.

'There, there, child.'

'You used to say that to me when I was small,' Agnes whispered.

'You may be a grown woman now . . . with a husband of your own,' her mother said between breaths, 'but . . . you will always be my child. Tell me what's wrong.'

'It's nothing,' Agnes said again in a small voice. 'Just, I wonder sometimes, about the mistakes I've made in life.'

'What do you mean?'

'I . . . I don't think I realised quite what I'd taken on,' she whispered, not sure if she was talking about Hedoné, or her mother.

'It was always going to be difficult,' her mother said, her voice saturated with kindness.

'But, I . . .' Agnes stumbled to a stop. How could she put her feelings into words, when she couldn't even pinpoint them herself?

This feeling of unease was new, but perhaps it was just seeing her mother like this. 'I suppose I just feel a little overwhelmed by everything,' she finished lamely.

Her mother took a long, slow breath. 'Dear Agnes,' she said. 'You will find your way through. You always do.' Her hand was cool and comforting on Agnes's. A small frown puckered the skin between her eyebrows. 'That little girl,' she said, her voice so faint, that Agnes had to bend to hear her, 'your stepdaughter. She visits me sometimes, always brings me jam, as if it were medicine.' She laughed softly, and Agnes heard the rumble of it in her chest. 'She is a lonely little thing. She needs someone to mother her, I think, someone to help remind her that she is a child. It must be ever so strange, being so young in a place like this. And I wonder if *you* don't need someone, too. Your husband has all his patients to tend to. Perhaps you should look to little Isobel,' she said, her voice so quiet now Agnes could barely hear her. 'Find solace in her needs, her wants. You never know, it may just be what *you* need, too.'

She smiled, a weary smile, squeezing Agnes's hand. 'You know, you have made me so proud, Aggie. We did all right, you and I, didn't we? We muddled through. And look where we are now. All thanks to you.'

The words were spoken with such kindness, such love, and yet Agnes only heard accusation in them.

'We did,' she whispered, the room blurring in a fusion of colour, like the view through a kaleidoscope she had been given as a child.

'We did,' her mother echoed, a small smile on her face, her eyes closing, sleep consuming her, and Agnes felt the touch of Matron's hand on her shoulder, though she hadn't heard the door.

'Come, Mrs Fairhaven, she needs to rest.'

Slowly, as if wading through water, Agnes got up, following the nurse obediently out of the room. In the corridor, she removed her mask.

'Do you think this is temporary? She was so lucid.'

Matron's eyes were, for once, full of compassion. 'They can be, sometimes. Bursts of energy. It might mean she is getting better, but . . .' She left the sentence hanging in the air between them.

'You mean, this could be the end?' Agnes said. 'She . . . she's dying?'

Matron ran a hand over her masked mouth. 'She is most unwell.'

'But surely Christian can do something?'

At the mention of the doctor's name, the nurse's eyes flashed with something that Agnes couldn't interpret.

'I suggest you go home now and rest,' she said, patting Agnes's arm. 'You won't be needed here: she won't wake up any time soon.'

'Will you fetch me, if she gets any worse?'

'Of course.'

As Agnes made her way down in the lift, she felt a rush of guilty relief at being away from the cloying warmth of the quarantine sickroom. She thought back to the day she and her mother had stepped off the train. Agnes had thought then that this place would be their salvation. Christian had talked of Hedoné House as a place of miracles, but now, unable to shake the image of her mother's lilac eyelids trembling, she realised that not even Christian had the power to save everyone, and she berated herself for ever thinking that someone like her could ever have a happy ending.

Chapter Twenty-Eight

Mother's health remained stable over the next few days. Still unable to visit, Agnes sought out Matron often, asking for updates. To distract herself from her worry, she took her mother's advice and spent more time with her stepdaughter. The little girl was so innocent, so oblivious to the sickness in this place, that Agnes found her company the perfect tonic. For brief interludes, she could almost pretend that she was someone else entirely – a governess to a wealthy family, perhaps, or an aunt visiting a lonely niece – far away from Hedoné's increasingly claustrophobic boundaries.

Together, she and Iso explored the very edges of the estate, Isobel clutching Agnes's hand and leading her eagerly to all her favourite places: the meadow where the Jersey cows grazed, their tails swatting at flies as they chewed; the corner of the lake where the water lilies grew, both of them kneeling down at its muddy edge, their fingers dipping exploratively into the delicate petals.

On a cool morning, the first frost lacing the grounds, Agnes was given something else to divert her attention from her mother's ailing health. She and Iso watched as the same racing-green Rolls-Royce that had brought her and Mother here in the summer went back and forth to the station like a yo-yo. Christian had invited some of the keener scientists and investors for another weekend, in the hope that they would commit to helping him further his cause.

There were only six men this time, and he and Agnes spent the day touring the estate with them, introducing them to select guests, Christian explaining his thoughts and visions for his sanatorium's future.

They were to dine with the men that evening at six o'clock, and at the cottage beforehand Christian presented her with a new dress for the occasion. It was made of plush velvet in a deep midnight blue, so dark it seemed to swallow all the light in the room. Agnes touched her hand to the soft pile, seeing how milky her skin looked next to it, her nerves mounting at the thought of what tonight might bring. Christian had told her how much hinged on the success of this evening. The Harringtons' money would only take him so far. He needed allies in the field of medical science, and far more funding than even Maximillian Harrington could provide. These men were the most powerful, most influential of the group who had visited before, though if Christian still refused to let them in on what the cure entailed, Agnes wasn't sure exactly how he would win their confidence. Perhaps he was planning to reveal all tonight, playing his one final, magnificent hand.

Despite her thoughts constantly flickering to her mother, Agnes wanted to be there, to witness her husband at his charismatic best. *And perhaps*, a small voice whispered inside her head, *you might learn something pertinent that could help save your mother.*

'By the way,' Christian said over his shoulder as he shucked on his tailcoat, 'I'd rather you didn't mention Hedoné's use of opioids at dinner tonight.' He glanced at her in the cheval mirror's reflection, the deep blue of his coat a perfect match to her dress, bringing out the colour of his eyes.

'But I thought it was perfectly legal,' Agnes said, surprised.

'Oh, it is — there's a piece of legislation called the Rolleston Report that states that morphine and heroin can be administered by a doctor for those considered needing it. It's not that. I . . . I just want to produce a full report before I announce my findings on the matter. It's the same with my cure — I don't entirely trust the other medical men not to take my idea and run with it themselves.'

Was that why he hadn't trusted *her* with the details yet? Did he think she might take his secrets and sell them to the highest bidder? The thought made her sad; for what was there in a marriage, if not trust?

Her husband seemed nervous, patting down his hair and fumbling with his cufflinks, and she went to him, taking his wrists one by one and securing each cuff, smiling as she saw the gold links were in the shape of hares.

'You will be wonderful,' she said, kissing him, and he rested his forehead on hers.

'What would I do without you?' he murmured.

Christian went on ahead to welcome the guests. Alone in the cottage, Agnes stroked the slippery velvet of her new dress. It occurred to her that his request not to tell the scientists about the opioids was an odd one. If their use was perfectly legal, then why would he not want to refer to it, to highlight its part in his grand experiment? Surely the whole point of this visit was to show in detail what Hedoné was getting right, and if opioids were part of that, they should be discussed. She understood that he didn't want the other doctors claiming it as their own idea, but surely what they were doing here was for the good of *all* patients, not some competition that needed a winner? And if Christian wasn't going to trust them even with this, then she was sure he wouldn't divulge the details of his cure. Which left Agnes wondering just what bargaining chip he thought he had with these men, and at what point he was planning on playing it.

At six o'clock, she stepped into the entrance hall. She was reminded of her first night out of quarantine, when she had arrived here alone, wearing a different dress, pale pink, not deepest blue.

The dining room seemed vast, with just one small table at its centre set for nine. She had noticed earlier that the guests were the same gentlemen who had been invited into the library for brandy after the last dinner. As Agnes circled, chatting politely, something about the scene felt erroneous. And then it hit her: she couldn't detect a single cough or clearing of the throat in the whole room.

How odd it was to be surrounded by perfectly healthy people. She had spent so much time in the company of Hedoné's patients that she had begun to think of them as normal, but of course they were anything but. These men were the normal ones, a mixture of ruddy faced and overweight, slim and muscled, and all of them bursting with rude health in comparison to the dear people she had got to know here.

She saw with dismay that the corpulent Doctor Camberwell was bearing down on her, the same terrible toupee upon his head that he had been wearing last time.

'Mrs Fairhaven,' he said, placing his meaty hand hungrily on her bare arm. 'How are we? Do we have any news?' He looked pointedly at her stomach, the hand on her arm warm and clammy, making her skin crawl.

Agnes laughed nervously. 'Oh, not yet, Doctor, but I'm sure we will soon.'

He nodded, the birthmark on his cheek creasing up as he smiled. 'Good, good.'

As they took their seats, Agnes was surprised to find herself at the opposite end of the table to her husband. Juno made a late entrance, sitting midway along the table, presumably placed there so that as many men as possible could ogle her. Across from Agnes, at the far end of the table, Christian was in his element, effusing lyrically about the sanatorium. Candles had been placed along the centre of the table, and as he gestured with his hands to make a point, his cufflinks caught the light, the little hares glinting delicately.

The food arrived, and conversation grew quiet for a moment while the guests began to eat.

'An excellent dinner once again, Doctor Fairhaven,' the man sitting to Christian's left said. He was neat and thin and rangy with a German accent. Agnes noticed how he cut his meat into precise portions. 'I was admiring the certificate on the wall of your office earlier, by the way.'

Christian took a sip of his champagne. 'Oh?'

'Yes. You learnt your craft at the same teaching hospital as a friend of mine. Gerhard Fischer? He was there at the same time as you, I wonder if you ever crossed paths.'

Christian put his flute down, the glass smeared and sticky from his hand, and Agnes wondered if beneath his confident exterior, he was feeling nervous. A lot must ride on this evening, after all.

'Quite possibly,' he said, 'but there were so many of us, and we were all so overworked, I doubt I would remember him, or he, me.'

'I shall have to ask him. What doctor did you study under?'

'Smyth-Patrick.'

'Ah, yes. An expert in the care of those suffering from *mycobacterium tuberculosis*.'

'As indeed is the wonderful Doctor Fairhaven,' Juno said, smiling seductively at the German doctor. She reached for Christian's wrist,

200

tapping at his cuff. 'I see you're wearing my gift, Doctor,' she added.

'Why, yes, thank you, Juno,' Christian said, his smile gone.

How odd, thought Agnes. Surely it belied the doctors' code of ethics to accept a gift from a patient?

'I always like to remind Doctor Fairhaven how important pretty things are here at Hedoné,' Juno said, turning to the table and catching the men's eyes. 'Luxury and beauty are so important, don't you think?'

Each one beamed back at her, infatuated.

What was Juno doing giving cufflinks to Christian anyway? Agnes knew Miss Harrington could be a bit peremptory at times, but still, it felt a little predatory. She looked around the table. None of the men looked put out by the behaviour. Agnes supposed that Juno wasn't just any old patient. If her father really had invested so heavily in Hedoné, then perhaps Christian was just trying to show favour by accepting her gift. It was strange that Maximillian Harrington wasn't here tonight, or at the last dinner, though Juno must be there in his place. She was certainly well-versed in the running of Hedoné.

After dinner, Christian got to his feet. 'The salon, I think,' he said. 'No need for you fine ladies to join us,' he added as they began to rise. 'We wouldn't want to bore you with yet more shop talk. Agnes, shall I escort you back to the cottage?'

'No, no,' she said, disappointed. 'I'm happy to make my own way back.'

Whatever Christian was planning on saying to these men tonight, it would be divulged behind closed doors amid clouds of thick cigar smoke.

Christian nodded. 'I thank you both for your excellent company. Do excuse us gentlemen.'

The men nodded their goodnights. A waiter opened a wide

double door that divided the dining room from the salon, and they filed through, the doors closing behind them.

'Well, that's that then,' Juno said, leaning back with a sigh. 'It went as well as can be expected, I suppose.'

'I thought you'd be invited through there with them,' Agnes said, half-jokingly.

'If your husband had his way, I might have been. He sees me as crucial to Hedoné's success, I think. But the other men aren't quite so forward thinking. I rather wonder if I was simply there to be looked at tonight.'

'And *my* sole purpose was to be seen as a vessel for Christian's future child,' Agnes complained bitterly.

'You're pregnant?' Juno said. She had begun to get up, but now she sank back down onto her seat, staring at Agnes.

'No, I'm not, as it happens!' Agnes said angrily. 'And *you* sound just like Christian.'

She regretted the words immediately. She remembered how Juno was with Isobel, trying to mother her in her own strange way. It must be so hard to be around someone who was actively trying for a child.

'I'm sorry,' she said quietly. 'It's just those men and their intrusive questions.'

Juno didn't reply, and Agnes thought she saw that strange vulnerability pass over her expression again, but then it was gone.

Juno got to her feet, as if the conversation had left a bitter taste in her mouth. 'You know, Agnes, you ought to be more careful how you talk to me. I wasn't here tonight because of my good looks alone. If you want to get on here, you and I need to rub along.'

And with that, she swept from the room.

Agnes stayed at the table, contemplating the conversation. She regretted her anger — she had forgotten for a moment who she was talking to. But how difficult she found the woman!

She looked at the clock, surprised to see that it was only nine o'clock. Agnes felt suddenly very lonely, and she wondered if Sippie was up. The pianist had recently had her quarantine hours lifted, which meant she was no longer confined to her room in the evenings, but Agnes knew how tired she still got. She would go to the guests' corridor, see if there was a light on under Sippie's door. A friendly face was exactly what she needed.

As she got up, Agnes heard a raised voice coming from the salon, and she went to the door, listening.

'That really isn't what this place is about,' Christian was saying, his voice heated.

'Really?'

Agnes recognised the German's voice, reedy and distinct.

'In Europe, Doctor Fairhaven, some people don't regard sanatoria as a place to rest and regain health, but rather somewhere to contain the sick, to keep them away from the rest of society.'

What an abhorrent idea, she thought, just as a chorus of 'Yes' and 'Good point' rang out from the other delegates. She waited for Christian to defend Hedoné, but when his voice came again, the anger in it was subdued, replaced by a hearty joviality.

'While that idea is a pleasing one, Herr Shultz — and I agree that while my patients are here, they are not endangering the public — the raison d'etre of Hedoné is not as a place to experiment or permanently quarantine, but to ensure patients have the best quality of life. Here, we are trying to rehabilitate them.' He cleared his throat. 'But I think we're going a little off topic — I was asking for investment, both financial and scientific.'

'Yet investment requires return,' Shultz countered. 'You led us to believe that giving our time and money would allow us a certain

203

amount of authority here. You promised we could pursue our own interests. What you have here, Fairhaven, is a very useful cageful of lab rats, ripe for experimenting on, and you know as well as I, that's exactly why we're here.'

Aghast, Agnes pressed her ear against the door, straining to listen.

'Indeed!' said Doctor Camberwell. 'What better test subjects could we have than those who are already so close to the grave? Experimenting with the dying rather removes the risk, doesn't it? Why, it's social Darwinism at its best.'

'The word "experiment" has a broad remit,' Christian said with a careful laugh. 'What sort of thing were you thinking?'

'We're not barbarians,' Herr Schultz said. 'And of course, we can observe many interesting results by simply watching your patients. For example, when we group highly contagious people together, we *increase* the chance of cross-infection.'

'Yes!' Doctor Camberwell agreed enthusiastically. 'How else do you suggest the world copes with the recent population explosion? The planet is on its way to becoming disastrously overpopulated, especially in poverty-stricken countries. Removing second-class citizens like the elderly and the sick from the equation is like cutting the infected flesh from a wound to allow it to heal.'

A queasiness began to spread through Agnes. She swallowed back her revulsion, feeling her body tremble in rage and disgust.

'I presume you're all familiar with the new Law for the Prevention of Hereditarily Diseased Offspring in Germany?' Herr Schultz said.

'Why of course,' Doctor Camberwell replied. 'I hear it's doing wonders for the health of your country.'

'It is indeed. You should think about adopting it in England. Take it to your government. I can provide you with documentation and research. I would be very happy to help you write a plan. I imagine you could even apply it to what you're doing here at Hedoné, Doctor Fairhaven.'

Christian's voice now had a tremor in it that Agnes had never heard before. 'I . . . I thought the law only refers to hereditary conditions?'

'Why yes, but in Germany, it includes idiocy and even alcoholism – and by the looks of the amount of champagne ingested here each day, I imagine half of your patients could be classified as alcoholic as well.' He gave a soft snort. 'Sufferers of tuberculosis have long been thought to have pre-existing genetic traits that led to them acquiring the disease. I cannot see why it can't be considered under the same bracket.'

'Your argument has merit,' Agnes heard her husband say in a mollifying tone, and tears of anger stung at her eyes. 'Sadly, one wonders if we'll ever be so advanced in this country. Britain is an embarrassment to modern science and—'

But Agnes had heard enough. She twisted away from the door in disgust, fear and revulsion churning in her stomach, filling her throat with nausea.

Chapter Twenty-Nine

Agnes stumbled from the dining room, the odious voices of the men still ringing in her ears.

She should never have agreed to come tonight. Her poor mother was lying above them, too unwell to visit, and here Agnes was, listening to men like that discuss the patients' lives as if they were next to worthless. And for Christian to not refute their words! She felt sick.

In the entrance hall, she came to a stop, everything she had heard seething in her mind. She hurried to the open front door, running down the steps and across the grass, her new shoes — velvet, to match her dress — quickly getting drenched in the evening dew, and she felt a surge of satisfaction.

While they had been dining, dusk had settled over the grounds in a violet haze that resonated with the soft buzz of insects. There were very few guests about as she made her way down to the lake's edge.

She turned to look back at the house. The dining room was being cleaned and tidied, the tables for tomorrow's breakfast hastily replaced. Agnes turned her attention to the salon, and the small group of men inside with mounting disgust. She was relieved that the French doors were closed this time, preventing her at least from hearing any more of their deplorable conversation.

At the lake, she slumped down, not caring if her dress got muddied, and gazed out across the water, letting it infuse into a blur as her eyes filled with tears. The evening grew black around her, and she was thankful that her dress was so dark, swallowing her up in the shadows.

She remembered something Christian had said to her once: *I control everything here. Everything.* Is this what he had meant? How far did this control stretch? What she had heard in there, they couldn't be *his* beliefs, too, surely? She knew her husband; had watched him working, caring, *curing*. She knew he needed to tread a fine line between his own beliefs and those of the people whose favour he was currying, bartering and negotiating in order to help make Hedoné a success. That was surely all this was.

From the darkness, Agnes heard the sound of a match being struck, the faint hiss as the flame flared and settled, and Sippie appeared, walking through the dusk light towards her.

'How was the big dinner?' she said, sitting down next to her on the jetty.

Agnes stared at the lake, feeling the tears building again, not sure what to say.

'Are you all right, Mrs Fairhaven?'

'I'm not at all certain, I . . .' She came to a stop. 'I thought I'd begun to understand what Christian was trying to do at Hedoné,' she said carefully. 'But those men at dinner just now.' She grimaced. 'They were awful, Sippie.'

'I've met a good few doctors in my time, and let me tell you, they can be arrogant and insufferable.'

'But it wasn't just that. Christian changed around them, too. They were talking as if . . .'

'As if what?' Sippie pushed, her voice soft in the darkness.

Agnes slowly shook her head, trying to make sense of it. 'The way they were discussing Hedoné, it was as if the guests here are just an experiment, as if they'd all forgotten you're human.'

She was suddenly wracked by another wave of nausea, as if her disgust had manifested itself in this sickness. She waited for it to pass, breathing through her nose, gazing out over the lake.

Sippie was looking at her enquiringly. 'Are you all right?' she said again.

'I'm fine. Just angry, I think.'

But beneath that anger, she felt unease. Now that she had begun to grasp it, Agnes couldn't shake the feeling that there was something very wrong with this place. She had seen a horrifying glimpse of another reality tonight. But which version of Hedoné could she trust?

She shook her head. Turning to look back at the house, she saw that the salon was empty now, and she imagined the men in Christian's office, admiring the expensive instruments and gilded certificate on his wall.

'I ought to go and check on my mother,' she said with a sigh, getting to her feet. She felt very weary now. She had a yearning to sit by her mother's bed, to take her hand and gaze at the face she had loved all her life. If Matron refused her entry this time, she would knock the door down.

'Of course, Mrs Fairhaven.'

'Oh, call me Agnes, please.'

Sippie's eyes flitted over her face, something in her expression changing, softening.

'Agnes,' she said. 'I feel I've got to know you a little in our time together. You and I, we understand how hard life can be, how difficult it could be again. As women, we have to navigate the world carefully, but that doesn't just stop because we're in this place. There are still dangers here, just as there are out in the real world. I suppose what I'm saying is that if you ever want to talk, I'm here. Don't forget that.'

Agnes nodded, attempting a smile.

'Take care of yourself,' Sippie said, squeezing her hand. 'You have a lot going on at the moment.'

At the main hall, Agnes opened her bag for the key to the lift, but at the same moment it began clattering into action of its own volition.

Matron's neatly polished shoes came into view from above, her wiry body descending as the lift settled.

'Matron, I was just . . .' Agnes began, then stopped.

Through the metal bars, she could see the nurse's face, the desolation in her eyes, and a swoop of fear lurched in her stomach.

'No,' she whispered. 'No.'

Matron put a hand on the gate. 'I'm so sorry, Mrs Fairhaven,' she said. 'I'm so sorry.'

They sat in the vacated salon, the sofa tables still littered with the men's drinks from earlier. A half-empty champagne bottle dripped rings on the piano's gleaming lid. Matron went to the cocktail trolley, sorting through the cut-glass decanters, their silver labels askew, and poured a glass of brandy. She sat down next to Agnes, pressing it into her shaking hands.

'She was sleeping. She would not have felt anything.'

'I should have been with her,' Agnes said. 'I should have realised.' She took a gulp of brandy, wincing as it caught in her throat alongside her guilt.

Matron shook her head. 'It could have happened at any time,' she said gently.

But still, what sort of person abandoned their mother in her last hours? Agnes had always thought of herself as the devoted daughter, sacrificing everything for her mother's wellbeing, and yet she hadn't even been there to hold her hand at the end.

'Darling.'

Agnes looked up to find her husband framed in the doorway, his face full of a desolate remorse.

'Christian,' she whispered, and despite everything she had heard behind that door, she felt her hopes clinging to him, like a life buoy on a sinking ship.

At the sound of her voice, he strode towards her, scooping her to him.

'Oh, my darling,' he said. 'Oh, my darling girl,' and Agnes melted into the familiar, comforting warmth of his arms, letting the feel of him eclipse everything else, numbing her reality if only for a brief, blissful moment.

Chapter Thirty

The Wappler Wand

Isobel Fairhaven has seen many things in this place. Things that a child should never see. She has tiptoed out in the middle of the night and glimpsed people, naked as God made them, slipping among the trees. She has seen Matron pull down her mask and extricate a piece of beef from a molar. She has spied Juno Harrington whispering with her father, her perfectly manicured hand gripping his arm.

Tonight, Isobel knows something is not right. Earlier, she had taken her usual route up to the quarantine floor to visit Mrs Templeton, only to find the corridor crowded, Matron holding forth at its centre, despite the late hour. With a feeling of unease rising in her thin ribs, she'd backed away, climbing quickly into the dumb waiter that ran through the levels of the house, and emerging one floor down, into the service room on the ground floor.

She comes to this room sometimes when she's hungry, eyeing the food as it is propelled up from the kitchens below. Isobel does not eat the same food as the guests, she lives on the meagre, simple fare of the staff. But she does not miss out: it's not unusual for a guest to find an oyster missing from their hors d'oeuvres, or a telling dent in their dauphinoise potatoes, as if an exploratory finger has scooped up a little to try.

Isobel knows that her papa has been entertaining tonight, a strange clutch of men with even stranger accents rising up through the building. They are so vitally important to Hedoné that she has been told she must not under any circumstances make herself known. She tiptoes out of the service room, crossing to the open door of the dining room, expecting to glimpse the men inside still, but they are nowhere to be seen. She wonders where her papa is now. Perhaps he is upstairs, attending to whatever is happening on the quarantine floor. That uneasy feeling in her chest starts again, and she thinks of Mrs Templeton, small and fragile amid all that frenzy.

She flits to the next door, the salon. It is being cleared of glasses now, the ashtrays and empty bottles taken away, the waiters working too diligently to notice the girl as she peeps at them through a crack in the door.

Slipping silently back along the corridor, Isobel comes to a stop outside the closed door of her father's office. She has been in here only once before, and then only because she was made to. It was a long time ago, when she was young and not so good at keeping out of trouble. Her governess at the time, a woman named Esmerelda, had discovered her in the library, curled up in an armchair, her unwashed hands leaving jammy fingerprints on the pages. She had been dragged to Papa's office straight away, the memory of that encounter still so painful that she can feel the sting of it on her skin even now. Esmerelda had been dismissed soon after, and since then, no governess has ever dared take her to Papa's office again, the rumours of his temper preceding him.

Despite those bad memories, Isobel remembers the beauty of the room, its delicate instruments sitting on sleek, shining pieces of furniture. Her fingers itch to touch the mechanisms inside, to try to understand just how they work. Whenever she finds herself alone in this stretch of corridor, she tries this door, but it is always locked. Not one to give up, she reaches up now and twists the handle.

And this time, it opens.

Inside, she flits to the first machine she sees, a handsome walnut box sitting on the huge desk. The words 'Wappler Electric Co Inc' are printed on a plaque on its top. The front of the box is open, and her small hands reach for the dials inside, enjoying the clicking sound they make as they turn. She picks up a strange wand-like device attached to the box via a braided cable, and sniffs it cautiously. It smells of singed hair and danger, and, curious, she flicks a switch. An eerie hum emanates from deep inside the machine, and the wand in her hand vibrates ever so slightly. She stares at it spellbound, reaching a finger towards the rounded end, then cocks her head, listening.

Footsteps.

Quickly, she flicks the switch off, her heart fluttering. As quick as she can, she unscrews the wand from its wire and pops it in her pocket, thankful to Miss Rose, whose sewing tutelage has enabled her to add extra storage to her nightdress.

The footsteps are growing closer. Cursing her rashness, Isobel scans the room, searching for somewhere to hide. At the last second, she ducks under the desk, squeezing herself into a gap between the bank of drawers, just as the door bursts open.

From her hiding place, she can only see the lower half of the man who enters: gleaming shoes, and the well-cut fabric of a dinner suit. But she knows it is her papa. His hands are tightened into fists, and she spots the tiny, gleaming gold cufflinks at his wrists that she has seen before, the ones in the shape of hares. He closes the door and begins pacing the room, muttering as he does so, and Iso holds her breath, trying not to make a sound.

'She's going to leave,' he mumbles, his breath coming in short, sharp gasps. 'I've let the old crone die, and now she's going to leave. Oh god, oh god. What should I do?'

Papa comes to a sudden stop, and Isobel draws deeper into the desk's cavity.

'Stupid man, stupid!' he says. With a jerk, he lifts his hand. There is a sound like a slap, and Iso flinches. She is quaking with fear. Her father always instils this feeling in her. She has tried to grow a thicker skin, a mask-like armour to cover her fear, but he always sees through it.

'But how did it happen?' he mutters, pacing again. 'I was so careful, damn it!' He comes to a stop once more, and this time, both hands reach up, disappearing from Iso's view. She braces herself for another slap, but instead, she hears a shuddering, wet breath. Is he *crying*? Her own emotionless father moved to tears?

'What am I to do?' he murmurs, his voice thick and wet and nasal. 'What am I to do?'

Outside the office, more footsteps. Papa falls silent, listening. There is the sound of his nose being blown, and then he strides to the door. With a brief repose, his hands bunching into fists by his side, he turns the doorknob with a quick jerk, and is gone.

When she is certain she is alone, Isobel backs out from under the desk and straightens up. Her father's office no longer feels beautiful. It is ugly, filled with ugly machines and ugly intentions. Iso's gaze settles on the wooden box on Papa's desk, and she feels rage stabbing at her like the needle and thread she uses in her sewing lessons. With a sudden flash of anger, she swipes the box to the floor. It lands with a clatter, the Bakelite facing breaking apart in a burst of sharp shards. Heart in her mouth, Isobel flees from the room, knowing only one thing: that she must be nowhere near this place when it is discovered.

Chapter Thirty-One

A soft beam of light stroked at Agnes's eyelids, urging her awake as she swam groggily into consciousness. For a brief, exquisite moment, the world felt the same safe place as it had been when she'd woken the day before. And then grief hit her like a thunderbolt.

Cautiously, so as not to wake Christian, Agnes got out of bed and stood for a moment, looking down at her husband's sleeping form. Dressing quietly, she let herself out of the cottage.

She emerged through the pine trees into the grounds. It was still dawn, the lilac blue shadows long, like caressing fingers trailing over the ground. Everything looked just the same, the trees, the statues, the house. And yet the world had changed, tilting on its axis.

She took the path to the memorial garden, climbing the steep hill that led up to the tangle of roses and the neat, polished slabs set into the ground. The early morning was overcast, the clouds an oppressive gunmetal grey. Flashes of the day before assaulted her vision, searing into the bark of the trees all around her. Those men, stuffing glistening food into their mouths. Their voices through the door. Matron, emerging in the lift.

As she came to the garden, Agnes stopped. Cobwebs shimmered between grass stems, dripping with dew, and her breath caught inside her, the rawness of remembering her mother's death once more, like a wound that sings with pain at the touch of a breeze.

She hadn't thought it would happen this soon. Christian had been so sure he could help her.

Agnes moved through the garden, too lost in her grief to notice where she was going. When at last she roused, she was standing in front of Meredith Fairhaven's memorial stone. The clouds had begun to disperse now, the hazy autumn morning sun breaching the tips of the pine trees above, and a ray of light shone down onto a smooth patch of grass nearby. Agnes knelt down, resting the flat of her palm against the ground, feeling the sun's warmth in it. This was the place. She would bury her mother just here. Pulling her thoughts together, she began to focus on the practical arrangements of a funeral. She and Mother had both known it would happen at some point, and Mother had been clear that Agnes must do as she wished. There was a church in the village down the hill, Agnes knew. A simple service, and then they would bring her here to this beautiful resting place. If she could bury her mother here, it would be another anchor, securing Agnes's position in this place.

For she knew she *must* stay here, despite what she had learnt last night. Where else could she go? She had nothing and no one else. No talent like Sippie, no way of making her own way in the world. Yet with still no sign of a pregnancy, Agnes sensed she was on fragile ground. She must rein in her anger at what she had overheard. Be the quiet, unassuming woman that Christian needed.

She got to her feet, looking at all the stones, wondering what sort she would choose for her mother, and her eyes settled on the memorial with the sparkling gemstones belonging to Elizabeth Thackeray.

Christian would of course tell her she could choose whatever she wanted, with no expense spared, but her mother would never want something so ostentatious. Mother's stone should be something uncomplicated that would endure the harsh winters and draw in the warmth from the summer sun. Something simple and comforting, the most honest stone she could find.

Since she last came here, someone had planted a small rose bush in front of Elizabeth's memorial. She touched one of the dark green leaves. Perhaps she could do something like this for her mother's grave. Something hardy and soothing, like lavender. She looked over at the patch of grass she had chosen, imagining the grave there. It felt fitting that her mother be buried so close to the memorial to Christian's first wife. They were all linked, after all. Family.

Christian was Agnes's only family now, she realised, which meant she must find her way to be at peace with what she'd heard. He hadn't been *agreeing* with the delegates, after all, only humouring them. His own views could not be so abominable. She must cling to this.

As she got to her feet, her eyes settled on Meredith's memorial stone, then back to the two graves across the glade. Christian had chosen to bury those two girls here, yet not his own wife. She remembered a conversation they'd had, back when she first arrived.

I had her buried nearby, he had said of Meredith. *I wanted Isobel to be able to visit her grave.*

Had he been referring to this place? There was no other burial ground within walking distance, the village church a few miles away, and as far as Agnes knew, Isobel never left the sanatorium's grounds.

Had she been wrong, and this was an actual grave? But surely the plot was too small for a body to be buried beneath it? No, it was just a memorial, like the others around it. Agnes's brow creased. Why would Christian have lied?

A trill of unease whispered through her grief, clearing her mind for a small, crystalline moment. She crouched down, running her hand over the slab, then, seized by a sudden, wild need to understand, she eased her fingers under its edge, trying to prise it up.

A small part of her expected it to lift easily, light and insubstantial, but it remained set into the ground, and she gave a single, soft laugh.

What on earth was she doing? Grief did this to you, she knew. After her father died, she had watched her mother dish up dinner each evening for him for weeks, leaving it on the table to go cold, only to scrape it into the bin the next morning.

Agnes patted the grass in front of the stone gently in apology, and her hand brushed against something poking up from the earth. Scrabbling her fingers into the ground, she pulled it out. It was a tiny piece of paper, rolled up like a scroll and tied with a ribbon. With shaking hands, she pulled at the bow, unfurling the paper, earth-stained fingers peppering its surface. The lettering was written in that same careful hand she had seen Isobel writing in the artificial-light room.

Dear Mama,

I miss you so. Papa says you are gone and won't come back. I got angry and told him hes wrong. Please tell me its not true?

All my love,

Your Isobel

Agnes's broken heart swelled with compassion. She remembered her last conversation with her own mother, when she told Agnes to look after the little girl. Perhaps Mother had been right, perhaps they could look after one another. They had both lost their mothers now, after all.

Agnes retied the ribbon as carefully as she could and pushed it back into its hiding place beneath the grass. Dusting her hands of earth, she got to her feet, just as the soft crunch of pine needles met her ears.

'I thought you might be here,' Christian said, emerging from the trees.

Crossing the garden, he took her in his arms, and despite her confusion, Agnes felt herself lean into him once more, breathing in his comforting, disarming smell.

'I can't believe I'll never talk to her again,' she whispered into his chest, grief overwhelming her. When she pulled away, she saw that his dazzling blue eyes were rimmed with red. She had not known that he'd grown to care so much for her mother.

Christian was looking down at Meredith's stone. 'I believe my own grief was helped by the creation of this garden,' he said. 'We'll have your mother buried here, just as I did with Meredith. That way, you'll always be able to visit her.'

'Meredith is buried here?' Agnes said. She turned to look at the stone.

'Sorry?' His eyelashes whirred.

'This is a memorial stone, surely?'

Christian's brow drew together, as if he was trying to make sense of what she was saying. But then his expression cleared. In the pale autumn light, his blue eyes looked almost silver.

'Oh! It does look like a memorial, doesn't it?' he said. 'I forget sometimes. Meredith was very modern in her thinking, and she chose to be cremated. I still think of her as being buried, which I suppose she is, though not in the traditional sense. Her ashes are buried here.'

Of course, Agnes thought. Cremation would not require such a large plot. How very modern indeed. She felt ashamed of her suspicions, and in her embarrassment she turned to look out at the garden.

'Who are all these people, Christian?'

'Guests, mostly,' he said. 'I felt it was only right to acknowledge them here.'

'And what about the two graves in the corner?'

'I told you before. They're paupers' graves. They had nowhere else to go.' Tentatively, he tucked a stray lock of hair behind her ear. 'Come,' he said, offering her his hand. Pulling her to him, he pressed his lips to hers, and she leant into the feeling of him, the safety of his arms around her, trying to blot out everything else that consumed her.

They took a different path back through the trees, the one she had seen Isobel use before, coming to a locked gate in the metal fence. Christian produced a gold key, unlocking it and relocking it behind them, then passed it to Agnes. 'So you don't have to slip through illicitly anymore,' he said with a raised eyebrow.

As they came to the edge of the grounds, the low morning sun broke through the clouds, streaming down over the house in rays of gold. The scent of the nearby rose garden drifted towards them, intoxicating at so early an hour. Agnes looked up at the house, its blue-velvet shadow still coating the lawn, and her gaze went automatically to her mother's bedroom, thinking of the time she had spent up there with her. No longer would she open that door to see her mother's sweet, hopeful face, eyebrows raised at the prospect of seeing her daughter once more, and she came to a stop, unable to tear her eyes from the window.

'I'll make sure all the guests are told,' Christian said softly. 'Perhaps you should take some time to yourself. There's no hurry to return to dining in the main house. The guests understand what it is to lose someone.'

'Thank you, Christian,' she whispered.

He took hold of her hands. 'I know you came here in part for your mother—'

Agnes started to object, but he spoke over her.

'I understand that marriage is a complex thing: we both of us had our reasons to marry. But I think so far, we have been happy, haven't we?'

He sounded so heartfelt, and she swallowed, nodding shyly. Up until last night he was right: she had been.

'The truth is, this place needs you, my love. *I* need you.'

Was she mistaken, or did his eyes flick to her stomach?

She felt his hold on her hands tighten a little, as if he was expecting an answer from her, and she managed a small nod.

They began to walk once more, her mind feeling so raw, so visceral, so fogged with grief. But through all of this, a single, clear thought emerged.

However uneasy this place made her feel, the poverty and desolation that waited for her outside the gates was far, far more frightening. If she wanted to stay at Hedoné, she must do whatever it took to ensure her place here was secure.

Chapter Thirty-Two

The scientists left early the next day. Agnes stood stiffly at the window of her mother's quarantine room, her jaw set, watching them depart. Behind her, a maid stripped the bed.

As the gleaming car disappeared down the long tree-lined drive, she noticed that the wrought iron gates remained open for a brief period, and she had a sudden, hysterical urge to hurry downstairs, to run from this place and everything that it represented.

But there was nothing out there for her now – no chance of a life, no chance to better herself. And so she remained, standing rigidly at the window, her face expressionless.

Her mother was laid to rest a few days later, after a simple church service in the local village. Christian, Agnes and Matron stood in the memorial garden in Hedoné's woods as the coffin was lowered into the grave. Her husband had thought it wrong to invite any of the guests. 'It would only remind them of their own ailing health, darling,' he'd said. And though privately she disagreed, Agnes did not put up a fight.

Christian remained resolutely silent throughout, and as the tears tracked down Agnes's face, it was Matron who tenderly clasped her hand, the touch reminding her so acutely of her mother that she had an urge to pull the strange, sharp woman into a tight embrace.

Afterwards, it seemed to Agnes as if time passed in strange, dreamlike fits and starts, perpetuated by Hedoné's rigid, familiar timetable. She measured the days in the perfect white tablecloths and gleaming, polished cutlery that appeared each morning in the dining room. In the empty champagne bottles that piled up each night outside the kitchens. In the fresh cut flowers that materialised each day in the entrance hall.

The days moved on, and each morning, Agnes felt her mind slowly pull itself a little further from the well of grief inside her. She supposed that this period of mourning had begun long before her mother had died, and perhaps now that Mother had been laid to rest, she might finally begin to look forward.

As September drew towards October, there was a sense of limbo among the guests, a collective shiver that passed across the grounds as each patient realised winter was edging closer. Gone were the days of sitting by the pool, sipping at cocktails.

A few weeks later, Agnes lay in bed one morning, sleepily watching as Christian secured his tie in the mirror. When the time came for him to kiss her goodbye, he leant in as usual, and she presented her lips to him. But instead of his kiss, she felt his hand on her stomach, the touch a little harsh, pressing and appraising her as if he were her doctor, not her husband.

'Do you think there is any possibility you could be pregnant?' he said, a little wearily.

She had lost count of the times he had asked her this. In truth, in her cloud of grief, she had not been paying attention to her body as closely as usual. Since Mother died, she and Christian had continued to try for a child, but something about their lovemaking had changed. It no longer felt passionate, its intensity dulled by her grief, by her burgeoning uneasy feelings towards Christian. And yet, she had never once said no to him.

Agnes shook her head numbly. How could he expect her to focus on the vital signs of her own body, when her mother's was still so fresh in its grave? 'I . . . I don't know, Christian,' she said.

Abruptly, he got to his feet, running a hand over his hair, pacing the bedroom.

'Are you doing this on purpose?' he said.

'Doing what?'

'Preventing a pregnancy.' He came to a stop, turning to her.

'No! No, I—'

'Do you not like it here, with me, Agnes?'

'Of course I do, I—'

'Because you're the epitome of health. All the tests have said so. I would have expected you to have conceived by now.'

Agnes sat back, shocked. Here was her worst fear, unfurling right in front of her.

Christian drew close, sinking down onto the bed, taking her hand. 'You are so beautiful,' he whispered. 'My sweet English rose.' He stroked a finger over her cheekbone, his voice tinged with sadness. 'I had thought you so perfect.'

'I'm sorry, Christian,' she whispered, hating how weak her voice sounded, but forcing herself to remain calm.

'I know you're still grieving, and perhaps that's why things haven't . . . taken. But . . .' He got to his feet, rubbing his hand over his face. 'But, Christ, how long can you grieve for? How long must we wait?'

He crouched down to her again, a marked jerkiness to the movement, panicked desperation in his eyes. He leant in, and for one awful moment, she thought he was going to kiss her, but he only put his lips to her ear.

'It would be best for all of us if we had a child,' he whispered hurriedly, and then abruptly stood again, running a hand over his mouth as if he wanted to take back his words.

A quiet roar began in her ears. 'I'm . . . I'm sorry,' she stuttered again. 'I'll try harder, I promise.'

But too late, Christian was already gone. Agnes flinched at the sound of the front door slamming closed behind him. She stared at the open bedroom doorway, only now realising that she was shaking.

Why was he *so* intent on having a child? She had known since she arrived how important a baby was to Christian. And she had wanted it too, for the safety and security that it would bring to her position here. But this reaction was new. *It would be best for all of us*, he had said. Not *both*, but *all*. Why? Who else was he referring to? Isobel? But she seemed perfectly happy without a sibling.

And all of a sudden, the idea of having a baby in this place felt terrifying. It would pin her here like a butterfly under glass, binding her to Hedoné and Christian more than any other tie could. She had thought this was what she'd wanted. But it was not just about her, was it? It was about bringing another, innocent, life into this tangled web. Could she in all good conscience do that?

She took a shower, hoping it would make her feel better, steeping herself in the countless oils and soaps that Christian had given her. Padding back to the bedroom, she pulled on a set of the expensive lace underwear that she liked best, and went to the window, gazing out at the pine trees, her eyes prickling with tears.

She had grown so used to this opulent lifestyle, to the nutritious food and the beautiful clothes, to the luxury at every turn, just as Sippie had wisely told her she would. The idea of leaving it all, of being plunged into poverty and goodness knew what else, was simply too frightening to comprehend. There was no other option but to keep trying for a child. And if, by some miracle, she managed to conceive, she would at least have someone to love, who might love her in return.

She sighed, leaning over to open her bedside cabinet in search of the scented body lotion that she loved so much. And then she stopped.

On her first day here, she had opened this cabinet to find it stocked with all kinds of sweet-smelling products for her use, as well as some sanitary towels, discretely stacked in one corner. At the time, she remembered being touched that Christian would be so thoughtful as to provide such things without being asked. But today, the sight of them brought on a different emotion.

Feeling suddenly lightheaded, Agnes sat down heavily on the bed, her heart trembling.

She had been here for over two months now, she realised. And yet she hadn't had need to use the sanitary products more than once. Hastily, she tried to work through the dates of her cycle. Had she missed her period? So much had gone on, she had lost track of time, but she supposed she must be a little late. Maybe more than a little.

She crossed to the dressing mirror and stood in her underwear, one hand on the flat white skin of her belly, assessing. A queer mix of despair and elation began to flow through her. This would be everything her husband had wanted, and more. It would cement her place here, allow her to stop worrying. It was a *good* thing.

So why was she filled with such horror?

Closing the cabinet, she sank back down on the bed, gazing at her pretty painted toenails, shell pink against the thick cream pile of the carpet. The simple fact was, she had chosen this life when she chose to approach Christian in France, knowing full well who he was, what he could give her and her mother. She had known exactly what she was doing. Or so she had thought. She had made her bed. And now she must lie in it.

Agnes dressed quickly, not caring what blouse she put on, her fingers slipping over the buttons. She hurried from the cottage, leaving the door behind her wide open, needing only to get outside, to gaze thirstily up at the sky, her frenzied thoughts spilling out in tiny, frightened ripples before her.

Chapter Thirty-Three

Outside, the wind whipped the tops of the trees as Agnes strode down the path, pine needles falling around her. One lodged itself in her blouse, prickling uncomfortably at her skin.

It would be best for all of us if we had a child.

What sort of a place would this be to bring up a baby, surrounded by the sick and the dying? And what sort of a father would Christian be? He rarely saw his daughter as it was, rarely interacted with her. Yet leaving Hedoné with a baby would not be an option. The world would not take to her kindly, a mother alone without the support of her husband. And besides, Christian was not one to let go so easily, she knew. If Iso was not allowed to go to boarding school, then this child would be clutched onto just as tightly.

Might it be a false alarm? Might her monthlies simply have been delayed due to the grief over her mother? Agnes scanned back over the last few days, remembering moments of nausea and crippling tiredness that she had taken for the side effects of sorrow and anger.

She came to a stop at the edge of the trees, looking out with bewildered fear over the grounds. How could a place look so wonderful and full of possibility one day, and so terrifying the next? How could it have altered so much, and yet, on the face of it, everything was just the same?

The wind changed direction, and in the distance, she heard the Jersey cows lowing. A maid came down the library steps, disappearing round the side of the house. The staff had their own entrance to their living quarters, hidden somewhere at the back of the house. Isobel and her governess lived there, she knew, and she wondered with a sickening twist of fear if her own child would end up there too, cloistered away from everyone who showed them any love.

She was suddenly infused with a need to see this secretive part of the house, a place she had never been privy to before. She started forward, taking the same path as the maid. Sure enough, there was an unobtrusive door here. Agnes pulled it open, feeling as if she were snooping. Walking cautiously down a slim, functional corridor, she passed multiple doors, coming at last to one with a colourful wooden plaque on it bearing the name Isobel.

Agnes knocked, the plaque shaking on its nail. There was no answer, and she paused, wondering what to do. A vision consumed her, of her own child's name here, badly screwed to a door in this dark and ugly corridor, and with a surge of panicked desperation, she pushed the door open.

Iso was sitting at a desk by a window, a set of paints and paper laid out in front of her, so engrossed in her work that she didn't look up. Agnes's eyes scanned the room in shock. It was a tiny, cramped space, threadbare and basic with no hint of the luxury of the rest of the house. How had she not realised this was how her stepdaughter lived? It would not do. She resolved to ensure that Iso was moved into their cottage with them, however long it took to persuade Christian. Perhaps she might even get permission for her to go away to school.

On the desk, a jar of pinkish water caught the sunshine pouring into the room, turning everything a swash of rose. Isobel was copying a lily, propped in an empty jam jar and purloined no doubt from one of the many bouquets displayed around the house. It looked like it had been there for days, mottled and wilting from lack of water. A single waxy petal had fallen, lying on the desktop, mouldering at the edges, and Agnes's nostrils were filled with the flower's cloying scent, made stronger by its decaying state. A waft of nausea shimmered over her.

She watched Isobel paint for a while. The picture was admirable, far better than anything Agnes could have accomplished.

'That's very good,' she said at last, growing weary as she waited for the child to finish. 'Perhaps your papa should engage you on a scholarship.'

Iso looked up, her face deadpan. 'The scholarships are only for those suffering from tuberculosis,' she said.

'Oh, yes, of course. How silly of me.'

Finding no other seat in the cramped bedroom, Agnes sat down on the edge of the bed. Her eye was caught by a photograph of a woman in a silver frame, standing on Iso's bedside table. She picked it up, and realised she was looking into Meredith Fairhaven's face for the first time.

She was an attractive woman, with a similar colouring to Agnes, perhaps a shade or two lighter, and a fine bone structure under the pale skin. Agnes supposed she would be considered what Christian referred to as an English rose, just like herself. She was looking out of the photograph with a kind, direct gaze.

'She was very pretty, your mother,' she said. 'She and you look very much alike.' Indeed, if only Iso's tight little face would open up more often, she might even be considered beautiful.

The girl did not appear to catch onto the compliment. She got to her feet and came over, studying the photograph in Agnes's hand, her hair tickling her cheek.

'You're sad about your own mother, aren't you?' she said, and Agnes looked up at her enquiring face, surprised by the girl's perspicacity.

'Yes. I am. I think we have that in common, don't we? Missing our mothers?'

The girl nodded.

'Have you written to her lately?'

'No. I can't write too often. It might make Papa angry if he caught me. I shall wait for her to write back first.'

'*Does* she write back?' Agnes asked, astounded by the bounds of the girl's imagination. Was this what happened when a child had no other children to play with? Was it right, this sort of unattainable belief? Would her own child in turn come out with similar spurious fantasies?

'She will when she can,' the girl said with a small sigh. Going back to her desk, she picked up her brush again, and Agnes placed the photograph back on the bedside table.

'Why would your papa be angry about the letters?' she asked her.

'He doesn't like me talking about Mama.'

'It upsets him?'

Isobel shook her head, a quick, darting movement. 'He gets in a rage,' she said, stroking a bright crimson splash of colour onto her painting, and Agnes noticed for the first time that the lily was the same type she had so detested that day in the entrance hall, the ones with stipples of red that had reminded her of blood. Its petals had sharp spikes, like tiny thorns, or piercing, serrated teeth.

'A rage?' she enquired, puzzled.

'He says I mustn't mention her in front of him.'

Agnes supposed that Christian's grief might be such that he

231

couldn't bear to talk about Meredith, but still, it wasn't fair to impress the same limitations upon his daughter. She thought with a sudden jolt of her mother's last, wise words. This girl needed her. Whatever happened with the baby that might already be growing inside her, Isobel was in as much need of a mother herself right now.

'Dear,' Agnes said, getting up and placing her hand on the girl's shoulder. 'Whether or not your mother writes back, you do know I'm here for you, don't you? You can talk to me about anything you wish. You can talk about your mother, or your father, or the patients here. Whatever you want. It must be difficult, always surrounded by people with tuberculosis. Lord knows, I find it so sometimes.'

'I don't mind it. I'm used to it.'

But surely it wasn't right for the girl to think that this was normality?

'I suppose it must begin to feel normal after a while,' Agnes said carefully. 'But Iso, you do know that most people *don't* have tuberculosis, don't you? Most people live long and healthy lives into old age.' She felt it important to remind the child of this. 'Anyway,' she said, seeing that the girl was lost in her painting again. 'I shall let you get on.'

She hovered for a moment, feeling a small pulse of affection for the strange little girl, and she dropped a kiss on her soft, silvery head.

As she left the room, Agnes felt an inexplicable lump of emotion well tightly in her throat, though she was not sure exactly why.

Chapter Thirty-Four

Agnes had the vague idea of visiting the library, of letting the news of her impending pregnancy sink in. Perhaps then she might go and see if Sippie was up. She needed advice, and the pianist, she knew, would be honest and sage.

She peered down the claustrophobic passageway, unsure how to access the main house from here. Retracing her steps back to the door she had come in through, she hurried out into the fresh air, relieved to be away from the dark stuffiness of the staff quarters.

Inside the main entrance hall, she took the corridor towards the library. As she approached Christian's office, she stopped. Perhaps she should just bite the bullet and tell him. It may be a false alarm, but if it was, then it might open the door to a discussion about whether this was the right time to have a child. And if she really was pregnant — and here her heart flipped at the thought — then it was important to ensure that she was taking the best possible care of herself, for the baby's sake. And to do that, she needed to let Christian know.

The sliding panel on the door was set to 'Do not disturb' and stepping closer, Agnes thought she could hear faint voices coming from within. She knew that Matron often met with Christian at this time to discuss the running of Hedoné, and, curious to know what they talked about, she glanced down the corridor to check she was alone, and then put her ear lightly to the door.

She could hear her husband's voice, low and smooth, coming from inside.

'. . . really don't think she suspects,' he was saying, and Agnes held her breath, straining to hear every word.

'Well, I should think not. We've been exceptionally careful.'

She froze. Filtering through the door as if it was whispering directly into her ear was the unmistakable voice of Juno Harrington.

'But she *is* clever, Christian,' Juno continued.

Christian, Agnes thought. Juno had always referred to him as 'Doctor' before.

'I have no doubt she'll find out eventually. I hear she's already been asking questions about how Meredith died. How long are you going to keep *that* little lie a secret?'

What did Juno mean? What lie? Agnes began to feel sick. She pressed her ear harder to the door.

'I—' Christian began, but Juno cut him off.

'Why on earth you couldn't have chosen a pretty, dim-witted young thing instead, I don't know. I wonder if the right thing to do would be to tell her.'

'Tell her? But surely not yet?'

'Of course not yet, but Agnes will *have* to know eventually, surely you can see that?'

At the mention of her own name, Agnes's breath caught in her throat. She tried to swallow, her mouth suddenly dry.

'We can't all live together in such close proximity and have her *not* know,' Juno continued. 'She will simply have to be told when the time is right. If we choose it carefully, then I'm sure she'll understand.

She'll have to. She has accepted everything else so far, albeit rather grudgingly.'

'Now come on, that's bally unfair.'

'Are you sleeping with her, Christian?'

Agnes's eyes widened. Inside the office, there was a pause, and she imagined Juno's quick mind assessing her husband, running over him like an x-ray.

'I knew it,' she heard the young woman hiss.

'I promise you, it's purely a marriage of convenience,' Christian rushed. 'But it must look genuine to Agnes, Juno. What would she think if I refused any sort of carnal relations?'

'Well, I hope you're at least taking precautions,' she said, her voice as sharp as a needle. 'You know that would throw a spanner in the works.'

Agnes clapped her hand over her mouth, trying to suppress her shocked gasp. Did Juno mean a pregnancy? But what could that impede? She pressed her hand to her stomach in confusion.

'Of course I'm taking precautions. I'm being careful, Juno, I promise.'

Agnes imagined Juno, those big brown eyes on her husband's face, considering.

'I suppose I'll have to trust you,' she said witheringly. 'But be that as it may, I do think it makes sense to tell her what we're doing eventually. It would be easier, her knowing. I do hate lying so. I'm sick of it.' There was a slight tremor in her voice. A breathless emotion that Agnes could not quite pinpoint. 'You know,' Juno said quietly, and Agnes strained to hear, 'despite the circumstances, I fear I've become quite fond of your wife.'

There was a beat of silence, and then Christian's voice, shot through with what sounded like sorrow. 'Yes,' he said. 'Yes, so have I.'

'You and I are having to be so much more careful, Christian, it's exhausting.'

At the sound of footsteps approaching the door, Agnes sprang away. She ran towards the library, slipping through the door and closing it behind her, her heart beating a tattoo in her chest.

She thought of the little golden hare cufflinks, the familiar way Juno always talked to Christian. How on earth hadn't she seen it?

But why had Christian married *her* if he was having an affair with Juno Harrington? Except, she knew the answer to that: doctors were not supposed to form relationships with their patients. Juno came from an extremely wealthy family. She imagined the Harringtons might have a problem with their daughter's so-called doctor taking advantage. Was Agnes's marriage just a ruse to hide their affair, then? Yet he had admitted to Juno that they slept together, and he had always seemed so intent on trying for a baby. But perhaps that was just a ploy to divert Agnes's attention from the fact that he was actually doing the opposite – trying to *refrain* from impregnating her.

If that was the case, it hadn't worked, had it, she thought with a sickening twist of realisation. It looked like she was pregnant, whether Christian liked it or not. And it sounded as if a pregnancy might be the one thing stopping him from ousting her from his life.

She pressed her ear to the library door. When she was sure it was clear, she slipped into the corridor and walked slowly towards Christian's office, listening intently for any sign that he and Juno were inside. The sliding panel was still set to 'Do not disturb', but she could detect no sound from within. She knocked quietly, but there was no answer, and with mounting trepidation, Agnes put her hand to the doorknob, expecting it to be locked, but it opened soundlessly. Quickly, she hurried inside.

The office was empty. On one wall, a large white lightbox had been switched on. Pinned to it was an x-ray plate of a pair of lungs. Agnes studied it for a moment. These were not her lungs, they looked as if they were full of clouds, and she realised that whoever they belonged to must be very ill. Were they Juno's? A brief glimmer of hope reared up. Had she been wrong, and it had only been a medical appointment after all?

Agnes went round the desk, trying the drawers, looking for clues of their affair, but every drawer was locked. She tried not to imagine Christian pushing Juno up against this desk, pressing himself on her, those sultry lips of hers curved into a lustful smile.

In one corner of the room was a wooden filing cabinet, and Agnes went to it with the vague thought of finding out more about Juno. She pulled open the drawer marked A–H, running her fingers through the files until she came to 'Harrington, J', but here she paused.

What was she doing? However angry and upset she was, she couldn't delve into the patients' medical files, it was a step too far. She was about to close the drawer, when the names on the graves flashed into her mind, Simpson and Clements. Though still unethical, it felt less objectionable to look at the files of those who were already deceased. Quickly, Agnes flicked through the drawer's contents, searching for Elsie Clements, but there was no one of that name in here. She slid the drawer closed, wincing at the loud screech the runners made, and opened Q-Z, looking for Betty Simpson. But again the search proved fruitless.

With one final burst of inspiration, she turned to the letter T. Here at last, she was successful. She pulled out the notes for Elizabeth Thackeray, the young woman who had drowned herself in the swimming pool.

Elizabeth Thackeray had died only a few weeks before Agnes

had arrived. The listed cause of death was drowning. A copy of a chest x-ray was clipped to the file. Poor Elizabeth's lungs were just as clouded as Mother's had been. Agnes scanned the paperwork. Elizabeth had had severe tuberculosis. A few days before she died, the initials AP(S) had been added to her notes. Agnes frowned at these, scouring her brain to think what they might stand for, but nothing came to mind.

She replaced the file and closed the cabinet. Straightening up, she stood, looking around at the room. Why were the two dead girls whose graves were in that sad little glade not in this filing system? Perhaps when someone died, their notes were put into storage. But that didn't explain why Elizabeth Thackeray's notes were still in here, unless they just hadn't got round to moving hers yet.

Agnes shook her head. This was all too much at once. Could she forgive Christian for his affair? Fidelity was not a given, she knew. It was plain fact that some husbands strayed, and when someone as beautiful and ambitious as Juno got their claws into you, what chance did you have?

Gazing round the room, she realised she had been right about something else. There was no photograph of Meredith Fairhaven here. It was as if, once his first wife had died, Christian had erased the woman from his life. Iso had said he grew angry whenever she mentioned her mother to him. And now, Juno was talking about the *way* she'd died, as if the guests had all been fed a lie. What had she meant? Could Meredith have died in a different, more sinister way? As far as Agnes could tell, only Juno, Christian and Iso had been here when she died. And Juno certainly seemed to be in on all of Christian's secrets. Had *she* had something to do with Meredith's death? Had they colluded together, the jealous lover and the prurient husband, intent on getting rid of her?

'Stop it,' she muttered under her breath. She was getting ahead of herself. Of course her husband wasn't a murderer.

She picked up a small photograph in a gold frame on Christian's desk. It was the engagement portrait that had been taken in France. How innocent she looked, how naïve. She had thought herself so clever, entrapping this wealthy man, and saving her mother all in one fell swoop. And she had got everything she'd wanted, hadn't she? Except that now, all of it was falling apart, drifting to the floor like the decaying petals of that despicable lily in Iso's room.

Had the affair been going on even when this photograph was taken? Of course it had, Agnes thought savagely. Of course it had.

She clenched her fists in frustration, feeling her nails press painfully into her skin. Deep in thought, she became aware of footsteps outside in the corridor. Hastily, she skirted the desk and sat quickly in the chair on the other side.

The door opened, and Christian stopped on the threshold. 'Agnes!' he said.

'Christian, darling,' she said, turning round and feigning surprise, hoping that her flushed cheeks would look like pleasure, not guilt.

She got up to greet him, and he came to her and gave her a perfunctory kiss on the cheek.

'What are you doing here?'

He was looking at her strangely, and Agnes wished not for the first time that she could see what was going on in that mind of his. Behind her, she felt the edge of the desk press against her legs.

'I missed you.'

Christian was looking at her in that measured, questioning way that he had, and she was suddenly reminded of what he and Juno might have been doing right here on this spot, only minutes before. Was he thinking of it, even now, as he looked at her?

Agnes stepped forward, closing the gap between them, and pressed her lips to his. She felt him react, and she kissed him more forcefully, trying to blot out any thoughts he might have of Juno. *I am your wife*, she was saying, *not her*, and he responded in kind, wrapping his strong arms around her and lifting her onto the desk.

'Is it the right time?' he whispered feverishly, his hand going to the belt of his trousers, and she knew, then, what she must do to keep him.

'Actually, I came here to tell you some wonderful news,' she said.

Christian pulled away, his blue eyes penetrating hers. 'Don't jest,' he said, his voice trembling. 'Are you saying what I think you're saying?'

'I am,' she said. She leant into him, her lips touching his ear, her voice every bit as soft and golden as Juno's.

'Christian darling,' she whispered. 'We're going to have a baby.'

Chapter Thirty-Five

As the evenings grew cooler, fires were lit in all the bedrooms. The staff brought thick furs out to the deckchairs so that the guests might stay outside as the temperature dropped. Those from colder climes relished the cool air, the men diving into the lake and beating their chests with abandon. The French guests retreated to their rooms, nursing whiskies and sitting close to the fires. Decorative torches on wrought iron pillars appeared, dotted across the grounds, and as the sun dropped low each afternoon, the soft flames began flickering, drawing cold hands and chilled faces to the warmth, as shouts of 'Who wants a hot toddy?' rang out through the gloam.

On a crisp morning, the mist catching in the pine trees like cobwebs, Agnes waited in the music room for Isobel. She had promised to sit in on her stepdaughter's piano practice, and as she waited, gazing out of the window at the grounds, her thoughts ran to Juno and Christian.

She had not found any more tangible proof of their affair, but it was easy to see it between them, now that she was looking. Christian behaved awkwardly around Juno, as if he was struggling to hide their secret. Juno had no such scruples. She positively relished those moments when she knew Agnes was looking at them, leaning in and touching him on the arm, brazenly visiting him in his office and shutting the door on the rest of the house.

Agnes presumed that Christian had not yet told her about their news – Juno was certainly not behaving any differently around her. And thinking back to the conversation she had overheard in his office, she could understand Christian's reasoning.

He had asked her not to disclose the pregnancy to anyone else yet, not even Matron. 'Best to wait until you're at a safer stage,' he had said. 'I'm sure all will be fine, our child is made of robust stock after all. But best to wait.'

He had been excessively attentive towards her ever since. Every day it felt as if the cloying, claustrophobic grip of his love grew stronger, binding her to him as a spider binds a fly. Could a man love two women at once? Or perhaps it was just his fixation with the baby inside her, and Agnes was merely a vessel to be protected at all costs.

As she became more used to the idea of the child growing inside her, she tried to spend more time with her stepdaughter. But whenever Agnes sought Isobel out, Juno seemed to have got there first, accompanying the girl on painting excursions out in the grounds, or dressing her up in the countless beautiful evening gowns she had hanging in her wardrobe, sitting her in front of her dressing table mirror and painting her face to resemble a china doll.

What was this role that Juno was exploring, the macabre parody of a doting mother? Was this her eventual plan, to replace both Meredith Fairhaven and herself? To be the mother that Isobel so obviously needed? And if so, where was Agnes's own baby in all of this? She imagined the beautiful young woman sweeping into the maternity room moments after the birth and scooping up the little thing, tucking it into the crook of her arm and cooing at it while Agnes lay, exhausted and helpless in her bed. She wondered again if

Meredith could have died, not, as everybody believed, from TB, but in a more underhand way. Surely Juno and Christian were not capable of that? But if they were, where did that leave her?

Gazing unseeingly out of the music room window to the grounds beyond, Agnes tried to dislodge this awful thought. She was getting hysterical. She felt the stirrings of morning sickness rising in her throat, a feeling that had begun to plague her each day, and she looked up to the ceiling, trying to quell it, blinking back the tears that seemed to come so suddenly and unexpectedly of late. It was a beautiful, high-ceilinged room, with ornate plaster roses and filigree sconces on the walls. Along one side stretched a fitted cabinet composed of hundreds of labelled drawers, each one filled with sheet music. Music stands stood here and there, abandoned sheet music upon them. There was no one else here, the only sound her panicked breaths as she tried to regain her composure. It occurred to her that silence in a music room felt very wrong.

The door opened, and Agnes wiped her eyes, expecting to see her stepdaughter.

'Sippie!' she said in surprise, blinking back her tears.

Sippie's gaunt face broke into a smile when she saw her. 'Agnes! I haven't seen you for an age.'

'I'm sorry — I haven't quite felt up to coming to dinner recently.' She came to a stop, noticing that the woman looked just as distracted as she felt. 'Is everything all right?'

Sippie's handsome face drew into a frown. 'Actually, it isn't. I'm worried about Georgie.'

'Georgie?'

'Georgie Murphy. He's been down in the infirmary for days now. Nobody seems to know what's going on.'

Agnes frowned. She had hardly seen the guests recently. What with the death of her mother and then the shock of the pregnancy, she had kept to herself, trying to process it all. Georgie. The young red-headed Irishman. Her thoughts fluttered from him to Leopold Rackham. As far as she knew, the guests had still not been told about Rackham's death.

Sippie sat down at the piano and lifted the lid. 'He wasn't in a good way when he went down there. He's so young, so very fragile.'

'I shall see what I can find out,' Agnes said.

'Thank you.'

Sippie put her hands to the keys and a cascade of beautiful, melancholy notes rose up. The sound caught somewhere inside Agnes's chest, filling her with a hopeful sense of urgency. She turned back to the window, looking out over the woods at the back of the house, at the tips of the pine trees wavering in the breeze. All too soon, the music came to an end, the room drifting into silence once more, and she felt herself tremble.

Sippie was gazing out of the window too, her hands resting lightly on the keys.

'Please don't stop,' Agnes said.

The music rose again, a liquid wave in the room. Outside, the grounds were deserted, most of the guests still asleep, and Agnes felt inside her a peculiar, beautiful ringing, a ribbon of nausea following it. She stumbled, pressing her hand to the glass pane, sweat breaking out on her brow.

'Agnes!' Sippie broke off her playing, hurrying to her. 'Are you all right?' she said, lowering her onto the sill.

'I'm sorry, I don't know what came over me.'

Sippie crouched down in front of her, looking at Agnes with that same enquiring frown she'd had after the delegates' dinner. 'You're pregnant,' she said, the frown melting away.

'What?'

'I have seven sisters back home, all older than me, and almost all of them had babies before I left for Europe. I don't know much, but babies and jazz, I do know. It's early days, isn't it?'

Reluctantly, Agnes nodded. 'It is. I'm still getting used to the idea. I can't quite take in the fact that it's happening at all.'

Sippie nodded. 'A baby at Hedoné,' she said with a smile. 'It's not something I ever thought I'd see.'

'No.' Agnes looked down at her hands, the gold wedding ring glinting in the pale autumn light.

'Though I did hear there *was* someone, last year, who got pregnant.'

Agnes looked up. 'You mean a guest?'

'Mmm hmm.' Sippie drew to her feet, her smile gone.

'What became of her?'

Sippie didn't answer immediately, but her eyes flashed to Agnes's face, a little fearful.

'You can tell me,' Agnes said.

'They say Doctor Fairhaven operated on her, aborted the baby,' she whispered. 'She was too ill to carry the child, so the guests were told.'

Agnes felt her breath catch in her throat. 'Do you know who she was, the woman?' she asked. For a brief, sickening moment, she wondered if Sippie would tell her it had been Juno.

'Her name was Sybil. Sybil Baxter.'

Agnes mentally scanned the guests, but she couldn't think of a Sybil. 'Where is she now? Did she leave Hedoné?'

Sippie shook her head. 'She died,' she said. 'A few months after the operation.'

'Oh no,' Agnes said quietly. 'Was she given a choice about the . . . the . . .' She couldn't bring herself to say the word.

245

'I don't know,' Sippie said. 'It was before my time here.' She pressed a gentle hand to Agnes's forehead. 'I'm sorry, I didn't mean to make you feel worse. But ever since I found out, it's been niggling at me. And after the delegates came, and our conversation down by the lake, I thought you ought to know.' She was whispering now, too, as if she sensed someone might be listening.

'Thank you. I appreciate your honesty.'

'It's just, the longer I stay here, the more I start to question things. There's something not quite right about this place. Do you feel it?'

'Yes,' Agnes said quietly. 'I do.' Lowering her voice, she added, 'Sippie, do you by any chance know what the initials AP, followed by an S would mean in a patient's notes?'

Sippie frowned. 'AP might stand for artificial pneumothorax. The operation that some of the guests have had to deflate one of their lungs.'

Of course! Agnes remembered the term from the first delegates' dinner.

'But the S, I don't know. Why do you want to know?'

'I don't know. Ever since the delegates came back, I've felt a little . . . unsettled about what's going on here. And now, with what you've told me about Miss Baxter . . .' She stopped, running over her thoughts, trying to make sense of it. 'When the scientists visited last time, they were discussing some kind of law in Germany. Something to do with the offspring of diseased people. So many things are changing over there at the moment, and yet, what they were talking about, Sippie, it all felt so wrong.' She shook her head. 'You lived there for a while, didn't you? Do you know anything about it?'

Sippie shook her head. 'Not that I recall. But then, it was a few years back. When I was over there, it felt dangerous for someone like me. They have very strong views on people who don't fit their idea of perfect. They say what they're doing is science, but really it's just one type of person saying they're better than the rest. I came here to get away from all that.' She went to the piano, running a hand lightly over its dark, gleaming case. 'But I can't believe your husband would bring those kind of ideas to Hedoné. He's trying to help us, not hurt us.'

Agnes nodded. 'I know. But he's so full of theories and ideas, and I wonder if sometimes he just becomes a little carried away with his own cleverness, forgetting that the patients' wellbeing should be at the heart of what he's doing here.' She sighed. 'I'm sorry, I shouldn't be burdening you with all this.'

Sippie sat down next to her on the sill, nudging her shoulder gently. 'It's all right. I would prefer to know. As I said, in my heart, I already knew something wasn't quite right.' She was looking at Agnes, her doe eyes penetrating her so that she had to look away. 'Mrs Fairhaven . . . Agnes?' she said quietly. 'Do you love your husband?'

'Sorry?' Agnes stuttered. 'Of . . . of course!'

'And do you trust him?'

'I . . .' Did she?

'It's just,' Sippie rushed in, 'now I'm living properly among the guests, I hear what they're all saying. They're trying to work out what happened in those few short weeks when the doctor was away on the Continent. Some are saying – and I'm not one to judge – that, well, that your marriage; it's all a bit too neat and tidy.'

Fear rose in Agnes's throat. 'What do you mean?' she whispered.

Sippie took her hand, her face serious. 'We're getting to be friends now, aren't we, you and I?'

'We are,' Agnes said guardedly.

'I think what the guests see is a poor young woman and her sick mother, both suddenly finding everything they ever needed. I suppose they just think it all feels a little too convenient.'

'You think I tricked Christian into marrying me?' Agnes said, her voice sounding too loud in the silent room.

'I'm only repeating what I heard,' Sippie said, squeezing her hand gently. 'But if it's true, then I have to tell you, I would have done exactly the same.' She was studying Agnes's face, searching for clues.

Sippie had always had a way of seeing the truth inside her. Agnes heaved a sigh.

'I didn't trick him. Not intentionally. But Mother was dying,' she said. 'We'd run out of money, and we were alone in a country that wasn't our own. I didn't set out to ensnare him, Sippie, I promise I didn't, but when I found out who he was, I suppose I tried to make myself more . . . appealing.' She looked into the woman's face imploringly. 'I was desperate,' she admitted quietly.

Sippie held Agnes's gaze as she digested this, then she nodded. 'That's what I thought,' she said.

'You're not disappointed in me?'

'Disappointed? No! Like I said, I would have done the same. Actually, I've been wondering something else, ever since I met you.'

'Oh?'

'I'm thinking it might have been the other way round.'

'The other . . .' Agnes said. 'I'm sorry, I don't follow.'

'Well, what if Doctor chose *you* because he needed a wife for . . . other reasons.'

'You think this marriage is . . . convenient . . . for Christian?' Agnes said slowly. Did Sippie suspect Juno and Christian of an affair, too?

The pianist's eyes were wide, filled with sadness as she nodded. 'I'm sorry if I'm being a little blunt – I always forget how restrained you English are, everything so stitched up in metaphor and politeness, it's sometimes a little hard to separate a compliment from a criticism here – but I need to tell you my concerns, Agnes.' She stopped, as if

248

to gird herself. 'The guests have said what a striking resemblance you have to the former Mrs Fairhaven. I suppose I asked you if you loved him, if you trusted him, because if you do, if you're happy here, then whatever reasons he had for asking you to marry him don't matter.'

Agnes considered this. 'I suppose . . . I love him for all that he's done for me,' she said carefully. 'And I loved what he did for my mother.' She paused, shaking her head with a sigh. 'But you're right, I've started to suspect that I'm here for a different purpose recently too.'

She didn't need to explain what she meant. Everyone must see how Juno was with Christian. Did *all* the guests know of their affair? Had it only been she who hadn't seen it? She felt suddenly very stupid.

Sippie nodded. 'All marriages are transactions. But that doesn't mean that they can't be successful. If what you have now is better than what you had before, then it's not necessarily important to know exactly what else is going on.' She took a quick breath. 'But if there ever comes a time when that love, that trust, is compromised, then perhaps you should scratch a little deeper.'

'What do you mean?'

Sippie glanced over her shoulder. Lowering her voice, she said, 'I think we both feel that there are things going on here, beneath the surface. Secret things. Terrible things. I wonder if we put our heads together, we might—'

She was interrupted by the door bursting open. Isobel ran in, trailed by her governess, and Sippie hurriedly got to her feet.

'It's been lovely to talk with you, Agnes,' she said, a small smile crossing her elfin features before it was eclipsed by a frown. 'Take care, won't you?'

'I will,' Agnes said, her mind still reeling from everything the young woman had said.

When Sippie had gone, she tried to focus on her stepdaughter's practice, the jarring scales rising and falling like painful breaths, but her eyes kept drifting to the window and the trees in the distance.

It was so beautiful here, so improbable to think that terrible things might have happened, might still be happening now. Had Mr Rackham really been so ill that they could do nothing more for him? He had looked and sounded so full of health when he shouted from the balcony. Agnes thought of the artist down in the infirmary now. He must be very ill. Was he dying, too?

It dawned on her that there was one person she could ask, other than her husband, who might know the answers to these questions. She got to her feet. Across the room, Isobel's tentative practice stumbled to a stop.

'It's very accomplished, Isobel,' she said, starting towards the door.

Once outside, she began to hurry down the corridor.

Chapter Thirty-Six

She found Matron on the quarantine floor, scrubbing her hands in the basin at the end of the landing, her back to her. The thick pile of the carpet silenced Agnes's footsteps, and she paused a few feet from the nurse, her eyes on that sharp little head with the veil perched atop it.

Could she trust this woman? They had never seen eye to eye, but she had watched the matron tenderly nurse her mother in her last hours. It had been Matron who had been there for her when Mother died, offering Agnes a calming brandy and a listening ear, taking her hand stiffly at her mother's grave and patting it awkwardly. She was not a nurturing, kindly woman, but she did, it seemed, care greatly for her patients.

'Matron,' Agnes said. The woman turned.

It was the first time Agnes had seen her up close since her mother's funeral, and she was shocked by the change in her. The nurse was stooped, her usually neat-as-a-pin hair escaping from beneath her veil, her whole demeanour worn down.

'Mrs Fairhaven,' Matron said, drying her hands on a towel. 'To what do I owe this pleasure?'

'I . . . I need your help,' Agnes said.

'Are you unwell, Mrs Fairhaven?'

Was that excitement she saw in the woman's eyes? Hope? 'I'm fine,' Agnes said, a little too sharply, and the nurse's eyebrows rose, her nose wrinkling in distaste. 'I'm sorry,' she added hastily. 'I'm a little anxious, that's all.'

She gathered her strength, bracing herself for what she was about to say. Testing Matron's loyalties was dangerous, she knew. The woman could go straight to Christian. But who else could she turn to?

'Matron,' she said, her voice so low it was barely more than a whisper. 'I've watched you work now for some time. Every day, I see how devoted you are to your patients; to your vocation. You strive to give the guests the best treatment, the best life. You know the people who pass through your rooms better than anyone else in this place. Better, dare I say it, than my own husband.' Agnes stopped, taking a quick breath, preparing herself for what she was about to say. 'Which is why I know that you *must* see that something here is not right.'

The matron gave a sharp inhalation as if affronted, her nostrils closing like a fish's gills. 'I don't know what you're talking about,' she whispered.

'But you must!' Agnes pleaded. 'I see it in your eyes. There are secrets here, you know there are. Secrets you don't know the answers to. Surely, you want to understand, just like I do?'

For a moment, she thought the matron was going to shake her head, but she only stood there in silence.

'Will you help me,' Agnes pushed. 'Please, Matron?'

This was too much for the nurse. She turned to the medical cupboard and began restocking the shelves. 'It is not my place to interfere with Doctor Fairhaven's business, Mrs Fairhaven,' she said, boxes and fresh masks tumbling everywhere. 'I am here to tend to the guests, that is all.'

'But that's *not* all!' The words shot from Agnes's mouth before she could contain them, and Matron's eyes narrowed again. Frantically backtracking, she added, 'It's just, I watched how carefully you tended to my mother. If I was as meticulous as you, I would want to understand what was going on here, to ensure my charges were safe.'

This caught Matron's attention, the boxes on the shelves forgotten.

'For instance,' Agnes hurried on, 'you never met Christian's first wife, did you?'

The woman shook her head. 'No. She died before I came here.'

'So, you don't know anything about how she died?'

'She had TB, Mrs Fairhaven.'

'You know that for sure?'

Agnes thought she saw a treacly flash in Matron's eyes, but then it was gone.

'Everyone knows that,' the woman said. 'It's why Doctor Fairhaven is so passionate about what he does here.'

Agnes let this go. 'Did you ever meet either of the two young women who are buried in the memorial garden in the woods, in the corner by the holly tree?'

Matron's eyes narrowed, but Agnes stood her ground, refusing to quail under her steely glare. 'Yes, of course. They were very ill.'

'With tuberculosis?'

'No, I don't think so.'

Agnes took a step back in surprise. 'Then what?'

'I don't know,' Matron said impatiently, lowering her voice. 'They weren't under my care. They never came up here, you see. They were Doctor's sole responsibility and remained in the infirmary until they died.'

'But, didn't you ask the doctor? Didn't you question what was wrong with them?'

The treacly flash in Matron's eyes was there again, and this time Agnes saw plainly that it was fear.

'I trusted him to take care of them in the appropriate manner,' Matron said. 'I was extremely busy with my work on this floor, looking after people like your mother.'

Agnes felt a tinge of guilt, but she pushed on. She had come too far to give up now. 'What was Leopold Rackham shouting about, at the window, that day he was taken to the infirmary?'

'I don't know,' the matron said stiffly.

'You didn't hear him? Because I saw you up there, in his room when it was going on. What happened to him, Matron, down in the infirmary?'

Matron relented. 'He should never have been allowed here in the first place,' she said. 'None of these poor souls should.'

A cold spike of fear travelled down Agnes's spine. 'Why do you say that?' she whispered. But Matron only shook her head.

'Please,' Agnes urged, her words spilling over one another in their desperation to get out. 'If you suspect something, then you must want to know the extent of it. I know Rackham died, and yet the guests still haven't been told. I think they just assume he left Hedoné. Are you really sure he was at the end of his life down there?'

Matron took a sharp intake of breath. 'Mr Rackham was very ill indeed,' she said. 'He was not my patient, but I do believe he *was* dying. But—' She stopped, as if she'd realised she'd said too much.

'But what? Please, Matron, I'm just trying to understand. I hear the artist, Georgie Murphy, is gravely ill now. He's been in the infirmary for a while. The guests are worried for him. I know it's not your place to take sides, but I wonder if perhaps you feel a little like I do? Perhaps you and I are working towards the same answers?'

Matron closed her eyes for a moment, pinching the bridge of her nose, but she did not speak, and Agnes took this as affirmation to continue.

'I know some of the patients have had a procedure called artificial pneumothorax, known as AP,' she said. 'Is that correct?'

'Yes. It deflates the lung, allows it to heal.'

'And if I were to see the letters AP followed by an S, what might that mean?'

Matron's brow furrowed. 'I . . . I don't know,' she said, looking down at her hands, her usually emotionless eyes filled with remorse, and Agnes saw that her palms were red raw.

'Please,' she pressed, her heart racing, sensing the woman was wavering. 'Please, Matron. This could save lives. I need to gain access to the old patient files. Those belonging to the guests who have passed away.'

Matron's eyes widened above her mask. 'I cannot help you with that. It is strictly confidential.' She began to stride down the corridor, shaking her head, but Agnes caught hold of her wrist.

'I'm not asking you to look at them yourself, only to tell me where the files are stored and help me gain access. Don't you want to understand what's going on here?'

The woman sucked air in through her mouth, her mask pressing against her lips so that for a brief moment she looked like she was screaming. 'Of course,' she said.

'Then help me,' Agnes urged. 'Help me get access to wherever the files are stored.'

'I don't have the keys to that room,' Matron hissed. Striding to the basin, she began scrubbing at her hands again.

'But you could get them?' Agnes said, following her over.

'It's more than my job's worth,' she said, and for the first time, her voice had a tremor in it. She was worrying at the skin of her palms with a nailbrush. A tiny drop of blood landed in the basin, starkly florid against the white china.

'But what about your responsibility to your patients?' Agnes pressed.

At this, Matron stilled. Heaving a sigh, she wrung the remaining water from her hands. 'If you do this, you must never, *never* mention that I helped you, do you understand?'

'Of course.'

'I don't have access to the keys, but I can get hold of them. Later tonight.'

Relief flooded through Agnes. 'Thank you. Thank you, Matron.'

'I shall bring them to you this evening,' Matron said. 'Meet me in the library at eight o'clock.'

Chapter Thirty-Seven

At eight o'clock that evening, Agnes paced the library, unable to settle. It was dark outside now, and moths fluttered near the ceiling, drawn in by the lights. In the grounds, the torches had already been lit, and she could see the guests as they filtered out from the dining room, wrapped in coats and stoles to stave off the cold, taking up their usual spot down by the lake. Juno was amongst them, and Agnes pulled back, keeping to the shadows, not wanting to be seen.

At the sound of the library door opening, she took her eyes from the open window. Matron slipped inside, quickly crossing the room and pressing an envelope into Agnes's hands.

'There *are* secrets here,' she whispered, so quiet that Agnes could barely hear her. 'You're right to question this place. I cannot say more than that because I don't fully understand it myself. But I feel what you feel. Something is rotten here. Very rotten indeed.'

She drew back, her eyes darting around the room, as if she were searching for eavesdroppers, then stepped closer, her words coming, harried and fast.

'Take the lift down to the basement, and turn left. It's the third door on your right. Best to go early in the morning. Doctor doesn't go down there at that time. I must go before I'm seen.'

She hurried to the door, and with a quick nod, she was gone, leaving Agnes standing at the centre of the library with the envelope in her hand.

Agnes awoke early the next morning having dozed and woken in starts throughout the night. She checked that Christian was asleep, then pulled the bedspread back and inched out of bed. Every tiny movement she made felt magnified. In the sitting room, she dressed, then let herself out of the cottage, slipping through the trees.

It was just past four o'clock, the sky above the trees a dark, magical blue that heralded the coming morning. She ran lightly up the steps of the main house, thankful that there was no need to unlock the door. In the entrance hall, she hurried to the lift and inserted the key Matron had given her. She pressed the gold button, the sound of the lift's motor awfully loud in the ringing silence. Agnes held her breath, waiting for someone to come running, but nobody came. And then the entrance hall had disappeared above her, and the lift came to a stop, and she was alone.

From the corridor ahead, she thought she heard a clanging sound, and she froze. Surely no one was up now? She strained to listen, but the passageway remained silent, and she pulled back the gate and stepped out into the empty corridor.

The basement was just as Agnes remembered, the lights in their pretty sconces illuminating the long hall, the artificial breeze rippling over her, raising goose bumps on her skin. To her right, she could see the door to the x-ray room. Beyond it were more doors, and thinking suddenly of Georgie Murphy, she ran as quietly as she could, passing door after door, checking the name on each one. Halfway along, she passed a small metal hatch hanging slightly open, a laundry chute. She pushed it closed, the same metallic clang she had heard earlier resonating through the passageway.

She came to a door at the end of the passage with a glass panel in it. Above the panel a plaque read 'Infirmary'. Agnes put her face to the window. The room was lit by a single spotlight in one corner. She could make out a hospital bed, the sides raised to contain the patient within. Georgie was lying under a sheet, his red hair the only bright smudge in the monochrome room. Even from here she could see how thin he was, the sheet moulded to his body, betraying every rib and hollow. Pity took hold of her. Was he dying, like Mr Rackham before him?

Knowing she could do nothing to help him right now, she retraced her steps. She passed the lift again, glancing at the doors on her right until she came to one marked 'Private'. The key fitted, and Agnes turned the handle and went inside, closing the door behind her.

For a brief moment she was enveloped in darkness, the air dry and dust-filled. Trying to contain her panic, she scrabbled for a light switch, finding it quickly and flicking it down. The room was flooded with brightness, the bare strip bulbs above buzzing angrily, and she blinked, startled by the sudden change.

It was a small room, lined with filing cabinets. She went to each one, scanning the cards on the front of each drawer, dismissing 'Pharmacy Orders' and 'Staff Files', before coming to a stop at 'Deceased Patients'.

She pulled the drawer open, running her fingers through the different names. 'Clements, Elsie' was near the front, and she lifted the pale green file out, pausing as she spotted 'Rackham, Leopold'. Quickly, she slipped this one out too. She opened Mr Rackham's notes first, running her eyes over the last page, reading the words written in her husband's hand, 'Cause of death: unexplained.'

Surely Mr Rackham's cause of death would be tuberculosis? Or, if not that, then some complication of it? If Christian was doing his job properly, he must have had a good idea of what caused the man to die?

In bewilderment, she turned to Elsie Clements's notes. These were laid out just like the ones she had seen upstairs. Her eyes scanned the page greedily, searching for the initials AP, but she couldn't see them anywhere. This must mean that Elsie Clements hadn't had an artificial pneumothorax. Agnes ran her eyes over the page again, looking for the elusive S she had seen on Elizabeth Thackeray's notes, but it was also absent. She was just about to return the notes to the cabinet when her eyes settled on something else. At the top of the page, in her husband's hand, were the words 'Admitted with terminal venereal disease'.

Somewhere nearby, a low, deep thrumming started up, punctuated by a series of loud, sudden bangs, and Agnes almost dropped the notes, the hairs on the back of her neck rising, only to realise that it was the boiler, cranking up to heat the water needed for the baths of thirty guests. She slid Leopold's and Elsie's files back into the cabinet, her mind on those terrible words. She knew what venereal disease meant, but surely that couldn't be right: Elsie had only been eighteen years old.

Next, Agnes pulled out Betty Simpson's notes. Here, she encountered an almost identical file, those same devastating words. It occurred to her that neither of the young women's files mentioned tuberculosis, just as Matron had theorised. But they both contained x-ray images. She slid the picture of Betty's lungs from beneath a paperclip. They looked just as Agnes's had, clear and pretty, not clouded, like the x-ray she had seen recently in Christian's office.

Frustrated, Agnes put the notes back. She was just about to close the filing cabinet and beat a hasty retreat, when something made her pause. She turned to the files again, running her fingers through them, the noisy hum of the boiler accompanying her thoughts, until she came at last to 'Baxter, Sybil', the woman Sippie had told her about, who had got pregnant while she was living at Hedoné. With a quick breath, Agnes opened the file.

Sybil had been very ill indeed. Her x-ray was so white it resembled the thick grey clouds that sometimes gathered over the sea in the distance. Agnes ran her finger down the notes, coming to a stop at the now-familiar initials, AP. But there was no S next to them. She ran her eyes over the complex list of medication and treatment. Then she spotted it, a lone capital S, dated a few weeks after the lung collapse operation. She had almost missed it because it was in the middle of another sentence. She read the line again, trying to make sense of what she was seeing.

'Termination', she read, the words again written in her husband's hand, and in brackets next to this he had added, 'S performed at same time'.

What was that damned S all about? She searched the clotted mass of poor Sybil Baxter's lungs, as if the answer could be found within them, and slowly, something began to knit together in her mind.

'No,' she whispered, the word coming out in a gasp of understanding, the file slipping from her hands.

Quickly she picked up the notes and replaced them in the cabinet. She began pulling out other files, searching this time for notes belonging to male patients. As she had thought, none of these contained an S. Next, she brought out files belonging to women, and again and again, she found it. S, S, S.

Beginning to feel sick, Agnes slammed the cabinet closed and, as the boiler's clanking hum grew to a crescendo, she ran to the door, thrusting it open, her mind on what she had just begun to grasp.

There was a clatter and a soft thud, followed by a yelp of pain, and she looked down in panic to see Juno Harrington on the floor, clutching her bleeding nose.

Chapter Thirty-Eight

'Juno!'

The young woman was collapsed on her knees, blood dripping between her fingers.

'That'll teach me to listen at doors like a common maid,' she said, pinching the bridge of her nose, her voice thick and nasal.

Agnes pulled a handkerchief from her pocket and pressed it delicately to Juno's face, too late realising it was her father's hankie, his initials quickly stained with the drip of blood.

She tried to think straight, her mind hurriedly searching out a reason for being down here, her heart beating in horror, but she knew it was pointless. Sliding down the wall next to Juno, Agnes sank onto the floor, sagging in defeat.

'Ho ho,' she said, letting out a mirthful laugh. 'Now I'm for it.'

'What on earth do you mean?' Juno said thickly, tipping her head back to stem the flow.

'I don't think it's very proper, finding the doctor's wife rummaging through patient files, is it?'

'On the contrary, I think it's rather beguiling. I always thought you a little prim and prudish, but now I see there's more to you than meets the eye.'

'Are you going to tell Christian?' Agnes asked.

'That depends,' Juno said, her eyes glittering. 'You've actually done me a favour. I wanted to look in here, to check that Christian's version of events corroborates with the paperwork. But rummaging through dusty cabinets really isn't my style – I've always preferred to get others to do my dirty work. Tell me what you read in there – all of it – and I promise I'll keep this little meeting to myself. But do be honest, Agnes: remember, I can read you like a book. I'll know if you're lying, and have no doubt I'll go to your husband.'

Agnes gave a resigned sigh. What choice did she have? A part of her was relieved, pleased she could talk freely at last to this woman. At least now their cards were on the table. Juno might even unwittingly reveal some of the secrets that Agnes was desperate to make sense of. She took a shuddering breath.

'The other day, I overheard you talking with Christian in his office. I know what's going on between you two. But not just that. I think there's all kinds of corruption at Hedoné, going on right under the patients' noses. I believe the patients are told about one operation, when in fact they are having two.' She looked queasily down at a spot of blood on her blouse. 'When they have routine operations here, the doctor is also doing something else, something to stop them from being able to have children. There's a word for it. Sterilisation. It's written in the notes as S.'

She turned to Juno, and the young woman met her gaze, a surge of respect blazing in her eyes. Her nose had stopped bleeding now, and she dabbed at it delicately before taking the handkerchief away. Even with a sore nose, she was achingly beautiful.

'Excellent work,' she said. 'I did wonder if you'd puzzle it out. I told Christian he should have gone for someone stupid. But no, no, he had to go for his clever English rose, didn't he?' She folded the handkerchief, spotted with her blood. 'I suggested to him that we should tell you, you know. That we should get it all out in the open. It was your husband who tried to keep it a secret, not me.'

'But I don't understand — why would you want to tell me about your affair? You don't think I'd have gone along with it, surely?'

'Affair?' Juno's laughter cracked down the corridor like a gunshot. 'We're not having an affair, silly thing. He's really not my type. Far too malleable.'

'But . . .' Agnes shook her head. 'If you're not having an affair, then what were you talking about in his office?'

Juno's eyes widened. 'But I thought . . .' She came to a stop, flustered. 'The other day, you were asking about the two girls that died. And I'm assuming you checked their records just now?'

'Yes . . . but I can't see what that has to do with all this?'

'You can't?' Juno gave a shake of her head as if she was suddenly weary of their conversation. 'Then you're not quite as clever as I had assumed.' Carefully, one hand cradling her nose in the handkerchief, she began to get up off the floor.

'Wait!' Agnes said, putting a hand out to stop her. 'I have a right to know what's going on here, Juno,' she said.

'A right? Oh Mrs Fairhaven,' she said, shaking her head, but she sank back down on the floor nonetheless. She looked pale, Agnes thought. Perhaps the loss of blood was making her lightheaded.

'People are being operated on without their knowledge,' Agnes pushed. 'Without their permission even! Don't you think that's wrong, Juno? Don't you *care*?'

At this last word, the young woman stilled. 'Of course I care,' she said quietly. She took the handkerchief from her nose, examining the red stain upon it. 'LT,' she said, reading the initials beneath the blood. 'Your father?'

Agnes nodded.

'He died of it too, didn't he? This disease?'

'He did.'

'And yet, *you* managed to avoid it. Christian said you were special, living in a den of sickness for years without even a sniff of illness about you. I do understand why he chose you, even if he doesn't think I do.'

'What do you mean, *chose* me?' Agnes said, but Juno did not hear her. She was gazing at the handkerchief, a whole galaxy of emotions flitting across her face.

'You have no idea how horrific this illness is,' she said. 'The fevers and the pain and the exhaustion. Constantly struggling to breathe, not being able to concentrate on anything at all. You have no idea just how hard we work, merely to stay alive.'

'Juno, I do understand,' Agnes said. 'I watched my own mother and father—'

'You *watched*,' Juno cut in. 'You watched! Don't pretend to know what it's like, just because you *watched*. You're perfect, Agnes, and yet you still consider yourself the victim.'

She took a breath, and Agnes saw how her ribs rose and fell, lopsided and painful.

'Let me tell you what it's like. When you have tuberculosis, your life as you know it is over. But here at Hedoné, that doesn't matter. We can do whatever we want here with the time we have left, and there are no repercussions, I could do anything, and nobody would care. I could kill myself right now and no one would mourn me.' Her voice cracked, and she lifted her face to the ceiling as if trying to stop the spill of tears.

'That's not true,' Agnes said gently. 'What about your family? Your father must care about you a great deal, he's putting so much money into Hedoné.'

'He doesn't care about *me*,' she said, her voice trembling. 'He cares about what others think, that's all. He cares about tax breaks and titles.' She gave a sniff, dabbing at her nose again. 'What Christian is doing here is revolutionary. We guests have everything we need. Everything we could ever want. Here, *we* are the normal ones. Nobody stares at us like we're freaks, turning their lip up in disgust if we so much as cough. So what if our doctor asks us for something small in return? I'm far too unwell to have a child of my own anyway. I saw what happened to poor Sybil when she found herself pregnant. That baby killed her. It sucked the life from her like a parasite. By the time Christian realised what was going on and tried to save her, it was too late, the damage was done.' She broke off, a tear tracking down one cheek, and she mopped it away, leaving a streak of red on her skin.

'But you don't know what might be around the corner,' Agnes said. 'There are ground-breaking new treatments happening all the time, Juno. I heard the delegates speak of a vaccine . . .'

'What use is a vaccine when you're already ill?' Juno hissed. 'And besides, what Christian is doing, it *is* ground-breaking. Don't you see? He's cutting out the rot, ensuring the next generation has a healthy start, born only from healthy parents.'

'It's wrong,' Agnes said.

'Oh, get off your high horse, Mrs Fairhaven. Right and wrong is never black and white, you know that more than most.'

'What do you mean?' Agnes said.

'You, who deliberately put yourself in Christian's path when you were in France. "Oh, Doctor Fairhaven, woe is me, please help my poor, sick mother." He told me all about it. Such a wanton act of desperation. Oh, how we laughed.'

Agnes felt suddenly lightheaded, trying to contain her horror at everything Juno was saying. 'What happened to the first Mrs

Fairhaven, Juno?' she said quietly. 'She didn't die of TB, did she?'

'Did you hear that listening in at doors, too?' Juno said, the ghost of a smile on her face. 'We should start a club, you and I. You know, in another world, I think we might have quite liked one another.'

'Did somebody kill her?' Agnes pressed.

Juno's eyes flashed. 'These aren't my secrets to tell, *Mrs Fairhaven*,' she said.

Was that a threat, Agnes thought? 'Did Meredith Fairhaven even have TB?'

Juno held her gaze, her brown eyes trembling. 'No,' she said at last.

Agnes took a step back. 'Does anyone else here know about these sterilisations?'

'No. Of course not.'

'And he's doing it without the patients' permission?'

'Permission?' Juno laughed, but it sounded different to her usual musical tone. It was a cold, calculated crack of pent-up frustration. 'If you learnt one thing from those meetings with the delegates, it's that we are worthless. We're women, Agnes. And worse, we're dying. We are the dregs of society. *Permission* indeed.'

She leant in suddenly, so close that Agnes could smell the decay on her breath, like the cloying scent of the lilies that she had tried to ban so many weeks before.

'None of the people here should have children. They would be too ill to look after them, and in all likelihood, their babies would be born with it. Have you ever seen children with this disease, Agnes? No, it's better this way, for all of us.'

'But tuberculosis isn't hereditary. Both my parents had it, and I never caught it.'

'You're an anomaly,' Juno spat. 'That's partly why Christian chose you.'

Chose. That word again. 'What do you mean?' she said, a hardness in her voice.

Juno leant back, resting her head against the wall. 'Do you know, in America, they sterilise those deemed unsuitable to procreate, just like this? Ill people, disabled people. In Germany they're about to pass a law to prevent people with bad genes marrying those with good. The Marital Health Law, they're calling it. But Doctor Fairhaven is going to do something far more ground-breaking even than this.' Her eyes sparkled, glistening with tears.

'And what is that?'

'He's saving my life,' Juno said.

'You mean, he's *curing* you?'

But Christian had told her that Juno could not be cured. Perhaps he simply spun different lies to different women, catching them all in his web eventually.

Juno gave her a withering look. 'Nothing so half-hearted,' she said, and Agnes's heart skipped a beat. 'No, Doctor Fairhaven is giving me a new chance at life.' She drew herself up, looking pointedly at Agnes.

'I don't follow.'

But Juno only put a finger to her lips, then pressed it to Agnes's own. Agnes pulled away, recoiling at the touch.

'Christian's right,' Juno said. 'It's probably best that you don't know. Not yet, at least.' There was a gleam of something like fanatical zeal in her eyes. 'It's been fun, this exchange. Like I said, I've wanted to tell you for a while, just to see your reaction. But make sure you keep our little chat just between us, won't you? You wouldn't want to suddenly have to leave Hedoné for any reason. After all, there's nothing out there for you now, is there, Agnes? I've checked. You're a real lone wolf now your mother's gone. No one would miss you if you suddenly went a little . . . quiet, would they? Understand?'

Juno held her gaze, and Agnes knew that she had her. She nodded, her face set.

'Good. Now, do help me up off this damn cold floor. I really don't want piles on top of everything else.'

She extended her hand, and Agnes took it, a looming feeling of terror beginning to set in around her heart.

Chapter Thirty-Nine

Agnes stumbled out of the lift. She had left Juno down in the basement, dabbing at her sore nose. The entrance hall was deserted. It must still be early. She stood at the open front door, looking out over the grounds. It was quite dark, that ghostly lilac blue of pre-dawn. She couldn't go back to the cottage now, Christian would see the truth written plain as day all over her face. She walked slowly down the steps. After a moment's hesitation, she set off in the direction of the memorial garden.

As she broke through the pines into the little glade, Agnes came to a stop. The sky, though still dotted with stars, was lightening into morning. The grass was bathed in dew, the barely visible shadows of the pine trees long and spindly, like reaching fingers stroking the memorials, bringing comfort to the dead. A thrush was perched on Elizabeth Thackeray's memorial, tapping a snail shell against the hard stone. Agnes went to her mother's grave, looking down at the smooth, solid slab.

'What should I do?' she whispered urgently. 'What should I do, Mother?'

Nearby, the grave of Meredith Fairhaven looked a little unkempt, the grass longer and less well cared for than she remembered. She thought of that beribboned note she had found there, and suddenly, without knowing how she got there, Agnes was on her knees in the dew-wet grass, scrabbling at the ground, her fingers teasing apart the damp green blades.

Something caught under her thumb, and she pulled back to get a better look. It was another piece of paper, not rolled up this time, but folded tightly and part buried in the soil. Carefully, she extracted it from the ground.

Her hands shook as she unfolded it.

Be patient, it read in an unfamiliar hand, *I will come for you soon.*

Agnes's heart began to stutter in her chest. She glanced over her shoulder to check she was alone. The glade was silent save for the sound of the thrush, tapping the snail on the stone, the crack as the shell began to break. She studied the note. It was not the same childlike hand that she had seen Iso write. It was hurried and fluid, small dots of spilled ink smattering the paper. She ran her fingers through the grass, searching for the previous note, but it was no longer there.

I shall wait for her to write back first, Iso had said. Not a colourful imagination, then, but plain fact. Was it really possible that this note was from Meredith? That she could actually be alive? But this stone marked her grave. The note was far more likely to be written by one of the staff, taking pity on the little girl out of some twisted sense of loyalty, or perhaps even by Christian, trying to protect his daughter from the full impact of her grief.

Agnes gave her head a shake. If Meredith *was* alive, then why was Christian stopping her from seeing her daughter? Her mind ran over all the possibilities, trying to make sense of this new mystery among all the others hidden in this house of horrors.

She heaved a deep, fearful breath, knowing there was only one way to determine whether the first Mrs Fairhaven was definitely deceased. Tucking the note into her pocket, she thrust her fingers round the edge of Meredith's plaque, digging her nails into the soft soil, and began tugging at the stone, trying to lift it up. She felt it shift slightly under her grip, and she pushed her fingers deeper underneath, pulling with all her might.

The plaque moved a little more, and she hefted her weight against it, levering it up until it was resting on one edge. She let it drop away, falling onto the grass next to the grave. Where it had been, the rectangle of soil was dark and damp, twisted with white shoots. Agnes stared at it for a split second, then began scrabbling at the earth. Clawing her fingers into the soil, she tore away the shoots, digging down until at last she felt something hard and smooth beneath her fingers. Carefully, she scooped away the earth, revealing the top of a burial urn.

Agnes sat back on her knees, reality rushing back. What on earth was she doing? Had she really thought there would be no urn here? Of course Meredith was buried here. Of course she was dead. What madness had overtaken her?

She looked down at her hands, plastered with dirt, at the black earth under her fingernails, and shame crashed over her. Everything she'd found out in the basement had skewed her sense of judgement, made her start questioning things too forcefully. What sort of a person dug up their husband's late wife's grave?

She ran a finger over the top of the urn. It was a simple, inexpensive piece of pottery, and as she stroked it, the lid moved fractionally, the sound so loud in the garden that she flinched. She went to set it back properly, then paused, and instead, took the urn's lid between her fingers. With mounting dread, Agnes lifted it up, peering inside.

It was empty.

A frisson of fear swept over her. She replaced the lid, scrabbling the earth back over the urn, packing it down with the palms of her hands. With effort, she lifted the memorial stone back into place, glancing behind her again, fear raising the hairs on her neck. She polished away the smears of soil on its surface and wiped her hands on the wet grass to remove the worst of the earth, then she got to her feet, her knees soaked with dew.

She barely registered the walk back to the house. When she emerged into the grounds, she heard voices drifting out from the open dining room doors. Breakfast must have begun. Not wanting to be seen in her muddied attire, Agnes followed the path round to the rear of the house, heading for the staff entrance.

She hurried down the dark little corridor, increasingly aware of her sweaty, dirt-smeared appearance. Passing Iso's door, she thought of the little girl inside, of the secret communes she was having with a mother who was not really dead.

Why had Christian lied? Was it he who had buried the empty urn? Had anything he told Agnes been true? What had Juno meant when she talked of the cure as being half-hearted? Simply that it was rare that it worked, or that it wasn't really a cure at all?

She brushed these questions aside, focusing on the task in hand. Matron's room must be down here somewhere. She was just about to start knocking on doors, when she heard a door a little further down open, and conscious of her appearance, Agnes drew back into the shadows, her heart ticking.

A woman in a bathrobe emerged, clutching a towel to her chest.

'Matron,' Agnes said, stepping out of the shadows, and the woman turned, her mouth opening in surprise.

For a brief moment, Agnes thought she had the wrong person.

Without her mask and veil, the matron looked entirely different. The lips that Agnes had always imagined to be thin and sneering beneath the cotton were in reality full and kind. They transformed the woman's face.

'Mrs Fairhaven,' she whispered. 'What are you doing here?'

'I need to talk to you,' Agnes said in a hushed voice. She saw the nurse take in her muddied, sweaty appearance. Quickly, the matron opened her bedroom door again and ushered her inside.

The room was small and cramped, a mirror image of Iso's. A single bed, neatly made, filled most of the space.

'Here,' Matron said, going to a small basin in one corner and filling it with steaming water.

She handed Agnes a nailbrush, and Agnes began to scrub at her nails, trying to remove every last trace of Meredith's grave.

'He's sterilising the women,' she whispered.

'What?' The woman's voice was a gasp, and looking up, Agnes caught her expression in the mirror above the basin, frozen with fear.

'The S in the notes. It stands for sterilisation.'

'But . . .' Matron's voice trailed off. She wrapped her arms about herself, those familiar sinewy chords of muscle flexing.

'I still don't understand it all. But there's more. I've just been to the memorial garden.'

Matron's eyes widened. She looked at the water in the basin, black with dirt. 'Mrs Fairhaven,' she whispered. 'What have you done?'

'Meredith Fairhaven's burial urn contains no ashes.'

The nurse sank down onto the bed, staring at Agnes in the mirror.

'I don't believe she had tuberculosis,' Agnes continued. 'Isobel writes to her. Leaves notes at the grave. She writes back. I think she's still alive.' She turned from the basin, droplets of water spattering the floor. 'I'm concerned for the guests, Matron, and I'm concerned for

Iso. And myself, and for you. I . . . I don't know what to do.'

In the pale morning light washing in from the small window, Matron's eyes met hers, reflecting back the mounting horror Agnes could feel beginning to flood through her.

The nurse got to her feet, offering her a towel, and she took it gratefully.

'There's something else you should know,' Matron said, her expression grave, and Agnes felt suddenly very tired. She put a hand to her temple, pressing at the insistent ache there.

'What is it?'

'I have reason to believe Doctor increased your mother's arsenic and opium prescription without my knowledge in the hours leading up to her death.'

'Arsenic?' Agnes said in alarm. 'But . . . isn't that poisonous?'

'Yes, in large doses, but we use it often in the patients' treatment here. Of course, he doesn't need to run everything by me, he is free to care for his patients as he wishes. But . . .' She took a breath, as if she was trying to work out what words to use.

Horror filled Agnes's head like a white blanket, blotting out everything else. 'But why would Christian do that?' she stammered.

Matron didn't reply.

Agnes looked around at the room, trying to force her thoughts into the semblance of a plan. At last, she said, 'I need to write a letter. Can you help me?'

The nurse went to a small dressing table, opening a drawer and taking out a piece of letter paper and an envelope. Agnes nodded her thanks. Sitting down, she picked up a pen and began to write. When she had finished, she signed and folded the letter, slipping it into the envelope. She sealed it closed, realising at the last moment that she didn't know the address.

'Here, let me,' Matron said, taking the letter. 'Doctor is careful about what correspondence leaves Hedoné. He has been known to open guests' outgoing mail before. I can post it next time I'm out of the grounds. Where shall I send it?'

Gratitude overwhelmed Agnes. 'Do you know the framed certificate that Christian has on the wall of his office? The one detailing the medical school where he undertook his training?'

'Of course.'

'It needs to go directly to the doctor named on that certificate.'

The matron nodded, slipping the letter into the pocket of her bathrobe.

'Thank you, Matron,' Agnes said. 'You cannot know what this kindness means to me. I must go, before I'm missed.'

As she got up, through the small window, she caught sight of the pine trees that led to the memorial garden, and her thoughts went to those two girls, dead in the woods, to the lies in the patient notes in the basement, the sterilisations and the secrets. Agnes thought of Leopold Rackham locked away in the infirmary, so recently deceased, and the poor artist, Georgie, still trapped down there now, and a swirl of dizziness overtook her. She gripped the edge of the table with her fingers to steady herself, her eyes on the pine trees outside.

All these little trails, each one a clue in itself, and yet she was still no closer to understanding the meaning behind it all. What lengths, exactly, was her husband capable of going to? And why?

Chapter Forty

The next few weeks passed by like a dream, a heavy malaise of fear cloaking Agnes wherever she went. The guests were busy planning a party for Guy Fawkes Night under Juno's careful direction, but the idea of celebrating anything felt absurd to her now, as if a veil had been drawn back, revealing the worst of society, the darkest, blackest rot running through its core. She viewed the guests' excitement with detached interest, her thoughts saturated by what she had learnt in the memorial garden and in the basement, her eyes idly flicking over each patient, wondering how many of these women had already been sterilised, how many were scheduled to be soon.

One bitterly cold day, after Christian had left for work, Agnes sat at her dressing table, gazing into the mirror, trying to decide what to do. There had been no reply to the letter she'd sent with Matron's help. She tried to push away the little shred of doubt that Matron had even sent it at all.

It occurred to her that she ought to be afraid of her husband. On the surface, he was no different, and this in itself was the most chilling thing of all. She wasn't sure if Juno had kept her side of the bargain and not told him of their exchange in the basement, but if she had, his behaviour certainly hadn't wavered towards her. He was his usual thoughtful, chivalrous self, not letting her lift a finger. Sometimes, Agnes wished she hadn't told him she was pregnant, and yet, she felt that it was this knowledge that was keeping her safe somehow, though what she meant by that she couldn't explain.

As she stared hard at herself in the mirror, she wished she could go back, could step into the life of Agnes Templeton from months before and warn her to stay away from the handsome, charismatic man she would meet in France. But she had never been prone to fancy. *She* had got herself into this position, and it was down to her to find her own way out.

She wished she had someone to talk to outside of Hedoné. Someone in the real world who could give her an unbiased opinion on everything that was happening here. But Mother had always required so much of Agnes's attention that she'd never really cultivated any friendships. And even if she had, with the knowledge that Christian was monitoring the outgoing correspondence, she would not have been able to write to them freely anyway.

She longed to talk to Sippie, to tell her everything that had happened since they last spoke in the music room. She knew she had a duty to tell the guests the truth if she was to help those that were left, and speaking to Sippie would set this in motion. But each time she'd set out to find her, Juno appeared, hovering over her like a bird of prey about to make its kill.

That evening when Christian came home, Agnes locked herself in the bathroom, feigning morning sickness. She had been experiencing nausea often, so it wasn't difficult. Though how much of it was really related to the pregnancy, and how much her current situation, she did not quite know.

'Are you sure you're all right?' Christian said through the door.

'Honestly, Christian,' she said brightly. 'Women the world over

278

have borne this sort of sickness for centuries before me. I'm made of strong stuff — you say it often yourself. Go on up to dinner without me. There's no need for you to miss out just because I'm a little off colour.'

Once he was gone, Agnes unlocked the bathroom door. She waited a few minutes, giving Christian enough time to reach the house, before slipping out of the back door. Here, instead of taking the usual path towards the statues, she set out in the opposite direction.

She walked for about a mile, pushing through the trees as they became more and more wild and unkempt. Deep in the thickest part of the woods, she thought she spied Isobel, far off in the distance.

It was not unusual to see her out in the grounds; the girl was always flitting around on some private mission or other. But it struck Agnes that she looked different, somehow. She wasn't climbing or running, or doing any of the usual frenetic activities that occupied her time. Instead, she was simply standing there, her head drooped like a wilting flower.

Agnes paused, pulled in two directions. It concerned her to see her stepdaughter like this. Had something happened? But she reminded herself that she was on a mission of her own tonight, and with one last quick, guilty backward glance, she pushed on through the trees.

Eventually, she came to the fence that marked Hedoné's boundary. It was higher than she had imagined, at least eight feet, with barbed wire coiled at the top. With one hand trailing it, Agnes began to walk the perimeter of the sanatorium's grounds, searching for a weak spot, but there were no fallen trees nearby, no breaks in the metal links like the fence near the memorial garden.

She came at last to the wrought iron gates, and here she stopped, looking up at the towering, twisted image of the hare entwined within them, its beady eye staring accusingly at her. She tried to push the gate open, to no avail. In frustration, Agnes ducked back into the woods, retracing her steps to the cottage before Christian came home to find her missing.

The next morning, she considered feigning sleep in order to avoid speaking to him, but she knew that she must broach a difficult subject, and Christian was always at his most receptive early in the morning.

'Darling,' she said sleepily, pretending she had just woken.

Christian was buttoning up his shirt in the mirror. He looked at her in its reflection, eyebrows raised.

'I was wondering, I'm feeling so sick at night at the moment, and I get so hot and restless. I thought perhaps I might move into the second bedroom for a while.'

'The nursery?' Christian said, adjusting his tie with a frown.

'Just for a short time,' she pushed on. 'I'd feel better knowing I wasn't disturbing you at all hours of the night. I feel so terribly guilty, when you have such important work to do. I'd hate to think I was endangering the guests' health with my own neediness.'

Christian conceded reluctantly, as she knew he would. She supposed that now they'd succeeded in conceiving a child, he did not have the need for her in his own bed anymore.

That first night, Agnes lay on her own, her relief at the distance between them tempered by the fact that she still hadn't got any closer to working out what to do. The obvious answer was to call the police. But Hedoné's only telephone was located in Christian's office, and although she had tried the door on a number of occasions, it appeared her husband had learnt from her last foray inside, and now kept it locked at all times.

On an unseasonably warm evening, the end of the summer heat held as if in the palm of a divine hand, Agnes made her excuses at dinner once more. Alone in the cottage, she paced between the four walls, feeling like a caged tiger, until the heat of the open fire and the claustrophobia of the place got too much, and she rushed out.

Out on the lawn she came to a breathless stop amid the statues. She could smell the heady scent of pine sap on the wind, mixed in with the smoke from the fires that had been lit in all the bedrooms to keep the cold at bay.

A sudden burst of voices, and she saw the guests spilling out from the dining room, making their way down to the lake. Dinner must already be over. Agnes hovered among the statues, hoping that the dusky light would keep her hidden. Peering round the statue of the ballerina, she watched them all with a keen sense of guilt as they settled in deckchairs and on rugs, wrapped up in furs and stoles. They made a beautiful tableau, silhouetted against the lake, and she was reminded of her first night here, seeing them from the window of her quarantine room. Sure enough, a discordant flutter of notes drifted up from their midst, a saxophone and a flute, the sound magical in the gloam.

A voice joined the music, a long, mournful note, piercing the misty air.

Sippie, Agnes thought.

She had never heard her friend sing before. The sound was more beautiful, more poignant than she could ever have imagined. She could hear in it her pain and sadness, the voice melodic and husky and carefree. All too soon, the song drew to a close, and silence fell over the grounds again, as if the sound had bewitched everything it touched.

How would Agnes find the words to tell these people what she had found out? Exhaustion wracked her body, draining her of energy, and she gazed unseeingly down at her feet, waiting for the feeling to pass.

'Agnes,' Sippie called out, spying her through the statues. 'Come and join us.'

Agnes fixed a smile onto her face and started forward. As she approached the lake she saw how they each turned to her, their kind, smiling faces warmed by the flickering flames of a nearby torch, and she felt an immense, bittersweet fondness for them all. Darkness was creeping in, and she sat down on the jetty, gazing out over the lake. The last of the waterlilies rested on the surface, the flowers tightly closed for the night, a low blanket of mist rolling towards them across the water.

Let it envelop me, she thought, *let it take me away from all of this.*

Sippie sat down next to her, wrapping a blanket around Agnes's chill shoulders. 'Look at that sky,' she sighed, gazing up at the immense black above them.

Agnes followed her gaze. It was beautiful, stars dotted across the black like specks of spilled salt thrown superstitiously over a shoulder.

'*Per aspera ad astra,*' she murmured sadly.

'Through hardship to the stars,' Sippie translated, her voice soft. 'I stayed at a sanatorium in France with that name: Ad Astra — *To the Stars.* Believe me, I'd really rather not be reminded that I'm headed to heaven sooner than I'd like.'

'It's easy to believe in the idea of heaven on a night like this,' Agnes said.

'Oh, I don't know. To believe in heaven is to believe in God, and what sort of a god would choose to kill people in this way?'

The other guests murmured in agreement, and the night drifted into silence. Agnes's gaze was fixed on the mist as it made its slow progress towards them across the water. The tops of the distant pine trees poked up from it like the myriad turrets of fairy tale towers. As the moon rose higher, the rest of the guests began to retire until it was just her and Sippie left. A waterbird screeched a throaty alarm call from somewhere nearby. Sippie put a cigarette to her lips, lighting it. Breathing out smoke, she passed it to Agnes. After a brief pause, she took it.

As the smoke hit her lungs, it made her feel lightheaded, and she embraced the feeling, wondering if it might make her float away with the mist. She lay back on the rug, sensing the echo of the sun's heat in the wooden boards beneath, warming her back. She gazed up at the great bowl of the night sky above her.

'Have you any news on Georgie?' Sippie said.

Agnes stirred, pulling her thoughts back. She had been so distracted by what she'd found in that room in the basement and in the memorial garden, she had barely given the young man a thought.

'I saw him, down in the infirmary a few days ago,' she said.

'How was he?'

'He looked peaceful. He was sleeping.' She fell silent, wondering how much to tell her, Juno's words of warning ringing in her head. Pulling herself up, she stared out over the lake. 'Matron told me something about my mother. It appears Christian gave her some very strong medication that may have played a part in her death.'

'What?' Sippie said in shock. 'But, why?'

'I don't know.' Agnes gazed up at the moon, its face wide open and innocent. 'Those two women whose graves are in the memorial garden, I've . . . heard . . . that they didn't have tuberculosis, and yet both of them died here under Christian's care. I've since found out that Leopold Rackham died too.'

Out of the darkness, she heard Sippie's intake of breath.

'It was a while ago, and I can only assume Christian didn't tell the guests because he didn't want to upset you all.' She shook her head, knowing how pathetic this sounded.

'Do you think the doctor had something to do with it?' Sippie whispered.

'I don't know.'

'Have you talked to him about any of this?'

Agnes shook her head. 'I'm frightened to,' she admitted. 'But something's going on, Sippie. Juno . . .' She stopped, cursing herself for mentioning her name.

'So, Juno knows too?' Sippie said, her face immobile. 'That makes sense.'

'Please, you mustn't let on I told you.' Agnes paused, unsure whether to go on, but who else could she tell? Who else might believe her? 'There's something between her and Christian. I thought they were having an affair, but it's more complicated than that. She told me Christian was doing something ground-breaking, but she refused to tell me what it was.'

'That sounds like Juno,' Sippie said, her voice hard as polished gold. 'She always did like to taunt. I'd wager she was the sort of child who liked to pull the wings off butterflies. Do you think poor Georgie has anything to do with all this?'

'I don't know. In truth, I have no idea what to think anymore.'

They fell into silence, gazing out over the water.

'Sippie,' Agnes said suddenly. 'Please don't mention any of this to the other guests. Not yet. I don't want to worry them.'

'I won't. Believe me, Agnes, I want answers as much as you do, but until we know for sure, I won't hurt them unduly.'

Across the lake, the wind caught in the trees, the sound eerily musical. In the distance, the sleepy crows looked down on them.

'A murder of crows,' Sippie whispered as they shuffled softly in the bare branches, their ragged wings dark and cloak-like, as if they concealed a flock of hidden truths.

Chapter Forty-One

The Filigree Lens

Isobel should be in bed, but nobody checks on her after nine o'clock. She has not been up to the quarantine floor since Mrs Templeton passed away. She cannot bear to see that bed, the sheets stripped away, and with them, every trace of the sweet old lady who she had begun to love.

She has felt sandwiched between death recently, trapped twixt the basement floor, where Mr Rackham died, and the quarantine floor. She hasn't been down to the infirmary for days, not since Mr Rackham went. It has felt too empty, too lonely a place to visit, and so her night-time wanderings have been constrained to the ground floor, slipping from room to room, standing barefoot in the guests' bedrooms, watching them sleep.

But tonight, she feels strong enough to head to the basement once more. Even now, after so many years without her mother, she still holds out hope that when she reaches the infirmary, she will find her there, waiting for her. It has been so long that she is beginning to forget what her mother looks like, to mix up her face with her stepmother's.

She remembers the day her stepmother visited her bedroom, the soft, gentle kiss on the top of her head. The only other person who kisses Isobel is Juno, but her kisses are cold and awkward and loaded with meaning. This kiss was different. It was infused with something Iso hasn't felt for a long time. She thinks it might be love.

Tonight, when she reaches the infirmary door, there is someone in there again, tucked up in bed. She sees long dark hair splayed across the pillow, and her heart misses a beat.

Could it be her mother? Could she have found her way back to the world that Iso inhabits after all this time?

She strains to see through the darkness. As her eyes grow used to the gloom, she sees that the hair isn't black, after all, but a muted red, knotted and dark at the roots with sweat, and for a moment, she feels only disappointment and anger. But any sadness is soon wiped away, replaced with pity. Quietly, she opens the door and steps into the room. She recognises this man. His name is Georgie. Not long ago, he asked her to sit for a portrait, and once, when he first arrived, he presented her with a little mouse that he had carved from a piece of wood.

Up close, he looks younger than she remembers, barely a man at all. He is shaking. He has paint under his fingernails, and his Adam's apple bobs up and down as he shivers and struggles to breathe. She puts the tip of a finger to a freckle on his cheekbone, and he opens an eye.

'I'm not a ghost,' she whispers, and he chuckles, a bubbly, wet laugh. By his side is a small enamel basin. In it, she sees what looks like raspberry jam, deep red and clotted, but she knows it is not. It smells of iron and decay, and it makes her stomach turn.

Pulling her eyes from the bowl, she takes a little pot of real jam from her pocket. She always keeps some on her now, just in case.

'Would you like some?' she asks him.

'I'd rather some opiates,' he whispers, still shivering vigorously. Their faces are inches apart and she can smell that smell that she should be used to by now, an underlying putrefaction, and yet it is too dreadful, too evil ever to grow familiar with.

He lifts a juddering hand and points to the cabinet on the wall, the one with the skull and crossbones on it. 'In there,' he says.

Obediently, she goes to the cabinet and stands on tiptoes, producing a key from around her neck, one of many she has procured on her nightly wanderings. She is familiar with this cabinet's contents, and she studies the array of bottles now, like sweets in a sweetshop.

'The little brown one,' he says, trying to lift his head, but it flops back on the pillow. 'On the bottom row,' he adds, but Isobel's hand is already reaching for it. 'I'll need a syringe and a needle and some water.' He is whispering, but his voice carries across the silent room. It is soft and lyrical like a song. Like a lullaby.

It is nice to feel useful. She finds the correct implements, her small hands closing over a silver filigree magnifying lens she has seen her father use to look into peoples' eyes. It will come in handy for examining insect wings, she thinks as she tucks it away in her pocket, and brings the requested items to the bed, holding the bottle still while he draws up some water. His hands are shaking so hard that he nearly pricks her with the needle. She wonders, as he mixes up the medicine, if perhaps he is a doctor, too, so proficient is he in his work.

'Thank you,' he says, glancing up at her, and then his eyes widen, hollow in his face. 'Aoife,' he breathes, his gaze locked onto her, eyes filling with tears.

Her name is not Aoife, but in this place, she has been many people. A daughter, a friend. She does not know who Aoife is, but something in the desperate way he is looking at her makes her nod.

'Ah Aoife, how strange that we should both find ourselves here.' His face grows suddenly tight with fear. 'You are not sick, little Aoife? You do not have the consumption, too?'

She gives her head a quick shake, and contentment spreads through his face in a flush of fever. He lays his head back on the pillow.

'Tell me, little Aoife, is old Bessie still producing much milk?' He licks his lips. 'I can taste it still. They give us milk here, but it's nothing compared to Bessie's. I remember it so well. Warm and sweet.' He smacks his lips, but his mouth is dry and it makes a terrible cracking sound. 'Do you remember, you used to curl up with her in the hay, squeezing the warm milk straight from the udder?' Before she can answer, he carries on. 'I wonder sometimes why I left, when heaven was right there.' He wipes his eyes, as if he is crying. They all cry down here, in the end. 'Ah, Aoife, how I have missed you. It is such a painful thing, missing the people you love.'

Isobel understands this. The pain of missing her mother is sometimes so execrable that it feels as if it will eclipse her. There is something about this man, about this room, that encourages confession, as if they are in a church, not down in the bowels of a house.

'Sometimes when I come down here, I hope I might see my mother,' she tells him. 'She was in here, you see, a long time ago. But I am glad you are here today. I am glad I have been able to help you.'

The man turns his head on the pillow, holding her gaze. His eyes are a strange, milky blue. 'I believe I shall see our mother soon, too, Aoife,' he says.

He takes the girl's hand, a quick, sharp movement that makes her jump. She tries to pull away, but his grip is strong, and something about his face scares her. Jerking her hand from his, she crosses the infirmary, panic making her run. She slips out of the door. Safe on the other side, she takes one last look at him through the window, her quivering, damp eyes on the flash of a needle as he presses it into his skin. With a stirring of dread, she turns and flees.

Chapter Forty-Two

Sippie bade Agnes goodnight, leaving her at the lake's edge to walk back to the house. Alone in the dark on the jetty, Agnes pulled the blanket tighter about herself, not wanting to go back to the cottage. Her breath misted into the air, mingling with the fog over the lake, and from behind her, she thought she heard the sound of a stifled cry.

'Hallo?' she called, peering into the darkness, a crackle of fear brushing her skin.

A small figure appeared, running towards her across the grass. As it drew closer, Agnes recognised Isobel. She was wearing a thin nightdress, her bare feet sending up a spray of dew in her wake as she skidded to a breathless stop on the jetty.

'Iso! What are you doing out here at this time? You'll catch your death.'

The little girl didn't answer. She swiped a hand through her tangled hair, her eyes catching the moonlight, and Agnes saw that she was crying.

'Whatever is the matter? Come, sit with me.' She patted the jetty. Pulling the blanket from her own shoulders, she wrapped it around the shivering girl, rubbing a hand over her back to encourage some warmth into her. She could feel Iso's spine beneath her nightdress. The little girl leant into her, and Agnes felt her tears begin again, wracking her body.

'Dear, whatever can the matter be?' But Isobel just pressed her face more insistently into Agnes's side. 'Come,' Agnes said, 'it can't be that bad.'

'They all die,' Iso whispered.

A shimmer of fright pattered across Agnes's shoulders. 'Who?'

'In the infirmary.' Her voice was muffled against Agnes's dress. 'I go there sometimes.' She pulled her small face away. 'I feel safe there. You won't tell Papa, will you? I look after them, you see, but they all die.' Her face screwed up again as tears overcame her once more.

'Of course I won't tell. But what do you mean, Iso? Who dies?'

The little girl sniffed. '*You* won't die, will you?'

'Me? Die? Of course not. I shall be here for you always.' She wasn't sure this was the right way to go about things, but Iso needed comfort at this moment, not truths.

'The man died,' Iso sniffed.

'What man?'

'Leo,' she whispered. 'I tried to help him; I promise. I gave him jam to make him feel better, but he died all the same. He said it was all lies, that there's no cure. And he was right, wasn't he? Wasn't he?'

The air around them seemed to sing with terror. Isobel scrambled to her feet, her breath coming in quick, panicked gasps.

'Mr Rackham said there wasn't a cure?' Agnes said.

Iso nodded.

What had Juno said, when she'd asked her if Christian was curing her? *Nothing so half-hearted.* Had it really all been lies, then? This whole place based on that single, unending lie?

Iso sniffed. 'Papa said he would fix Leo. He said he knew how.'

She was panting now, great, heaving sobs, and Agnes scrambled to her knees, reaching out for the child. 'Papa told me he would fix them all. But I watched him, I watched what he did, and they died all the same.'

Agnes got to her feet, crouching down in front of the child, gripping her thin shoulders. 'What do you mean?' she said carefully. 'You watched Papa do what?'

Iso tried to pull away from her.

'Isobel, I want you to think very carefully about this. What is your papa doing?'

'Everyone leaves,' Iso said, and her voice was infused with sadness. 'Mama left. She stopped writing back.'

A tinge of guilt crept over Agnes. The note, tightly folded, that she had found at the grave. It must still be in her skirt pocket. 'But she's alive, isn't she?' she urged. 'Your mother?'

Iso's little face paled even more. 'She told me I mustn't say anything,' she whispered. 'She told me it was our secret.'

'But you know you can trust me. I would never tell, I promise. Where is your mother, Iso?'

The girl was taking little gasps of air between her sobs now. She took a step back, her heel touching the edge of the jetty.

'She said she would come for me. But she hasn't . . . she didn't . . .' She shifted back again, and Agnes flung an arm out, catching her by the wrist.

'You must try to calm down,' she said, more forcefully than she meant to. 'You're working yourself into a hysteria.'

'I'm scared,' Iso whispered between shuddering breaths. 'I'm scared, Mama.' And then she turned to the lake, the blanket dropping from her shoulders, and launched herself into the water.

Agnes stood for an agonising moment, her brain not quite

registering what had happened. She turned to the grounds, to the house beyond.

'Help!' she called. But the house was silent, cloaked in darkness.

She turned back to the lake. The lily pads had closed over the water again, concealing the place where Iso had jumped.

'Iso!' Agnes called, scouring the lake. 'Isobel!' But there was no sign of her, and knowing there was nothing else for it. Agnes took a deep breath, and dived into the water.

She knew in an instant that she had made a terrible mistake. The cold was like nothing she had ever experienced before. She was aware of an explosion of bubbles around her as her breath was expelled from her body. Disorientated, Agnes twisted, clawing, swirling in the great dark chasm of the lake, trying to work out which way was up, her lungs roaring to breathe. Her hair had unpinned itself in the impact of the dive, and ribbons of it plastered themselves to her neck, clutching at her throat. Her foot touched the bottom of the lake, soft and silty, and she kicked down to propel herself upwards, only to find her toes disappearing into the mud. She tried to peer through the murky depths, searching desperately for Isobel, and bright spots began popping in front of her eyes.

The coldness of the water was like a violent scream that drove through her brain, pushing her down, down, and she let it, her hands and legs splaying outwards as the searing in her lungs dissolved into numbness. As if in a dream, she caught sight of a hand, ghostly and white, a ribbon of weed laced between the fingers. Her mind finally realised what she was seeing and she reached out. With a surge of effort she took hold of it, kicking downwards, and propelling herself and her delicate cargo up.

Up, through the silty water. Up, towards the stars, and she thought to herself, *ad astra, I am coming*, and then she was lying on the lake's edge, taking great gasping breaths like a fish out of water. Beside her, the tiny fragile body of Isobel lay, her thin chest rising and falling, her silver eyelashes splayed with beads of water. 'Thank God,' Agnes said between ragged breaths. 'Oh, thank God.'

Chapter Forty-Three

Agnes awoke in an unfamiliar bed. Something was clawing at her mouth and nose, hissing and sucking at the flesh there, and for a moment she thought she was still below the water, some strange monstrous lake dweller attached to her face, sucking out her soul.

Matron's sharp, thin face appeared, eyebrows raised. The black little eyes that Agnes remembered so well were soft with kindness. Agnes tried to speak, and the nurse pulled what she realised must be an oxygen mask down from where it rested over her nose and mouth.

'There, there,' Matron said. Her voice, like her eyes, was gentle.

'What happened?' Agnes asked, her own voice thick and groggy.

'You saved her, Mrs Fairhaven. You saved little Isobel.'

Agnes closed her eyes in relief.

Her head pounded, and there was a pressure in her eye sockets. Deep inside her belly she felt a heavy dragging feeling, pulling at her tired muscles. She put a hand to her head and found a strand of weed clinging there.

'Where am I?' she asked.

'You're in Austen,' Matron said, placing a thermometer under her tongue.

'Is Iso . . .' she tried to say, but the words got lost around the glass instrument.

'She's all right,' Matron said. 'She was in the infirmary overnight, but they've just brought her up to Mansfield.' She took the thermometer from her mouth, securing the oxygen mask back in place. 'Now, you must rest.'

Exhaustion coursed through Agnes, tugging at her eyelids. As she closed her eyes, her final thought was of Iso just before she had thrown herself into the lake.

She called me Mama, Agnes thought, before her body and soul gave into the delicious pull of sleep.

She was awoken by a quiet knock on the door. Through sluggish, heavy eyelids she saw her husband stride in. Fear and panic threatened to overtake her as she recalled the conversation she had with Iso last night. What had Christian done to Leopold Rackham? Could he really have murdered him, as Iso had implied?

He was wearing last night's dinner suit, the jacket removed, the shirt wrinkled. Tiredness pulled at Agnes, rolling in waves, numbing the fear, and she felt her eyes close again involuntarily.

'How is she?' she heard him say in a hushed voice.

'She has a fever.' Matron now. 'She'll live. She was lucky. And she's strong.'

Agnes opened her eyelids a crack. Across the room, her husband was drawing something up into a small syringe from a glass bottle. She watched with a torpid beat of alarm.

'Is that really necessary, Doctor?' Matron said.

'I want her recovery to go as smoothly as possible,' he said, holding the syringe up and flicking it. The light from the window caught it, the clear liquid inside glimmering. 'We must contain the fever, Matron. Agnes must be in the peak of health, you understand that, surely.'

Matron's dark eyes blazed. 'Of course, but—'

'She is living in a place rife with illness, and she has just suffered a terrible shock,' he interrupted. 'We must keep her well.'

'With respect, Doctor, this is not the infirmary.'

'What does that mean?'

Through half-closed eyelids Agnes watched Matron pull her taut frame up to her full height. 'This floor is my domain,' she said. 'We have always agreed on that. I don't believe Mrs Fairhaven requires any more medication. I've already given her an analgesic, and her temperature is beginning to come down. I don't understand what the point of—'

Christian whipped round, his hand shooting out, gripping tightly onto the nurse's wiry arm. 'With respect, *Matron*,' he said, his voice as sharp as the needle he was holding, 'you are right; you *don't* understand.' His face was a mask of rage, his mouth twisted with malice.

'B . . . but I understood you and Mrs Fairhaven were trying for a child,' Matron stuttered. 'You know that this medication can be dangerous to expectant mothers. If there is any chance that she is pregnant, however small, then surely you should not give it to her?'

It was as if Christian had been slapped. His body visibly wilted, and he took a step back. 'Good god, what am I doing?' he whispered.

'I know this is out of love,' Matron said gently, her voice measured. 'But you are exhausted.' Cautiously, she extracted the syringe from his hand. 'Agnes needs to sleep, Doctor, that is all. And so do you. Come, leave her be. I shall send for you when she is fully rested.'

She ushered him to the door, and Agnes pressed her eyelids together, feigning sleep. She heard the door open and close. When she opened her eyes again, Matron was standing by the bed, looking down at her. She was not wearing her mask, and Agnes saw lines of worry etched across her face.

There was another knock on the door, and a maid came in carrying a small tureen. Matron took it and dismissed her. She put the bowl on the bedside table and helped Agnes to sit up, pulling the oxygen mask from her face. That groaning ache in her stomach pulsed again, incessant and just out of reach. Everything felt hazy, as if she had been held in a dream for days.

'Thank you for defending me,' she whispered, sinking gratefully back against the pillows. 'You . . . you knew I was pregnant, didn't you?'

The matron nodded.

'When did you realise?'

'Probably before you did,' she said.

Her voice was even softer, laced with a sadness that Agnes did not quite understand, and she looked down at her hands twisting in her lap.

'He is so obsessed with the idea of having a child. This,' she touched her stomach, 'might be the one thing that keeps me safe.'

Matron didn't reply. She perched on the edge of the bed and began spooning the broth into Agnes's mouth. It was warm and rich as it slid down her throat, and she tried not to think of the silted lake water she had swallowed only a few hours before.

'I stayed in this very room when I first came to Hedoné,' Matron said suddenly.

Agnes looked up. 'You had to quarantine?' she said.

Matron nodded. 'Myself, and my mother both did.'

'Your mother came here, too? Did she have tuberculosis?'

She shook her head. 'No, although she was very ill. We came here together. I wouldn't have come if the doctor had not allowed my mother to come too.'

Like me, Agnes thought.

'I wonder now if he used her to ensure that I would come. With hindsight, it is easy to spot patterns, isn't it?' She shook her head, a small, sad smile on her face.

'What made you decide to come?'

'I was working at a rival sanatorium in Austria. Doctor Fairhaven found me there.'

'You were a matron there?'

The woman shook her head, spilling a droplet of soup onto the quilt. 'No. I was just a nurse back then. Doctor . . . made me an offer that was very hard to refuse.'

'A promotion?'

'Not quite. He caught me stealing.' She lifted the soup spoon to Agnes's lips.

'Stealing?' Agnes said. She pushed away the proffered soup.

Matron set the bowl back onto the cabinet. 'My mother was desperately ill. I think you of all people know only too well that when someone you love is ill, you'll do anything to help them.' The words sounded accusatory, but there was no malice in them. 'I was taking supplies from the sanatorium and selling them to pay for her care.'

'And Christian caught you at it?'

She nodded. 'He threatened to tell the hospital. I would have been fired, and my mother might have died. He told me that he would keep my secret, but that I would need to come back to England with him and take on the role of matron at his new sanatorium. I think he had been studying me for a while. He wanted someone capable, but who would also turn a blind eye.'

'What happened to your mother?' Agnes asked, steeling herself.

'She died, not long after we arrived.'

Like my own mother, Agnes thought again, her heart sinking with dread. 'Why are you telling me all this?' she said to the nurse.

'Because ever since you came here, Mrs Fairhaven, I have been battling with my conscience. At first, when you arrived, I thought you must be like him. I thought you shared his views, his morals. But over time, I began to wonder if that was in fact not the case. And then, when you came to me about the patient files, I saw that we were on the same side.'

She got to her feet and went to the window, looking out over the cold autumn day.

'All these years, I've tried my hardest to keep the patients safe. I keep new patients in quarantine for as long as possible, to ensure they are in my care, so that I can keep *him* at arm's length.' She turned back to the bed. 'He always waited until they were downstairs before interfering, you see. It was only once they were firmly embedded in the life here that the operations started, the trips to the infirmary. But then, what happened with your mother changed all that. He's never interfered with one of my charges before.'

'Do you think he was trying to kill her?'

Matron shook her head. 'I don't know. But you saw him just now. He makes mistakes. He lets his emotions take over.'

'He could have killed my baby,' Agnes said.

At these words, Matron sat down on the bed again, taking Agnes's hand in her own. It was rough and chafed from so much washing, but Agnes appreciated the touch anyway.

'About your pregnancy,' Matron said. 'I'm afraid there are signs that it may no longer be viable.'

That pulse of something like pain, deep in her belly again. 'What do you mean?'

'Just as I say. I believe you are no longer pregnant. I have given you pain relief to help you cope, and I can continue to do so should you wish me to.'

'I . . . I'm not pregnant?'

'Only time will tell for sure, but, I think . . . not anymore.'

Deep inside her, Agnes felt that urgent throbbing pulse again. She put a hand to her stomach, feeling it gripe hollowly through the pain medication. Now that she was concentrating on it, it felt familiar, this pain, the shape of it similar to the ache that wracked through her each month. She pressed tentatively at her thoughts, trying to make sense of how this news made her feel. It should be a relief, except that, in these last few weeks she had grown used to the idea of having a child, clung onto it amidst the terror of this place.

'Was it my fault?' she asked in a small voice.

'Miscarriage is rarely anyone's fault. You were only a few weeks gone. So often, these things were just never meant to be.'

Agnes lay back, pushing away her emotion, trying to focus on the bare facts. The pregnancy was her last link to Hedoné, which meant that she was no longer tied to this place. As soon as she regained her strength, she would leave, for no matter how hard it would be outside Hedoné's walls, anything was better than a life trapped here.

'I imagine this news might bring mixed feelings for you,' Matron said gently, her voice barely above a whisper. 'Though I doubt very much it would please Doctor.'

'No,' Agnes agreed.

The nurse took up the soup bowl once more, carefully ladling up another spoonful. Her wrist caught the light, and Agnes saw the unmistakable raw imprint of her husband's fingertips on her skin.

'I shall keep the truth from him for as long as you need,' Matron said.

'Thank you, Matron.'

'Don't forget, though, Mrs Fairhaven, that he is a medical man.

He may well guess soon enough.'

Agnes felt suddenly cold. What would he do, if he found out she was no longer carrying his child? Whatever else these last few weeks had been, they had felt like a buffer, a bargaining chip, protecting her from the worst side of him.

'Now, you must try to sleep. You should build up your strength. I fear you will need it.'

She pressed her hand to Agnes's forehead, a kindly smile on her face, and Agnes lay back against her pillow, letting out a tense breath, feeling a tautness in her throat where she had held onto the air last night for too long. Overwhelmed by tiredness, she closed her eyes once more.

All night, Agnes tossed and turned, the analgesics she had been given conjuring strange, nightmarish thoughts that roiled through her head, the images watery, as if she were trapped still beneath the surface of the lake. One moment, she was looking at her husband's handsome face smiling at her, the next, he had sprouted sharp, needle-like teeth, those dazzling blue eyes blackening to pools of darkest ink.

By morning, the medication had begun to wear off, and Agnes's temperature was back to normal. Other than a slight bruise on her elbow, she was given a clean bill of health.

'I wanted to keep you up here for longer,' Matron said. 'But sadly Doctor Fairhaven has other ideas. He came back when you were sleeping, demanded I discharge you last night, but I wouldn't hear of it. I managed to negotiate a little more time, but I'm afraid Doctor will be escorting you home after lunch today. These painkillers should help with what is to come,' she said, pressing a small bottle into Agnes's hand. 'I'm hopeful that it will be manageable. I shall try and visit you soon. Be sure to hide those away.'

Agnes tucked the bottle into her nightdress.

Just after eleven, Juno came to see how she was faring, worry etched into her face.

'Oh Agnes,' she said on seeing her. Turning to Matron, she said, 'Now, you're sure you've done everything needed? Mrs Fairhaven must be in the peak of health.'

Agnes looked up at the familiar expression, the same words that Christian had used yesterday. Her luncheon arrived then, and Juno left soon after.

After lunch, Matron doled out more analgesics and took her temperature, adding it methodically to the chart. Agnes watched the nurse absentmindedly stripping the bed and cleaning the equipment, trying at the same time to make sense of the strange feeling of unease inside her. Behind them, she heard the sudden click of the door as it was unlocked, and Christian strode into the room.

She was surprised to find that he was not the monster she had imagined in the dark hours of last night. He looked full of energy and vitality, his blue eyes sparkling, his face clear of the lines of exhaustion that must pepper Agnes's own. It truly was a mask, she realised properly for the first time, and who knew what unbearable truths lay beneath it. Her heart began beating fast, a sheen of sweat breaking out on her forehead, but she tried to compose herself, smiling up at her husband as he came towards her.

'Temperature and pulse perfectly normal, Doctor,' Matron said.

'Thank goodness,' he said. 'Are you ready to return home, darling?'

'Yes please, Christian,' Agnes said, tilting her head up to meet his kiss. 'Quite, quite ready.'

Chapter Forty-Four

At the cottage, Christian settled Agnes on the sofa.

'I'm perfectly fine, Christian,' she said, batting him away as he attempted to take her pulse. 'Just a little tired, that's all.' She tried to keep her voice steady, wondering if he could sense the lie.

'You're not perfectly fine,' Christian said, raising a spark of fear inside her. 'You are carrying our baby and you have been in very cold water. Goodness knows how long you were under for. You must rest, for your sake and the child's.'

'Don't be silly. I've been discharged,' she argued.

'Please, Agnes!' he cut across her, his voice reverberating out in the little sitting room, making the windowpanes ring, and Agnes shrank back into the sofa. He had never raised his voice to her before.

'Just . . . do as I say,' he whispered. 'Just this once.' Anger no longer fuelled his words. Instead, he sounded frightened.

Agnes looked down at her lap, trying to compose her face, to make it blank and unreadable.

'Please,' he said again, sinking down in front of her and taking her hand. 'Please just trust me. I know the human body intimately, how it works, how it survives. I have noted each and every physical change this pregnancy has had on you.'

She dared not lift her eyes to meet his. How long before her body would betray her? How long until he knew she was lying to him?

'Darling.' Christian scooped her gently against him. 'Just do this one thing for me.' He drew away. 'You haven't told anyone about the pregnancy yet, have you?'

'No.' It wasn't a lie, exactly. She hadn't *told* Sippie, after all. Or Matron.

'Good, good. Let's keep it to ourselves for just a little longer. Tomorrow, I shall take you down to the infirmary and perform a few tests, just to check if everything is as it should be.' His voice was jittery with a nervous excitement. 'And then perhaps we can announce it.'

'Tests?' Agnes said in alarm. 'You mean, to confirm whether I'm pregnant?'

'No, no,' he laughed, tucking a stray hair behind her ear, 'we know you're pregnant. It's more to ensure you are keeping as well as could be. See if I need to add anything to your diet, that sort of thing.'

Agnes thought of that room, of poor Georgie, lying unconscious. It would be good to check in on him, let Sippie know he was being well looked after.

Christian drew her to him again, and she tried not to stiffen in his arms. 'We need to ensure you are in the peak of health,' he murmured into her hair. 'The peak of health.'

Those words again. Fear fought with exhaustion, and she lay back against the cushions, her eyelids heavy.

Carefully, Christian scooped her legs up onto the sofa, tucking a blanket around her tired body.

'I cannot tell you how happy I am that you are all right,' he said. But as Agnes closed her eyes, surrendering to the pull of sleep, she thought how his voice sounded, not happy exactly, but relieved.

*

The next morning, Christian left early as usual. The pains in Agnes's stomach were abating, and she made her way slowly to the front door, desperate to look up at the sky, to remind herself of the world outside. As soon as she was strong enough, she would put plans into place for her escape. It made sense to ask Matron to bring her a key to Christian's office. Agnes wished she had thought of asking her when she was up in quarantine, but the pain medication had fogged her brain. Once she gained access to the office, she would telephone the police, and then she would finally tell the guests everything she had learnt.

Agnes went to open the door, but found that it was locked.

How strange. She supposed Christian must not want anyone to disturb her while she was resting. She looked around for her purse, seeing it propped on the mantelpiece. He must have put it there; she hadn't needed it while she was recuperating in the main house. Slipping open the clasp, she searched inside for the set of keys that he had given her on her first day out of quarantine.

They weren't there.

Trying to contain her panic, Agnes hurried to the sitting room windows, thinking of her first day at Hedoné, when she had clambered through the open window of Mansfield Suite and out onto the balcony. The windows here were all closed, and with mounting dread, she saw that each and every one of them was locked.

It was like that first day in quarantine all over again, except that this cottage was not a hospital; it was her home. And there was no chance now of her carrying any illnesses that might pose a threat to the guests; she was not a threat to anyone at all.

Except perhaps to Christian.

Agnes forced herself to remain calm. Her eyes raked the room, searching for anything that might help her predicament, and her gaze settled on a letter sitting with the other incoming mail on the console table, her own name on the envelope.

Nobody wrote to her at Hedoné. Nobody knew she was here. Had Christian not seen it? Surely if he was checking outgoing mail, then he would be checking incoming mail too. He must have missed it in his hurry to leave for work; his own mail was here, too, untouched.

She picked up the letter, sliding the paperknife under the envelope, slitting it open.

Dear Mrs Fairhaven,

Thank you for contacting me with your concerns about a Doctor Christian Fairhaven. I am writing to inform you that we have never had anyone of that name study medicine at our institution.

The letter fluttered to the floor. Hastily, Agnes picked it up, glancing at the door before continuing.

We did however have a Christopher Fairhaven study here in 1923, but his education was cut short due to his poor grades and an obsessive preoccupation with mycobacterium tuberculosis.

His 'English rose theory', as he called it, described how it was possible to predict who would be less susceptible to contracting the disease. He postulated (quite wrongly in our opinion) that if a patient's posture, build and skin imitated those with TB – or in other words, had the delicate beauty of an English rose – then they could effectively hide in plain sight from the illness. There is some evidence now

that points to some people being more immune than others.
But this is not due to their looks, but usually because they
have been exposed to a small amount of tuberculosis at an
early age. Christopher wrongly believed that this small
exposure went on to show itself in the person's complexion,
hence the 'English rose' description.

Suffice to say, this sort of conjecture has no place in
science, yet Mr Fairhaven would not give up on the idea,
and he was asked to leave, long before he qualified as a
doctor. If I am correct, and we are speaking of the same
man – and, as you attest, he is continuing along this line
of treatment – then I would ask you to please write back
with immediate effect, detailing where he is practising, and
I shall—

Agnes was interrupted by the sound of a key in the front door.
Quickly, she stuffed the letter into her blouse, replacing the knife on
the console table and stepping away just as Christian came in.

He was pushing a wheeled chair in front of him – the same one
her mother had used; she recognised the design of deep blue peacock
feathers on the plush upholstery. Had he chosen it on purpose, a
little nudge to remind her what he might be capable of?

'Darling,' he said, tucking the key into a pocket of his white
doctor's coat and patting the plush seating. 'Come on, let's go and
get those tests done.'

At the house, they passed a few guests on their way to breakfast,
Agnes feeling strangely vulnerable in the chair. She sensed them do a
double take as they saw who was sitting there, and she dropped her
eyes in embarrassment.

At the infirmary, Christian opened the door, pulling the chair in behind him, and she leant round, trying to see inside, but he pushed her back gently. When at last he turned her, her gaze went straight to the bed, a small, hopeful part of her still expecting to see Georgie there. But it was empty, and she felt a leaden weight drop in her stomach.

Christian wheeled her to a corner, and she sat, staring at the bed, the sheets crisp and freshly made. She pulled herself from her reverie to find him taking a stethoscope from around his neck, and with panic, Agnes thought of the secreted letter, burning at her chest.

'Christian darling,' she said as lightly as she could, 'my lungs are not the reason we're here today.'

'Oh! Of course not,' he exclaimed. 'A habitual reflex.'

With relief, she saw him hang the instrument back. He went to a clinical cabinet and came back with an empty syringe and tourniquet. Crouching down beside her, he took her arm in his warm hands, and began gently to clean the crook of her elbow.

'Has the artist who was in here been moved up to quarantine?' Agnes said.

A red flush appeared on Christian's neck. How strange that she had once thought it so becoming.

'I'm afraid Mr Murphy died, my darling, two nights ago.' He did not look up, concentrating hard on cleaning her skin.

'What?' The word came out in a rush of breath.

'He had been very unwell. I thought it best not to tell you in your fragile state. I didn't want to upset you. I'm so sorry, Agnes.'

She stared unseeingly at the room, her gaze settling at last on a cupboard on the wall opposite, a skull and crossbones pasted onto it. It stared back at her, its vacant eyes challenging her to react more forcefully to the news, but she felt her shoulders droop, no fight left in her.

'What happened?' she whispered. But she realised she already knew. *Papa told me he would fix them all,* Iso had said. *But I watched him, I watched what he did, and they died all the same.*

'Christian, what happened?' Agnes pressed.

As he raised the needle, he looked up at her, and his blue eyes looked haunted. 'He just . . . gave up,' he said.

Chapter Forty-Five

Agnes remained locked in the cottage. Christian's tests must have proved sufficient, for he didn't mention them again, though she noticed that the meals brought from Hedoné's kitchen began to change, rare steak and plenty of fresh vegetables, the usual pot of salt absent. The silver medication cup that she had first seen up in quarantine began to make an appearance once again, the pills inside growing in number each day, and always accompanied by a large glass of thick Jersey milk.

'Nutritious and health-giving,' Christian said encouragingly, nodding at yet another bland, plain meal. 'Eat up.'

Agnes tried hard to at least sample everything that was put in front of her, knowing she must keep up her strength for her own gain, but her appetite was non-existent. The door to the cottage remained locked, and as each day passed, and she faced yet another day held prisoner, she began to feel the very last of herself ebbing away.

She thought of her stepdaughter often. Christian had told her that Iso was still recuperating after the incident in the lake. She had been put in Mansfield Suite, and Agnes thought of her little body dwarfed by that large bed that Agnes's own mother had occupied not too long ago. She wondered about Isobel's mental state. Had

311

she meant to harm herself by jumping into the lake that night? Her poor mind was obviously quite as precarious as many of the guests' physical states. Quite rightly, Agnes thought, having lived so close to so many people flickering on the edge of mortality for so long.

She hoped that little Iso was at least allowed visitors. No one had visited the cottage, though of course, she couldn't let them in if they had. What was Christian's plan? To let her waste away in here forever? She had managed thus far to pretend to take the tablets he gave her, but she could not keep up the pretence forever. Nor, she realised, could she pretend indefinitely that she was pregnant.

Christian had still not informed the residents about Georgie's death. When she'd queried this, he'd told her he would tell them after the Guy Fawkes party. 'Let them have one more night of happiness before we spoil it,' he had said.

Agnes spent her days sitting by her locked bedroom window, looking out at the trees on the other side. She had felt lonely many times in her life, but this was different. For the first time in her twenty-eight years, she had relinquished all control over herself, and with none of the guests allowed in to see her, she was alone with her thoughts too. She used her time to concoct ever more vicious and just punishments for the man who held her here.

The only upside to this ban on visitors was that Juno was also included. Agnes was not sure how she would face the woman now if she saw her. Sometimes, when the wind was in the right direction, she thought she heard a jubilant shout from the grounds, the thwack of a croquet mallet on a ball followed by a burst of laughter. Beyond the pine trees, the guests must be continuing on with their lives. She knew that Christian hadn't yet told them about the pregnancy. They all must just assume she was still recuperating after her episode in the lake.

The day of the Guy Fawkes party arrived. As Christian got ready for work that morning, Agnes pleaded one last time to be allowed to go, even if just for a little while. In the long, endless hours of solitude, she had gone over and over what she would do if she managed to break away from her husband's tight grasp for just a short moment. There would be no time to find Matron, and her plan was a simple one: to run to the back of the house and find Christian's office window, breaking the glass and climbing in to reach the telephone.

When she'd asked about the party before, Christian had been against the idea of her going, but today he was in a jovial mood.

'It might actually be a good time to announce the pregnancy,' he said, nodding to himself as if it was all his idea. 'I shall bring the wheeled chair. We can't have you expending too much energy quite yet.'

'I'm strong enough to walk, Christian,' she said. 'Honestly. I'd prefer it.'

'Now, now, Agnes, don't question my methods. Doctor knows best, after all,' he said, and she gritted her teeth and smiled, not daring to contradict him lest he rescind his offer.

'I'll dress for dinner up at the house tonight,' he said. 'I've a busy day ahead. I shall come and collect you after I've eaten. Oh, and by the way, I've left a little surprise for you on your dressing table.'

After he'd gone, Agnes went to the bedroom. On the table, next to her hairbrushes and perfumes, she found a long, thin box made of the palest blue kid leather. Unlatching the tiny clasp, she found nestled inside a diamond choker on a bed of velvet.

'For my dear wife,' the note read. 'To celebrate our wonderful news. C.'

She looked at it for a long moment, her face devoid of emotion, then abruptly strode from the room, closing the door behind her.

That day, the hours seemed to crawl by. Agnes felt a crackling in the air like an electrical charge, a pent-up fizz of tension inside her as she counted down the minutes to the party. In the evening, the moon rose early, full and clear, flooding the woodland with its ethereal light. When she opened her wardrobe, she saw that yet another new dress hung there. With a sigh, she took it down, not bothering to examine it before putting it on.

There was a knock on the front door as she was fastening the gown.

'Agnes?' came a hushed call on the other side.

'Sippie?' Agnes said, rushing to the door. 'Is that you?'

'Come to the window,' Sippie said.

Agnes hurried to the sitting room window. Sippie appeared, picking her way through the pine needles. Her face was set with a grim determination, her aquiline features beautiful in the darkness.

'He's locked me in,' Agnes said.

'I know. We all know.'

'Sippie, you must listen,' Agnes hurried. 'Georgie Murphy is dead.'

The young woman's face slackened, her sloe-dark eyes fixed on Agnes's. 'What happened?'

'Christian said he just gave up, but I don't believe it. He only told me after I came out of Matron's care, but I think it happened a few days before.'

Sippie's eyes brimmed wetly, but she blinked it away, her jaw set. 'Georgie always came across as so frail,' she whispered, her voice emotionless. 'But he had fire in him.' She gave a small breathy sigh. 'I came to tell you that I'm leaving. Tonight. I can't stay here any longer. I wanted to come and say goodbye properly.'

'Oh, Sippie,' Agnes said, her eyes filling with tears.

'I have to leave, Agnes. But I'll get help. I'll go to the police, as soon as I'm out, I promise.'

Agnes smiled her gratitude, but inside, the tiny spark that Sippie's appearance had ignited snuffed out. The police would not listen to this woman. Sippie had said it herself; she was an ill, black woman with a strange, foreign accent, in a country that was not her own. They wouldn't believe her, not without proof.

Proof. 'One moment,' Agnes said. Quickly, she rushed to the bathroom. Pulling back a tile from behind the basin, she edged out the last of the hidden medication that Matron had given her, reaching behind it and pulling out the letter the doctor had sent.

'Come to the door,' she said, hurrying over and slipping it through the gap underneath, before going back to the window.

Sippie followed her, scanning the letter in the light from the cottage, her eyes widening as she read it.

'Thank you for this,' she said, tucking it away. 'It'll help. I know it will.' She glanced over her shoulder. When she looked back, her eyes were wet with tears. 'Come with me, Agnes,' she said, her face filled with hope.

For a brief moment, Agnes saw another life unfurling before her, one of hardship, but also of possibility. But then Iso's face swam into her vision.

'I can't,' she said. 'Not yet. Not without Iso. And I need time to find out all I can before I leave. For the guests as much as myself. You go. I'll find you, I promise.'

Sippie gazed hard at her through the window, her eyes blazing, but she nodded.

'I will miss you so, Sippie,' Agnes whispered. The pane of glass between them felt suddenly like a wall, a barrier between two different worlds.

Sippie cleared her throat. 'Will you be all right?' she said, her voice raw.

'I will,' Agnes said, trying to make herself believe it.

'Is there anyone I can get a message to once I'm out? Any family or friends who might be able to help you?'

Agnes shook her head. 'No,' she said. 'No.'

They stood on either side of the glass, each looking at the other, neither quite able to tear herself away.

From far away through the trees, there was the sound of voices. Sippie looked over her shoulder.

'Dinner must be over,' she said. 'I have to go.' She gave Agnes a quick, harried smile, and then hurried away, back through the woods.

Agnes walked slowly back to her bedroom. Sitting at her dressing table, she gazed at her face in the mirror. It looked hollow and gaunt, as if she was one of the guests, not the wife of the doctor who reigned over it all. She lifted the diamond necklace from its box, the brilliant jewels flashing in the soft light, securing it about her neck. The choker was tight on her throat like a collar. At the centre, a much larger, angular diamond rested on her clavicle, and she stared at it in the mirror's reflection, unable to pull her eyes away, the feeling of it so heavy against her body, as if it might snap the delicate bones there at any moment.

Chapter Forty-Six

Agnes did not know how long she sat at the dressing table, gazing at her reflection. The sound of the key in the door roused her from her contemplation.

Christian, she thought with a start. But when she turned, it was not her husband in the bedroom doorway, but Matron.

'I cannot stay long,' the nurse said in a hushed whisper. 'Doctor Fairhaven won't let me come and see you, he says he's perfectly able to attend to you himself. How are you, Agnes?' Her eyes went pointedly to her stomach.

'I'm all right,' she said. 'The pain's gone, mostly.'

'That's good.' Matron drew closer, searching Agnes's face. 'Are you eating enough?' she said, pressing a hand to her brow. When Agnes didn't answer, she continued, 'I hear he's allowing you out tonight for a short while, to the party. I have something for you, here.'

She took hold of Agnes's hand, placing a little white pill in her palm, and Agnes looked down at it, frowning.

'More medication?' she said wearily. 'I think I'd be happier if I never saw another pill again, Matron.'

'It's not for you.'

Agnes looked up. 'What do you mean?'

'It's a sedative.' Matron took a step closer, her voice hushed. 'If you crush it up in his drink tonight, he won't be in any state to stop you, should you decide to leave Hedoné. It's a low enough dose that he'll think he's merely exhausted after a busy day, but it should give you time enough to make your escape, if you decide that's what you want.'

Agnes looked at the tiny pill in her hand.

'I . . . I can't leave yet,' she said. 'There are still things I need to find out. The guests deserve to know the whole truth. And I can't go without Isobel.'

Matron nodded. 'I thought you'd say that,' she said. Detaching the jangling set of keys from her belt, she held them up. 'These will give you access to the quarantine floor, to get Miss Isobel.'

'But, won't you miss them?'

'I have a spare set.' She lifted the largest key. 'For the gate. And here,' she added, pushing a handful of notes into Agnes's hand. 'To tide you over.'

Agnes looked down at the money, then back to the face of the strange, severe woman, overwhelmed by her kindness.

'I mustn't linger,' Matron said. 'I just . . .' She paused, looking at Agnes. 'I just wanted to see that you were all right. And you are. You're made of strong stuff, Agnes Templeton.' She smiled.

When she left, Agnes stayed sitting at her dressing table. Then swiftly, as if something had clicked in her mind, she got to her feet, the small white pill clutched tightly in her hand.

Later, when she heard the key in the door again, she sat back down at the dressing table, pretending to make last-minute adjustments to her appearance. Christian appeared, pushing that damned horrid wheeled chair ahead of him. He came to stand behind her, reflected in the mirror as she secured a pin in her hair. Leaning down, he dropped a kiss on her clavicle.

'You look wonderful,' he murmured. 'Do you like your gift?'

Agnes put a hand to the huge diamond at her neck. 'It's beautiful, Christian,' she said.

In truth, she thought it ugly, like a chain about her throat, as if he were trying to bind her evermore tightly to him. What did he imagine he had bought with it? She gripped the heavy stone in her palm, trying to stifle the glare of the facets as they caught the light.

'Are you ready, then, Cinderella?' he asked her, his hands on the gleaming handles of the chair.

'I thought perhaps we should have a drink together first, just us. This is a momentous day, after all, Christian, announcing our child to the whole of Hedoné.'

She got to her feet, lifting two glasses of champagne from the dressing table, hoping that the tremor in her hands wouldn't betray her guilt. She passed one to Christian.

'To us,' she said, trying to conjure those heady days in France, to imbue her gaze with the adoration she had felt for him once, all those weeks ago.

'To us,' he replied, lifting his glass and drinking deeply.

As Christian pushed her through the trees, Agnes felt the weight of the necklace pressing against her windpipe every time she drew breath. Deep in her stomach she felt a rhythmic clenching churn, but whether from the vestiges of the thing that had happened inside her, or the fear of everything that was happening outside, she did not know.

Above the trees, the moonlight found the diamonds at her neck, their facets throwing splinters of light onto the ground, illuminating their way. As they came to the end of the tree-lined path, a strange premonitory feeling rose inside her, like a beast awakening.

Across the grass, the bonfire had been lit, the air filled with the scent of pine resin. The guests were all outside, drawn hypnotically to the flames. Christian pushed the chair through the statues, and Agnes looked up at them, towering over her. They looked different in the fire's reflected flames, a deep blood red instead of their usual pale stone. As Christian began to wheel her over the uneven lawn, she felt again the heavy weight of the choker as it bounced at her throat, the diamond's facets throwing the reflected flames back, staining her bare skin the colour of sunset.

Near the bonfire, she felt the chair come to a stop. Ahead, the guests had not yet seen them, all turned to the fire, their hands outstretched, warming themselves.

'My dear esteemed guests,' Christian said loudly.

At his voice, they all turned, delight painting their faces when they saw Agnes, pity threaded through it as they took in the chair she was sitting in.

'I should like to say a few words to you all,' Christian continued. Silence fell across the grounds, the only sound the crackling spit of the bonfire. He nodded to a nearby waiter to begin filling up people's glasses.

'I am pleased to say that my darling wife, Agnes, is making a full recovery after her heroic rescue of my daughter from the lake, and I should like to make a very special announcement.' He took Agnes's hand in his own. 'I am extremely happy to tell you all that we are expecting a baby.'

Cries of congratulations echoed across the grounds. The guests drew towards them, shaking Christian's hand and bending to kiss Agnes on the cheek.

Through the flurry, she saw Juno. She was standing under a birch tree, a silver fox fur tied tightly at her throat, observing the scene before her in that careful, measured way that she had. As Christian's speech came to an end, Juno snatched a glass of champagne from a passing silver tray, gazing into its depths for a moment, before draining it with a quick tip of her head. As if she felt Agnes's eyes upon her, she looked up, but in the darkness it was impossible to make out her expression.

A sudden crash above, and a firework display began. Great glittering bursts exploded in splintery clouds. Cries of wonder cascaded across the grounds, the smell of gunpowder mingling with the bonfire smoke, potent and intoxicating. Out of the corner of her eye, Agnes saw Christian stifle a yawn. Was it the sedative beginning to work? She could see the fireworks reflected in his eyes as he gazed upwards along with the rest, his hand resting on hers on the padded arm of the chair.

She wondered what he was thinking as he surveyed this paradise of his own creation. His face, as always, was expressionless, and she felt a pinch of regret at how their marriage had unravelled. What great secret was he hiding, this man that she had once thought she could love? Tears stung at her eyelids, and she turned her hand, linking her fingers with his one last time.

Chapter Forty-Seven

The Leather Diary

Isobel has been held in this quarantine bedroom for days. It is a luxurious room, far nicer than her own, but it is not in her nature to be contained. She has a key for this room, secreted under a floorboard in her bedroom, in a little nest of objects that she has procured over the years, jewellery and medicine bottles and half-eaten jars of jam. She has not yet been able to source another key with which to escape, but tonight is the night of the fireworks, and for once, the balcony doors have been left open so that she can enjoy the spectacle.

She sits on the edge of the bed, the little wooden mouse that Georgie Murphy carved for her in her hand. She supposes that Georgie must have died; he was not in the infirmary when she was recuperating in there after the lake, and she has not seen him since from her quarantine window. There seems to be so much death at the moment. Mrs Templeton died in the very bed she is sitting in now. Whenever Isobel tries to sleep, she dreams of the old woman's sweet, crinkled face next to her on the pillow, and she wakes up, drenched in sweat, silent tears running down her cheeks.

Outside, darkness has begun to descend over the grounds, and she jumps down from the bed and slips through the door to the balcony, waiting for the display to begin. As the first crash splinters across the sky, she drags a sun lounger across the floor and climbs up onto the outer ledge. There she stands, arms raised for balance like a ballerina, her toes clenching against the wood, looking up at the sky. The fireworks make her dizzy with exhilaration. She can see the guests far in the distance, clustered around a huge bonfire, their faces raised up to the magnificent display. No one will be looking this way tonight.

She begins to walk, trapeze-like along the balcony ledge, her arms outstretched until she reaches the end. Here, she draws herself tightly back, then leaps, her body scaling the gap between this balcony and the next. She lands on the wooden floor of the next-door balcony and straightens up like a gymnast.

Isobel peeps through the window to the bedroom next to hers. It is empty, as she knew it would be. She tries the door and finds it unlocked. Quickly, she crosses the room and opens the door into the hallway. From here, her route is easy, familiar. She pulls open the laundry chute and climbs inside, relishing the cold feel of the metal against her skin. She calculates that there is no laundry at the bottom of this chute. It will have been emptied early today on account of the staff watching the fireworks. She must be careful as she climbs down, there will be no jumping tonight.

She descends cautiously, stopping halfway and opening the chute's hatch onto the ground floor. From here, she can see the doors to the guests' bedrooms. It is rare that this floor is so empty. Usually, even if the guests are not here, there are maids, cleaning the bedrooms, staff patrolling to check everything is as it should be. But tonight, even the lowliest maid has been given the night off.

Isobel climbs out of the chute and makes her way down the wide corridor. She passes many doors, whispering the name of each guest as she goes. Eventually, she comes to the last door on the left.

'Juno Harrington,' she whispers.

She does not have a key to Juno's rooms, for the woman guards her privacy so fiercely that there is only one copy. But in her time here, Isobel has become quite accomplished at picking locks — something she learnt from a former governess who was fond of secretly helping herself to the guests' trinkets. Stealing is a hobby that Isobel has come to enjoy too, little trophies that she knows won't be missed, her small acts of rebellion making her feel alive in a house that rarely acknowledges her.

She slips through the door, and into the beautiful sitting room. The walls in here are painted to look like a jungle, and Iso feels the eyes of hidden animals on her as she moves noiselessly through the room. She goes to the leopard-skin rug and pats its great head, not liking the way it stares, its eyes glassy and unblinking. On the coffee table, amid a pile of magazines, she spots a small leather book. It is open, the spine cracked, the pages beneath a little creased and filled with handwriting.

It is a diary.

Curious, Iso flicks through the entries. Juno's writing is as beautiful as she is, an elegant copperplate that is both intricate yet easy to read.

We had a new guest arrive today. A rich old aristocrat who said he knew my father. He took a good long look at my chest and immediately offered to buy me a diamond ring if I did certain things to him. I laughed in his face. Why are all men such ignorant bores? He couldn't see that he had nothing to offer me. Money does not excite me. Not anymore.

Iso turns the page, leafing through the diary. She spots her own name, and she reads hungrily.

I'm not entirely convinced that Isobel doesn't know her mother is still alive.

I catch her looking at me sometimes, and I wonder if she thinks I'm a part of it. She's a crafty little thing. She reminds me of myself at that age. Forget about her father, this girl is wise beyond her years. She won't suffer fools gladly.

Isobel does not know what this last comment means, and she turns the page, searching for any more mentions of her. But instead, another name jumps out.

I admit now, he was right to choose Agnes. I do like her. She's obviously playing her own game. But this of course means we'll need to be careful. I keep trying to tell Christian, but he has this horrible tendency to believe his own hubris. He is undeniably an attractive man, and he really thinks she's fallen in love with him.

Despite this, I do wonder if this time, we haven't found the answer to all our troubles. I've felt so ill this last week, I don't know how much longer I can wait . . .

Iso looks up, sensing a stillness. Outside, the fireworks have come to an end. The staff and guests could be back at any moment. Quickly, she closes the diary, tucking it under her arm, and with a last pat of the leopard's head, she slips from Juno's suite. In the passageway, she scrambles back into the chute, and begins to climb further down, towards the basement.

As her feet touch the cold tiles of the basement floor, she hurries to the infirmary, glancing through the little window, fearful that there might be someone in there. But the bed is empty, and she slips inside.

Isobel hasn't been in here since she was a patient herself, eight days ago. She pulls herself up onto the bed, the diary clutched in her hand, intending to continue reading undisturbed. But the bed is extraordinarily comfortable, and as she curls up on it, she is comforted by the thought that her mother lay here once too. The climb down to the basement has tired her, her muscles weakened from so many days of bedrest, and Isobel closes her eyes, clutching the diary to her chest.

Just a short nap, she thinks.

Chapter Forty-Eight

As the last firework fell silent, Agnes dropped her husband's hand.

The grounds around them seemed all at once bewitched by an expectant silence, as if everyone was holding their breath. And then at last, deep in the woods, she heard it, a strange dreamlike beat. It was so low that it was barely a noise at all, more like a pressure, a percussive thumping like a heartbeat in her ribs and chest, and Agnes put a hand to her stomach, feeling it deep in there, too. Next to her, she felt Christian stagger, gripping the handle of the chair.

'Are you all right?' she asked.

'Just a little dizzy,' he said. 'I might go and sit down for a moment. Will you be all right without me?'

'I'll be fine,' Agnes said, clasping her purse in her lap, feeling the press of Matron's keys inside.

Christian stumbled away. The drumbeat grew faster, swelling with intensity. A few of the guests began dancing round the bonfire, their silhouettes moving slowly in twisting shapes, revolving around the great mound of fire. And then the magic of it seemed to capture everyone, and suddenly the night was alive with shouts and halloos of excitement as the party began in earnest.

When she was sure Christian was out of sight, Agnes got to her feet, kicking the chair away from her in disgust.

'Good evening, Mrs Fairhaven.'

Juno was standing close by, two glasses of champagne in her hands. 'Care for another drink?' she said. 'Or should you be taking Guinness now instead, to fortify the baby?'

Her voice had that mocking tone that so often laced her laughter, her eyes a little bright, a wildness to them as she handed a glass to Agnes.

'To Hedoné,' Juno said, lifting her champagne flute. 'And all that it has achieved.'

'To Hedoné,' Agnes agreed, clinking her glass to Juno's.

The two women sipped their drinks, regarding one another over the cut crystal.

Juno gave a small sigh, surveying the party. 'We really know how to put on a show here, don't we?'

'Indeed you do, Juno,' replied Agnes icily.

'Touché,' the young woman whispered with a ghost of a smile.

They stood in silence, watching the bonfire. More people were dancing now. Some held sparklers, the fizzing white lights so bright that they looked like fairies flying in the dark. The noise had intensified, great whoops of excitement as the carousing guests became more inebriated.

'Congratulations on your wonderful news, by the way,' Juno said.

Agnes did not reply. She gazed at the fire. Out of the corner of her eye, she could see Juno's face, her smooth skin flushed by the flames.

'Tell me,' Juno said, 'did you know it would scupper mine and your husband's plans, this child?'

'I'm not as calculating as you are, Juno,' she said coldly.

'Really? You've scored yourself a rather luxurious little life here though, haven't you? And managed to find a husband who could care for your dying mother. And now, with a baby on the way, your good fortune is set to continue. If that's not calculating, then I don't know what is.'

Agnes spun round in a sudden fit of anger, her champagne ribboning from her glass. 'You call this *good fortune?*' she hissed. 'Why are you doing this, Juno? What have I ever done to you?' She caught a glint of surprise in the young woman's eyes. '*Is* it me? Or is it bigger than that? Some great wrong you feel the world has dealt you? Because I would bet that every last guest here has felt that same way. In fact, I'm sure your life must seem wonderful in comparison to their own.'

She waited for Juno to deny it, for that soft, mocking laugh. But instead, she felt the woman's trembling eyes lock onto hers, shining wet with tears.

'What a beautiful necklace,' Juno said, her voice clotted with emotion. Reaching up a shaking hand, she tapped the large stone at Agnes's throat with a blood red fingernail. 'If that isn't a declaration of commitment, then I don't know what is.'

Agnes ignored her, staring at the fire, not trusting herself to speak.

'And now, of course, you're going to have a baby,' Juno said. 'A perfect, healthy child for the perfect, healthy couple. You know, when you first arrived, Agnes, I did wonder if, after all this, we might become friends one day.' She gave a soft breath of laughter. 'But it's never going to be, is it?' She tipped back the last of her champagne, her face set with an immoveable hardness.

'You know he lied, Juno?' Agnes said, still gazing at the fire.

'Oh, we all lie, Mrs Fairhaven.'

Agnes turned to her. 'He isn't even a qualified doctor; did he tell you that?'

A flicker of doubt crossed Juno's face.

'He was thrown out of medical school because of his obsessive theories about TB. I wrote to his old university, and they confirmed it: he's a con artist, Juno, a dangerous, blundering con artist.'

'Oh, Agnes, really, lying does not become you. You lack the finesse to pull it off.'

'I'm not lying!' she exclaimed. 'Christian is not what he says he is, not to me, and certainly not to you. Whatever he promised you, it's all lies. I know this baby is a problem for whatever plan you're concocting. But he's known about the pregnancy for weeks, and yet he didn't tell you, did he?'

Juno remained silent, staring down at her empty champagne glass, and Agnes realised this was her chance.

'What exactly is it that he promised you?' she said. 'Why am I here?'

She held her breath, waiting. A small frown puckered Juno's neat eyebrows, and her lips parted, her chest rising as she drew in a breath. Hope reared inside Agnes.

But Juno only gave her head a small shake. 'Do excuse me,' she said, thrusting her empty glass into Agnes's hand. 'I can't be seen to be conversing with just one person all night, however scintillating the conversation.'

As she walked away, Agnes noticed how she weaved slightly as she pressed through the crowd. She wondered how much of it was inebriation, how much shock at the news of the pregnancy.

Agnes surveyed the grounds, looking for Christian. She needed to make sure that the sedative was working, and then she would go and collect Isobel. As the party wore on, and the guests' energy wound down, she assumed that they would all congregate in the glade. Then she would tell them all that she'd learnt. Agnes wondered with a pang of regret if Sippie had already left, a small part of her hoping she had been delayed. If she hurried, she and Iso might be able to leave with her.

She began to make her way round the bonfire, searching for Christian. All around her, people were chatting excitedly about the fireworks and the party. They congratulated her on her news as she hurried passed.

Agnes followed the path to the woodland glade, her way illuminated by the string of bulbs above. The clearing had been transformed for the party, as per Juno's extravagant instructions. Everything was gold, the seating, the parasols, even the trees had been slathered in gold paint. Golden tables nestled on the ground, and huge gold-framed mirrors were strung among the trees, giving the impression that the space looked much larger than it was. A few guests were here already, sitting in armchairs, and stretched out across sofas and cushions, chatting animatedly. Christian was passed out on a sofa. Agnes checked on him. He was fast asleep, a thin trail of saliva pasted to his jaw.

Nearby, she saw trays of prepared drugs on a table, and she had a memory of Georgie lying on the same sofa that Christian now occupied, the needle sliding into his skin. Before she could stop to question what she was doing, she had slipped a couple of syringes into her purse.

Agnes hurried back towards the bonfire, breaking through the trees. Hedoné loomed golden in the distance, lit up like a beacon. There was a light on in Mansfield Suite. Good. Isobel must not have gone to bed yet, which would make things easier. Agnes's mind turned to practical things; what clothes the child might need, which shoes to take with them. She had not made any plans for when they were out, but she supposed that they should begin to search for Meredith, to reunite her with her daughter.

With these thoughts running through her mind, she set off across the lawn towards the house.

Chapter Forty-Nine

A few guests were still dancing around the bonfire as Agnes passed it, their frenetic movement increasing in speed and urgency. They were wearing masks now. Great hulking animal heads spun past, a fox and a deer and the huge white face of an owl.

She spotted Juno again beneath the same silver birch as earlier, and despite her haste, Agnes paused. The young woman was slumped on the damp grass, watching the ongoing party with a detached interest, her eyes barely open. Agnes glanced at the house, then back to Juno, and then, swearing inwardly to herself, she changed direction, hurrying over.

'Juno, are you all right?'

At first, she wasn't sure if she heard her. But then Juno lifted her head, a slow smile breaking across her face.

'Agnes!' she said. She got unsteadily to her feet, swaying slightly, a half-drunk glass of champagne gripped in her fist. She put a hand to the tree trunk to steady herself. 'Do you know, Mrs Fairhaven,' she said. 'I think I may be a little tipsy.'

She tried to trace a finger down Agnes's nose, but her usual grace deserted her, and she stumbled, losing a splash of champagne. A slow ringing began in Agnes's ears, a dawning idea.

'Perhaps we should go somewhere quieter,' she suggested.

'Yes,' Juno replied, 'I should like that.' The words came out in a sigh.

They made their way across the grounds, Agnes kicking aside spent firework cases, Juno clutching her champagne as if her life depended on it. They passed a Guy, made by the guests in a fit of frivolity but forgotten now, slumped in a wheelbarrow. As they wound through the statues, Juno's fingers gripped Agnes's arm, her hand damp and trembling as she walked unsteadily across the soft ground in her heels. The champagne glass in her hand fizzed droplets onto the grass ahead of them, and Agnes lifted it from her grasp.

She surveyed the grounds, searching for somewhere quiet and dark. Steering Juno down towards the lake, she lowered her gently onto the wooden planks of the jetty. Juno stretched out her hands greedily for the champagne glass and took a deep sip, her eyes half-closed, long eyelashes fanning her cheeks.

Agnes sat down next to her. The heady beat of the party was far away now, as gentle and repetitive as breathing, and her gaze was drawn to the lake's still surface, smooth and glassy.

'I've never really enjoyed champagne before,' Juno said. She was studying her crystal flute, her eyes slightly crossed. 'But it is really rather lovely, isn't it? Just think of all those bubbles fizzing inside you.'

This comment was so un-Juno-like that Agnes felt a small, hysterical bubble of laughter rear up inside her. She quashed it back, focusing on what she must do.

Juno put a hand on Agnes's knee. 'I should so like us to be friends,' she said.

Even through the silk, Agnes could feel the cold clamminess of her touch. She didn't answer straight away. She could feel herself changing, her face becoming hard and immobile, as if a mask had grown over her skin there like the ones belonging to the guests dancing round the fire. She felt her heart begin to beat faster.

'Perhaps we could,' she said at last. 'But friends are honest with each other, aren't they, Juno? Can you be honest with me?'

Juno's face took on a look of anguish. 'You'll hate me,' she said, a petulant whine in her voice like a child's. 'I know you'll hate me.'

'I won't,' Agnes hurried, taking both Juno's hands in hers, trying not to recoil at the feel of them. 'I promise I won't, just tell me the truth about why I'm here.'

They gazed at one another in the moonlight, their hands still joined. *This is it,* Agnes thought.

Then Juno's face changed, morphing into a look of sobered anger. 'I'm not that drunk, Mrs Fairhaven,' she said, dropping her hands. 'Like I said before, you're not as good a liar as I am. A few glasses of champagne aren't enough to get me to divulge my secrets.'

In frustration, Agnes turned to look at the house. She picked up her purse with a sigh, clicking it open to search for the ring of keys that Matron had given her, and her eyes settled on the syringes she had taken from the clearing.

One can have all kinds of enlightening conversations under its influence, Juno had told her once. *There's something quite wonderful about losing one's inhibitions like that. Our truths become so much easier to bear.*

Juno had not noticed her silence. She was gazing out at the lake, lost in thought, and as Agnes touched a finger to the smooth glass syringe, her heart gave a tick of fear. Would it be enough to get her to talk? Could she do it?

'Hello, Sippie dear,' Juno said suddenly, blinking out at the night, and Agnes looked up with a jolt of joy to see Sippie's silhouette appearing from the darkness.

'Hello, Juno,' Sippie said, coming to sit with them, her eyes growing wide as she glimpsed the syringes in Agnes's purse. She caught Agnes's gaze, and they stared at each other for a long moment, before Sippie gave a single, sharp nod.

Juno had gone back to gazing at the lake, completely unaware of the silent exchange taking place behind her. Quickly, Sippie slipped the two syringes from Agnes's purse, placing one on the jetty, and expertly tapping a fingernail against the other. The sharp glint of the needle caught the moonlight, and Agnes found she couldn't look away, bewitched by the opiate's shine.

Silently, Sippie passed it to her. *Ready?* she mouthed.

Agnes's heart skipped a beat. *Was* she ready? Time was running out. When would they ever get another opportunity like this?

Swallowing back her fear, she nodded, her head jerking up and down in overlarge movements, as if she no longer had control over her own body. She felt outside of herself, looking down at the scene like a god among the stars.

Sippie took a firm hold of Juno's slender arm. At the touch, Juno's head whipped round, her eyes locking onto the syringe in Agnes's hand. She went very still.

'What are you doing?' she whispered.

'I'm sorry,' Agnes said, tears filling her eyes. 'We just want the truth, Juno.'

Juno stared at her for a long second, then gave a shrug. 'Do what you want,' she said. 'There's no point me hiding anything from you anymore. You'll find out soon enough anyway.'

Sippie's hand tensed as she held fast to Juno's arm, trapping the blood there with her taut piano-playing fingers. Her arm was so thin, almost concave in places, the bones far too prominent, and Agnes worried they might snap.

'Here,' Sippie whispered, touching the crook of Juno's elbow, where a lilac vein was visible, and Agnes pressed the tip of the needle to the skin.

Juno kept her unblinking eyes on Agnes's the whole time. As she pushed the drug into the woman's arm, something in Juno changed. She shuddered, the breath she was holding spooling out into the night in a film of fog that flowed over the lake. Her body visibly slackened, her eyelids fluttering closed.

'Juno?' Agnes said, pulling the syringe out in terror, suddenly fearful.

Juno's face was waxy, her eyes still closed. And then a smile spread slowly across her face. 'I had forgotten how lovely this feels,' she said with a sigh, and Agnes breathed out in relief.

'Go on,' Sippie whispered urgently. 'Talk to her. This might be your only chance.'

Juno's head had fallen forwards. 'Juno?' Agnes whispered, taking her hand.

At her name, the young woman lifted her head, but her eyes remained closed.

'You told me Christian was going to do something ground-breaking. He was going to give you a new chance at life. What did you mean?'

Slowly, Juno opened her eyes. She stared unseeingly for a moment, her pupils large, so that Agnes wondered if she had heard her at all.

'Oh Mrs Fairhaven,' she said at last, lifting a finger and tracing it down Agnes's cheek. 'You have always been so very innocent, haven't you?'

'Juno, please,' Agnes begged.

But Juno only gave a sigh, her head wobbling on her neck as if it had grown too heavy for her body. Her chin dropped down to meet her chest, hair tumbling over her face.

'Tell me about the cure, then,' Agnes pushed. 'It's not real, is it?'

From beneath the curtain of rippling hair there came a crack of laughter. 'Of course not,' she said. 'It's just what he tells them to lure them here.'

She lifted her head, focusing on Agnes for the first time.

'He's curing *me*, though,' she said.

'What?' Agnes whispered.

'*Really* curing me, I mean.' The young woman's expression was frightening, her stare disconcertingly direct, her face for once filled with a terrifying ugliness.

'How?'

'I tricked him,' she said, her voice barely more than a whisper. 'I tricked him into doing something he would never have attempted if left to blunder along here on his own. Something ground-breaking.'

'What is it, Juno?'

'He's replacing one of my poor, damaged lungs with a nice, clean healthy one,' Juno said.

'What?' Agnes said, her voice rising in shock. 'But Christian wouldn't do that. It's too dangerous.'

'You don't know him, Agnes. Not really. Christian would do anything for Hedoné. For me.' She smiled, that strange, robotic smile, lacking in the grace that usually came so naturally to her.

'But surely it's not possible, moving a lung from one body to another? It's like something from science fiction.' Agnes looked to Sippie, but Juno was already nodding.

'It is possible,' she said. 'It's been done before. In rabbits.'

'Rabbits?'

'Rabbits represent resurrection, did you know that?' She lifted her face to the night sky, staring at the stars. 'All I want is to be resurrected,' she whispered, as if to herself. 'It's all I have ever wanted.'

Agnes didn't answer, staring at Juno in disgust.

'And now of course, he has begun to trial it. He's experimented on two women. Perfecting his art, you might say. For are we not all artists here, in some way or another?'

'Betty and Elsie,' Agnes whispered, feeling sick. The two graves, hidden in the trees.

Next to her, Sippie was looking at Juno with an expression of appalled realisation.

When she spoke, her voice was husky with emotion. 'Elizabeth Thackeray,' she said. 'She knew, didn't she? How did she find out? Or did you tell her what you were planning to do?'

Juno swept a trembling hand over her face. 'She didn't understand,' she said, and her voice for the first time was infused with regret. 'She was going to take it to the papers. Everything I had worked so hard to secure, gone, like that.' She clicked her fingers. 'So I did the only thing I could,' she said, touching a finger to the pinprick of red on her arm. 'And then I pushed her into the pool.'

Agnes sat back, reeling. Far off, she could hear the distant cries of excitement from the guests, but it might have been another world for all it meant.

A faraway look had come into Juno's eyes. 'I paid for her memorial myself. I wanted to do something, I suppose, to make up for it all.' She smiled. 'She always did love diamonds.'

Agnes shook her head, trying to focus on the facts. 'But those two women Christian experimented on — they died, Juno. They both died.'

'They did, eventually,' Juno said. 'Such a shame. They weren't healthy enough to survive, you see. They came from poor stock. But this time, he's found a much healthier body. One that is strong and virile, unlike the others. He believes he can do it, and better yet, he thinks he can keep both of us alive. You see, this one has a good heart.'

She stretched a trembling hand up and touched it to Agnes's breast, a look of zeal in her eyes, of desperate hope, and Agnes felt a crackle of terror.

'Whatever happens,' Juno said, 'however long I survive, I will have been at the forefront of modern science. You will remember that, won't you, dear Agnes, when all this is done?' An odd smile spread across her face.

Agnes sat back, reeling. Her mind harried over everything Juno had told her, knitting it all together, filling in the gaps. 'Who is this person, Juno?' she whispered, her thoughts flitting over every face she had seen since moving to Hedoné: the waiting staff, the maids, the carers. 'Who is the donor?'

But beneath all this, a terrible feeling was stirring, raising its monstrous head. She watched in silent, dawning horror, as Juno's face composed itself into a picture of serene beauty.

'Why, it's you, Mrs Fairhaven,' she said, a small smile of satisfaction spreading slowly across her face.

Chapter Fifty

Agnes hurried through the velvet black grounds. She and Sippie had scooped Juno up and placed her in a nearby deckchair, covering her with a blanket. They left her, head lolling, laughing softly to herself, her unfocused eyes gazing up at the night sky.

'She's deranged,' Sippie said, catching up with Agnes, her voice husky with shock.

'She's not deranged, she's just desperate and frightened.'

It was late now. Across the grounds, Agnes could see that the area surrounding the bonfire was empty of dancers, the beat that had throbbed through the air gone. Instead, the sound of a violin drifted from the trees beyond, just audible over the crackle of the bonfire.

'We ought to tell the guests now, while they're all together,' she said. 'Who knows what Juno's capable of? She's already told us she killed her best friend to keep her secrets intact. We need to let them know before she sobers up, before Christian realises we know.'

She knew it would be better to wait for the morning, when the guests had slept off their excesses, but this was a luxury they did not have.

As they emerged from the trees, they saw that the party had begun to wind down. Guests were lounging on the sofas and stretched out on the rugs. Christian was not among them.

'I'll talk to them,' Sippie said. 'You go and pack your belongings, and then find Isobel. I'll meet you at the front steps.'

'And then what?' Agnes asked.

'Then we leave.'

Across the glade, a young man was gazing into a huge mirror strung from the circle of trees, reciting Shakespeare to himself, and Agnes looked on, captivated by his gaunt, beautiful face illuminated by the bulbs above.

'But soft,' he said, looking up and seeing them reflected in the glass, 'what light through yonder window breaks?'

It was such a gentle, magical scene, and she steeled herself for the horrors that they were about to unleash. Swallowing back her fear, she squeezed Sippie's hand.

'I shall see you soon,' she said with a quick smile, and then she turned and began to run.

The cottage was in darkness as she approached, but she knew her way by now without the need for a light. She found Christian, crashed out on the bed, a ray of moonlight across his face.

As quietly as possible, she pulled her old carpet bag out of the wardrobe, comforted by the sight of the familiar swirling pattern on the worn fabric. She began to pack, taking only her old clothes, her thin cardigans and darned skirts, thankful she had not got rid of them. She left the sumptuous silks and wools and jewel-encrusted dresses in the wardrobe, feeling a satisfied sense of detachment.

When she was finished, Agnes looked down on her husband. In sleep, without the worries and secrets that he so cautiously guarded, he looked peaceful, tranquil, even. He looked like the man she had met on the French Riviera, and for a brief, exquisite moment, she allowed herself to grieve for all that was lost.

And then Christian's eyes opened, and a hand shot out, clamping onto her wrist.

Agnes jumped back, her heart pounding like the explosion of fireworks earlier.

'Agnes,' he murmured, those startling blue eyes fixed on hers, then on the bag sitting on the dressing table. His eyes widened. 'What are you doing?' he whispered.

'Let go of me,' she said through gritted teeth, surprising herself at the authority in her voice.

'Are you leaving me?' he whispered. Letting go of her wrist, he scrambled up in bed, putting a hand to his temple, flinching.

'Of course I am,' she spat. 'I *know*, Christian.'

'You know what?'

'Everything. Juno told me. The sterilisations. The experiments. Where I fit into it all.' A queasiness spread through her as she recalled Juno's words.

'It's not what you think,' he said. 'I promise, Agnes. I swear. I would *never* hurt you, you must believe me. Juno—'

Agnes swung round. 'Don't you dare say her name,' she hissed. 'You lied about everything. You used a false cure to lure people here, so you could experiment on them, sterilise them!'

Christian swallowed, his Adam's apple jerking unpleasantly in his throat. He put a hand to his head again, wincing.

'Feeling a little unwell?' Agnes said. 'It's not nice, is it, being given medication you didn't ask for.' Christian looked up at her, bewildered. 'I sedated you,' she said savagely.

'You . . . sedated . . .'

'Rackham knew, didn't he?' she cut in, impatient for the truth. 'He knew what you were doing to those women in your care. He wanted to warn them all, but instead you shut him up in quarantine. He

343

ended up dead for his efforts!'

Christian took a great, shuddering breath. 'I only ever tried to save people, Agnes, I promise. Everything that happened – the whole spiralling mess – it was only because Juno—'

'Oh, Juno, Juno, Juno,' Agnes said, furious now. 'When are you going to take responsibility for your own actions, Christian?'

'She blackmailed me!' he said, his own voice rising. 'I would never have done any of it, I swear. I had no choice.'

'There's always a choice,' she said coldly.

'No,' Christian said, and the conviction in his voice surprised her. 'Please,' he whispered. 'Just let me explain.'

Agnes went to the window. Through the trees, a thin line of palest lavender had appeared, the first sign of morning. She could see her husband's reflection, hunched on the edge of the bed, cowed and fragile.

'Go on,' she said.

'It was Juno who approached me to run Hedoné House three years ago. She'd read a paper I wrote while doing my medical training, and knowing my interest in tuberculosis, she sought me out. She came to me with an offer from her father. If I would agree to explore the idea of sterilisation at Hedoné, then he would back me; would protect me, even. I could be at the forefront of scientific research. He would invest money into this place, allowing it to become the most luxurious, ground-breaking sanatorium that had ever existed in Britain. I was already having to perform medical abortions; this operation was barely a step further.'

'Oh, I see! So, you did this for *science*.' Agnes gave a scoffing, scornful laugh.

'No.' He shook his head vehemently. 'Have you ever seen a pregnant tuberculous woman, Agnes?' he asked her quietly. 'Because I have. I've seen many, and I promise you, it is never a good outcome. Most often the woman dies before the child is born. And if they live, well, it is a long and painful decline. A life worse than death.' He swallowed, as if nauseous. 'I agreed to operate on just one patient. A young woman so terribly unwell with the disease that there was no doubt she would have died had she become pregnant.'

Agnes took a step back in horror, tears stinging her eyelids.

'And then, afterwards, when I told Juno the operation had been a success, she said she had lied: that her father had no idea what I had done, and that he would be appalled if he knew. She told me that she had enough evidence to go to the police. I was finished, unless I continued to do as she asked.'

He ran a hand over his jaw.

'Her father had access to all kinds of scientific papers, even those not yet published. She had been reading up on a procedure, a dubious experiment regarding the transplantation of lungs from a healthy body into an unhealthy one. She wanted me to attempt it on her. Up until then, it had only been performed on rabbits.' He broke off, looking down at his hands, twisting his wedding ring.

'But surely you told her it was impossible?'

'Of course I did. But this is Juno Harrington we're talking about.' His face took on a snarl of hatred. 'Juno enjoyed baiting me. She designed this whole place to ensure I was always reminded about what I must do. She twisted rabbits into the gate's design, dotted golden rabbit buttons throughout the house, beadily staring at me wherever I went. She even gave me rabbit cufflinks. Each time I lifted my hands, they caught the light, reminding me again and again of what she wanted from me.' He sighed. 'In the end, I told her that I would attempt the lung operation, with one stipulation: if I were to agree to do it, I would only transplant one lung so that the donor 'could still live.'

'How gracious of you,' Agnes spat. 'And yet two women died.'

Christian sighed, a great shuddering sigh that drew all the breath from his body. 'No,' he said. 'It wasn't like that.'

'Then what was it like? I've seen their graves, Christian. Are you telling me I'm wrong, that they're not dead?' Hope flared within her. Could the graves be empty, like Meredith Fairhaven's? Had he tricked Juno all along?

But Christian looked up at her, his eyes sunken in his face. 'Of course they're dead,' he said. 'They were already dying when they arrived here.'

Agnes spun back to the room. 'But I've seen their notes,' she said. 'They didn't have TB. Their x-rays were clear.'

'They were prostitutes,' he said. 'Riddled with venereal disease. I brought them here from the slums they were living in, and I cared for them until they died. I gave them a good death, Agnes, letting them go in as dignified a manner as possible.'

'But . . . why?'

'I needed Juno to believe that I was experimenting on women, perfecting the transplantation process. I hoped that when she saw that two women had died, she would give up on the idea. But Juno Harrington is not a normal human being. When she first started all of this, she suggested I use Meredith's lungs. She was fixated with the idea. Ours had never been a happy marriage, but I would never have done such a thing to my wife. So I pretended to Juno that Meredith had TB. But of course, she saw straight through that lie. In the end, I forced Meredith to leave. I threatened her — it was the only way I could ensure she would be safe.'

'You're still married?' Agnes whispered.

'Yes. But only on paper.'

Agnes twisted away from him, aghast at the levels of duplicity.

'But sending Meredith away was for nothing,' Christian said. 'It simply made Juno more determined.' His face collapsed in a grimace of guilt. 'And then after the two prostitutes died, she told me that I needed to find someone stronger, that when I next went to the Continent to find scholars, I should also search for a new subject, a healthy subject.'

Agnes stared at him, knowing what was coming.

'And then I found you,' he finished, and she sank into a chair in horror.

'So, you brought me back here with the intention of cutting me up?'

'No!' He raised his hands in supplication. 'Please, Agnes. I was never going to operate on you. I hadn't even planned to take you as my wife. You were a decoy, that's all. But a few days after I first saw you, the idea came to me, and I realised it was the best shot I had. I hoped that once we were married, you might become pregnant. Even Juno wouldn't want me to operate on a healthy woman carrying a child. It bought us time, at least.'

Agnes paused at this, shocked at the layers of lies he was capable of. She thought of the number of times he had asked her if she might be pregnant, feeling sick as she saw how tightly she was stitched into his plan.

'So, what were you going to do? Lock me up in the infirmary until I wasted away, so you could pretend to Juno that you'd failed again?'

'No! Never!' His eyes were wide with horror.

'But that's what you did with Georgie Murphy, and all the other patients who died down there, wasn't it? I don't know if you intended to kill them, or if you just wanted them out of the way. What's the saying? Out of sight, out of mind?'

Hysteria was beginning to set in now, her head buzzing with the adrenalin of it.

'At what point exactly did you begin to kill off your patients, Christian?'

His face changed, a look of shock coming over him. 'Kill them? No, you have it all wrong. I didn't kill anyone, I swear it.'

He sounded so genuine. Was he really that deluded?

'You overdosed their medication, Christian. Matron told me.'

Her husband's face paled. 'No. Georgie Murphy died from an opioid overdose, that is true,' he said. 'But he was found with a syringe in the infirmary. He did it himself. I don't know how he got the medicine from the cupboard; it's always kept locked. The others were just too desperately unwell to live. I would never give my patients too much medication. I *know* tuberculous bodies, Agnes, I *know* them.'

'But,' she stuttered, 'those men at the delegates dinner — Herr Schultz and his abhorrent ideas — you agreed with them, with all their disgusting talk of patients being like lab rats, worth so much less than everyone else.'

'Just because I was interested in his theories, doesn't mean I would go ahead and start euthanising the guests!'

'That's not what Iso told me,' she said quietly.

Christian's brow drew together. 'What would Isobel know of my practices?'

'She's been breaking into the infirmary, visiting your patients. They're so sick and starved that she's been feeding them jam. Giving them the love and care that you've denied them.'

'That doesn't make sense, why would she . . .' He stumbled to a stop, and his face was suddenly full of an unimaginable horror. 'Jam,' he whispered. 'Oh no. Oh, no, no, no.'

'What is it?' she said, but he only turned to her, contrition etched into his features.

'Oh god, Agnes, what have I done?'

She had expected anger and denial, but this reaction was neither of those things. He began pacing the room, his expression stricken with guilt, and Agnes bunched her hands into fists in frustration.

Enough, she thought. She began collecting up her belongings. Lifting her bag, she cradled it in her arms.

'What are you doing?' Christian whispered, his face white.

'I'm leaving.'

'Agnes, wait.'

He stumbled towards her, landing hard on his knees and reaching for her hands, but she shrank back against the doorframe in revulsion. Striding around him, she went to the dressing table, gathering her old hairbrush and pins and dropping them into her bag. Unhooking the clasp of the diamond necklace, she dropped it in after them, rubbing at her neck where it had lain, relieved to be able to breathe properly again.

'Agnes,' Christian said again, still bowed on the floor. 'I never set out to hurt you. I promise I didn't. Tell me how to fix this.'

She turned from the dressing table, looking down at him, cowering before her. 'How do you fix this?' she said. 'You let me go.'

Chapter Fifty-One

Agnes closed the door of the cottage and hefted her carpet bag into her arms. She realised she was trembling. On the doorstep she paused, looking up at the sky. It was nearly dawn.

She followed the path back to the grounds. It was very quiet. The bonfire had nearly burnt itself out. She stumbled over a discarded mask on the grass in the shape of a rabbit's head. Kicking it aside in disgust, she turned to look at the house.

Hedoné sat, long and low, dark against the backdrop of pine trees. Agnes thought of Isobel up there on the quarantine floor, and she started towards the house, stepping over spent sparklers and champagne glasses. A sharp crackle behind her, and she turned, peering through the dawn light.

The smouldering remains of the bonfire glowed like hot coals, a charred skeleton of twigs and branches silhouetted against the pale lavender sky. Something right at the top still flickered brightly, half consumed by flames.

It looked like a person.

In panic, Agnes dropped her bag and began to run towards the bonfire. As she reached it, her heart gave a moan of relief. It was only the Guy.

The stuffed effigy had been thrown atop the smouldering heap. As she peered through the swirling smoke, she thought she could make out two startling blue eyes painted onto its cloth face.

Christian, she thought, with a flash of satisfaction. This must mean that Sippie had told the guests. Quickly, she crossed to the clearing in the woods, passing the wheeled chair she had arrived in, upended on the grass, the pretty upholstery ripped and ragged.

The glade was empty, the mirrors reflecting her image back to her again and again, and she hurried back through the trees, skirting the edge of the bonfire, before coming to a stumbling stop.

The sky was lightening now. Far ahead, the house stood, pale and magnificent in the dawn. She could make out the silhouettes of what must be the guests, clustered on the grass around the house, and among them, three or four bright dots of fire. Confused, Agnes went closer, trying to make sense of what she was looking at. As the sky brightened, she saw that the dots were flaming torches, held aloft in the guests' hands. She could hear them spitting and crackling now, like a travesty of the sparklers she had seen earlier, and as she watched, that same pulsing drumbeat began again, an eerie, percussive throbbing. But now it felt different, more insistent.

Like a call to arms.

Agnes began to run.

She flew across the grounds, losing her shoes as she stumbled through the grass, the lawn below her blurring as she willed herself to speed up, speed up. She could see the guests properly now. They were all wearing the animal masks again, their faces hidden behind grotesque snarling wolf heads and long-eared rabbits. And then, when she was still too far away, one of them launched a torch at the house.

'Stop!' Agnes called out. 'Stop! Isobel's in there!' But she was

351

too far away, the sound of the drums and the chants of the crowd drowning her out.

More torches were being lit now, and as she looked on helplessly, more and more guests began throwing them at the house. One hit a wall and fell back in a shower of sparks. Another arced up towards the building, and this time Agnes watched transfixed as it disappeared in through an open bedroom window.

She came to a terrified halt , her eyes fixed on the muslin curtains that billowed out into the dawn air. Through the window, she caught sight of a glimmer of gold.

Juno's bedroom.

Was Juno in there? Agnes turned, searching the lawn down by the lake, trying to work out if the young woman was still down there, but it was too dark to see. She turned back to the house, and her eyes settled on the bedroom above Juno's, and another, more desperate thought took hold of her.

Iso.

She began to run again, unaware that the grass had given way to shingle beneath her bare feet. She kicked aside a shard of a broken champagne glass, not feeling it slice into her heel. As she reached the crowd, she found Sippie in the middle, desperately trying to talk sense into the guests.

'Iso is still in there!' Agnes shouted into her ear. All around her, the guests were yelling, chanting, bellowing their anger, and she began grabbing at people, trying to reason with them, but they were beyond that now.

A great whoop of excitement went up, and she turned to look at the house. The curtains at Juno's window were enveloped in a tongue of fire. Agnes stood, pinned to the spot as it licked and danced its way across the fluttering fabric, consuming it in seconds. And then a crack like gunshot rent the air, followed instantly by a great spray of glass from the next room along as the windows exploded.

The guests all fell silent, the drum beat vanishing, the only sound the splintered glass pattering to the ground. And then a sudden, growing roar, as the fire began to charge unseen through Hedoné's rooms.

'Iso!' Agnes screamed, running as close to the house as possible. Smoke had started pouring out from Juno's windows, drifting up towards the balcony above. Sippie joined her, taking up the call.

And then, from somewhere deep in the house, a siren, low and quiet at first, then spooling out into the grounds with an urgent, strident call. Staff were swarming out of the far exit in their nightclothes. They formed a line from the lake to the house and began passing buckets of water along. Seeing this, some of the guests joined them.

People rushed past, water sloshing as the buckets were borne towards the fire. Through the smoke, Agnes saw the door to the entrance hall standing open, and she ran towards it and stumbled up the steps.

The fire had already reached the great cavernous hall, the heat of it pushing her backwards. She turned away from its force. Across the grounds, she sensed movement through the smoke, somebody running towards her. Christian.

'Isobel is in there,' Agnes shouted, her voice scratchy from the smoke, and he turned to her, his eyes wide with fear.

Something passed between them, an understanding, a transaction. And then Christian nodded once. Turning to the house, he raised an arm to protect his face, and disappeared inside.

Agnes stumbled back down the steps, towards the balcony that led to Isobel's room. As she drew close, her knees buckled, and she collapsed onto the grass, all strength draining from her.

Time slowed, the seconds drawing out like an unwound clock. The world changed, the sound deadening, movements torpid. At one point, Sippie's face swam in front of hers. She was shouting, but her voice seemed far away. Agnes looked down and saw that her foot was bleeding and her dress was ripped and spattered with blood. But none of it mattered anymore. She lifted her gaze to the house, and waited.

Chapter Fifty-Two

She waited for long minutes, gazing up at Isobel's balcony. Smoke was pouring out of the upstairs quarantine rooms now. The windows of Juno's room were black and charred, the space inside a gaping void.

Tears tracked down Agnes's cheeks, but still she waited. Christian must have found her by now. Surely at any moment he would emerge with his daughter in his arms.

The sun began to rise over the sea, as unconnected to this nightmare as if it belonged to another world. Something fluttered out from a shattered downstairs window, catching on the breeze and soaring high into the sky. It glittered momentarily in the emerging sunlight, a scrap of gold leaf from the wall of Juno's bedroom, and Agnes gazed at it, hypnotised, as it ribboned up, higher and higher.

And then, behind it, high up on a balcony, she saw a figure.

'Iso,' she whispered.

She was on her feet in an instant, searching through the smoke, her sore eyes blinking away grit and ash. But the figure that emerged was not her stepdaughter.

Christian had a handkerchief pressed to his mouth. 'She isn't here,' he called down, his voice cut off as he coughed against the smoke.

She could see the terror on his face.

'She must be!' she cried.

'She's truly not. I've searched every corner.' Through the smoke, she saw her husband put a hand on the balcony, clutching it as if it were the bow of a sinking ship, and for a brief moment she thought he was about to climb over the edge, to try to jump to safety. But then he jerked his hand away. Turning back to the bedroom, he disappeared again, lost to the smoke.

Where could she be? Agnes ran through the rooms of the house in her mind. The music room, the library, her stepdaughter's bedroom. And then it came to her.

The infirmary.

I go there sometimes, Iso had said to her the night she jumped into the lake. *I feel safe there. You won't tell Papa, will you?*

Agnes stumbled across the grass, running to the entrance hall. The fire there had almost burnt itself out. She could see the lift through the smoke, the gate open from Christian's ascent to the quarantine floor. She scrabbled in her purse, finding the keys that Matron had given her. Would the lift still work? With one last look out over the grounds, Agnes ran forward.

The heat in the hall was all-consuming, the air devoid of oxygen. Fingers fumbling, she inserted the key, pressing the button for the basement, sensing the warm imprint of the rabbit against the pad of her thumb. She stood, her muscles taut, hoping, praying that the mechanism would work. With a sound of gears crunching, the lift rumbled into life, and Agnes let out a breath of relief. The compartment slid down from the upstairs floor, settling in front of her, and she hurried inside.

As the lift drew to a stop on the basement floor, she peered into the corridor. It was cooler down here, the pretty sconces on the wall flickering on and off, plunging her momentarily into darkness and light, and Agnes shuddered. The lift was the only way out. She must find Isobel and get back to safety before the electricity failed completely.

She hurried down the corridor, the air getting hotter the further she progressed. At the infirmary door, she peered through the little window.

The room was consumed by flames. The ceiling had given way, and Juno's bed jutted down at a sharp angle from above. Flecks of gold leaf fell like rain. The cupboard on the wall that she remembered from her last visit had begun to melt, the skull and crossbones on its door warped and dripping like a surrealist painting.

And then Agnes saw her. Isobel was huddled in a ball under the infirmary bed, her head buried in her arms. Agnes pushed open the door, bracing herself as the heat forced her back.

'Isobel!' she called, shading her face from the heat.

Her stepdaughter looked up. 'Mama?' she said, her voice so small and frightened that it made Agnes's heart clench.

'Iso, we must get out of here. Now.'

The girl was only a few feet away. Agnes reached out her hand. 'Come, Iso,' she stuttered.

But Isobel gave a frightened shake of her head. A great cloud of smoke curled towards her and she began to cough.

'Iso, we don't have long,' Agnes pleaded, as the fallen bed above them gave a creak, shifting a few inches further into the room. Beyond the far wall, something heavy crashed to the ground. 'Please,' she begged again, her voice cracking. 'I need you to try. For me.' She cast around, trying to chivvy the child along. 'If you come with me now, we'll leave this place. We'll go and find your mother, I promise.'

The girl lifted her chin, and Agnes thought she could see a trickle of determination in her silver eyes.

'That's it,' Agnes said, reaching out as far as she dared. 'Come along, take my hand. You're so close.'

Slowly, Isobel uncurled herself and crept out from under the bed. She got to her feet, her nightdress billowing about her. Above her, the falling bed creaked again.

'Quickly!' Agnes cried, and Iso broke into a run, closing the gap between them, her thin arms wrapping tightly around Agnes's waist.

'Good girl,' Agnes said. 'Oh, good girl.'

She pulled her from the room, closing the door behind them to contain the fire. Holding hands tightly, they ran back along the corridor, the lights above them flickering. At the lift, Agnes inserted the key and pressed the button, pulling Iso into the compartment with her. She waited, her heart racing, but nothing happened.

'Damn it,' she whispered, jabbing at the button again.

From down the corridor, there was a sudden, splintering crash as the glass in the infirmary door burst outwards. Agnes felt the heat of it almost immediately. She stabbed at the button again, just as the lights went out, plunging them into darkness. Around them, the low hum of the lift's inner workings cut off.

'No,' she whispered. She pressed the button again, scrabbling for it in the dark. 'No,' she sobbed. Not now, not when they were so close.

In the pitch black, she felt Iso's small hand take hold of hers.

'Mama,' Iso said, 'this way.' She felt the insistent tug of her hand as the girl stepped out of the lift.

'What are you doing?' she whispered.

'Come, Mama.'

She was pulling her back towards the infirmary, back to the heat and the horrifying roar of the fire.

'We can't go that way, Isobel, there's no way out.'

But her hand was insistent. 'Come, Mama,' she said again, and her voice was so calm, so full of peace and trust, that Agnes gave in to it.

She let the girl lead her, back towards the infirmary. It was impossibly dark, the only light the pulsing threat of fire ahead. The heat here was abominable. Halfway to the infirmary, Iso came to a stop. She put her hand to the wall, and opened a hatch, and Agnes's heart gave a bound of joy.

Iso began climbing up into the space, and Agnes ducked her head in and looked up. It was a laundry chute. In the darkness, she could make out the shine of the metal walls. It was angled ever so slightly, but still, it would be a perilous fall.

The girl began to climb, moving at a lightning pace as if she had done it many times before. Agnes watched her disappear into the darkness. There was a dim flash of light above, and then she was gone.

'Iso?' Agnes called, but there was no answer, just the echo of her own voice, reverberating off the metal walls.

Cautiously, she pulled herself into the tight space. She tried to copy how the girl had climbed, pressing her hands and feet flat to the metal, and slowly, painfully, she began to move upwards, her muscles singing with the effort.

A flash of light above her, and Isobel's face appeared, silhouetted against another hatched doorway. 'Hurry!' she called down, her voice reverberating in the metal chute.

Agnes climbed. She could feel the metal beneath her palms getting hotter the higher she went. She dared not think how close the fire was up here. Her cut foot, sticky with blood, slipped, and she dropped down a little way before her limbs reacted, anchoring her in place.

Slowly, inch by inch, she moved up the chute, her teeth set, her face fierce with determination, until finally, she tumbled through an opening, the fresh air from the entrance hall doorway clawing its way into her lungs. With a rasping breath she collapsed onto the polished marble floor, the thoughts in her mind softly scattering like the ash she could feel falling on her face, her hands, her hair.

Chapter Fifty-Three

'Mama?' Agnes felt Iso's small hand pulling at her. 'Mama, get up. It's Papa.'

Agnes staggered to her feet and followed blindly through the smoke. Ahead of them she saw a body, slumped on the floor.

'Christian,' she croaked, dropping to her knees, her hands cupping his skull, fragile as an egg. In the thick, miasmic air, she could not tell if he was breathing.

'Help him, Mama, help him.'

Getting to her feet, Agnes placed her hands under his arms and, with her last remaining strength, began to pull.

She dragged him across the marble tiles, her teeth gritted, grunting with the effort, the smoke scorching her throat. Out of the front door. Down the steps, the child, whimpering now, leading the way. As the ferocious heat of the fire began to abate, Agnes sank down onto the dew-heavy grass, its cool touch like a welcome breath. She bent to listen at Christian's mouth, her ear so close she brushed the stubbled jaw.

'Make him better.' Iso's voice was filled with sadness.

Agnes placed a hand on his stilled chest, searching for signs of life.

'Please, Mama, please. Make him better.' The girl was crying now, silent, gasping sobs, but Agnes did not hear her. She lifted her husband's soot-blackened hand, feeling his wrist for a pulse with every nerve ending. Nothing.

'Give him jam,' the girl said, and Agnes roused.

'Jam?' she repeated, blinking at her stepdaughter.

Isobel fumbled at her neck, pulling out a little key on a chain. She held it up, the reflection of the flames winking on its shiny surface.

'What's this?'

'The skull cupboard.' The words were hardly audible in the torrent of tears coming from her now, and a growing feeling of alarm ribboned through Agnes. She thought of the hollow, staring eyes of the skull and crossbones on the medicine cupboard.

'What do you mean, Iso?'

'Mor-fine,' Isobel said, sounding out the word she had clearly read but never heard. 'It makes them better.' She sniffed. 'Papa used to give it to me when I was little, mixed with jam. I gave it to the guests.' She swallowed, wiping her face. 'The sweetness takes the bitter taste away.'

Fear spiralled through Agnes's smoke-clouded thoughts. '*You* gave this to the patients, Iso?' The girl nodded, sniffing back her tears. 'How much?'

She shrugged. 'I just shook it on the jam,' she said. 'I mixed it up. It helped. It always helped. Mr Rackham liked the blackcurrant best. He liked it when I fed it to him.'

Slow, dawning horror stirred through Agnes. 'And my mother?' she whispered.

'She . . . she said it tasted like ambrosia,' Iso whispered.

Agnes gazed at her stepdaughter's ash-blackened face. 'Oh, sweet girl,' she murmured, drawing her close, feeling the weight of her blameless, helpless innocence.

Behind them, a gasping breath, and she broke away, staring at Christian. His chest was rising, his dry, parched lips working up and down as if he was trying to speak. She bent low to him, putting her ear close to his mouth.

'Take . . . her,' he whispered.

Matron was suddenly there. 'Move the girl away, Agnes,' she said. 'She shouldn't see this.'

Numbly, Agnes did as she was told, taking Isobel by the hand and leading her away from her father. Halfway to the lake, they stopped. The girl climbed into Agnes lap, wrapping her arms tightly about her neck, and Agnes found herself clinging back, staring dazedly around her as the scene played out in front of them, as fragmented as the diaphanous flakes of the burning house spiralling into the air all around.

She did not know how long they sat, holding one another. She was aware of people milling about them. The roof of the house had begun to sag in on itself now, and Agnes gazed at it, strangely unemotional. Someone handed her water in a champagne flute, and she trickled it into Iso's parched mouth, before gulping the last of it down herself, feeling it cool her scorched throat.

Carefully, Agnes helped Iso to her feet, wiping at a dark smudge of soot on her stepdaughter's cheek. She remembered with a pang how her own mother had done the same for her on the train when they arrived here. The child was hugging a small, leatherbound book to her chest, her arms crossed over it protectively.

Matron appeared out of the smoke, ghostlike in a long nightdress. Taking her stethoscope, she commenced to examine Iso. Agnes looked over to where her husband lay. She could just make him out through the smoke.

'Is he . . .' she began.

Matron looked up, her mouth set into a thin line, then looked pointedly at Isobel, and Agnes gave a nod of understanding. Isobel did not need to know right now.

Taking the stethoscope, the nurse placed it against Agnes's chest. 'No lasting damage,' she said. She turned to look at the house. 'This was not the end I expected.'

'Nor I,' Agnes replied, gazing at the skeletal remains of the building.

Matron pressed a piece of paper into her hand. 'Sippie asked me to give you this address. She said to look for her there.'

Agnes glanced up at Matron, blinking ash from her eyelashes. 'She's gone?'

'She said it was too risky for her to stay any longer, and I don't blame her. There are going to be questions,' Matron said. 'Police. Doctors.'

Doctors. Agnes shuddered. 'Thank you, Matron,' she said. 'For everything you've done.'

Matron nodded, briefly taking Agnes's hand in her own. Across the grounds, a shout for help went up, and she hurried away, disappearing into the crowd of people.

Far away, the jangling bell of a fire engine rose, growing louder, and Agnes drew her stepdaughter close. 'I think it's time we found your mother,' she whispered.

She collected up her carpet bag, abandoned on the grass, and they began to walk across the grounds, passing the chalets and deckchairs, making their way down towards the path that curved around the lake.

Near the water, a lone deckchair was standing on the grass, far away from all the others. As they approached, Agnes came to a stop.

Juno Harrington was lying where they had left her, a blanket covering her slim body. One thin arm hung down towards the grass, a silk scarf tied tightly as a tourniquet. A spent syringe lay nearby.

Juno's almond eyes were open, staring glassily at the lake. In death, she was even more startlingly beautiful than in life.

Agnes touched the toe of her shoe to the syringe, wondering for a moment where Juno had got it. She remembered vaguely as if it were a lifetime ago, her purse, and the syringes she had stowed inside. Had Juno seen that second one, and been so allured by the feeling of the drug in her veins that she decided she must have more? Or had she simply realised that she'd said too much, and, knowing her time was up, ended things on her own terms?

Agnes put her arm around Isobel and steered her away from the lake and the deckchair and the dead girl. As they began to walk down the smooth, straight road that led out of Hedoné's grounds, a fire engine hurtled past, alarm bells clamouring. Ahead, the wrought iron gates she remembered so well from her first day stood open, no longer any electricity to lock them in place. Agnes could just make out the shape of the leaping rabbit twisted into the ornate metal, its beady eye staring at her as if awaiting her departure.

Something — a sound, a voice — made her turn back, and her trembling gaze met with the building one last time.

It was consumed by fire now, more gilded than it had ever looked. The early morning sky was obliterated by a blanket of smoke. Agnes thought of the opulent marble and mirrors and gold leaf inside, all now devoured by flames.

It no longer resembled a luxurious hotel. It looked instead like the set of a play, its flimsy façade too weak to hide the rot and canker beneath, and as she stared unblinkingly up at it, a feeling of hope rose inside her.

She pulled Isobel to her, dropping a kiss on her soft, silvery head.

'Come,' she whispered, and together, they walked through the gates to the world beyond.

Chapter Fifty-Four

Three Months Later

The walk from the station was a long one, the rain stinging her skin, the clouds above a mercurial, oppressive grey.

Agnes had seen no houses for the last mile of winding, twisted roads, as if no one cared to live too close, and as she came to a stop at the metal gate, she realised why. The place looked like a prison. Quite rightly, she supposed. If it weren't for the sickness that burrowed deep inside each resident, many of its inhabitants would be locked away.

She put a hand to the towering gate. There was no wrought iron scrollwork there, only thick, dark, impenetrable bars. Lifting the heavy latch, she hefted her weight against it. It inched forward with a screech that set her teeth on edge.

The building was set high on a hill, like Hedoné House had been, but there the resemblance ended. Above the main entrance, the Latin phrase *Nil nisi bonum* towered in foot-high lettering. It was an outdated, unfashionable building, desperately in need of a paint.

Or a gild, Agnes mused, the thought raising a smile to her lips.

There was no entrance hall, only a small reception, a wizened old nurse standing behind a desk. Her eyebrows were prickly with determination, the biggest thing about her.

'Yes?' she said, the cloth of her mask bunching up over her jaw, and Agnes was reminded fondly for a moment of Matron.

'I'm here to see a patient. Christopher Fairhaven?'

The name felt alien on her lips, and for a moment, she hoped that she'd got it wrong, that the patient in here was another man altogether. In the first few weeks after she'd left Hedoné, she had not known or cared if Christian had survived. But recently, something had begun to eat away at her. A need to know, to understand.

It wasn't hard to find out where he had been taken. The newspapers had been filled with the scandal, and though she hadn't wanted to read them at the time, Sippie had kept them for her just in case.

'Name?' the nurse said.

'Miss Templeton.'

The woman ran her finger down a list. 'Ah yes,' she said, picking up a cloth mask from a tray on the counter. 'Put this on please.'

Agnes followed her down dark, green-painted corridors, past countless doors, each inset with a glass panel stippled with wire mesh. A strip light above them buzzed loudly. Groans and shouts echoed from behind the doors they passed, the wet sound of coughing, a short, sharp scream of pain. They drew to a stop near the end of the corridor, and she forced herself not to peer in through the murky glass.

'It's actually good that you came today, Miss Templeton,' the nurse said. 'We don't believe he has very long left to live, which, I suppose, is a blessing, given the circumstances.' She paused, taking in Agnes's moth-eaten cardigan, more darn than holes, and her skirt, too thin for this time of year. 'Are you a relative?'

'A very distant one.'

'How kind of you to visit. You're his first ever visitor, in fact.' The woman glanced up and down the corridor, checking it was clear, her bushy eyebrows lifting slightly, and Agnes had the distinct impression that she was licking her lips beneath the mask. 'Did you know him well?'

'Not well,' Agnes said truthfully.

The nurse looked disappointed.

'I only know what was reported at the time. That, and the publication of Juno Harrington's diaries, of course. Did you read them?'

'No,' Agnes lied, though she had taken the diary to the news building herself. She supposed that Juno had always wanted to make her mark, to leave an imprint long after she was gone. But not even Juno could have imagined the fame that would befall her in the end. Not, as she'd hoped, for her role at the forefront of modern science, or even for her acting skills. All that had been eclipsed in the blink of an eye by the words she had foolishly written in that little diary, saved from the fire. Agnes often still marvelled at how blinkered Juno had been, to leave such detailed insight into her most private thoughts lying around. But then, she had always thought herself untouchable.

Agnes had been back to Hedoné just once since she and Isobel limped away from the burning building. As she'd stepped through the open gate, she'd barely given the burnt-out shell of the house a second glance. Instead, she had picked her way through the trees to the memorial garden.

She'd climbed the hill in silence, parting the sharp wire fencing and emerging at last into the oval glade. There, Agnes had placed a bouquet of dried lavender at her mother's grave, and stood for a moment, eyes closed in contemplation. With a quick inhalation, she'd turned away, searching the garden until her eyes lit on a small, scrubby patch of grass. Taking a wooden memorial plaque from her bag, she had placed it unceremoniously on the ground. It boasted no diamonds or gold leaf, only a name, Juno Harrington, the cheap wood plain and simple. Agnes had noted with pleasure how ephemeral it looked, destined to fade and rot to nothing over time, and she had smiled.

The nurse touched the pane of glass in the door, wiping away a smear that looked decidedly like saliva, then rapped smartly on it, making Agnes jump.

It was answered almost immediately by a small, fair-haired nurse. She looked too young and innocent to be doing such a thankless job, and Agnes was reminded with a twist of pity of herself on that first day at Hedoné.

'Nurse Williams, Mr Fairhaven has a visitor.'

The young woman nodded, a quick, nervous flinch.

'I must ask that you do not approach the patient,' the older nurse said to Agnes. 'As I'm sure you're aware, he should by rights be in prison. I shall leave you in Nurse Williams's hands.' And with one last look at her, she marched off down the corridor.

'Come in,' the young woman said, and Agnes stepped into the room.

It was a small, dark space, barely a room at all. The single window was wide open, a blast of cold February air cutting through the antiseptic smell like a knife. There was only one patient in here. He was sitting in a wheeled chair, facing away from her. The chair was much less luxurious than the one Agnes and her mother had used at Hedoné. Next to it, a large oxygen canister rested on wheels, the rubber tubing hissing unpleasantly.

'You have a visitor, Christopher,' the nurse said, her voice light and kind.

The man in the chair moved his head slightly, as if in acknowledgement, but he did not turn.

'He's very weak,' the nurse whispered. 'Go on.'

Agnes stepped forward.

The man in the chair was barely recognisable as her husband. He was gaunt and sickly, a facsimile of his own patients at Hedoné. As she moved into his line of sight, she thought she saw something in his eyes change. A flash of recognition, of fear. Or perhaps love.

'The fire did this?' she said, looking to the nurse, shocked.

'It exacerbated it, certainly.'

'I . . . I don't understand.'

'The tuberculosis.'

Agnes felt the air in her lungs stop moving, a pressure in her chest making her ears ring unpleasantly. 'Tuberculosis?' she whispered.

'His lungs are riddled with it. We think it's reached his brain now too. Apparently, his mother died from it when he was a child. He nursed her all by himself until he eventually contracted it, too. He recovered quite quickly. Or so he thought. It caught up with him in the end. It would be a kindness to let him die peacefully now, but he's due to be sentenced in a few weeks, and our job is to keep him alive until then.'

Agnes gazed at the limp husk of the man before her, his blue eyes weeping and bloodshot. He had thought himself immune. Was it this brush with the illness as a child that had sparked his obsession with TB? He had gambled with his own life ever since, thinking he was invincible.

She imagined the lungs inside his shrunken chest, clouded and scarred and oddly beautiful in their own way, tainted by the illness he had lived so close to for so many years.

'Do they know what the outcome of the sentencing will be?' she whispered, not taking her eyes from him.

'They say likely hanging. It might have been a leaner sentence for the sterilisations. But then all those patients he overdosed . . .'

Overdosed.

Agnes thought of the night of the fire, of Christian and herself, standing on the steps at the blazing entrance hall, the silent transaction that had taken place between them: his life for Isobel's, her promise to always keep his daughter safe.

She had visited Isobel a few days ago, now safe with her mother. As they'd said goodbye on the doorstep, Iso had wrapped her small arms about Agnes's neck, clinging to her, her silver hair tickling her face. She had smelt of jam even then. Her mother said it was her favourite treat, a spoonful of jam to sweeten the day.

Agnes wondered if the girl would work it out one day; what she had done. But if she did, Agnes had sworn to herself that she would be there to help her through it. Whatever had happened at Hedoné House, the blame did not lie with the girl.

'Is he in pain?' she said.

'Most probably. He can't talk any more, you see, but he's still able to tell us how he feels, aren't you, Mr Fairhaven? He has a way of getting his meaning across with those bright blue eyes of his. We try to keep him as comfortable as possible, but there's only so much morphine a body can take, and these chairs aren't the most luxurious things to spend your last days in. Here,' she said, handing Agnes a pillow. 'This should help prop him up. It seems as if he grows smaller every day. He's so bony now, he needs all the support he can get.'

Agnes took the pillow in both hands, and as it came into Christian's line of vision, she thought his eyes took on a spark of something she recognised, a glimmer, for the first time, of the man she had known.

Far off in the building, an alarm went off. The nurse glanced at the door.

'I'm needed elsewhere,' she said. 'Will you be all right on your own with him? I shouldn't be too long, and he's perfectly harmless.'

Agnes nodded wordlessly.

The nurse left, closing the door behind her, and she took a step closer to the man in the chair. The oxygen mask over his nose and mouth hissed threateningly, and with sudden daring, she reached out, gently lifting it over his head.

His face looked oddly vulnerable without it. She studied him, searching for her husband, both the man she had left that night at Hedoné, and the man she had met in the South of France. The sun chose that moment to break through the dark clouds, a ray of light piercing the room, stroking itself over her skin. Its searching warmth caressed her body, calming her; gilding her.

She felt Christian's gaze running over her, as if he was remembering each and every contour, and then his trembling eyes settled on her hands.

Agnes looked down, thinking he must be looking at the bare finger where her gold wedding band had once been. With a jolt of surprise, she saw that she was still clutching onto the pillow. Slowly, she lifted it to Christian's eye level, watching his expression for any sign of change. For a moment, his face remained immobile. But then, so slight it was almost imperceptible, she thought she saw him nod.

Sometime later, Agnes walked back down the corridor, her heels ringing out on the concrete floor. At the desk, she nodded goodbye to the nurse. She stood at the open door for a moment, drawing in a long, restorative breath, before striding assuredly from the building.

When she reached the gates, she did not look back.

Acknowledgements & Author's Note

This novel has been quite a personal journey for me. During the covid pandemic, as someone who was classed as clinically extremely vulnerable, I spent most of my time safely tucked away in my house, feeling very afraid of the outside world. When I eventually emerged, I needed to work through my own thoughts on what those dark months had meant personally to me. It was then that this story began to take shape.

I have cystic fibrosis, a lung condition that is in some ways very similar to covid. It is life-limiting, invasive and exhausting. For years, people with CF have worn masks in hospitals and doctors' surgeries, we have kept windows open to ventilate rooms, and made sure to steer clear of people with coughs or colds to ensure we remain as well as possible.

But I didn't want to write about CF – that seemed a little self-indulgent. And I didn't want to write about covid either – it still felt a little too real.

And so, as a historical writer, I looked to the past. Humans have faced pandemics for as long as we've been on this earth. I wasn't so much interested in the medical side, as the emotional facets; the people who went through it, their lives continuing despite an illness that ravaged through them and their loved ones.

It was then that I hit upon the idea of writing about tuberculosis. Like covid, TB was also classed as a pandemic. It killed thousands of people, often for similar reasons – poverty, and lack of cleanliness and fresh air. All three of these illnesses are linked by one thing: the ability (or not) to breathe. And so, *The House of Fever* was born.

Most people with a chronic illness or disability will tell you that theirs is boring. It's such a small part of who we are that we really don't want to think about it any more than we have to. And yet, it *is* a part of me. And without it, I would not be the person I am today. CF doesn't define who I am, but I also cannot ignore it. I wanted to write a book about people who all happened to have the same condition, just as the CF community is filled with very different people who all share one small commonality. Because of my own lung condition, I have felt quite qualified to write this story, but I do not profess to being a specialist. Any errors are my own.

Thank you to my wonderful agent, Juliet Mushens, and to my editor, Cicely Aspinall, who knows me and my dark mind far too well by now!

Thank you to Seema Mitra, Emily Burns, Louise de St Aubin, Charlotte Philipps, Eldes Tran, and the whole of the HQ team.

Finally, a thank you to my wonderful CF specialist team at the Norfolk and Norwich University Hospital. A lot of this book is about people in the caring profession. Thankfully, my own care has been exemplary. I've never met a nurse like Matron, nor a doctor like Christian (thank goodness!), and if it wasn't for the incredible care I have received over my lifetime, I would not be here to write this novel.

If you were enthralled by *The House of Fever*, you'll love Polly Crosby's hauntingly beautiful novel, *Vita and the Birds*

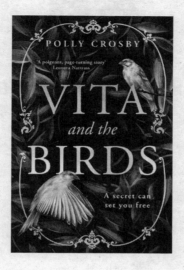

1938: Lady Vita Goldsborough lives in the menacing shadow of her controlling older brother, Aubrey. But when she meets local artist Dodie Blakeney, the two women form a close bond, and Vita finally glimpses a chance to be free.

1997: Following the death of her mother, Eve Blakeney returns to the coast where she spent childhood summers with her beloved grandmother, Dodie. Eve hopes that the visit will help make sense of her grief. The last thing she expects to find is a bundle of letters that hint at the heart-breaking story of Dodie's relationship with a woman named Vita, and a shattering secret that echoes through the decades.

What she discovers will overturn everything she thought she knew about her family — and change her life forever.

'A poignant page-turning story, beautifully written'
Leonara Nattrass

ONE PLACE. MANY STORIES

Bold, innovative and empowering publishing.

FOLLOW US ON:

@HQStories